The Onion Girl

By Charles de Lint from Tom Doherty Associates

The Onion Girl

Charles de Lint

A Tom Doherty Associates Book
New York

THE ONION GIRL

Edited by Terri Windling

A Tor Book
Published by Tom Doherty Associates, LLC
175 Fifth Avenue
New York, NY 10010

www.tor.com

Tor® is a registered trademark of Tom Doherty Associates, LLC.

Library of Congress Cataloging-in-Publication Data

De Lint, Charles.
        The onion girl / Charles de Lint.
              p. cm.
        "A Tom Doherty Associates book."
        ISBN 0-312-87397-2 (hc)
        ISBN 0-765-30381-7 (pbk)
        1. City and town life—Fiction. 2. Women artists—Fiction.
    3. Young Women—Fiction. I. Title.

PR9199.3.D357 O55 2001
813'.54—dc21   2001041445

Printed in the United States of America

0 9

for all of those who
against all odds
made the right choice

Author's Note

I hope regular readers of my books will forgive the reappearance in these pages of the short story "In the House of My Enemy," but having dealt with this element of backstory once already, I didn't have the heart to recast the events for this book simply to say it in new words. Jilly goes through enough already with what happens to her in this novel.

Special thanks to Holly Cole who, while she didn't write "The Onion Girl," which gives this book its title, certainly made the song her own with the interpretation she did on her CD, *Dark Dear Heart*; Fred Eaglesmith for all those little pieces taken from the edge of life and for making them so heart-felt and real, and for letting me quote from his unrecorded song "It Was You"; Jane B. Winans for sharing her professor's comments on fairy tales; Gillian O'Meagher for bravely sharing her own horrendous experiences of surviving a car crash; Paul Brandon for reminding me of Jilly and Natty's friendship; Andrew and Alice Vachss—Andrew for his ongoing support and Burke, Alice for all those intriguing animal stories; Honey Vachss for inspiration; David Tamulevich and Cat Eldridge for those wonderful packets of CDs they keep sending me, God bless 'em; Charles Vess, Rodger Turner, Pat Caven, Terri Windling, the Kunzies, and the Red Rock Girls for general goodwill and keeping me sane (or happily not, as the case might be); Karen Shaffer for bravely sharing her own war stories, and for kindly vetting the manuscript and being her red-slippered marvelous self; and to MaryAnn, as always, for her love, comfort, and support, her astute reader's eye and red pen, and for getting me to add those two chapters.

For those readers who continue to write and ask for musical references, inspiration was obviously well served by Holly Cole and Fred Eaglesmith, as noted above. (Which makes me think, I'd like to hear Holly cover a

Fred song.) But I was also charmed and swayed by any number of other albums over the year and a half it took to write this book. A few of the highlights were: *Places In Between* by Terri Hendrix; *Covenant* and *Over and Under* by Greg Brown; *Transcendental Blues* by Steve Earle; *The Green World* by Dar Williams, *Too Much Plenty* by Beki Hemingway; *Somewhere Near Paterson* by Richard Shindell; *Fists of Flood* by Jennifer Daniels; *Broke Down* by Slaid Cleaves; and *To the Teeth* by Ani DiFranco.

When I'm actually sitting down to write that first draft, however, the music tends to be instrumental, or in a language I don't understand. Along the lines of World and Celtic music, I was listening to: Robert Michaels; Kevin Crawford; Lúnasa (my favorite Celtic group, bar none—thanks, Paul, for that initial introduction); Kathryn Tickell; Lisa Lynne; Alan Stivell's *Back to Breizh; Tone Poems III* (a CD of slide and reso-phonic guitar and mandolin overseen by David Grisman); Kim Angelis; *Small Awakenings* by Kathryn Briggs; *Pipeworks*, a wonderful CD of Northumbrian piping by Rua's Jimmy Young; Los Lobos; Lila Downs (she has the voice of a Latina angel, not to mention a demon); Badi Assad . . . well, you get the idea. I was all over the place.

This past year or so I also rediscovered the joy of Bill Evans's record-ings for Riverside, particularly *Moonbeams* and *How My Heart Sings!*, and I can't seem to keep *Beyond the Missouri Sky* by Charlie Haden & Pat Metheny, Bill Frisell's *Good Dog, Happy Man*, or *The Tatum Group Masterpieces Volume 8* (featuring Tatum with Ben Webster) out of the player. I also keep returning to CDs by Miles Davis, Oscar Peterson, Thelonious Monk, and Lester Young.

The above only scratches the surface, but I hope it will point my fel-low music junkies to some of the pleasure I received from those artists.

If any of you are on the Internet, come visit my home page at www.charlesdelint.com.

—Charles de Lint
Ottawa, Autumn 2000

They (fairy tales) make rivers run
with wine only to make us remember,
for one wild moment,
that they run with water.

—G. K. CHESTERTON,
from *Orthodoxy*

It was you, it was you, who said that dreams come true
And it was you, it was you, who said that mine would, too
And it was you who said that all I had to do was to believe
But when your ivory towers tumbled down, they tumbled down
on me

—FRED EAGLESMITH
from "It Was You"

It's the family you choose that counts.

—ANDREW VACHSS

Jilly

Once upon a time . . .

I don't know what makes me turn. Some sixth sense, prickling the hairs at the nape of my neck, I guess. I see the headlights. They fill my world and I feel like a deer, trapped in their glare. I can't move. The car starts to swerve away from me, but it's already too late.

It's weird how everything falls into slow motion. There seems to be time to do anything and everything, and yet no time at all. I wait for my life to flash before my eyes, but all I get is those headlights bearing down on me.

There's the squeal of tires.

A rush of wind in my ears.

And then the impact.

2

Once upon a time . . .

That's how they always start, the old fairy tales that I read as a child. It's the proper place for them to start, because right away you know you're going to be taken somewhere *else*.

So.

Once upon a time there was a little girl who wished she could be anywhere else in all the wide world except for where she was. Or more preferably still, she wished she could find some way to cross over into whatever worlds might lie beyond this one, those wonderful worlds that she read about in stories. She would tap at the back of closets and always look very carefully down rabbit holes. She would rub every old lamp that she came across and wish on any and everything . . .

I've always been aware of the otherworld, of spirits that exist in that twilight place that lies in the corner of our eyes, of faerie and stranger things still that we spy only when we're not really paying attention to them, whispers and flickering shadows, here one moment, gone the instant we turn our heads for a closer look. But I couldn't always find them. And when I did, for a long time I thought they were only this excess of imagination that I carry around inside me, that somehow it was leaking out of me into the world.

In terms of what Professor Dapple calls consensual reality—that the world is as it is because that's how we've all agreed it is—I seem to carry this magical bubble world around with me, inside and hidden from the world we all inhabit. A strange and wonderful world where the implausible becomes not only possible, but probable. It doesn't matter if, most of the time, I'm the only one that can see it, though that's probably why I paint what I do; I'm trying to show the rest of the world this weird little corner of reality that I inhabit.

I see things from the corner of my eye that shouldn't be there, but are, if only for a brief, flickering moment. At a flea market, an old black teapot turns into a badger and scurries away. Late at night, a lost boy sits on the windowsill of the second-floor nursery in the apartment beside the Chinese grocery down the street from my studio, a tiny spark of light dancing about his shoulders as he peers in through the leaded panes. Later still, I hear the muted sound of hooves on the pavement and look out to see the dreadlocked gnome that Christy calls Long, his gnarled little fingers playing with a string of elf-knots that can call up the wind as he rides his pig Brigwin to the goblin market.

Oh, and the gargoyles . . . sitting high up on their perches, pretending to be stone while having long conversations with pigeons and crows. I've caught them twitching, moving from one position to another, the sly look that freezes mid-wink when they realize I'm watching.

But then I've always had a fertile imagination and it was many years before I realized that most people don't experience these extraordinary glimpses the way I do. For the longest time I thought they simply wouldn't admit to it.

But the trouble with magic is that there's too much it just can't fix. When things go wrong, glimpsing junkyard faerie and crows that can turn into girls and back again doesn't help much. The useful magic's never at hand. The three wishes and the genies in bottles, seven-league boots, invisible cloaks and all. They stay in the stories, while out here in the wide world we have to muddle through as best we can on our own.

3

The world feels all mushy when I open my eyes. My eyelids are sticky, encrusted with dream sand, and nothing has a defined edge to it. Colors are muted and my ears are blocked. I feel dislocated from the rest of my body. I'm aware of it, but it doesn't seem to really be connected to me anymore. That's part of the blur. I have the sense that I don't really want to connect with my body because that'll just open me up to a world of pain.

I'm vaguely aware that there's something pushed up my nose. An IV drip in my arm. Limbs weighed down with I don't know what.

I realize I must be in a hospital.

Hospital? Why would I be in a hospital?

I hear a small pathetic whimper and realize that I made that sound. It draws a huge face into my line of vision, features swimming. Slowly the face becomes normal-sized, though still blurry.

"S-Sophie . . . ?"

My voice comes out in a weak, slurred rasp. My mouth doesn't seem to work properly anymore.

"Oh, Jilly," she says.

My ears pop at the sound of her voice. My hearing clears. There's something I need to tell her. A dream I had.

"I . . . feel . . . weird."

"Everything's going to be okay," she says.

Then I remember the dream. The fuzziness and strange feelings go away, or at least distance themselves from me like I'm experiencing them through the wrong end of a telescope. I try to sit up, but I can't even lift my head. Not even that troubles me.

"I've been there," I tell her. "To Mabon. I finally found a way into your dreamlands."

She looks like she wants to cry. I thought she'd be happy for me. I've been wanting to go there forever, into her cathedral world where everything feels taller and bigger and brighter—*more* than it is here. She visits the city of Mabon in her dreams and has a whole other, really interesting life there. Christy calls it serial dreaming, where every time you fall asleep you pick up where you left off in last night's dream, but it's more than that. What, exactly, none of us really knows. But I've always believed it was a real place and now I know for sure because I've been there, too.

"I couldn't find you there," I tell her. "I wandered around for ages. Everybody I asked knew who you were, but they couldn't tell me *where* you were."

"I was here," Sophie says. "With you. In the hospital."

I don't clue in at all.

"I was wondering about that," I say. "Who's sick?"

"There was an accident," Sophie begins. "A car . . ."

I tune her out. I don't like cars. There's something bad about cars, but I can't remember what.

"Jilly?"

I try to focus on her voice, but suddenly there's this great abyss inside me and it just keeps pulling me down into it.

Down and down and down . . .

4

Where is that nurse? Sophie Etoile wondered, looking over her shoulder at the door to Jilly's room. It felt like ages since she'd pushed the call button.

She turned her attention back to Jilly and brushed a damp lock of curly hair away from her friend's brow. Jilly was gone again, but at least her breathing seemed more normal. The doctor had said that when she came out of the coma, she would probably fall into a second period of unconsciousness, but it would be more like sleep. Now all they had to worry about was the possibility of paralysis when she came around again.

The call Sophie had gotten three nights ago had been her worst nightmare come true. The way Jilly was forever wandering around the city at all hours of the day or night, not caring about the danger, Sophie'd always worried that it would only be a matter of time before Jilly got hurt, though she'd been thinking more along the lines of a mugging rather than this—an early evening hit-and-run on a Lower Crowsea side street. Sophie had often joked that Jilly must have a guardian angel looking out for her. Well, if that was true, either her angel had taken the other night off, or Jilly's run of blind good luck had finally run out.

It broke Sophie's heart to look at her friend. Always lively and vibrant, Jilly was almost unrecognizable at the moment. Her skin was sallow, except for the bruising on the left side of her face where she'd struck the pavement. They'd had to shave the hair on the side of her head to properly clean her scalp. Her left arm and right leg were encased in plaster casts. Her torso was wrapped with bandages because of the ribs that had been cracked. Tubes from her nostrils tied her to an oxygen unit in the wall. More tubes were plugged into her body, running from an IV pole that held plastic bags of fluids. Wires connected her to a bank of machines that were gathered near the bed like a crowd of curious onlookers, their conversation conducted in lights and beeps and monitor lines. Her heartbeat was displayed by three waveforms undulating on a screen.

Being in here made Sophie nervous. She and Wendy and a number of Jilly's other friends had taken turns sitting with her while she was in the coma, and Sophie was more than happy to do her part. But Sophie also had a unique problem in that mechanical and electrical devices sometimes developed odd symptoms around her. Digital watches could simply flash a random time while ordinary wristwatches ran backward. She'd once crashed Christy's hard drive simply by switching on his computer. Though she wasn't connected to a cable service, her television could bring in cable signals, which would be fine except that the TV set also changed channels randomly.

When Jilly first learned about this affliction of Sophie's, she'd insisted that Sophie give it a name. Something fanciful, rather than gloomy.

"I don't know that I want to make friends with it," she told Jilly. "Then it'll never go away."

"It's not a matter of going or staying," Jilly had replied. "It's a part of you. This'll just make it easier for us to talk about it. You know, like our own secret code."

Jilly liked codes almost as much as she liked mysteries, and after any number of long conversations on the subject, Sophie finally gave in. They ended up calling it Jinx, because while it was a friendly sounding word, it still warned of its potential for disaster. And it *was* easier, at least among their circle of friends, to simply say "Jinx" when Sophie wasn't to be trusted around anything that could possibly be influenced by this peculiar trait of hers.

But giving the affliction an identity didn't make it any easier for Sophie to deal with the way Jinx slipped in and out of her life, or make her any less nervous in situations such as the one she was in at the moment. So while she was here in Jilly's room, she made sure not to touch or even stand too close to any of the equipment that was keeping her friend alive. Except for the call button. Had she screwed that up as well? Was the nurse now on his way to some room at the other end of the intensive care unit?

She was about to try again when the nurse came hurrying into the room.

"Sorry," he said. "I would have been here sooner but there was a problem with another patient's ventilator and the monitors at the station didn't show an emergency in here."

Jilly was going to enjoy being looked after by this nurse, Sophie had decided when she first met him. Daniel was as handsome as a soap opera doctor, tall, dark-haired, ready smile, gentle eyes. If you had to be sick, you might as well have a dreamboat for a nurse.

"Why did you call for me?" he said.

He didn't look at her as he spoke, his gaze traveling over the array of monitors before settling on Jilly's bruised features. Sophie eased his obvious concern by explaining what had happened.

"Did she seem lucid?" he asked.

Sophie had to smile. With Jilly, how could you even tell? But she nodded.

"She was a little confused," she said, "but she recognized me right away and knew she was in a hospital. She didn't seem to be aware that she'd been hurt."

"That's not too unusual in a case like this," Daniel told her. "There's often a certain amount of disorientation, even amnesia sometimes, but it rarely lasts long. I'll have the doctor come in to check her over."

And then he was gone again.

Sophie looked back at Jilly. She seemed so fragile lying there, like a broken doll, her guileless features no longer so slack now that she'd slipped from coma into a more natural sleep. But it was still heartbreaking to see the damage that had been done to her, to know how much work lay ahead before Jilly might be her old self once again.

The two of them could have been sisters. They were of similar height, with the same slender build, though Sophie was a little bustier. Her hair was a soft auburn, tamed into ringlets, while Jilly's was usually a tangle of darker curls. Wendy likened Jilly's quick, clever features to a Rackham pixie, Sophie's softer ones to a pre-Raphaelite's painting, and strangers often mistook one for the other, then remarked on the family resemblance when corrected.

Wendy was the missing third member of their little tribe of, as Jilly liked to describe them, "small, fierce women." She was blonde, so less easily mistaken for either of them, but of a similar body shape and height, and just as tangle-haired. Though the three of them were unrelated by blood, they were sisters all the same. In the heart, where it mattered. Others had come to join their tribe —and they had become close and greatly loved, to be sure—but the three of them were its root, the core from which all their other relationships blossomed.

Rising from the bedside, Sophie bent over and brushed her lips lightly against Jilly's brow, then left the room to make some phone calls.

·   ·   ·

"Oh, my god," Wendy said. "It's like the best Christmas present anyone could get."

Sophie laughed. "And yet, it's almost summer."

She could feel Wendy's good humor come across the phone line and wasn't surprised by it. Her own body felt lighter with the weight that had been taken from it and she was more than a little giddy herself. Even the phone was behaving for her, allowing her to talk to Wendy instead of trying to connect her to someone in Japan or Germany.

"I'm coming down right now," Wendy said.

"She's asleep," Sophie warned her.

"I don't care. I was so worried."

Sophie understood. None of them had wanted to even consider what would happen if Jilly hadn't pulled through, but it hadn't been far from any of their minds all the same. Life without Jilly in it was unthinkable, but as someone had once said, fair was only the first third of fairy tale, and the world had its own agenda that didn't take anyone else's into account.

"I'm going to make a few more calls," Sophie said. "Would you mind letting Christy and maybe Sue know before you leave? I'll call the professor and the others."

"Don't forget Lou."

"I won't."

"Or Angel or—"

"Wendy."

"Okay, okay. I'll make my calls and then I'm on my way."

Sophie smiled as she hung up. She fed another quarter into the phone and dialed the next number on her list.

Be nice to me, phone, she thought. Don't give me any trouble tonight.

For once something mechanical seemed willing to give her a break.

When Sophie finally returned to Jilly's room she thought she saw two girls peering in through the window, dark faces pressed against the glass, hair standing up in sharp spikes. She hesitated in the doorway, trapped by the impossibility of their presence, then blinked, and they were gone.

She crossed to the window and looked out, but there was no one there, of course. The ICU was on the third floor and there was no fire escape outside the window. When she lifted her gaze she saw a pair of crows in the distance, winging off against the Crowsea skyline.

Jilly would say it was the crow girls, but Sophie knew better. All she'd seen was an odd reflection on the glass. She might have an active dream life, but she didn't let it carry over into what the professor called the World As It Is. It drove Jilly crazy, but the only magic Sophie saw in the world was what people made for each other. Still, what she thought she'd seen had been disconcerting, if only for a moment.

You're just not getting enough sleep, she told herself, rubbing at her temples.

The doctor came in then and she concentrated on what he had to tell her after he'd examined Jilly.

5

Once upon a time . . .

The forest seems familiar to me right away, but it takes me a moment to realize why. I stand there, absorbed by the towering trees that surround me on all sides, trees bigger and stranger than they have any right to be. There's next to no undergrowth, just these behemoths, their trunks so wide that five of me couldn't touch hands around them. Light pours down from the dense canopy above in golden shafts and that's when I know where I am. The cathedral effect reminds me of what I call the place that Sophie goes traveling to at night.

I'm back in the dreamlands again. The cathedral world.

It's not the city of Mabon that Sophie founded here, but a magic place all the same. It would have to be, wouldn't it, with trees like this. They must be close cousins of what Jack Daw used to call the forever trees, the giant growth that made up the first forest when the world was born.

I can't believe that I'm finally able to cross over into the otherworld like this. While I'd prefer to be able to go in my body, dreaming my way across is certainly the next best thing. But I would like to learn how to choose where I end up, the way that Sophie can. I'll have to ask her how she does it.

Thinking of Sophie reminds me that I just saw her . . . or was that a dream, too? She really didn't seem herself. Way too sad, for one thing. I know everyone can't be as exuberant as I tend to be, but couldn't she have shown just a little more enthusiasm that I'd learned how to cross over, too? Because now we can have adventures in the dreamlands together. And I'll finally get to meet her mysterious boyfriend Jeck, that handsome crow boy that she can only be with in Mabon.

Sometimes I just don't get her. How can someone be so full of magic and still deny it the way she does? You only have to look at her to see the faerie blood in her, to know that she's as magical as anything you could find in or out of the cathedral world.

A little niggling thought comes worming up through my happiness. It's got to do with that last time I saw her. I remember her starting to say something about accidents and cars, but I don't want to go there. I don't want the World As It Is to intrude on the magic I'm experiencing right now.

I take a deep breath and look around some more, trying to empty my mind of everything except what's happening at this moment. I want to exist in Zen time. No past, no future. Just now. Just being here.

I think I'm alone until I smell the cigarette smoke. I turn in a slow circle and finally see a thin drift of it coming from the far side of one of the nearby trees. I head over, happy to have something new to focus on. When I get there, I find a guy sitting with his back against one of the trees, legs sprawled out in front of him. He's wearing jeans, scuffed work boots, and a T-shirt with faded writing on it that I can just make out. Oh, and he's got the head of a coyote or wolf, but I know who he is all the same.

"Hey, Joe. I haven't seen you for a while."

Joseph Crazy Dog's the only guy I know who'd be wearing that "Don't! Buy! Thai!" T-shirt in the dreamlands. Like they have boycotts here.

Unlike Sophie, he's up-front about his otherworld origins. The funny thing is, no one pays much attention to that. Most people just assume he's this city Indian come down from the rez, living on the street, and he won't take his meds. Or they know him as Bones, sitting in Fitzhenry Park, telling fortunes with a handful of what gave him his name, scattering the rodent and bird bones on a piece of deerskin, reading stories in how they fall. Stories about what's been, what is, or what might be.

The wolf head shimmers while I'm standing there, morphing into the face I know with its dark, coppery cast and broad features. Square chin, eyes set wide, nose flat. His long black hair's tied back in a single braid festooned with feathers and beads. I've always loved his eyes. They shift like mercury, one moment the clown, one moment the wise man. Impossible to capture in a painting. I know; I've tried.

Joe shrugs in response to my greeting. He takes another drag from his cigarette as I sit down beside him.

"You know how it is," he says. "I'm always crossing back and forth and you've been busy."

"It seems like I'm always busy. Maybe I spend too much time trying to be too many things for too many people."

"You wouldn't be the first, though you do seem to have made more of a career of it than most. Could be this accident of yours is the spirits' way of telling you to spend a little time on yourself for a change. Kind of like forcing the issue."

"What accident?"

"See, that's what I mean. You just don't pay enough attention to yourself."

Sometimes Joe can drive me crazy with his obliqueness.

"Is this one of your lessons?" I ask.

Joe's been working with me on and off for a couple of years now to prepare me to be able to cross over into the spiritworld like he does, walking in my body. The way that came about was out of this long conversation we had, back when Zeffy and Nia got lost in the otherworld. I wanted to accompany Joe while he was looking for them, but he wouldn't let me.

The way he put it was, "It's dangerous for anybody, walking there in their own skin, but especially for someone like you. You're like a magnet for the spirits, Jilly. Got a light inside you that shines too bright. I've told you, I can teach you how to navigate that place, but you've got to give me a few years so you can study it properly."

"But Sophie just goes there," I said to him then.

"Sure she does," he told me. "Only she doesn't go in her skin. She dreams her way across—she'd have to, seeing how she shines about as bright as you—and that's the only way you can go, too, until you learn more."

"I don't have those kind of dreams."

"Maybe you just don't remember them." He smiled at me, those crazy eyes of his grinning. "That light you carry's got to have come from somewhere. I don't know many people who shine so bright without having touched a spirit or two along the way."

"I guess," I said. "I only wish I could be the one to decide when it happens."

"You've got to accept your blessings as they come. Most people don't even get one, and when they do, they ignore it, or explain it away."

"I'm not ungrateful to be here," I tell him now. "No matter how I got across. But I can't help wanting more. I want to know that I can keep doing it. I want to be here like you. For real."

"This doesn't feel real to you?" he asks.

"You know what I mean."

He nods. "I guess I do." He puts out his cigarette on the heel of his boot and stows the butt away in his pocket. "We always want more than what we've got."

"I don't mean to sound greedy," I tell him. "But I don't want two lives like Sophie does—one in the World As It is, and one here. I'd feel too schizophrenic. I don't know how Sophie does it."

"One's real for her," Joe says, "and one's a dream. She puts each experience in what she figures is its appropriate compartment and it all comes out tidy."

That describes Sophie to a "T." She's as neat as I'm messy. I don't know how she does that either. I can't open a tube of paint without some of it immediately migrating to my fingers, my hair, my jeans . . .

"Tidy," I repeat. "That's sure not me."

Joe laughs. "You don't have to work at convincing me about that."

I could just whack him sometimes.

"I mean I can't divide my life up neatly like that," I say. "If I'm going to have access to the spiritworld, I want to be able to bring my sketch-book across with me and then bring it back again. I'd like to carry over a tent and food and things so that I could stay awhile and not have to worry about shelter or eating roots and berries."

The thing about traveling to the dreamlands the way Sophie does is that you can't bring anything with you. You can't bring anything back. Only the experience.

"I hear you," Joe says. "And we've been working on that with what I've been teaching you."

"I know. But finally being here, even just like this . . ."

I see the understanding in his eyes. That understanding's been there all along, but I had to explain how I feel all the same.

"It's hard to be patient," he says.

I nod.

"We can work on it," he says. "Being able to dream yourself over's going to make everything go a lot quicker."

"When can we start?" I ask.

He gives me an unhappy look.

"First we have to deal with that accident," he says.

I start to shake my head. I don't want to talk about it, whatever it is. But Joe's not one to let you bury your head in the sand.

"You've got a hard road ahead of you," he tells me. "Maybe your being able to cross over like this is compensation for all the work you've got waiting for you back in the World As It is. Or maybe that bang on the head knocked loose whatever it is that lets people cross over in a dream."

I am shaking my head now. Joe just ignores it. He fixes that steady gaze of his on me, the clown gone. He's all serious.

"I brought in a couple of different healers," he says. "Even asked the crow girls to look in on you. They all say the same thing. You've got to do the mending on your own. See, the problem is, there's an older hurt, sitting there on the inside of you, and it's blocking anybody's attempts to speed the natural healing process of what's wrong on the outside."

"What are you saying?"

I don't admit to anything, but some part of me knows what he's trying to tell me. Just thinking about it makes me feel the pull back to the world I've left behind. I don't want to go back.

Joe hesitates, then tells me, "It's like a part of you doesn't want to get any better."

"I'm not even sick."

"Well, you don't have the flu," he says, "but you got banged up something bad. There's no point in either of us pretending otherwise. And you and I both know there's old hurts you've just hid away. Maybe you can turn up the wattage of that shine of yours to fool most people, but you don't fool me."

"What kind of hurts are you talking about?"

"If I knew, maybe I could help."

"You know the story of my life," I say.

He gives a slow nod of his head. "But I don't know how you feel about it."

"This is such bullshit."

Joe sighs. "I'm just telling you how it is. If you didn't want to know, you shouldn't have asked."

It's true. Joe rarely offers advice without first waiting to be asked. The trouble with advice is that it's usually something you don't want to hear.

I have to look away. I let those wonderful trees fill my vision. Already they seem less present. Or maybe I am. I can feel the tug of my body, and it's stronger. I don't want to go back. I know what's waiting for me now.

"I'm sorry it worked out this way," Joe says.

I nod. "Me, too," I tell him.

"You deserve better."

I shrug. I don't think the world works on merit. At least, not as much as we'd like it to.

"We'll find a way to beat it," Joe tells me.

And if we can't?

But I don't say the words aloud. I touch his hand.

"Don't you worry about me, Joe," I say. "I'm a survivor."

Then I let the pain reach across into the dreamlands and pull me back to that hospital bed. I hear his voice as I go, a faint sound, growing fainter.

"There's more to life than just surviving," he says.

I know that's true. But I also know that sometimes just surviving is all you get.

6

It was getting to be like old home week, Wendy St. Clair thought as their friends continued to arrive. The waiting room was crowded, getting close to standing room only as the last seats were taken. There were so many familiar faces, Wendy felt she was at one of Izzy's or Sophie's gallery openings, except for the fact that everyone was far too glum.

And Jilly wasn't here.

If there was something special going on in your life—a reading, a book signing, a gallery opening, a gig—you could always count on Jilly to be there to help you celebrate. Just as she was also there when the world bore down too hard and you needed a friend, someone to commiserate with. But tonight Jilly was a couple of rooms away, wires and tubes connecting her to the life support and monitoring machines, the Rackham pixie transformed into a creature from an H. R. Giger nightmare, and it was her friends who had gathered to lend each other what support they could, and to celebrate, in their quieter way, Jilly's having come out of the coma.

Professor Dapple, Christy, his girlfriend Saskia, and Alan were on one couch at the end of the room, with red-haired Holly sitting on the coffee table in front of them, looking perfectly at home between the piles of old magazines stacked on either side of her. Sophie, Sue, Isabelle, and Meran had commandeered the other couch that ran along the longer wall. Desmond and Meran's husband Cerin were sitting on the floor between the two. Cassie had a Formica and metal chair that must have been borrowed from the cafeteria, while Wendy herself was sharing the only other seat with Mona. It was a stuffed chair with squared cushions and arms that was a really dreadful color of olive green. The two of them were taking turns sitting on one of the arms and the seat cushion.

While they were missing a few faces—Geordie and Tanya were still in L.A. and Cassie's husband Joe . . . well, who ever knew where Joe was?—it was still quite the turnout. But then Jilly inspired this kind of loyalty. If she was to die, half the city would probably show up for her funeral.

Wendy put her hand to her mouth, even though she hadn't spoken the words aloud.

Oh, god, she told herself. Don't even think such a thing.

Mona touched her arm. "Are you okay?"

Wendy nodded. Before she could fumble an explanation as to what had made her suddenly go so pale, the door to the waiting room opened and Lou Fucceri and Angel came in. Lou smelled like cigarette smoke, Angel of a blend of cardamom and ylang ylang oils.

It was odd seeing the two of them like this. They hadn't been an item for almost twenty years, but whenever Wendy saw them together, it was impossible for her not to think of them as a couple. Neither had gone on to get married, or even had a long-term relationship since they'd broken up, but they hadn't tried to fix whatever had gone wrong between them either.

Wendy thought it was their jobs. They both had careers rooted in heartbreak and frustration, neither of which allowed much emotional strength left over to work on a relationship. Because of those careers they had locked horns more often than not, disagreeing on the letter of the law and how the people who broke it were best served.

was a career policeman. He'd risen to the rank of lieutenant
Jilly first met him as a rookie street cop—when "my life began
.in," as Jilly put it—without asking for or taking favors. He was a tall,
broad-shouldered Italian whose people had a long history of either entering law enforcement or working for the Cerone family on the other side
of the law, which could make holidays and birthdays strained affairs at
the best of times.

Angela Marceau was a counselor for street people and runaways. She
had a walk-in office on Grasso Street and wasn't above bending, if not
outright breaking, the law if the safety of one of her charges was at stake.
Wendy had first met her years ago and Angel was as gorgeous now as
she'd been back then. She had a heart-shaped face, framed by a cascade
of curly dark hair, and deep warm eyes. Her trim figure didn't sport
wings, and she leaned more toward baggy pants, T-shirts, and high-tops
than she did harps and shimmering gowns, but some of the street people
claimed she really was a messenger from God, come down to help them.
She certainly had the Botticelli image down, updated for present times.

"Has she come to again?" Angel asked after she and Lou had said
their hellos.

Sophie shook her head. "But she's out of the coma. The doctor said
she's just sleeping now."

"She'll need all the rest she can get after that sort of trauma."

"Rest, Jilly," Mona murmured from beside Wendy. "Somehow you
don't expect to hear those two words in the same sentence."

"Has there been any word on the driver of the car?" the professor
asked Lou.

Everyone fell quiet to hear his response. Lou got an uncomfortable
expression and a horrible feeling shivered through Wendy.

Don't tell us, she wanted to say. If it's more bad news, just don't
tell us.

But they had to know. That was the only way to face your fears. You
can't stand up to the night until you understand what's hiding in its shadows, someone had told her once.

"There's been a complication," Lou finally said. "Dispatch got a call
late this afternoon from Jilly's landlady . . ." He looked old, sagging in
on himself, as though having to describe what had happened was more
than he could bear. "Somebody trashed the studio. I mean they really had
themselves a time. They cut her paintings into ribbons, pulled everything

out of her drawers and shelves, and went to town tossing it around. The place looks like a hurricane hit it. Everything reeks of turpentine and solvents. But it's the paintings . . ."

He shook his head. All those years on the street, with all he must have seen, and still this had obviously gotten to him. Maybe because it was personal, Wendy thought. Because it had happened to a friend.

"Who could ever do this to Jilly?" he said. "Who could hate her that much?"

His last few words were drowned in a general hubbub of disbelief and concern. Wendy glanced at Isabelle and saw the pained look on the artist's face. They were all upset, but Isabelle, who'd lost most of her paintings in a fire years ago, was the one who knew better than any of them just how devastating this would be for Jilly.

"This is connected, isn't it?" Sophie said. "To the hit-and-run."

Lou turned to her. "What makes you say that?"

"I can see it in your face."

"You think someone ran her down deliberately?" Meran asked. Her voice echoed the shock they were all feeling.

No, Wendy thought. That couldn't be true. It was just too awful to contemplate.

"Until we find the driver," Lou said, "it's impossible to say." Then he sighed. "But it doesn't feel right to me. First the car, now this business with her studio. The incidents are just too close to each other to feel like a coincidence."

"But you're talking about someone actually trying to kill her," Saskia said.

Angel shook her head. "No, they want to erase her. Her and her work . . . To make it be like she never existed."

"I don't believe it," the professor said.

He took off his glasses and gave them a brief cleaning they didn't need before putting them back on, his gaze fixed on Lou's grave features.

"No, it can't be true," Cassie said. "How could it be true?"

Lou just gave them all a tired look.

"Does she have enemies that any of you know about?" he asked.

There was a long moment of silence.

"This is Jilly you're talking about," Sophie said.

"I doubt she's ever hurt anyone in her life," Meran added.

"Certainly not deliberately," Lou agreed.

the other couch, Christy nodded. "Which would mean you're
...g for someone with an intense dislike for the relentlessly cheerful."

That woke faint smiles throughout the room, but they didn't last long
... Jilly's friends considered the idea of someone hating her so much that
they would want to cause her this much pain. Enough so that they would
destroy her life's work and deliberately run her down with a car.

"Just think about it," Lou said. "Keep your eyes and ears open. And
if you think of anything that could help us, if you hear or see anything,
call me. I don't care what time of the day or night it might be."

7

Once upon a time . . .

I open my eyes and I can't move. It's not just because of the casts on
my left arm and right leg. There's no feeling under the leg cast. There's no
feeling in my right arm either. That whole side of my body is paralyzed
and numb. It's so weird. I can feel the fabric of my hospital gown and the
bedclothes against my skin—but only on the left side. On the right,
there's nothing. I can move my head, stiffly, with an effort, my left leg,
the arm in the cast, though that sends a shiver of pain through me.

I remember how it was before, when Sophie was looking down at me.
I couldn't move then either. Now I know why. I remember the car and
the impact.

There's no one in the room with me, but I can hear voices from
nearby.

I look down at my useless right arm, my hand, my *drawing* hand,
willing it to move. I can't even feel it.

There are lots of fairy tales. I remember the professor telling me once
how people need to be storied to get over their fears. We were talking
about the elements of fairy tales and their relevance to the World As It Is,
the here and now in which we all live. It was just the three of us—Christy,
the professor, and me—sitting in that old-fashioned drawing room of the
professor's that he uses as a study.

People who've never read fairy tales, the professor said, have a harder
time coping in life than the people who have. They don't have access to
all the lessons that can be learned from the journeys through the dark
woods and the kindness of strangers treated decently, the knowledge that

can be gained from the company and example of Donkeyskins and cats wearing boots and steadfast tin soldiers. I'm not talking about in-your-face lessons, but more subtle ones. The kind that seep up from your sub-conscious and give you moral and humane structures for your life. That teach you how to prevail, and trust. And maybe even love.

The people who missed out on them have to be re-storied in their adult lives.

Maybe that's what's happening to me. Faithfully though I read them when I was a kid, and have kept reading them all my life, maybe I need to be re-storied again anyway. Because there's something missing in my life, too. I don't need Joe or anyone else to tell me that. I've always known it.

I'm an onion girl, like in that song Holly Cole sings. And what I'm most afraid of is that if you peel back enough layers, there won't be any-thing left of me at all. Everyone'll know who I really am. The Broken Girl. The Hollow Girl.

Maybe the stories can fill me up.

So.

Once upon a time . . .

I try to move my right hand again. It's like it doesn't exist.

I can't imagine a life in which I can't paint and draw.

Once upon a time . . .

I'm in the fairy tale where the girl gets hits by a car and then lies in the ICU ward of the hospital, waiting to die. Or at the very least, life as she knew it is over and everything is forever changed.

I'm not sure I want to know how the story ends.

Once upon a time . . .

Raylene

Pinky Miller's about my best friend, so I guess that's why I put up with her the way I do. I mean, she's as like' to get me into trouble as out of it and there's no way around it. She's pretty much a strollop, and not the sharpest tool in the shed neither, but she's got a lot of heart. Always stood by me, leastways.

Like the time we ended up at this tailgate party on the Sutherlands' back forty. We were still in high school at the time, fifteen going on twenty, the pair of us. I was always small, but big in all the right places, if you know what I mean, and Pinky, well, you look up "statuesque" in the dictionary and you'd find her picture.

We was popular with all the boys, but I never put out like she did. Back in those days my big brother Del'd have tore a strip off me if he ever heard I was letting anybody get past second base. He was always telling me I had to save myself for that special guy and we both knew who he was. The boys I dated didn't mind. I gave a righteous hand job and there was always Pinky, happy to oblige whoever I was with if her own fella got himself a little wore out, and they got wore out more often 'n not.

Pinky's been like that pretty much since we hit puberty. There were three things a girl had to live for, she'd tell me, men, money, and partying, and not necessarily in that order. "Think about it, Raylene," she told me once, at a time when we might've been going to college if we'd had the grades, the interest, or the money. "You can't have a party without men and the foldin' green to buy the party favors, am I right? Now given my druthers, I'll take a backwoods boy any day of the week, hung like a horse and ready to rock 'n' roll. But for the finer things in life—and I'm talkin' perfume and jewels and pretty party dresses here—give me some old fuck with a fat wallet. It's just economics, you understand?"

But in those days we was dating high school seniors and the dropouts that hung out at the pool hall. Rich was something you saw on TV, not something anybody who lived in our section of Tyson could ever claim to be, so we had to make do. We was white trash, plain and simple. I don't mean we thought we was white trash, but that's what we was all the same.

See, we lived not only on the wrong side of the tracks, but past the Ramble, past Stokesville—which the ignorant still call Niggertown—all the way out on the butt end of Tyson in what the townies called Hillbilly Holler. Had us run-down clapboard houses that the wind was as like' to blow over if we didn't burn 'em down our own selves, with hand pumps in the kitchen and outhouses 'round back. We had phones, and power when it wasn't being shut off, but the sewers and water mains stopped our side of Stokesville.

What makes a body live there? you're wondering. What makes you think any of us had a choice?

Anywise, that night I was with Lenny Wilson, a handsome enough boy except for that spray of zits on his forehead. He wore his dirty blonde hair slicked back like he was right proud of those zits, but he dressed sharp and he was funny. Always made me laugh, leastways. He was a high school dropout like pretty near everybody in our crowd already was, or soon would be, and I guess he was going on twenty, but he was okay for an older guy. He settled for the hand job like it was all he needed and never pushed too hard for more.

There was maybe eight or nine of us in the field that night. We had pickups backed up to each other, nice and cosy like, a little fire ˌ in the middle where they met, shooting up sparks—hillbilly fire-ˌs, Lenny called them. There was plenty of beer, a little pot, and ˌd tunes coming in on the radio. It was still early so most of us was ˌust dancing, or necking, or lying there in the bed of one of the pickups, looking up at the stars.

The music was pretty loud, and I guess that's why we didn't hear a fourth vehicle come bouncing across the field until it was pretty much blowing gas fumes up our asses. By then it was too late to do anything 'cept shiver and quake.

There was three of them sitting side by each in the cab. Russell Henderson, Bobby Marshall, and Eugene Webb. All of a kind, dark slick hair, weasel-thin, and about as mean as you can imagine, and if you're like me, you can probably imagine pretty good. None of the boys we was with had a hope in hell of standing up to these hardcases. I'd bet even Del'd have backed off 'less he could take 'em on one at a time.

"We're lookin' for a party girl," Russell said with a grin. He studied us, one by one, that cocky gaze of his finally settling on me. "Now you see, Eugene? I told you we was gonna find us some fresh meat tonight."

Pinky and me, we was sitting on the tailgate when they drove up. 'Bout now I was shaking so hard I thought I'd pee my panties, but Pinky just lounged against the side of the truck bed, hands in the pockets of her jacket.

"You sure this is the way you want it to play?" she asked Russell.

"Now don't you be frettin'," he told her. "You and me, I ain't for-gettin' the fun we had in the past. I mean, you don't meet that many girls who'll take it up both ends and still ask for more."

Pinky gave him a smile.

"Your call," she told him.

He reached for me and the next thing I know she was swinging her feet to the ground. Her hands came out of her pocket and there was a switchblade in one of them, the blade popping out and locking in place like a piece of dark magic. What happened then happened so fast it took everybody by surprise, especially Russell. She stuck that knife in him, hard, deep in his gut, then gave him a little push. By the time he dropped to his knees and the other two were moving in, she had the knife free and was moving it back and forth in the air between them, spraying drops of blood.

This was a side of Pinky I'd never saw before that night. I mean, she always talked tough. I just never realized how hard she could back the words up. But I guess those boys knew. The one that got himself gut-stuck, all the fight was taken out of him, that was for sure. Bobby and Eugene grabbed hold of him and held him up between them.

"This ain't over," Eugene told Pinky before they dragged Russell away.

"Hell, no," she told them. "Whatever gave you that notion? I'm of a mind to go by where you sorry fucks live and burn them shacks down. Listen to your mamas squeal while they're fryin'. That about what you had in mind when you're sayin' this ain't over?"

Eugene dropped Russell's arm and started for her, stopping when that weaving dance with the switchblade stopped and the blade pointed at him, still wet with Russell's blood.

"A smart man'd know when to quit," she said, "but you're just a big dumb fuck, ain't that right? Let me tell you what's going to happen here, Eugene. I'm goin' to be wearing your balls for earrings if you don't turn around and haul your sorry ass out of here."

I didn't know which was troubling Eugene more, that it was a girl facing him down, or that the rest of us was there to see it happen. But I knew this, he was scared of Pinky and scared of that knife. More scared of dying than he was of losing face.

"Fuck you," he said. "Fuck you all."

He reached down and grabbed Russell's arm again and helped Bobby carry him back to their pickup. Pinky eased her way 'round to the cab of the truck we'd been in the back of and pulled down the hunting rifle that was up on the rack behind the seat. By the time Eugene and Bobby had reached their own truck, she was standing there with the rifle in her hand now, just a-waiting.

That was Pinky for you. Like I said, she's not real smart in a whole bunch of ways, but she's cunning. She knew them boys might have them a coon gun up on the rack of their own truck and she just outthought 'em, same as she outbraved them. Eugene and Bobby got Russell into the cab, climbed in their ownselves, and they peeled outta there, tires spitting up sod and dirt. I wouldn't have liked to have been Russell on that ride, holding in his guts as the truck went jolting back across the field.

"You can't never back down," Pinky told me as she laid the rifle on the tailgate. "You back down and they're gonna walk all over you. Not just today, but every goddamn day. You trust me on that one, Raylene."

I didn't say anything, but I nodded. I already knew that. I'd been backing down seems like my whole life and it never got better. Never helped much and only got worse. It's like every time you get pushed a little further, the one standing over you's just gotta find something meaner to do, like he's daring you to stand up for yourself, but he knows you never will.

Pinky reached down and picked up her switchblade from where she'd dropped it on the ground. She gave the blade a wipe, then closed it up again.

"Where'd you learn to be so brave?" I asked.

Pinky laughed. "Hell, Raylene. I got me four brothers—only one more'n you. When we ain't fightin' with each other, they're showin' me how to fight anybody wants to hurt me. Don't Del or those other brothers of yours teach you nothin'?"

He teaches me more'n enough, I thought.

"Nothing I want to learn," I said. "Not from Del. Tell you the truth, Robbie and Jimmy and me—we's all scared of him."

Pinky shook her head. "That ain't right."

She hefted her switchblade in her hand, then offered it to me.

"Here," she said. "It's about time you learned a thing or two 'bout takin' care of yourself."

Them boys showing up like they did pretty much shut the party down for the night. Pinky, she was still a-raring to go, but all the fun had leaked out of it for the rest of us. Pinky and me, we got us a ride home, had Lenny let us off a half mile down the road because Pinky said she and me, we had some talking to do. We watched Lenny's taillights disappear down the road, then Pinky started to explain the finer workings of my new red-handled switchblade.

"You gotta practice gettin' it open fast," she said. "Sometimes that's all you need, just to have it out and be ready to use it afore anybody knows what's what. Most times, that's all you're gonna need to do."

I nodded. I don't know as I'd ever be able to cut anybody like she just done, but that knife sure felt good in my hand.

"Now, when you do need to use it," she went on, "you hold the blade edge up, and cut up with it. Natural inclination's to cut down, but all you're gonna do is hit you some ribs. Cuttin' up, you go clean through all the soft stomach tissue. And you keep this sweetheart sharp, you hear me? I'll get you a whetstone and show you how. You don't want to be dependin' on nobody but yourself."

It went on like that for a while, Pinky talking, more serious than I ever heard her before, me nodding and listening, holding it all in.

"You know how to shoot?" she asked me after we got done talking about knives.

I shook my head.

"That's somethin' else I'm gonna have to teach you. Time might come when you gotta walk out into the dark, and if you're walkin' on your own, a gun makes for mighty fine company. See, most of the hard-cases you're gonna meet, they ain't used to no pretty girl that can stand up and be just as hard as they are. Harder even. But they see you know how to use what you're holdin', and you ain't afraid to use it, ain't nobody gonna hurt you." She grinned. " 'Less you like it a little rough."

"You been with those boys before," I found myself saying. "Russell and Eugene and all."

"Oh, yeah." I couldn't see her eyes in the dark, but her voice was as hard as I imagined they'd be. "We had us some history. But they just ain't much good at learning the difference between fun and pain."

Well, that night when Del come into my bedroom, like he's been doing three or four times a week ever since my older sister run off and he needed himself a new special girl, I was waiting with that present of Pinky's in my hand. I knew I couldn't outright kill him—that'd probably be a sin, killing your own brother, don't matter what he was doing to you—but I meant to hurt him bad.

I'd had me some of Pa's liquor when I got home, to fortify me like. Back then I didn't have much courage I could call up on my own. But I was primed that night. The old man and Ma was out someplace, don't ask me where. But I knew that'd mean Del'd be sniffing around my bed as soon as he got his own self home. Jimmy and Robbie were sleeping down the hall, but they wouldn't say nothing. I could holler like a cat on fire and they'd still stay in that room of theirs, too scared of Del to even think of helping me. Or maybe they'd be jacking off to the sound of my crying. I don't know. It's not like we ever talked about it or nothing.

I held in my head what Pinky told me afore she headed off home earlier. "You get into a situation," she said, "you gotta hold this thought in your head: 'It don't matter if I live or die.' That's what gives you the edge. Bullies, they're pretty much all the same. Scared under all that meanness and bluster. But they can read you good, smell the fear on you like an old coon hound." She grinned. "But they can smell the fearlessness, too. They know when you don't give a shit what happens to you. So you hold your head up, Raylene. Look 'em in the eye and remember what the Injuns say: 'It's a good day to die.' "

I said that to myself as I stood there with that red-handled switch-blade in my hand, moonlight coming in through the window glinting on the blade.

"It's a good day to die."

And damned if it didn't feel that way. Part of me was still a little girl, scared as all get out, but part of me was something else. Part of me was a piece of the night, lying in wait for the monster to come. Lying in wait with a big shiny knife in my hand, and wasn't it a pretty thing?

The door opened without a creak. Del oiled those hinges on a regular basis his own self. I stood there against the wall by the door, watching him creep across the floor to my bed.

"Hey, there, Ray," he whispered. "Rise and shine, little sister. I done got you a present."

He was fumbling with his zipper when I stepped up behind him. He smelled of beer and cigarettes and something else. A dark, animal smell.

"You playin' shy?" he said, reaching out with his free hand to give me a shake.

But there weren't nobody there. Just some bunched-up old jeans and shirts to make it look like I was sleeping.

"I'm right here, Del," I said. "And I got me a present for you tonight."

I let him turn around. I let him see the moonlight in my eyes and the shine on that blade. I tell you, I was feeling big and tall, like one of them mountain men you'd see come down from the real hillbilly hollers. I wanted to drive that new knife of mine right in his gut, just like Pinky done with Russell, but all my courage drained away at the look on his face. I never seen him so mad. I was froze solid, like I had roots growing outta the bottoms of my cowboy boots.

He was drunk and I guess that's what saved my life, though it didn't seem so at first. He just up and backhanded me across the face. Split my lip and sent me skidding back against the window frame. Then he stood over me and laughed. I was so scared I maybe did wet my panties some and I was gripping the handle of that switchblade so tight my knuckles were whiter than the moon hanging outside the window.

But he was swaying while he laughed. Hurting something always made him giddy and I guess being drunk just made everything seem funnier to him.

"Lookit you, Ray," he finally said. "Damned if you ain't a sight. I think maybe I'm gonna take that little knife away and stick it up your hole. Whatcha think about that?"

He crossed the floor and I didn't know what I was doing, just knew I had to do something. So I swung out with that knife of Pinky's, honed sharp as a razor. I caught him in the back of his knee, slicing through his jeans and skin and muscle like it was butter. He howled and went down and I scrabbled out of the way.

"Jesus, fuck!" he cried. "You cut me, Ray!"

Something went click in my head then, changed me. He reached for me and I slashed again, opening up the palm of his hand. And it felt good. Seeing his blood. Hearing him moan.

Big, bad, scary Del. He was just lying on the floor, whimpering now.

"You sound like a girl," I told him.

"I . . ."

I bent down so my face was close to his, but not so close he could grab me.

"This is gonna be our little secret, ain't that right?" I said, echoing the words he done told me more times than I can ever remember.

"I . . . I'll fuckin' . . . kill you . . ."

I'll give him this. He was hurt bad, but he wasn't scared. Maybe he was too drunk and mad to be scared. Or too dumb. I don't know. I didn't much care.

"I'm right sorry to hear you feel that way," I said.

I stood up again and I give him a kick. Those cowboy boots of mine have got them a point, so I know it hurt. He just cried out, backed away. Dragging his leg. Cradling his hand where the blood come bubbling up, making a slick mess.

" 'Cause now I'm gonna have to kill you," I told him. "And that worries me, 'cause I'm thinkin' it could be a sin. What do you think, Del? Is killin' your brother a sin? And if it is, what I'm workin' on here is tryin' to decide if it's a bigger one'n the things you done to me, your own little sister."

"You . . . you get me a doctor . . ."

I shook my head. "I can't do that, Del. I'm too scared to go walkin' around a big dark old house like this, all on my own like."

I didn't know it could feel so good, standing over someone like this and knowing you had the power of their life or death in your hands. If I'm a broken thing, like one of them shrinks at the jailhouse told me once, then this is the place I got broke. Not all those other times, when Del came sniffing 'round me, but that night. The night I learned how to hurt back.

I coulda killed him. Maybe I should have. But I guess I still didn't have it in me yet. There was a shake starting up in my legs and I knew I had to get me outta there afore I fell down my own self. He made another grab at me and I kicked him again, waving the knife in his face. He went down and I turned, grabbed the bag I'd packed before he got home, and I lit outta there, pounding down the stairs in my boots, the bloody knife still in my hand.

I made it maybe as far as the end of the lane before I got all weak in my knees. My legs went to jelly and I dropped down on all fours, my head bent down in the ditch, puking up beer and liquor and whatever sour crap was left when the alcohol was gone. I wasn't no pretty sight by the time I'd dragged myself down to Pinky's house and banged a handful of gravel up against her window.

"Damn, if you ain't a quick study," she said when I managed to tell her what I'd done.

That was the first time I run off from home, same as my sister afore me.

But that was a long time ago, some thirty years or better now, I guess.

Russell survived the cutting Pinky give him and he and his hardcase buddies kept up their wicked ways, but they never come 'round bothering us again. Oh, they beat the crap outta Lenny and a couple of the other guys'd been there in the field that night, and I heard they had themselves a party with Cherie, but they stayed clear of Pinky and me.

Del didn't die.

He told our parents and the police that he'd come upon a burglar, sneaking in through my bedroom window. He couldn't tell the truth. The can of worms that would've opened wouldn't have let him come out smelling like a hero the way his own story did. Course Jimmy and Robbie backed him up.

When the police found me at Pinky's and dragged me back home, I said I didn't know nothing neither. I stood there in Pinky's front hall, my own eye half shut and swollen from where Del'd hit me. It was just coincidence I picked that night to run off like I did, I told them, and they swallowed the lie. What were they supposed to think? That the slip of a girl I was, bra size notwithstanding, coulda beat up a big ol' boy the size of Del?

Del didn't bother me for a while. But he'd give me looks. Ma'd give me looks. Jimmy and Robbie. Only the old man went on the way he always did, pretending nothing was wrong.

I still hate them all. Del, well, he goes without saying. Pa for being so pussy-whipped and not protecting me. Ma for taking Del's side, blaming me when I first ran crying to her, a little scared girl, looking for comfort. Jimmy and Robbie, well, they was always no-account. I don't know that I hated them. I don't know that they even registered at all. I mean we was all victims, right? Just like our sister afore us.

I think maybe I hate her the most of all, for running off the way she did. If she hadn't lit out, Del would've stuck with her and never took up with me. I know that's true. He told me often enough.

Jilly

Sophie found Mona Morgan waiting for her by the mouth of the alley that ran along Jilly's building on Yoors Street. The comic-book artist had her hands in the pockets of her green cargo pants, her head tilted back to study the second-floor window that Jilly used as a door to her fire escape "balcony."

"I would've given you the key last night," Sophie said when she joined Mona, "if I'd known you'd be early."

"I just got here," Mona told her. She ran a hand through her hair. The short blonde spikes were showing an inch of dark roots. "That's where they went in, I guess," she added, indicating the window.

Sophie nodded. "Lou said he boarded it up before he left last night."

"This is so awful," Mona said. "I just dread going up there."

"Me, too."

Mona had offered to help clean Jilly's studio loft when she'd heard Sophie and Wendy talking about it at the hospital last night. Wendy would have come as well, but she had a regular job writing copy and doing proofreading at *In the City* now. The weekly arts and entertainment newspaper ran on a tight schedule that didn't leave a whole lot of room for creative time management. It wasn't like the old waitressing days when she could simply trade off a shift with someone and make it up later. These days, only Jilly still worked part-time at Kathryn's Café.

Sophie sighed. Or at least she had been up until four days ago.

"Did you go by the hospital this morning?" Mona asked as the two of them returned to the front of the building.

They walked past a few abandoned storefronts to the narrow entranceway that led to the second floor, pausing just inside the door so that Sophie could collect Jilly's mail. It was mostly junk: flyers, a catalogue. There were also a couple of bills and a letter with an L.A. postmark. From Geordie, Sophie saw when she turned it over to look at the return address. That would have been mailed before the accident, she thought as they climbed the stairs to Jilly's loft.

"I went by first thing," she said in response to Mona's question. "I wanted to catch the doctor while he was making his rounds."

"What did he say about . . . you know . . ."

"The paralysis?"

Mona nodded.

"Pretty much the same as last night," Sophie said. "Every case is different. She could shake it off today, in a week, in a month . . ."

"But she's going to be okay."

"Of course she is," Sophie lied, as much to Mona as herself.

The truth was she didn't know if Jilly would ever be okay again. The results of the accident, especially the paralysis, seemed to have stomped Jilly's normally irrepressible spirit right into the ground. Understandable, of course, considering what she'd been through, but it was so disconcerting to see Jilly like this, lying there, staring up at the ceiling, answering in monosyllables, her few words mumbled because the paralysis had also affected one side of her mouth.

"Is she a fighter?" the doctor had asked Sophie before they parted this morning.

Four days ago Sophie would have had no trouble answering yes.

"Because it's the ones who are most determined," the doctor went on, "who recover most quickly . . ." He gave a sad shake of his head. "When they give up, nobody can help them."

"I won't let her give up," Sophie had told him.

But that was easier said than done. How did you *make* someone want to live?

"I don't want to be here," Jilly had said, lying there, broken and pale. Half her head shaven, the words spilled out of a crooked mouth. At least the tubes had been removed from her nose and she was no longer dependent on machines to breathe.

"I know you don't," Sophie told her. She was sitting on the side of the bed, wiping Jilly's forehead with a damp cloth. "None of us wants you to be here. But you don't have any choice right now."

"I do have a choice," Jilly said. "I can go back to sleep. I can go back to the dreamlands."

It was the most she'd said to Sophie all morning.

"That's not a solution," Sophie said. "You know that, don't you?"

But Jilly only closed her eyes.

"Sophie?" Mona asked. "Are you okay?"

Sophie had paused halfway up the stairs, tears brimming in her eyes. She shook her head. Mona came down to the riser she was standing on and put her arms around her. For a long time they stood there, holding on to each other.

"Thanks," Sophie said finally, stepping away. "I needed that."

"Me, too."

Sophie's gaze went past Mona, up the stairs to Jilly's door.

"Let's get this done," she said.

It was both worse and not as bad as Lou had made it out to be. At least half the paintings were untouched, so the loss wasn't as complete as when, years ago, Izzy had lost all her work in the fire. But looking at the art that had been damaged, it was difficult for either woman to understand the sheer savagery of the sick individual responsible for the wreckage. There would be no fixing those paintings. Most of them hung in tattered ribbons from their frames. The remainder had even had their frames broken and splintered. Fifty or sixty of Jilly's gorgeous paintings, all destroyed beyond repair. Some were works in progress, but most were ones she'd just loved too much to be able to sell.

The reek of turps and solvents that stung their nostrils when they entered the loft came from some bottles that had been broken near Jilly's easel, almost as an afterthought, it seemed. The sharp sting in the air was enough to burn their eyes, but at least they hadn't been poured over the furniture the way Sophie had feared from Lou's terse description the night before.

Jilly's other belongings—her clothes, books, everything—were scattered around as though a squall had blown in off the lake and through the apartment. Only the kitchen area was relatively untouched. Some glasses and mugs had been broken there—they must have been in the drainer which Sophie found lying on the floor under the kitchen table. Except for that small bit of damage, the doors of the cupboards and fridge were all still closed, guarding their contents.

After a quick circuit of the loft to assess the damage, they opened the windows facing onto Yoors Street to help air the place out, removed a couple of boards from the back window to create some airflow, and got to it. They began with picking up the broken glass and porcelain, mopping up the turps and solvents from around Jilly's painting area.

"At least no one had a dump on the floor," Mona said as she wrung out the mop in a bucket.

Sophie turned to her with a handful of fired clay and porcelain fragments that had once been mugs and raised her eyebrows.

"Like what happened to Miki last year, remember? The people that trashed her place peed on her clothes and furniture and smeared feces everywhere."

Sophie grimaced. "God, I'd forgotten about that."

"It's the kind of thing you want to forget," Mona said. "Like this." Her gaze traveled the length of the room. "All these beautiful paintings . . ."

"I don't know how we're going to tell her," Sophie said.

"Or *who's* going to tell her."

Sophie nodded glumly. She rose to her feet and dumped the handful of mug fragments into the big plastic cooking oil container that Jilly used as a garbage bin. When she glanced back at Mona, it was to find the other woman still gazing at the paintings.

"This is weird," Mona said, finally looking over at Sophie.

"What is?"

"The paintings that are destroyed. They're all Jilly's faerie paintings. The landscapes and city scenes—none of them were touched." She crossed the room and laid one of the damaged paintings on the floor, arranging the torn strips so that its subject could be seen. "You see? This has got a couple of those gemmin of hers in it. That one's of a dandelion sprite."

Sophie joined Mona and looked down. The painting Mona had roughly reconstructed was one of Babe and Emmie—a couple of faerie that Jilly claimed she had met in the Tombs, that junked-out part of the city north of Grasso Street that looked like it had been bombed. Sophie lifted her gaze and regarded the other paintings with a new eye. It was true. Whoever had done this really hadn't cared for the faerie art, destroying it, while leaving the rest untouched.

"So what are we supposed to think?" she said. "That it was some critic?"

"I can't imagine that," Mona told her. "But then I can't imagine anybody doing this kind of thing in the first place, so what do I know."

Sophie sighed. "I can. All you have to do is open the newspaper and you get a daily dose of all the horrible things people can do to one another."

Mona laid the ruined painting on top of another.

"What are we going to do with them?" she asked.

"God, I just don't know. But we have to do something. I don't want them to be the first thing Jilly sees when she gets back."

If she got back. It might be a long time before Jilly was able to navigate the stairs leading up to her loft. Maybe never. The professor had already offered his house for her convalescence, though how well Jilly and Goon, the professor's cantankerous housekeeper, would get along was anyone's guess. Goon was impossible at the best of times.

"Is there room in that closet?" Sophie added.

Mona went to look and gave a start when she opened the door.

"What?" Sophie began, then saw that it was only the life-size fabric mâché self-portrait Jilly had made in art school that had startled Mona.

Mona gave her an embarrassed grin. "I forgot about the mâché clone."

"Is there room in there for the paintings?"

"Not really. What about the storage area in the basement?"

"We can only go check," Sophie said. "Let's finish cleaning this stuff up first."

.   .   .

"Why hasn't she ever moved?" Mona asked as they folded away the last of Jilly's clothes.

The smell of turps still hung in the air, but the air circulation had helped, and it didn't seem any stronger than it usually did when Jilly was working on a painting. The floor was cleaned and mopped, all the broken glass put away. Jackets and Jilly's few dresses hung in the closet, books restacked on their shelves in as much order as Jilly ever kept them in, which was none. Knickknacks were back in their usual places, or at least as well as either Sophie or Mona could remember.

"Surely she could afford a bigger place by now," Mona went on.

"For the same reason she works"—Sophie refused to say "worked"—"at Kathryn's—she doesn't like change. For all her spontaneity and love of the strange and unusual, there's something comforting for her when things stay the same."

Mona nodded. "That's true. She was really broken up about Geordie moving to L.A. Is that what you mean?"

"Well, Geordie was special."

"An honorary member of your small fierce women tribe."

"That, too."

"They spent a lot of time together, didn't they?" Mona said. "All those aimless rambles and late-night coffee klatches."

Sophie nodded. "And she was also sweet on him."

"You think?"

"I'm sure." Sophie straightened up and looked across the room at Mona. "Though you'd never get her to admit that, not even to herself. The kind of happiness that comes from a relationship is something that's always eluded her. It's the intimacy, I suppose. It takes her back to . . . well, you know."

Mona nodded.

"So even if she did ever admit to herself that she liked Geordie in that way, she'd never have acted on it because she'd be afraid to spoil what they did have."

"And now he's with Tanya."

"Mmm. So it's a moot point, I guess."

Sophie had rarely been in the basement of the Yoors Street building that housed Jilly's studio and Mona had never gone down there. It was a dark, cavernous space, with only low-watt overheads to push back the shadows and who knew how many years of clutter, making an adventure of the simple walk from one end of the room to the other. The old furnace was enormous, squatting in the corner like some drowsy dinosaur in comparison to the more sleek and contemporary models available now. Dangling from hooks attached to the tall ceiling were stepladders, snow shovels, coils of extension cord, as well as any number of less readily identifiable items, all of which made passage along the length of the room that much more hazardous.

The tenant storage areas were all along one side of the wall, square cells constructed of tall chain-link fencing and wooden support beams, each with its own padlocked gate. True to Jilly's haphazard ideas concerning security, the key to her area hung on a nail beside its lock. The small room was full of boxes as well as some furniture and two more fabric mâché sculptures from her art school days: a rather crudely rendered gargoyle that stood upright, rather than crouching in a traditional pose, and the seven-foot-tall, even more crudely rendered Frankenstein monster that Jilly used to haul out and place on the landing outside her front door on Halloween.

"Whatever happened to the neat old bike Jilly used to have?" Mona asked as they moved boxes to make room for the damaged paintings, stacking them along the back wall.

"She set it free."

"She what?"

"It was after Zinc died. Remember how he used to cut the locks on bikes so that they could go free?"

Mona nodded. "I remember."

"So a year or so later, Jilly just leaned her bike up against the wall of the alley under her fire escape and set it free."

"Did it really . . . you know, go off by itself?"

"Oh, please. Someone just took it. The same way they took all those bikes that Zinc 'freed.' "

Mona paused with a box in her hand to look at her.

"You don't believe in magic at all, do you? Even with your dreamworld?"

Sophie shook her head. "Not the way you and Jilly do. Mabon's just that: a dream. I realize my serial dreams are weird, but they're not impossible."

"I've only ever had the one magical experience."

"I know. I read about it in your comic. It made a good story."

"But it really happened," Mona said. "This little grotty gnome of a man really did turn invisible and squat in my apartment."

"I believe in a different kind of magic," Sophie said. "The kind we make between each other. The kind that comes from our art and how it can change us. The world doesn't need any more than that."

"But what if it has it all the same?"

Sophie shrugged. "Then I'm missing out on it."

"I don't think so. Not with Mabon, and the way stuff goes wacky around you."

"Jinx is purely physiological," Sophie told her. "It's got something to do with the way my electromagnetic field interacts with that of clocks and machines and things like that."

"Maybe," Mona said.

Sophie smiled. "Well, it's not because of fairies."

They went back to moving the boxes.

Hours later, they were finally done. All the damaged paintings had been brought downstairs and stacked up in Jilly's storage area and the apartment was tidier than it had probably been in months. Mona had put on a pot of tea. When it was done, the two of them sank down on either end of the sofa and put their feet up on the pillow that lay between them.

"I think Daniel likes Jilly," Sophie said.

She looked at Mona over the tops of her knees, tea mug cradled on her stomach. Her fingers felt stiff and her back and shoulders were aching a little from the unfamiliar labor of moving all those boxes and paintings.

"Who's Daniel?"

"You know. The hunky nurse in the ICU. He was asking me if she had a boyfriend last night."

Mona smiled. "Big surprise. Everybody likes Jilly."

"Not everybody," Sophie said.

They looked around, remembering the damage the studio had sustained. Sophie thought of what Lou had told them, his suspicions that the hit-and-run and the vandalism were connected.

"What are we going to do about all of this?" she finally said. "How are we ever going to figure out who's got it in for her?"

Mona slowly shook her head. "Maybe the person we should be asking is Jilly."

"Except that means we have to tell her about the paintings."

"We have to do that anyway," Mona said.

Sophie turned away and looked around the loft. She missed the faerie paintings. For all that she couldn't buy into the reality of fairyland the way so many of her friends did, she'd always liked the enchanted feeling she got sitting in Jilly's studio, surrounded by all those impossible denizens of the dreamworld as they were portrayed in Jilly's art. She sighed. Magical creatures and faerie were so much a part of Jilly's life, so integral to how she viewed the world. How was she ever going to deal with the loss of all her paintings of them?

It would kill her at the best of times, but now, stuck in the hospital and—please, god—temporarily unable to paint or draw because of the paralysis . . .

"I mean, sooner or later, she's got to know," Mona said.

Sophie nodded. "I know. And I guess it'll have to be me that tells her. But I'm just dreading it."

"You don't have to do it alone," Mona told her. "I can come with you. Or I'm sure Wendy would."

"Or maybe Angel," Sophie said. "She always seems to know the best way to give bad news without it seeming to be so completely devastating. And Jilly's always listened to her." She gave Mona a small smile. "I mean, Jilly's always a good listener, but Angel's like Joe. She can get away with telling Jilly stuff she doesn't want to hear."

"I knew what you meant," Mona said.

2

Once upon a time . . .

It's a relief when I can finally fall asleep and see Joe again in the dreamlands. Everyone else's been tiptoeing around me like I'm this fragile china teacup. And I guess maybe I was, considering how easily I broke. But all that's left now are the broken shards of china that the doctors have bandaged and arranged in the shape of a body on my hospital bed, so there's no need for hushed voices and concerned gazes anymore. There's nothing left to break. My heart doesn't count.

My happiness at finding Joe doesn't last. He's in mild loco mode, the way he gets when his trickster side starts to swamp the wise man.

"You know how we'd get along better?" he says. "If everybody'd just remember how we're all related. White, black, Asian, skin. No difference. All the bloodlines go back to that one old mama in Africa."

The idea of blood relations isn't high on my list of things to care about.

"Your point being?" I ask.

"No point," he says. "I'm all smooth edges."

"I just need a break," I tell him. "That's why I'm here. I know I have to face up to what's waiting for me in that hospital bed, but can't I get a little distance from it first? I need this. The cathedral wood. The enchantment. Air that tastes like it has weight and substance."

Joe looks at me and doesn't say a word. He's the only person besides Geordie who can make me feel guilty without even trying. And I know what he's aiming at here. It's the hurt that sits inside me; the hurt that first got born when I was a little girl.

"The trouble with distance," he finally says, "is that you always need more of it."

"You know it's not like that," I say. "I've spent my whole life trying to be a person who wouldn't fit into the kind of family I grew up in. To care more instead of caring less. Or not at all."

"You have to work at that?" Joe asks.

I nod. "I did at first. I was all the rough edges you say you don't have."

That gets me a smile. Like he isn't all edges himself. I've seen people pass him by on the street, their gazes quickly averted, troubled by the weird lights that can dance in his eyes.

"I really do care about people now," I go on, "but that's something I had to learn. I had to let go of all the hurt and old baggage and teach myself to meet each day with anticipation and a smile. To look for the best in people, instead of the worst, because when you look for the best, you can bring it out in them."

"Not to mention in yourself."

I nod in agreement.

Joe lights a hand-rolled cigarette that he takes from the pocket of his jeans. The tangy smell of tobacco and sweetgrass comes drifting over to where I'm standing.

"But you never let the hurt go," he says. "Not really. You hid it away inside instead."

Me and Geordie and all the other damaged souls that refused to give in to the darkness.

"Same difference," I say.

"You really think so?"

I'm about to brass it out, but this is Joe. I can never put anything past him.

"I don't know," I tell him. "It's how I could deal with it. I could never forget."

I take a breath to ease the growing tightness in my chest, get a little sustenance from the air. All these years it's been, and it still won't fade or go away.

"I can never forgive them, Joe."

Blue smoke trails up from his mouth as he exhales. He nods.

"I know," he says. "But you've got two things broken now, and the way the healers tell it to me, the new hurt's not going to mend until you deal with the old one." His gaze fixes on me, serious. "We've got to do something or you're going to end up with nothing."

"I've got this," I say, waving a hand to take in the trees of the dreamlands.

"And if you *don't* mend, back there in the World As It Is?" he asks. "See, that's the problem with traveling here in the spirit—you need that anchor your body makes. Without it, your spirit's got to move on."

He's talking about me dying, I realize. The thought doesn't really scare me—it's hard to be scared in this place, where mystery already lies so thick on everything—but all the same, it wakes a nervous murmur that snakes up my spine.

"Where do we go?" I ask.

He shrugs, takes another drag. "That's something nobody living really knows," he says. "Not even here. And the dead don't hang around to explain."

We fall silent. I've known Joe for so long that even our silences are companionable, but there's a strain in the quiet today. Something pushing against the peacefulness. It's my broken body and the old hurts that nobody can mend.

"I'm going away for a while," Joe says. "There's a woman I know that can maybe help, but she's hard to find and you know what time's like in this place."

Not firsthand, but I've heard about it often enough from others. Time's like water here, sometimes moving faster, sometimes slower than it does in the world where my body's lying in a hospital bed and can't even sit up, never mind walk around like I can here.

"I'll be okay," I tell him.

"I'll get one or two of the cousins to look in on you," he says. "Keep you company when you cross over here. Maybe show you around while I'm gone."

"Like the crow girls?" I ask, unable to keep the eagerness out of my voice.

"What makes you think we're related?"

Just that you're all three shapeshifters and tricksters, I think. But I only give him a shrug in response.

"Maida and Zia will get you into more trouble than you're already in," Joe says. "They don't mean any harm. It's just the way they are."

"Well, I like them."

Joe grins. "What's not to like? They sure do keep the world interesting."

He takes a final drag on his cigarette and puts it out against the heel of his boot. The butt goes into his pocket.

"I'll be as quick as I can," he says.

"Thanks, Joe."

I give him a hug. It's funny, I think. A hug is such a simple thing. We take it for granted along with everything else, like walking and picking up a pencil and breathing. Until we can't do it anymore. Back in that hospital bed, I can't even take a drink by myself.

"Don't spend all your time here," Joe says as he steps back. "Promise me you'll work hard when they start you on rehab."

"I will. But first—"

"You need a little distance. Yeah. I hear you."

He puts his index finger against my forehead and gives me a little push.

"Ya-ha-hey," he says.

Then he takes a sideways step and he's not with me anymore. It's like he stepped behind an invisible curtain.

"Ya-ha-hey," I repeat softly.

I close my eyes and take a long, deep breath of this enchanted air before I let myself wake up again in the hospital bed.

3

When Sophie got to the hospital just before dinner the next evening, she discovered that Jilly had been moved from the intensive care unit into a regular room. She and Desmond had come straight from teaching at the Newford School of Art, so they arrived at the hospital lugging knapsacks of art supplies and portfolios. Once they had the directions to Jilly's new room, they returned to the elevator where Sophie pressed the button for the fifth floor, two up from where they were. The elevator immediately took them straight down to the cafeteria in the basement.

"Stupid thing," Sophie muttered.

She reached for the button again, but Desmond mouthed the word "Jinx" and caught her hand before she could touch it.

"Better let me," he said, "or we'll be riding this thing all night."

Sophie sighed and leaned back against the wall. Desmond grinned at her, teeth flashing white against his coffee-brown skin. As usual, he was wearing nothing more than cargo pants, a T-shirt, and a thin cotton jacket, even though the wind was brisk enough outside tonight to take the temperature almost down to freezing. But Desmond always dressed as though he were still living on the Islands. The woolen tam that was pulled down over his dreadlocks might be considered a concession to the cold, except he wore it on the hottest days of the summer as well. His tams were invariably in the African liberation colors of red, black, green, and yellow, but Desmond wasn't a Rastaman. He didn't even have a Jamaican accent, his family having emigrated to Newford when he was barely seven.

They met Angel in the hall when they stepped out of the elevator. She managed a small smile for them, but it didn't reach her eyes.

"How is she?" Desmond asked.

"If it was anyone else," Angel said, "you'd think they were in pretty good spirits. But this is Jilly, and for her, it's like a major depression. Don't let the smiles and jokes fool you. She's hurting."

Desmond sighed. "Makes you wonder about all these plans God's supposed to have for us, doesn't it?"

"God doesn't do anything to us," Angel said. "He doesn't have to. We're too busy doing it to each other."

She lifted a hand, then stepped into the elevator. The doors whispered shut.

"Angel's hurting, too," Desmond said.

"We all are."

He nodded. "Amen to that."

The new room was a double, but the other bed was unoccupied, so Jilly had the space to herself for now. Windows took up the whole side wall. They started at about waist height and rose all the way to the ceiling, offering a wide view of the city's skyline. From this height they could see all the way to St. Paul's Cathedral. Beyond its square finialed towers a jagged mountain range of tall office buildings hid the lakefront and Wolf Island.

"Some view," Desmond said.

"They send tour groups through here a couple of times a day," Jilly told him.

She gave them the crooked smile that was the best she could manage these days, then her gaze dropped to what they were carrying. Sophie watched Jilly struggle to keep the smile in place.

We should have left all this stuff in the hall, she thought, realizing too late how it would only remind Jilly of what she'd lost.

You're going to get better, she wanted to say. You'll be drawing and painting again before you know it.

Except what if she couldn't?

"So how were classes today?" Jilly asked.

"Oh, you know," Desmond told her. "It's the same old. They all want to be able to paint, right now, without putting in the time to learn how."

"Who's taken over my classes?"

"Izzy and I are sharing them at the moment," Sophie said. "Just until . . ." They can get someone to replace you, she almost said. "You get back."

"I think they should be looking for someone a little more long-term than that," Jilly said.

Desmond shook his head. "Ah, you'll be out of here in no time."

Jilly hummed a few bars from "Wishin' and Hopin'," a song that Ani DiFranco had recently covered for the soundtrack to *My Best Friend's Wedding*. They'd rented the video only last week, but Sophie'd slept through most of it.

"So talk to me," Jilly said. "What's going on at the school? I feel like I've been in here for months."

"Well," Desmond said in that slow drawl of his. "You know Hannah's always had this thing for Davie Fenn, right?"

"Oh, tell me about it. I was seriously thinking of going into high-action matchmaker mode with the pair of them."

"No need," Desmond told her.

Sophie nodded. "She asked him out on Saturday and he ended up spending the night at her place."

"Plus," Desmond added, "there've been many sightings of them holding hands and kissing in public places."

"Oh, god, I'm missing everything," Jilly said. "Details. I need some juicy details . . ."

It was good to see Jilly more like her old self, Sophie thought, even if she did mumble some of her words and couldn't bounce around the room the way she normally did. That was probably one of the oddest things about her being laid up like this. She was so still.

But after a while Desmond had to go, and Sophie saw the false good cheer for what it had been.

"There was a letter from Geordie in your mailbox," Sophie said, digging among the paint tubes and brushes in her knapsack. "I brought it along."

"Can you read it to me?"

"Of course." Sophie hesitated. "It's postmarked before the accident. You know he wants to be here, but he has to finish up that studio work first. He told Wendy that he'll be flying in on the weekend."

"I miss him."

Sophie nodded. "We all do," she said.

Though not the way Jilly would.

The letter provided a tonic in a way that Jilly's many visitors couldn't. It was filled with Geordie's wry observations on life in L.A., gently poking fun at the Hollywood crowd he was mingling with because Tanya was in the movie business. Underlying it all was a general affection for Jilly that no one could miss.

Jilly's eyes were shiny by the time Sophie got to the end of the letter.

"Do you think he's happy there?" she asked.

Sophie shook her head. "Not really. But I guess he's making the effort for Tanya's sake."

"He wasn't going to go," Jilly said. "I'm the one who talked him into going."

"But why? I know how you feel about him."

That crooked smile pulled at Jilly's lips. "For all his scruff, Geordie likes a little glamour in a girlfriend. Just look at the women he's always been attracted to. Remember Sam?"

"She was gorgeous," Sophie agreed.

"Exactly. I can't compete with that."

"You wouldn't have to. First of all, you're just as gorgeous."

"Right. It's this gift I have."

Sophie ignored her. "And secondly, you've got way more going for you than just that. The two of you, you were natural for each other."

Jilly slowly shook her head. "I could never be physically close to him. Not the way he'd want. Or deserves. You know how I freak when things start to get intimate."

"Maybe it would have been different with Geordie."

"Maybe," Jilly agreed. "But I couldn't take the chance that it'd spoil what we did have."

Except now he's gone and all you've got is him at a distance, Sophie thought. He's somebody else's lover, where he should have been yours.

But there was no way she'd ever come right out and tell Jilly that. She didn't have to. She could already see the knowledge sitting there in Jilly's eyes.

When Wendy arrived with Christy and his girlfriend Saskia, Sophie folded up the letter and put it in the drawer of Jilly's nightstand, then gathered her things and said her good-byes. But she didn't leave the hospital. Instead she took the stairs down to the cafeteria and got a sandwich and a cup of tea. She was on her second cup when Wendy came in, got herself some tea, and joined Sophie at her table.

"How did it go at the studio?" Wendy asked. "Did you get it all cleaned up?"

Sophie nodded. "It's probably tidier than it's been in ages."

"It must have been so hard, having to deal with all those paintings . . ."

"It was the most awful thing you can imagine. But there was something odd about it as well. Only the faerie paintings were destroyed. Whoever did it left all the other ones alone."

"Why?"

Sophie shrugged. "Why would anybody do it in the first place?"

"You should tell Lou," Wendy said. "It might be a clue." She laughed. "I'm rhyming again."

Sophie smiled. "Well, you are our resident poet."

"I do try. Maybe I should become a DJ. Rappin' Wendy, she's really quite friendly."

Their laughter died away quickly. It was hard to maintain good humor at a time such as this. The guilt of having any fun at all while Jilly lay immobile upstairs reared immediately.

"I will tell Lou," Sophie said. She took a sip of her tea, studied Wendy over the brim of her cup. "How did you find her tonight?" she asked.

"I've never seen her this bummed before. And it's so weird, when you think about it. Jilly's always the one who rises above things. Everyone comes to her with *their* troubles."

"The eternal den mother."

"Well, it's true."

Sophie shrugged. "I know." She took another sip, then set her cup down. "But what really worries me is how all she wants to do is sleep and visit the dreamlands. It's like nothing here means much to her anymore, now that she has access to that other world."

"As things stand," Wendy said, "she hasn't exactly got a whole lot waiting for her here."

"She's got us."

"You know what I mean."

Sophie sighed. "You're right. But the real trouble is, she's so caught up in mucking about in the dreamlands that she's not putting any real effort into getting better. All she does is sleep."

"The doctor said she needs to rest—didn't he?"

"He also said she's got to *want* to get better."

But Wendy wouldn't let it go. "What harm is there in her getting a break from how horrible everything's become for her?"

"The dreamlands aren't real."

"But they feel real, don't they? Isn't that what you always say about your dreams? It's like they're another life."

" 'Like,' not 'they are.' "

Wendy shook her head. "You've even got a boyfriend there."

"But it's not *real*." Sophie tapped the table. "This is real. This is what she has to concentrate on now or she's never going to get better. They can exercise those paralyzed muscles, but if she doesn't put some effort into it as well, nothing they do is going to help."

"Come on," Wendy said. "It's not like she wants to be paralyzed."

"Oh, god. I know that. It's just . . ."

"You can't stand watching her slip away from us."

Sophie nodded.

"The really sad thing is," Wendy said, "if that's what she wants to do, there's nothing we can do to stop her."

That was what scared Sophie the most.

"I was always afraid of this," Wendy said after a moment.

"Of what?"

"That if Jilly ever actually got access to fairyland, she'd go and never come back."

"I can't imagine the world without Jilly," Sophie said.

Wendy sighed. "That's the trouble. I can. And it would be a horrible, boring place."

"We can't let her go."

Wendy only nodded. She didn't have to repeat what she'd said earlier. Sophie could still hear the words ringing in her head:

If that's what she wants to do, there's nothing we can do to stop her.

4

I can't seem to explain why I need to get away as badly as I do. This broken body that everybody comes to visit in the hospital might seem reason enough, but I've never been one to wallow in my misery. I'm just not built that way. If there's a problem, I fix it. If I don't know how to fix it, I find out how.

And I'll do the same with the hand I've been dealt now.

But all my life I've wanted to be the kid who gets to cross over into the magical kingdom. I devoured those books by C. S. Lewis and William Dunthorn, Ellen Wentworth, Susan Cooper, and Alan Garner. When I could get them from the library, I read them out of order as I found them, and then in order, and then reread them all again, many times over. Because even when I was a child I knew it wasn't simply escape that lay on the far side of the borders of fairyland. Instinctively I knew crossing over would mean more than fleeing the constant terror and shame that was mine at that time in my life. There was a knowledge that ran deeper—an understanding hidden in the marrow of my bones that only I can access—telling me that by crossing over, I'd be coming home.

That's the reason I've yearned so desperately to experience the wonder, the mystery, the beauty of that world beyond the World As It Is. It's because I know that somewhere across the border there's a place for me. A place of safety and strength and learning, where I can become who I'm supposed to be. I've tried forever to be that person here, but whatever I manage to accomplish in the World As It Is only seems to be an echo of what I could be in that other place that lies hidden somewhere beyond the borders.

So now that I can cross over, if only in my dreams, it's all I can do to come back to the World As It Is and be the Broken Girl again. Even if I was perfectly healthy, I'd have trouble returning. This is my chance, maybe the only one I'll ever get. If it took a hit and run and a crippled body to get me there, I can deal with it. Because I'm not escaping from, I'm escaping to.

I know everybody's worried. I love my friends, and I hate making them feel so bad, but I can't seem to find the right words to explain what this opportunity means to me. I don't think any of them, except for maybe Geordie and Joe, know how much I need the otherworld.

Though, if I'm going to be honest, the aftereffects of being hit by that car, the paralysis and broken bones, don't make time spent in the World As It Is all that appealing right now. I'm so used to being active, to dealing with my problems on my own, that the helplessness of being the Broken Girl is killing me. I can't even exercise on my own. I've only got movement in one leg—a lot you can do with that, right?—and my left arm, though it's weighed down with a cast.

This morning the physical therapist came by to see me, along with

Daniel, that handsome nurse Sophie claims is sweet on me. He's just got a good bedside manner.

Because of budget cuts, the therapist's workload is too big and he can't always be here to do it himself, so he's showing Daniel how to exercise my paralyzed arm and leg, a combination of movement and deep muscle massage. It's supposed to be done at least twice a day. More often, if possible. So this afternoon, Daniel comes by for the second session of the day and it's driving me crazy, his moving my leg, my arm, my neck like I can't, chatting all the while. Time was, I'd be happily chatting back. As Geordie says, I can be terminally friendly. I may have had to learn how to like people, back when I rejoined the human race, but it's not hard anymore because I genuinely do like them now.

But at this moment, I just want to be alone. I don't want Daniel manipulating my limbs like I'm some kind of puppet. I don't want to visit with my friends who are all suddenly acting awkward and stiff around me. It's like, be careful around the Humpty Dumpty Broken Girl. Humpty Dumpty walked down the street. Humpty Dumpty got knocked off her feet. We've just put the pieces all back together, but the glue's not holding so well and the slightest draft of air could easily make her fall all to pieces again.

When Daniel finally leaves, I shut my eyes. I remember being surprised at how easily Sophie's able to fall asleep, but I think I understand now. When you know that falling asleep lets you cross over, how can you not train yourself to drop off at a moment's notice?

One moment I'm the Broken Girl, lying in her hospital bed, and the next I'm myself again, whole and mobile, standing in the forest of forever. The cathedral woods. It's only a dream, you say. And that's true. But I don't care because when I walk off under those giant trees, every breath I take is like food, sustenance for my soul.

What I want to do is travel deep and deeper into the dreamlands, to find that place that I know is waiting for me here. My home. But I promised Joe I'd take it slow, that these little sojourns here are to catch my breath before I concentrate on the real work at hand: healing the Broken Girl. Then I can look for home. And I know he's right. If my body dies in the World As It Is, I'll be taken away from the dreamlands, too, heading off on that final journey that we all have to take one day. I don't know what's waiting for us when we die—something better, something worse. I only know I'm not ready to find out yet.

So I take it easy. Today I've decided to go sketching.

Before the accident, this is something I always made time for. Even when I might be too busy to paint, I'd work in my sketchbook, going out and drawing for no reason except for the pleasure of feeling the pencil rub across the paper, searching for the lights and darks with the graphite until the magic happens and recognizable shapes appear on the paper. I guess drawing's something I've always taken for granted. Even when I was a kid, it was just something I did, like breathing. But I'm really paying attention to it now. I know a lot of the pleasure I'm feeling at this moment is from the simple fact of being able to do it. The Broken Girl can't even pick up a pencil.

I got my sketchbook and a nice Wolfe's carbon crayon in Mabon. I still don't know why I sometimes find myself there, sometimes here, in the woods. I wandered around the city for a long time, looking for Sophie or her boyfriend Jeck, but while I met a lot of interesting people, I couldn't find them. I wonder about the people I meet. Do they originate in the dreamlands, or are they here like me, taking a vacation from their body? I haven't asked because it doesn't seem polite.

The last time I crossed over, I decided to give up looking for Sophie for the time being. Mabon's even bigger than Newford and Newford's pushing six million by now. Since I don't know my way around, finding Sophie feels kind of hopeless. I figure we'll meet here when we do. And for now, well, I like Mabon, but the forest draws me more.

The last time I found myself in the city, I tracked down an art shop where I got my sketchbook and pencil. I asked Jamie—the clerk behind the counter, according to his name tag, if he hadn't switched it with a co-worker—if he could tell me how to get from Mabon to the cathedral woods. He liked that name for them. Even in the dreamlands, which is such a cathedral world in itself, that forest is something special again.

"This works sometimes," he said, leading me to the back of the store.

We were in the store's shipping/receiving room, everything in a clutter the way it so often is in the parts of a store that are hidden from the view of the general public. Jamie reached for the handle of a door set in the wall on the far side of the room and opened it, but there was only an alleyway there.

He closed the door and turned to me.

"I'm sorry," he said. "I forgot to tell you that it helps if you're expecting it to be on the other side of the door. The place you want to go, I mean."

I started to ask how that could be, but then gave him a nod. This was a magic world. Magic happened in it.

I gave him a smile. "Of course it'll be out there," I told him.

He opened the door again and there it was. The alleyway was gone and the cathedral wood was just a few steps away.

"You're good," Jamie told me. "If it happens for me at all, it usually takes a few tries."

So that's how I got my purchases into the cathedral wood. Before I crossed back over to the World As It Is and let the Broken Girl wake up, I set them down by the trunk of one of the big trees in the plastic shopping bag they'd come in. Returning today, they were still here, waiting for me.

I don't even try to capture the majesty of the giant trees. Instead I work on smaller, more manageable subjects. A cluster of mushrooms, bunched around a dead tree limb. Some moss growing on the thick bark of one of the giants. A study of nuts, leaves, and a blue jay's feather that I'll admit I rearranged for a better effect. The light's so amazing here. Rendering it in black and white, I don't even miss working with color.

I'm so involved in what I'm doing that it takes me a while before I realize there's someone standing behind me. I turn slowly and blink at the strange little fellow who's been watching me for who knows how long. I'll give him this much: he knows how to be quiet.

"Hey," he says.

"Hey, yourself."

He's about my size, a little shorter than my own five-foot height, but not by much. Trim and muscular, where I'm just thin. His face is broad—which on that small frame makes it look big—dark brown eyes wide-set and prominent, nose stubby, mouth generous, and from the laugh lines, quick to smile. His hair is as curly as mine, but dark red and short, and his skin is the color of cinnamon. He kind of fits my mental image of what Robin Goodfellow would look like—you know, the Puck from English folklore—except he's dressed in jeans and leather, and has a tattoo of a lightning bolt in a circle on the back of one hand, an unenclosed lightning bolt on the other.

"So, do you want to draw me?" he asks.

I have to smile. It's hard not to respond to his good humor.

"Sure," I tell him. "Why not? Do you know how to pose?"

He strikes a muscle-builder's stance. I try not to laugh.

"You're not drawing anything," he says. His voice sounds strained from holding his breath.

"How about something a little more natural?"

He lets out a stream of air and collapses on the ground, then flops against a big tangled root, lounging there like he's been in that position for hours. He'd make a good cat.

"What's your name?" I ask as I flip to a new page in my sketchbook.

"Toby Childers, the Boyce. What's yours?"

"Jilly."

"That seems like an awfully small name."

I give him a shrug. "I'm a small woman," I tell him.

Joe once told me that when I finally did cross over to the dreamlands that I should be careful about who I give my name to, and how much of it I give them. Names are power here, though I think that carries over into the World As It Is as well. Ever notice how much easier it is to deal with a problem once you can put a name to it? It doesn't make the problem go away, but at least you know what you're dealing with.

Toby smiles, like he knows what I'm thinking, but I just continue with my drawing. He's got easy features to draw, but I'm having trouble fitting the head to the body. If I render it the way it really is, it seems too exaggerated.

"You're new to the Greatwood," he says.

"Pretty much."

"Do you want to be my girlfriend?"

I look up from my sketchbook. "Not really."

"Too bad," he tells me. "I've got a penis, you know."

"Most males do."

"Mine's special."

"Most of them think that as well."

"But mine can do tricks."

I sigh and decide to change the subject. He strikes me as an innocent, but you never know with faerie types. He could just be seeing how far he can push before I get mad. Why? Who knows? They're the original inscrutables.

"You called yourself 'the Boyce,' " I say.

"That's me."

"So is it a name or a title?"

He shrugs. "More like a title, I suppose."

"So what is a 'boyce'? Is it like a duke or an ear—"

He starts to hum the old rock song "Duke of Earl."

"—or more like a doctor or a mayor? You know, some kind of professional."

"You're very pretty."

I sigh. "Looks are an accident, so that's hardly an accomplishment. It's not like they're something you earn."

"But pleasant, nevertheless. At least from my perspective."

"Um."

"You don't seem very taken with me."

"I don't really know you."

"And you're not very gracious receiving compliments."

"I'd rather be known for what I do than for how I look."

"So you don't look in mirrors at all?" he asks. "You don't primp and preen before a big date?"

I shake my head. "I don't really go out on many dates—so you see, it's nothing personal. And I'm usually too busy to worry about how I look. People can take me as I am or not. Their choice."

"I choose to take you."

I give up on my drawing and close my sketchbook. The root he's leaning against curves around behind me in a long fat twist of wood. When I lean back on it, it's like we're sitting on some enormous woodland couch. I hold my sketchbook closed on my lap and study him for a moment.

"So are you one of Joe's cousins?" I ask.

Something passes over his features quicker than I can read.

"I'm a cousin," he says.

I didn't know the difference then.

"And what do you do—when you're not chatting up strangers you meet in the woods?"

"It depends on the day of the week," he tells me. "On Gormdays I go riding my bike along the hedgeroads. Soowieday I always have a coffee with my friend the Tattersnake and browse the bookstores in Mabon. When the Wiggly comes, I usually sleep in late because there's so much to do at night."

He keeps a straight face, but I don't buy any of it.

"You're making all that up."

"I did, I did!" he cries. "I made every bit of it up!"

He leaps to his feet and throws a handful of leaves at me, dancing back out of range in case I mean to retaliate. I stay where I am and brush the leaves from my hair and clothes.

"Except I do have a friend," he adds.

"This Tattersnake, I'm assuming."

He shakes his head. "Oh, no. You can't be friends with the Tattersnake. That's like trying to be friends with the stars or the moon—ever so filled with the potential for disappointment."

"Why's that?"

"Because they're so bright, and they hang so very high."

"So Tattersnake lives in the sky?" I ask.

"It's not a name, it's a title," he corrects me. "Like I'm the Boyce."

"Which you never did explain."

"That's true. I didn't."

I can see that this is one of those conversations that could go on forever, but nothing ever really gets said.

"Well, I'm glad you have a friend," I tell him.

He nods, then gives me an expectant look.

"What?" I say.

"Aren't you going to try to guess who it is?"

"I couldn't even begin."

"That's right. I forgot. You're new here. You don't know anybody."

"I know Joe," I say. "And I've met a few people in Mabon. Do you know Sophie? She's one of my best friends back in the World As It Is."

"Everyone in Mabon knows Sophie," he begins. His voice trails off as his gaze strays over my shoulder, then he simply says, "Jolene."

"That's your friend's name?" I ask.

His only reply is to turn around and bolt. He's so fast that for one moment all I can do is sit there, watching his little figure suddenly dwindle off into the distance, disappearing among the trunks of the giant trees. I wonder, was it something I said? Except then I hear the breathing, slow and deep and steady, the way you'd imagine a big stone outcrop to breathe if it could. When I turn around it's to find a woman the size of a bear standing behind me. Bigger, even. She seems as tall as the trees, though maybe that's only because of my vantage point.

I scramble to my feet, but standing doesn't help. She still looms over me and I feel no bigger than a child, and about as powerful. Her legs and arms are like tree trunks, her torso massive. I feel like she could just pick me up and put me in a pocket if she had one. I don't see any in the buckskin dress she's wearing. It's the size of a small tent but still only comes down to her knees.

She looks more Native than Toby did. Broad-faced and dark-eyed, skin a reddish brown, hair hanging over her ample breasts in two long, dark braids that are decorated with beads and small, brightly colored feathers that must have come from orioles and jays and cardinals. She's barefoot and doesn't so much seem to be standing where she is so much as growing out of the ground the way the trees do.

I can't read the look she's giving me. Is she angry, finding me here in the woods? Maybe they belong to her and I'm trespassing. Toby sure didn't stick around to find out, or maybe he already knew. I wish he'd bothered to warn me. Then I remember the last thing he said before he bolted.

"Is . . . is that your name?" I ask. "Jolene?"

She gives me a slow nod. "People call me that. Animandeg asked me to look in on you."

There's only one person that would have asked anyone to check out for me that I can think of.

"Do you mean Joe?" I ask.

My relief is immediate when she gives me another of those slow nods. I still don't know why Toby ran off at the sight of her, but at least now I know she's not going to eat me or something.

"That name you used," I say.

"Animandeg?"

"Yes. Is that Kickaha for 'crazy dog'?"

I know that's what they call Joe up on the rez.

She shrugs. "A truer translation would be 'crow dog,' but since crows are all half-mad anyway, I suppose it's close enough."

Crow Dog actually makes sense, since when Joe's in his mythic-face mode, sometimes he's got a crow's head on his shoulders, other times that of a wolf or a coyote. Mind you, Crazy Dog always made sense, too, since Joe can play the fool as readily as the wise man.

"So I guess you're another of Joe's cousins," I say.

She studies me for a moment. "Who else has been claiming kinship to Animandeg?"

"There was only the little fellow who ran off when you came," I tell her. "He said he was Toby Childers, the Boyce."

"And he said he was our cousin?"

This seems important to her, so I go back over that part of my conversation with Toby.

"Actually, no," I admit. "He just said he was a cousin—the same way he said he was the Boyce."

She seems to relax when I say that. She takes a step forward and I swear I can feel a tremor in the ground when she moves. It makes me wonder why I never heard her approach. When she sits down, there's another one, followed by a distant rumble that seems to come from deep underground. All her movements are slow, but liquid. She may be large, but she's comfortable in her body and knows it well.

I sit back down and pick up my sketchbook from where I dropped it. Jolene has such a beautiful face, I want to draw it, but I don't have the nerve to ask if it's okay. When she doesn't say anything for a while, I start to feel a little nervous again, which is odd, since I can usually be as comfortable not talking with someone as talking with them. But everything feels akilter at the moment, so I try to think of something to say.

"What does that mean, 'the Boyce'?" I settle on. "It doesn't sound Kickaha."

"It's Gallic," she tells me. "It means 'one who lives in the woods.'"

"Gallic? You mean French?"

Again one of her slow nods. Then she adds, "You seem surprised."

"I just thought this place was, I don't know. The Native spiritworld. Joe sometimes calls it *manidò-aki*, so I guess that's what makes me think it's particular to the Kickaha."

That gets me a smile. "That is one of its names. But at the same time it's the heart home of all spirit, not simply that of one clan, or one people. It's as if the Christians claimed heaven for their own."

"Actually, they do."

She laughs. "That's right, they do, don't they? It's like making war in the Peacemaker's name—they get so many things wrong. Crazy Crow says that's the trouble with writing stories down. Everything gets locked into history, even mistakes, and the stories can't breathe anymore."

I'm getting confused now. "By Crazy Crow, do you mean Joe?" I ask.

She smiles. "I don't think so. But Crow's an old name among the cousins. Old Crow, Crazy Crow, Crow Dog, the crow girls. And it doesn't help that they keep stepping into each other's stories, wearing each other's faces. I think maybe only Cody's worse than them."

"And Cody is?"

"Coyote. The dog with a thousand names."

"I know some of those stories," I tell her.

She laughs. "Everybody does."

Since she doesn't seem to mind answering questions, I keep asking them.

"What do you mean by the cousins?" I ask.

"Now that can be confusing, too. It's like asking Bear to give you one name for honey when he has a hundred hundred of them, one for every flower the bees have visited and then all the combinations you can get when their pollen gets mixed up in the hive."

"I can get like that talking about colors," I tell her.

"That's right, you're a painter. That's a good way to tell a story—everybody can find their own way through when they look at a picture."

"You were telling me about the cousins."

"Well, now. When we say the cousins, we're usually talking about ourselves. You know, the People. The ones who were here first when Raven made the world. But sometimes we mean anyone who has a bit of our old blood in them. And sometimes we mean those who have a shape close to our own. So when Bear sees some old grizzly scratching his ass against a pine tree, he'd call him a cousin. But he's not a direct relation, you see."

"I think so." That makes me think of Toby again. "So the little man who ran off when you arrived. When he called himself a cousin, what did he mean?"

"I don't really know," Jolene says. "Not without talking to him. But he wouldn't be claiming blood kinship, unless he's looking for trouble."

"Why would that be trouble?"

"It's like someone saying they're your friend when they're not, and trading in on that to maybe take advantage of you. To be trusted on someone else's word and loyalty instead of your own."

I certainly trusted him quickly enough, I think, even with his talk of penises and girlfriends and all.

"Who would your cousins be?" I ask. "I mean, if it's not being rude to ask."

She laughs. "You can ask, but I don't know the answer. I've just been who I am for a very long time. Alberta says I must have just come out of the ground, because I've always got a bit of dirt on me."

"Alberta," I say. "She's a deer woman, right?"

"Now how would you know that?"

It's coming back to me now, where I've heard some of these names before. Jolene and Bear, Alberta and Crazy Crow.

"There was a storyteller named Jack Daw," I say, "who used to live in a bus near the Tombs. He's been gone for a few years and there's a red-headed girl named Katy Bean living in the bus now, but when he was around, he used to tell me all these great stories about the animal people like you're talking about. How they were here first, and how they're still walking around today, still a part of stories. Alberta was in a couple of them. And so were some of those other names you've mentioned. And you were, too—or at least he had a character in his stories that was named Jolene. He used to say she could be as little as a minute or as big as a mountain, depending on . . . well, I'm not really sure what."

"Oh, Jack," Jolene says. She looks sad when she says his name. "But that was me, I guess. Sometimes I'm big and sometimes I'm small."

"I miss Jack. I always wondered where he went."

"We all miss him," Jolene says.

"Do you know if he's all right?"

"He went into the Grace," she tells me.

"What's that?"

"It's where we came from. It's where we all go to when our time's done."

I've never heard it put like that before. The Grace. A wave of sadness comes over me, realizing that Jack's dead. Doesn't matter if maybe he's okay, because he's still gone on. For those of us left behind, we only have our memories of him left to hold on to. I guess the small comfort I can take out of all of it is this: maybe I'll get to see him again when it's my turn to die.

Because that's one thing I'm sure of, being here in this wood, traveling to Mabon. We have spirits. We have a soul. Something that survives when the body's done.

"Am I a cousin?" I find myself asking Jolene.

She gives me a long, slow study. "Well, now. You've got something bright in you that makes a cousin sit up and notice, but I can't tell what it is. If you were here in body and not just spirit, you'd be calling all sorts of things to you—cousins, spirits, friendly beings, and those with more hunger in them than you'd care to feed."

"That's what Joe says."

"But even just dreamwalking, you've got a shine. It's what let me find you so easily."

"But I'm not a cousin."

"Didn't say that. Truth is, I can't tell. Usually we can smell each other—except it's with some kind of inner sense—but when I look at you the shine gets too bright and I just can't see far enough."

We sit quietly for a while and now I don't feel the need to fill the silence with words. This little bit of time we've spent together, talking, getting to know each other, seems to have been enough to set me at ease.

"So what're you doing here?" Jolene asks after a time. "Animandeg—Joe says you're mending, but you don't look too hurt to me."

"It's my body that needs the mending—back in the World As It Is. I need a break from what's happening to me there."

"So you're just messing around here."

"I guess. Though I want . . ."

My voice trails off.

"What do you want?" she asks.

Her voice is gentle, comforting, like a warm rain, like the mother's touch I never knew. And maybe it's because of that, or maybe it's the air in this place, but I find myself telling her the things I've only told Joe and Geordie, about the safe haven I know's waiting for me somewhere here, somewhere in the otherworld.

"You can find that place," she tells me, with a slow thoughtful nod. "But it's not here, not in this wood. This is just where the story begins."

"What do you mean?"

She smiles. "What do you think this forest is?"

"I don't know. But I feel like I could live off the air forever and never have to eat or drink."

"Maybe. But it's more than that. I've heard it called Nemeton—an old word in some other old tongue which means sacred place or grove—but most people just call it the Greatwood. It's the forest perilous. The dark wood that you have to get through. Like I said, the story begins here, but where it takes you, you can only find out by putting one foot in front of the other and see where you end up. This is the forest of dark journeys and memories, and you have to be brave and steadfast to travel through it to the other side."

"Like in a fairy tale."

She nods, then says, "And if you're ready to take the journey, you should just go."

"Joe says I should heal my body first. But it's complicated."

"Joe would say that. And he's probably right. But if it was me . . ." The massive shoulders rise and fall and she smiles. "Well, I've always been more impetuous myself."

Regarding the solid bulk of her, I can't imagine it. But then I remember those stories Jack told me about when she's the other Jolene, small and wilder even than the crow girls, and I see something of that side of her in her eyes. A mad-happy light. Joe has that same look in his—part clown, part shaman.

"So you think I should go," I say. "Start my journey now."

She shrugs. "Only if your heart tells you it's time. It's not a matter of the sooner you start, the sooner you'll get there."

"Because it's the journey that matters."

She gives me an approving smile. "Exactly."

"I think I'd better wait on Joe's say-so. He's never given me bad advice before." I laugh. "Mind you, I won't say I've always *liked* his advice."

"As I said," Jolene tells me. "You must do what you feel is right. But don't forget, Joe feels what he feels, not what you do."

She gets to her feet then and it's like a mountain standing up. Like one of the giant trees around pulling up its roots and going walkabout.

"Time I was moving on," she says.

I stand up, too. "Thanks for looking in on me."

"I always have time for Joe's friends," she says.

She reaches out and tousles my hair, and I get that I'm-only-a-kid feeling again. A last smile, then she does Joe's disappearing act, takes a step behind an invisible curtain, and she's gone. I stand there feeling the tremors fade underfoot. So that's how she slipped up on Toby and me earlier. It's a trick I want to learn, but before I can, I have to fix the Broken Girl.

I know I should be getting back, but I take the time to do some sketches of Jolene from memory. The light never seems to change here, so it's hard to tell the passage of time. I'm probably at it longer than I should be because I've filled a half-dozen pages before I finally put the sketch-book and pencil back in their plastic bag and stash it away in a nook made by some roots. I brush my hands and let myself go back.

When I wake up as the Broken Girl it takes me a moment to get used to the fact that I'm trapped in my bed again. It always does. The paraly-sis on my right side is the hardest to reconcile. And the numbness. That half of my body's just flesh on bone, nothing I can actually feel or relate to. Mobility and free will only exist in the dreamlands. I know that. But every time I come back, I have a little panic attack all the same. Then I remember and all the colors of the world go gray once more. That's how I see life as the Broken Girl. In shades of gray.

I think about my encounters in the wood. Randy little Toby in his leathers and tattoos. Jolene, as enormous in her serenity as she is in size.

"Well, that was weird," I say.

"What was?"

I manage to slowly turn my head and see that Wendy's sitting in the visitor's chair. She has her journal open on her lap, her fountain pen in her hand.

"My latest adventure in the dreamlands," I tell her.

She caps her pen, then uses it to keep her place in her journal.

"So tell me about it," she says.

I smile. There's magic in this world, too, I remind myself. I've seen faerie girls who call themselves gemmin, living in an abandoned car in the Tombs. I've been to an underground kingdom of goblinlike creatures called skookin that exists beneath the city. I've met crow girls who can shift from one shape to another.

And even my friends aren't immune. Sophie has faerie blood. Geordie once dated a woman that he lost to the past, while the Kelledys—Cerin and Meran—came here out of the past. Sue had her dog Fritzie talk to her one Christmas Eve. Christy and the professor have had more magical encounters than I've got fingers and toes. And Wendy . . . Wendy grew a magical Tree of Tales from an acorn one winter and fed it on stories. Come spring she had to move it from the pot in her house to Fitzhenry Park where it's this huge spreading oak now. But she still feeds it stories.

"It's one for the tree, all right," I say and tell her about Toby and Jolene and all.

5

Wendy watched Jilly's face as her friend spoke. Sharing her adventures in the dreamlands was about the only time Jilly had any animation in her features or voice these days. But while Wendy was as afraid as Sophie of losing Jilly to the dreamlands, she didn't begrudge the time Jilly spent there. At least the dreamlands were giving her some happiness in a world that had otherwise gone all desperate and miserable.

Wendy had a different concern about the place that Sophie, and now Jilly, could visit in their dreams. It made her listen to Jilly's latest adventure, half caught up in the marvel of it all, half in wonder at just how vivid Jilly's imagination could get. Because the truth was, Wendy wasn't quite so sure about the dreamlands herself. When she and Jilly listened to Sophie's stories about Sophie's time there, it was different. Then she had Jilly's enthusiasm and unqualified belief to dispel any reservations about how real or not it might be. She was able to simply go with the flow of the story and it didn't matter whether the dreamlands were a place that existed independent of the World As It Is, or only in Sophie's imagination.

But with Jilly telling the story, and no one sitting with Wendy to nod and smile and clap her hands in wonder, it was harder. Little nagging "as ifs" kept getting in the way of her enjoyment. But after a while she realized that today her discomfort didn't have so much to do with believing or not believing, as it did with trying to listen and at the same time deal with the worries of Jilly's injuries and what had happened in her studio. It was hard to hear about little elfish men with tattooed hands and enormous earth spirit mamas when she knew that all of Jilly's faerie paintings had been destroyed. Perhaps even by the same person who had put Jilly in the hospital in the first place.

"What kind of an animal would I be?" Jilly asked and Wendy sat up with a guilty start. And the context of that odd little question was . . . It took her a moment to make the connection.

"You mean as in Jack's animal people?" she said.

"I'm not saying I am one of them," Jilly said. "But if I was, what kind do you think I would be?"

This was more like the old Jilly, Wendy thought.

"Probably a monkey," she said. "Or a cat. Or a crow, since you're so enamored with them these days. Maybe a black monkey-cat with crow wings. What do you think I'd be?"

"Oh, definitely a hummingbird."

"A hummingbird?"

"Don't pull that face," Jilly said. "Joe says that they're considered to be one of the creator animal spirits, and you're a born poet and story-teller, so that fits. They're very powerful and beautiful, and harbingers of joy—all stuff that you do."

It was odd how other people saw you, Wendy thought. She didn't feel like any of those things herself.

"I don't care," she said. "I'd rather be a mouse or a mole. Something small and unassuming that lives in a cozy little burrow." Then she smiled. "Or I could be a mouse with hummingbird wings to go with your winged monkey-cat, though you'd have to promise not to eat me."

"But I could chase you sometimes, just in fun."

Wendy smiled. "Only until I ask you to stop, and then you'd have to stop right away."

"Oh, I'd love to draw the pair of them," Jilly began. "Buzzing around in the air like . . . like . . ."

Her voice trailed off and her gaze went down to her hands.

"You'll be able to draw again," Wendy said.

"But what if I can't?"

Wendy thought of those ruined paintings that Sophie and Mona had put away in the basement of Jilly's building. Bad enough that they were all destroyed, but the thought of Jilly never being able to bring all her magical characters back to life again in other paintings was too depress-ing to contemplate.

"You have to," Wendy said. "You just can't not get better."

"Maybe I don't have a choice."

Wendy shook her head. "I hate it when you talk like that. It's so not you. Where's the fierce and positive musketeer who never lets anything keep her down?"

"She turned into the Broken Girl," Jilly said. "Who, whenever she finally does get out of here, is going to be the seriously Broke Girl because I don't know how I'm even going to start paying for all of this."

"Your health insurance is covering it," Wendy told her.

Jilly gave her a puzzled look. "I don't *have* health insurance."

"You do, actually. The professor first got it for you when you were in university and he's been keeping your policy up-to-date ever since."

"But—"

"You just never knew because you never get sick."

"I can't believe how good he is to me," Jilly said. "Why's everybody so good to me?"

"Because like attracts like," Wendy told her. "I've never met anybody who does as much for other people as you do."

Except as she spoke, the ruined paintings came to mind again and she felt her chest tighten. No, like didn't always attract like because there was no way Jilly could have done something so bad to someone to make them retaliate in that way.

"You're making me blush," Jilly said. Then she looked more closely at Wendy. "What's the matter?"

"Nothing."

"No, there is. You're keeping something from me." '

"It's not for me to tell," Wendy began.

But if not her, then who? No one wanted to tell Jilly—why would they? It was such a horrible thing to have to relate on top of everything that Jilly was already going through here in the hospital. But sooner or later someone was going to have to.

Wendy got up from her chair and came to sit on the edge of the bed. She took Jilly's left hand and stroked the fingers where they came out from under the cast.

"I'm going to hate this, aren't I?" Jilly said.

Wendy nodded. "But you've got to be strong."

"Oh, god. It's about the paralysis. It's permanent."

"No, it's not about any of this," Wendy said. "It's about your paintings. Someone broke into your studio after the accident."

6

I don't know why I don't take it worse than I do. I guess it's because I already feel so divorced from my life here in the World As It Is, that when more horrible things happen, they don't feel like they're happening to me. They're happening to the Broken Girl.

"You're sure you're okay?"

Wendy repeats the question for about the hundredth time while she puts on her coat and stows her journal away in her backpack.

"I'm not even close to okay," I tell her and offer up a weak smile. "I mean, look at me, lying here like a lump."

"I meant about the paintings."

"I know you did," I say.

Somehow, losing the faerie paintings doesn't feel like much of a surprise when I've already lost my painting arm. The truth is, I can even detect an element of relief welling up from underneath the initial shock that hit me when Wendy first gave me the awful news. Because that's one more tie connecting me to the World As It Is that's gone. But I can't tell her that. It'll just make her worry even more.

"Things'll work out the way they're supposed to in the long run," I tell her. "We might not like all the details, and the trip's not always fun, but we'll make do. That's part of the blessing and curse of being alive."

Wendy looks so small and sorrowful, standing there by the door, her backpack trailing on the floor as it hangs forgotten by one strap from her hand.

"God, you sound so fatalistic," she says.

"I know. And it's not me," I add before she can say it.

"Well, it isn't."

I give her a sympathetic look. "I've been through worse," I tell her.

"I can't imagine worse," she says.

Then she's gone, swallowed by the hallway.

"I'm glad you can't imagine worse," I say softly to the empty room. "No one should have to. But that doesn't stop it from happening to us all the same."

I stare up at the ceiling. Sometimes when I lie here I try to count the dots in the ceiling tiles. If I can ever count them all in one tile without losing track, then I can multiply the dots by the number of tiles in my room and I'll know just how many dots there are up there. Maybe I can even figure out how many there are on this floor. Or in the whole hospital.

It's something to do when I'm lying here in the bed. It's either that, or remembering, and remembering always seems to take me too far back in my life, back to the dark ages, before my life began again.

This evening the dots don't hold my attention. Instead I start thinking about how I first started drawing. Not the pathetic little sketches I tried to sell for spare change when I was living on the street, but further back, when I was just a child.

Sometimes I think children want to paint and draw more than they want to learn how to talk. I don't know what it is that seduces them—my memory doesn't go that far back, or at least it isn't that clear. I remember doing drawings, but not the impulses that had me pick up the crayons. Maybe it was as simple a thing as the colors. Crayons and water-based paints, all bright and impossible to resist. But I was just as happy with a pencil and an old shopping bag. So maybe it was seeing the world and having this urge to put a fragment of it down on paper. I can even remember using twigs to scratch out drawings in the dirt in the yard behind our house.

Lucky kids get born into families where their messy attempts at art are praised and cherished, taped up on refrigerator doors, maybe even put into a frame and hung on the wall. They live with people who care about them, twenty-four hours a day, seven days a week.

I wasn't a lucky kid.

I don't say that for sympathy. It's just the way it was.

Today my memory takes me back to this one afternoon, I guess I was five or six. Probably six, because I was already in school, or at least kindergarten. We were doing what I liked best, using poster paints on great big pieces of newsprint. I remember the teacher was so nice to me that day. We were supposed to paint what we liked best and there were kids around me doing their pets or their family or whatever. I was painting this old tree that's in the fields behind our house. Whenever I could, I'd sneak out of the backyard and lie in the grass under that tree and stare up into its branches, imagining faeries.

The teacher came by and stood behind me for a while, watching me work. I'm looking at this memory through the gauze of a lot of years, so I don't remember the real details of my painting, but I guess there was something in it that impressed her.

"You have so much talent," she said. "It wouldn't surprise me if you become an artist when you grow up."

"I love art class," I told her.

"What are these?" she asked, pointing to little globs of yellow paint that were clustered around the tree.

"Faeries," I said. "But they're so small I can only show them like dots."

She ruffled my hair. "Don't ever lose your sense of wonder," she said as she went over to look at another kid's work.

I rolled that newsprint up very carefully and brought it home, just bursting with pride. When I got in the door, I wasn't thinking and ran into the kitchen with it, calling out to my mother. It wasn't until I was in the kitchen that I realized the mistake I'd made. It was only midafternoon, but she was already drunk. She yelled at me for running in the house, yelled at me for making noise, then wanted to know what that was that I was holding. I tried to hide it from her, but it was too big. She unrolled it on the kitchen table.

"This what they're teachin' you in that school?" she demanded. "Paintin' pitchers instead a somethin' useful like keepin' your head outta the damn clouds?"

Then she tore it up. Tore it up, threw the pieces on the floor, and slapped me for crying.

"Now, little missy," she said. "You all just put that in the garbage where it belongs and don't you never be bringin' crap like this home again."

That memory has never lost its ability to hurt. Not because it happened to me, though every time those events come back, I want to take that little girl I was and just hold her tight against my chest, kiss the top of her head like it never happened to me, and tell her that she'll get through this. If she hangs in there, things'll get worse for a while, but then they'll get better again. All those images will get put down on paper and canvas.

It hurts because it reminds me of all the other kids who've had that kind of experience and worse. Who are still having it today, right now, right at this moment. Children are the brightest treasures we bring forth into this world, but too large a percentage of the population continues to treat them as inconveniences and nuisances, when they're not treating them as possessions or toys.

And people wonder why I prefer drifting off to the dreamlands to being in this world.

I sigh. This is depressing me. I should just go to sleep and cross over into the cathedral world. But I'm beginning to recognize that Joe's right. My crossing over as much as I am isn't to give myself some breathing space. It's escape, pure and simple. Now that I can do it, I could just pack up and go there forever. Let the world carry on without me.

But that's not the way I'm built, I guess. I stopped running away from trouble a long time ago, Joe's comments notwithstanding. I know I've got to deal with the difficulties I've got here before doing any serious traveling in the dreamlands. The problem is, beyond dealing with the physical ailments that have turned me into the Broken Girl, I don't know what else I can do. I thought I'd already come to terms with what happened to me as a kid. I can't change what happened to me. And I've spent a lifetime doing what I can to make sure it doesn't happen to other kids.

But I guess that's not enough.

I try to move my paralyzed arm. My leg. I try to just *feel* something there. *Anything*. If my inner hurt has to be cured first, I'm going to be stuck like this forever.

Great. Now I'm even more depressed.

I wonder if I can sleep without crossing over, because any time I spend there is only going to tempt me to spend more. I'll have to ask Sophie how that works when she comes by tomorrow.

For now, I don't fight it. I close my eyes, but instead of drifting off, the paintings come. I see them floating in my mind's eye, all those faerie paintings that Wendy told me somebody trashed. My gemmin and subway goblins, junkyard fairies and gargoyles, moving from their high stone perches.

I open my eyes but the room's a smeared blur from my tears.

And then I start to see paintings I haven't done yet. Toby and Jolene, for starters. That sweet image of Wendy and me as flying animals.

I don't have Isabelle's gift. I can't make numena from my paintings—those spirits that her art calls over from somewhere else and clothes with bodies that can move and interact with people in the World As It Is so long as their paintings remain intact. It's like she opens a door between the worlds with the way she uses her pigment. But something is still born from my work. It might not literally bring spirits to life like Isabelle's paintings can, but it still does something. If nothing else, it reminds people that everything has a spirit, even an empty lot or a trashed car. Or maybe it reminds them of what it was like to see the world as a kid, which isn't such a bad thing either. We could stand a little more wide-eyed innocence in the world.

I live and breathe art. I can't imagine not being able to do it. Where other people write in journals to mark the passages of their lives, I use my sketchbooks. When you flip through them you don't get a sense of story the way you do with Mona's comics. Two of her strips, "My Life As a Bird" and the shorter "Spunky Girl" that runs every week in *In the City*, are literally a day-to-day commentary on what happens in her life.

But the stories in my sketchbooks are there for me to see. I can look at a page and call back exactly where I was when I did it, what I was thinking, what I was feeling, what was going on in my life. I started keeping a sketchbook when I was in university and until this hospital stay, there hasn't been a day gone by that I didn't draw something in whatever one was currently on the go.

That's gone now. It's all gone. Art can't be a journey for me anymore. It can only be something that other people do, a journey they take, and all I can do is watch them go. See what they bring back.

I'm weeping in earnest now. I can't stop. I can't even blow my nose. I start to choke on the buildup of phlegm, but I'm too embarrassed to call for a nurse. I manage to turn my head and cough the mucus out onto the pillow beside me. It oozes down my neck, onto my shoulder. But that doesn't help. I still feel like I'm choking.

Finally, I bury my pride and push the call button for a nurse.

I just can't stop crying.

Joe Crazy Dog

Manidò-akì, *1999*

There are no maps in the spiritworld. When the Great Spirit decided to make *manidò-akì*, I guess she wasn't thinking about us needing to find anything specific in here. What she gave us was just a patchwork quilt of spirit lands and dreamlands and the *manidò-tewin*, the spirit homes of everything that lives or ever has lived in the World As It Is: animal, vegetable, mineral; waterway, landscape, building. Everything's got its own *manidò-tewin* here. Some people call them *abinàsodey*, a heart home, your own piece of the quilt that's as familiar to you as your own heartbeat, the one place that's always going to be yours.

But the deeper you go, the wilder and more unpredictable the landscape becomes. Go far enough and it's like you're on some other planet where the natural laws all run counter to everything you know.

Places like Sophie's Mabon, the minutes tick away pretty much at the same rate they do in the World As It Is. Connecting these kinds of regions is a spiderweb of paths that stick to the same timeline that the two worlds can share. Work at it and you can also find other, secret roads where the hours stand still, or fold back in on themselves so that no time passes from when you step on the trail to when you get off again. There's places like that, too, small acres and whole territories, even. The Greatwood— that echo of the first forest where Jilly's been spending so much of her dreaming time—is one of them. But stray beyond those trails and timeless regions, and you don't know what you'll find.

Mostly it's quicklands, places where time runs faster than it does in the World As It Is. You can spend a year there and only minutes pass by in the world you've left behind. But there are tracts of slowtime, too. Stay overnight in one of them and you could come back like Rip Van Winkle to find that a hundred years have gone by. Not a good idea if you've left anything you care about back in the World As It Is.

People like me, we can smell the difference. I stay out of the slowtime pockets because there's too much I like waiting for me in the world I leave behind. If I've got to move through the wild, I try to go by the quicklands. With my blood, I've got the time to spare. I'm not immortal, but we're a long-lived people. It's in the blood, but it's also a side effect of spending time in this place. Something in the air, I guess.

But though time can stand still, or even run backward in *manidò-akì*, it just keeps marching on in the World As It Is. So when I leave Jilly in the Greatwood, I stick to the secret roads, covering as much ground as I can in an ever-widening spiral. I'm hoping for a quick end to this. I don't expect to just run into the woman I'm looking for, but if I'm lucky, I'll hear some gossip, catch a whiff of news that'll lead me to her.

I'm not lucky.

I don't want to brag, but I'm good at this, navigating *manidò-akì*, finding people, places, things. Some of us just have a knack for it and I've been doing it for a long time. But it can take patience, and time, and I'm running out of time so far as Jilly's concerned. The way she's feeling these days, she's liable to just cut the thread, thinking she's going full-time into the dreamlands, but all she'll be doing is finishing this lifetime and moving on to what comes next.

So after a couple of days of this, I take myself back to the World As It Is to get some guidance. I can read the bones, but I can't throw them for myself—they're like any augury system; they just don't work as well when you use them for yourself. I need someone else to do a reading for me.

·   ·   ·

Cassie looks up and smiles when I step out of the bedroom of our apartment. Time was, and not so long ago, we just made do with squats. We were nomads, living half in this world, half in *manidò-akì*. Everything we owned we could carry on our backs. We'd camp out in the dreamlands, find ourselves an abandoned building to squat in whenever we got back to the city.

But Cassie's been getting the nesting instinct lately. She wants babies. She wants a cabin in the hills, a bottle tree out front to scare off the witches and welcome the spirits, just like the tree the old woman had—the one who gave her the cards. I'll make sure it happens, just like I make sure she spends time in the spiritworld to stretch out the years she's been allotted for this lifetime. For now we make do with a basement apartment in the north end of Upper Foxville, but it's already filled up with more things than we could fit in the back of a pickup truck. Mind you, we don't have any kind of a vehicle either.

"Hey, stranger," she says and comes over to give me a hug. "I've missed you."

"I've missed you, too."

How could I not? There's a comfort and love in these arms that I won't ever find anywhere else, not in this world or any other. I was never much for believing in soul mates until I met her.

She still looks to be in her mid-thirties, a dark-eyed, beautiful woman with coffee-colored skin and hair that hangs in a hundred little beaded braids. Always one for the subtle colors, tonight she's wearing a pair of purple sweatpants and a hot-pink T-shirt. Her sneakers are bright yellow. That's my Cassie, always blends into a crowd.

"So did you have any luck finding your grandmother?" she asks.

Nokomis isn't my grandmother. It's just what the People call her. But I don't bother correcting Cassie.

"Not yet," I say. "That's why I need your help."

"I'll get the cards," she tells me.

They don't look like much, these cards of hers that were handed down to her by that old black woman in the cabin with the bottle tree. Cassie's got other, fancy Tarot cards that she uses for regular readings, like when we're out on the streets doing our fortune-telling shtick. These are different. Battered cards with a blue floral pattern on the backs, held together with a rubber band, face sides all blank.

We sit down on either side of the coffee table. Cassie pulls the elastic

off. She fans the cards out and offers them to me, face side down. I know
the drill. I let my need fill me. I attune myself to it and the spirit that fills
the room—mine, Cassie's, the one that flows between us. Then I take
three of the cards, one at a time.

The first card's blank face starts to shimmer and an image appears,
showing a dog with a coyote shape to its body, its mottled fur a half-
dozen shades of brown and muted red and ocher. It's got a crow's head
and seems to be trotting through the bush down some game trail.

"Me, I guess," I say.

"You recognize where you are?" Cassie asks.

I shake my head. "Probably *manidò-aki*."

"Past or present?"

"No difference, really," I say with a short laugh. "I've been there
and I'll be going back. What I'm looking for is some guidance on *where*
to go."

Cassie nods and we study the second card. The image taking shape
there shows a pack of wolves worrying at what looks like the flank of a
white horse. All we can see is the dead animal's hindquarters. There are
crows and ravens nearby, waiting their turn.

I look up at Cassie. "Any ideas?"

"Cousins?" she asks. "Maybe they can direct you?"

"And the horse?"

She shakes her head. "It might not mean anything beyond the fact
that the ones that can help you will have just made a kill. You know how
literal the images can be."

"I suppose."

I get a bad feeling from that card, but nothing I can put my finger on.
Maybe it's just the dog in me. Horses and dogs, we've both been partners
to humans, which kind of makes us kin to each other as well. Doesn't feel
right, feeding on kin.

I study that second card for a moment longer, then turn my attention
to the third one. The image on this card shows a full moon, reflected in
the dark water of a seep-fed pool that's high on some mountaintop in red
rock country. As I study the image, I can see time passing on the lower
slopes, the seasons flowing one into the other. There's only one place I've
ever seen them do that.

"That's in the quicklands," I say.

"And the reflection of the moon?"

"You don't get more earthbound than Nokomis, but she always did have a fondness for lunar imagery. Her contact with the Grandfather Thunders, I guess."

Cassie straightens up and looks at me across the table.

"Does this help at all?" she asks.

"Indirectly. I thought she'd be deep in the wild. This just confirms it."

"You know the cards," Cassie says. "They expect you to help yourself as much as they help you." She picks up the cards, shuffles them, just the three. "We could try again."

"No," I say. "I can tell this is about as clear as it's going to get. Looks like I've got some hard traveling ahead of me. The quicklands pretty much go on forever."

Cassie returns the cards to the deck and wraps the rubber band around them again. I enjoy watching the quick, easy movement of her fingers.

"This could take some time," I add. "Sure you won't come with me?"

She shakes her head. "I'm filling in with Laura at the hospice. They're still short-staffed."

"I thought you'd gotten some new volunteers."

"We did, but they're too sick to do much, and everybody else seems to think they're going to catch the disease by working there."

"Idiots."

"Mmm. You want me to pack you some food?"

I look at her sitting there across the table. I don't know how long I'll be gone, but any amount of time is too long.

"Thought I'd wait until the morning to leave," I say.

A slow smile builds on her lips, then spreads across her face. She doesn't say a word. Just takes me by the hand and leads me into the bedroom.

In the morning, I've got frybread, beans, and a pair of big mugs of coffee ready by the time Cassie comes wandering in from out of the bedroom. She rubs the sleep from her eyes and gives the coffee an approving look.

"This is why I keep you," she tells me.

"And here I thought it was for my superior dancing skills."

"You are a good dancer, actually."

"Ya-ha-hey," I tell her and dance a plate of breakfast over to the table for her.

She's wearing an oversized, tie-dyed T-shirt as a nightie this morning that's so bright it makes my eyes water. When I blink, I see beadwork patterns instead of stars. Cassie takes an appreciative sip of her coffee, then looks at me over the rim.

"Did Jilly say anything about her paintings when you were talking to her?" she asks.

"Nothing specific. I know it's driving her crazy that she can't even pick up a pencil where she is in the hospital."

"Somebody broke into her studio and destroyed all her faerie paintings."

My worry for Jilly goes up a couple of notches. Something like that might be all she needs to send her off into the dreamlands for good.

"How's she taking it?" I ask.

"No one's told her yet."

"That's good."

"Maybe, maybe not," Cassie says. "I think she should know. It'll hurt, but knowing the truth is always better in the long run. And it might harden her resolve to get serious about healing herself."

"If it doesn't drive her deeper into *manidò-aki*."

"I think she's stronger than that."

I give a slow nod. "I hope you're right."

"But there was something funny in her studio," Cassie goes on. "I got the key from Sophie and had a look around before I came home last night. You know, to see if I could pick up any sign the vandals might have left behind."

Cassie's a sensitive as well as a card reader. When she talks about sign, she's talking about spirit traces that most people would never feel. She can read people and places better than most of the cousins I know.

"What did you find?" I ask.

Cassie doesn't answer immediately. I know she's going back to the studio in her head, looking for the right words to explain what she'd felt when she was there.

"You know there's that brightness in Jilly," she says finally.

"Like a star sometimes," I say, "and I still don't know what it is. The glow of a big spirit, I'm guessing. Big and strong."

Cassie nods. "Whoever trashed her paintings was just as strong, but instead of a brightness she—I'm pretty sure it was a she—has a dark light burning in her. But the weird thing is that the sign she left behind could have been left by Jilly."

"But dark instead of bright."

"If that makes any sense."

"So what're you saying?" I ask, though I can already see where this is going.

Cassie hesitates before she answers. Moves her coffee mug around in a circle on the table.

"It's like Jilly trashed the paintings herself," she finally says.

"Except she was in the hospital, right? I mean, the time frame—"

"No, Lou says it happened when she was still in the coma." Cassie's gaze lifts from the table and settles on me. "Could her spirit have come back out of the dreamlands and done it? I mean, without her even knowing it?"

"When it comes to *manidò-akì*," I say, "anything's possible. They don't call it the Changing Lands for nothing. But that'd make no sense. Why would she do it?"

"I don't know," Cassie says. "But the sooner you find this grandmother of yours, the better it'll be."

I don't like the idea of leaving this behind, unsettled. Because thinking on what Cassie's told me, it sounds too much like a shadow twin, the cast-off bits of a person that, in the right set of circumstances, can take on a personality of its own. My people have too many stories about these shadow twins and the trouble that can follow them. It's like a dark wind fills them and they're liable to do anything. Mostly, they turn on the ones that cast them in the first place.

But I know Cassie's right. I can't worry on that right now. Best thing I can do is find Nokomis and see if she can help.

We finish our breakfast. I pack some of the frybread, grab a fat pouch of tobacco and a couple of packages of rolling papers from the cupboard. There's time for one long soul kiss with Cassie, and then I'm gone.

I head straight for the quicklands when I cross over, covering ground at a steady lope. I'm not much for skinchanging, and maybe I could travel a little faster in an animal skin, but this human body of mine has put in a lot of miles. I can keep up a pace like this for days if I have to. But I'm wearing a dog's head, for the sharper senses. Sight, smell, sound.

Doesn't matter how many times I travel through the quicklands, I never get used to them. Seasons can change from one step to the next. One minute you're crunching across a thin cover of snow, your breath frosting in the air, the next it's like high summer, hot and humid. The landscape can shift, too. Grassfields become desert in the blink of an eye. Turn up an arroyo, and you're in a pine forest. Half a mile later, you're scrambling up some steep incline like a mountain goat, pebbles and rocks clattering away from underfoot. Step onto the top and you're in an echo of the Greatwood.

After a half day of this I find myself on a trail running through rough bushland like you'll find up on the rez north of Newford. There's a faint prick of familiarity whispering in the back of my head as I follow it, but it's not until I step into a clearing that I realize why.

This is the second card from Cassie's reading. The crows and ravens lift up on black wings when I come out of the forest, startled by my appearance, but the wolves just sit up from the carcass and fix me with steady, considering looks. I make a closer study of their kill and see it isn't some white horse they took down, but a unicorn.

My first impression was that these wolves were cousins, but the dead unicorn puts the lie to that. There's some things the People just don't hunt, doesn't matter how hungry we are. And we'd never make a sport of it like this. This pack isn't feeding on the body. They're just tearing at it for the fun. The main show was running it down and making the kill.

That tells me what they are. Human dreamers. Crossed over in their sleep and went hunting. There's no alpha male, but I spot the female that's leading them.

How it works is, a human can dream true, but might not even know it. Still, that doesn't stop her from crossing over to our world when she sleeps. Most people drift in and out of *manidò-aki* at various times of the night, but they can't sustain their presence, and they can't control who they are or what they do. It's no different than dreaming for them. But you get a few like this alpha female that can maintain a shape, call up a hunt. Probably she just likes to hurt things. Can't do it in the World As It Is, so she does it here. Calls other dreamers to her and they go chasing mysteries, looking for blood.

For them it's nothing more than a dream, but that's no excuse. It doesn't make it right. Because the unicorn and whatever else they manage to kill, this is their world. They're real here. They die here.

But I'll give the alpha female this: she's got brass. She leaves the unicorn carcass and starts walking stiff-legged toward me, her muzzle dripping blood, a challenge in her eyes. The rest of her pack fan out behind her.

I don't know what she's thinking and just shake my head.

The dreamlands are going to shit. Bad enough these little pissants killed themselves a piece of some old mystery that they figured was no more than an animal, but they've got to be either blind, stupid, or just plain not give a damn to start in on me. Maybe I've got me a dog's head, but I'm wearing clothes and not walking on all fours. Take me on and they've just moved up from bullying hunters to murderers.

Except I'm not some innocent mystery, going to run till they've worn me down. They don't know what they're getting into and I'm just pissed off enough to do them some serious damage. Rough them up and then close the door in their heads that lets them cross over.

But before they can attack, somebody else comes ambling into the clearing and I know him.

It's Whiskey Jack. He's tall and lean, dressed in jeans and cowboy boots, buckskin jacket. Dog-headed like me, but wearing a flat-brimmed hat the color of a crow's wing with a leather hatband, decorated with turquoise and silver. A couple of long, black, beaded braids hang along either side of his head, bouncing against his chest as he walks.

Whiskey Jack and I go way back. Follow the family tree far enough, and you can find where we're related on the canid side of the family. It makes for an uneasy relationship at times with a lot of the canid, seeing how the other half of my family carries corbæ blood. But it still makes us cousins, and Jack and me, we've run together from time to time.

The wolves have stopped their approach on me. The alpha female loses some of her cockiness with two of us to contend with.

"Aw, Christ," Jack says, taking in the dead unicorn. "What'd you have to go do that for?"

I get the sense that the alpha female has never run into any of the People before, least not when they're doing a mix-and-match with their skin-changing like we are.

"You better make tracks," Jack tells her when she starts to growl, "or I'm going to tear that pelt off your body and use it to wipe my ass."

He finishes with a snarl and the pack bolts. We stand there for a long moment, listening, tasting the wind. But they're not circling back.

I think about that alpha female. There was something about her that nudges at my memory but I can't grab hold of it. Then it's gone and Jack's talking to me.

"Hey, Crazy Dog," he says. "Or are you calling yourself Bones these days?"

He walks over to the carcass as he talks. Bending down, he closes the animal's eyes, runs a hand along the bloodied flank. The look in his eyes tells me that those wolves better think twice the next time they get the urge to come hunting in the dreamlands.

"You know how it is," I tell him. "People call us what they want, but we don't need names to know who we are."

I take out my tobacco pouch and roll a couple of smokes, offer him one. He stands up from the body and takes a fancy Zippo lighter out of his pocket.

"Won it in a card game with Cody," he says when he sees me looking at the lighter. He grins. "You know Cody. A poker face he hasn't got."

He lights my cigarette, then his own.

"Been a long time," he adds, blowing out a stream of blue-gray smoke. "I haven't seen you this deep into *manidò-akì* since we went chasing water ghosts with the corn girl sisters."

"I've been busy."

"You still opening doors for people?"

"Opening them for some, closing them for others. Whatever's needed."

Jack shakes his head. "I don't know what it is, but I can't get my head around this idea of having a calling. Must be the corbæ blood in you."

I smile. "Must be. Where are you headed?"

"Steamboat Harley's place. I've got my eye on a puma girl he's got working the bar."

"Watch she doesn't hang you up by your toes."

"Naw. Ray says she's sweet on me. What about you?"

"I'd rather just be friends," I tell him. He laughs, then I add, "I'm looking for Nokomis. Have you seen her? I think she's doing the buffalo walk but I don't know where."

I tell him about the image from the third card, the reflection of the moon in the pool of dark water, up on that mountaintop. Last time

Nokomis was in the high country, she walked one of the lost trails, following in the footsteps of the buffalo spirits that the Europeans slaughtered. It was possible she was doing it again. Sadness and old hurts can always call her, bring her with healing in her hands and a blessing in her eyes.

"She's not White Buffalo Woman these days," Jack says. "Last time I saw her she was back to Grandma Toad, but that was pretty much a year or so ago."

Some spirits are impossible to keep track of, they change skins so often.

"And you've heard nothing since then?" I ask.

Jack shakes his head. "You should ask Jolene."

"I already did."

"Then you got me. What do you want with her anyway?"

"I've got a friend needs a blessing."

"Best blessings come from inside," Jack says. "Nokomis'll just tell you the same thing."

"I know. It's complicated. See, the inside's broken, too—an old hurt—and we can't get to fixing the outside till we deal with that."

"What happened to her?"

"Family trouble. Deep bad medicine, the kind that scars the marrow."

Sympathy enters Jack's usual mocking gaze.

"That's something that might never get fixed," he says.

I sigh. "Don't I know it."

"And trying can just call up more trouble."

"This one's worth the trouble."

"Your woman?" Jack asks.

I shake my head. "My sister. At least she is now."

"I'll put the word out," Jack tells me. "Let the Old Woman know you're looking for her."

"I appreciate that."

"In the meantime," he adds, "you could take a swing by Cody's *manidò-tewin*. That mountain of his has a moon pool on the mesa top and the two of them used to be tight."

I think of that third card of Cassie's and nod.

"How's Cody feel about corbæ these days?" I ask.

Like I said, there's an old rivalry between canid and corbæ, goes way back to the first days. Some canid like Whiskey Jack here just ignore my crow blood, but Cody's old school. He and Raven have been feuding since time began. I've had a run-in or two with him in the past myself, so now I just stay out of his way.

Jack laughs. "Didn't you hear? Cody's got himself a magpie girlfriend these days."

"Hard to imagine."

"I swear it's the truth."

We have another smoke before we take full canid shapes and start to dig a hole in the dirt beside the dead unicorn. We work at it until the grave's deep enough to hold it, then shift back to human form and roll the body in.

"Damn shame," Jack says.

I nod. Creatures like this can't leave the dreamlands. There's so much medicine caught up in that horn of theirs that even if they can make the shift to human form, the horn stays there on their brow. Makes it kind of hard to stay unnoticed in the World As It Is.

But they're rare in the dreamlands, too. I only ever saw one before this. It was back when I was a kid, before I'd ever crossed over into the World As It Is. I was out scouting with one of my uncles one night, the two of us sailing high on crow wings, when he suddenly banked and went into a long, descending curve that took us to the top boughs of an old pine tree. I don't know where exactly we were. Deep in the wild, for sure.

"Look," he said.

And then I saw it. High on a crag of granite, horn shining silver in the moonlight. It lifted its head and sang to the moon. The sound of its voice was sweet as honey, but it made the marrow in my bones tremble and resonate like I was feeling distant thunder. *Animiki.* The Grandfather Thunders.

"You want to say a few words?" Jack asks.

I look down at the body, trace the curve of the horn with my gaze.

"Safe journey," I say.

Jack bows his head and adds an "Amen," then we fill the hole back up again. It makes a small, rounded hillock when we're done. Jack draws a pattern in the fresh dirt, a warding to keep predators away.

"You know any unicorns?" Jack asks when we're done.

I shake my head.

"Me neither. I guess I'll pass the word around when I get to Harley's and hopefully somebody'll let his kin know how it went down. And if anyone asks, I'll be sure to share the scent of that alpha female with them. See how she likes to be hunted, the next time she crosses over."

I nod. It's the right thing to do, but it doesn't make me feel any better. It's like spreading the shadows, instead of shining a light into them.

Talking about shadows makes me think of something.

"Hey, Jack," I say. "You know much about shadow twins?"

He shrugs. "No more than the usual stories. Why? You had a run-in-with one?"

"Not so's I know. I'm just trying to remember something. The one that casts the shadow—does she know about her twin?"

"I don't think so," he says. "But I'm no expert."

"Know anybody that is?"

He has to think a moment. "Jack Daw," he says finally. "Except he's—"

"Dead. Yeah, I know."

"You find the Old Woman, you might ask her," he says. "There's not much she doesn't know."

"But sometimes there's not much she likes to share, either. I remember her telling me once, 'Don't look to other people's stories; live your own' "

"There's that. But I don't know that I agree." Jack looks off into the woods. "I know this much about shadow twins. When they go bad, it's because the one that casts the shadow hates something about himself."

I nod. When someone hates you, it takes a big heart to not return that hate. I know Jilly's got things in her life she hates. And for sure she's got a big heart. But if she's got herself a shadow twin, how big is *its* heart going to be?

"You think that she-wolf we chased off could have been one?" Jack asks.

I hadn't even thought of that.

"I doubt it," I tell him, but more for something to say. Right now I've got more important things on my mind than human dreamers like her.

Jack nods and tips a finger against the brim of his hat. "Well, you take care."

"Good luck with your puma girl," I say.

He laughs. "Hell, Joe. You don't need luck when you've got my good looks and charm."

"Not to mention modesty."

"That, too."

I watch him go, then turn back to the grave we dug. I bend down and lay my hand against the dirt. Closing my eyes, I can hear that song I heard with my uncle so long ago. It comes whispering up out of my memory, and then I see the horn again. The image lies across the back of my eyelids, the gleaming white flanks, the white mane and tail, the horn rising like a spiral of white fire in the moonlight.

Sitting back on my haunches, I roll a cigarette and light it. I take a drag and offer the smoke up to the Grandfather Thunders before I place the burning butt on the dirt beside Jack's warding.

I sit there for a while, watching the smoke trail up into the sky until the cigarette goes out. Then I stand up and head off myself, deeper into the quicklands.

Raylene

Everything changed after that business with Del and the knife. It was like when Mama decided they weren't going to bail my sister outta juvie no more, starting her in on her round a foster homes. Mama flat disowned her and we was none of us supposed to talk about her, or even mention her name. I was still pretty small, but come the first couple of lickins, I learned to keep my mouth shut. After a while it weren't so hard, 'cause that's 'bout the time Del started coming into my room of a night and I learned to hate my sister just like everybody else did.

For me, it was the way she just up and run off on me, and I guess for Del it was pretty much the same reason, 'cept I'm guessing he was more pissed that he'd gone and lost him his little homegrown girl-toy. I never really knowed why the rest of 'em felt the way they did. Jimmy and Robbie never much talked to me, and 'specially not after Del started paying his midnight visits. I doubt the old man even noticed she was gone for the first few months; he never did pay much mind to any of us kids. I guess he

just give up on the lot of us, what with the two oldest becoming delin-
quents straight off, that being Del and my sister, and then Jimmy and
Robbie not showing much inclination to walk the straight and narrow
neither.

And Mama? Hell, she was a mean drunk anyway and she just hated
us girls—on general principles, I reckon, since I sure never done her no
wrong.

I remember it was different before they took my sister away. Hell, I
adored her then. She was like the mama none of us had—the kind you see
on a TV show, you know. Not the soaps, but the sitcoms and such like,
where the mama cares for everybody more'n she cares for her own self.
My sister was like that—for me, anyways. We'd hide out, the two of us,
in the fields behind the house, and she'd tell me stories she made up, or
she'd read me outta her books. I didn't have me a clue, what was happening between her and Del then.

I gotta laugh now. I remember being jealous of how close they
seemed and all, and then feeling confused 'cause I could also tell that she
just plain didn't care for him neither. She made out like it weren't so, but
I could tell different.

"How come you don't like Del?" I'd ask.

"Oh, I like him well enough," she'd say, but there'd be a mean burn
in her eyes, just at the mention of his name.

"I seen the looks you gived him."

" 'I've seen the looks you give him,' " she'd correct me.

I figure that's partly why I talk the way I do, her always correcting
me like she done. Once she took off and left me behind, anything she
cared about, I'd do the opposite. Like once I knew she wasn't coming
back to me, I took them books of hers out to the old tree where she'd
read to me and I burned them and that damn tree down, started a fire
that spread into the field and just kept on a-coming. It pretty near took
out the house, and woulda done it, too, if the wind hadn't up and
changed at the last minute. The fire department sure never bothered
coming out.

I can read and write fine, but I don't bother much. When I was still
taking my schooling, I'd sit there in art class with my arms folded against
my chest. Because those were the things she cared about—books and
drawing.

And about that time's when I started to make a point of sounding like the white trash we was. But it wasn't just 'cause of her that I keep it up. Thing is, while I know better, I like sounding ignorant. Talk like this and people figure you're about as dumb as a fencepost, which suits me fine. Makes it all that much easier to take advantage of 'em.

I suppose if I'm going to be fair, I got to say that maybe my sister didn't have much choice, things working out the way they did. And I guess she tried to warn me about Del. She'd say, "You be careful around him," and I'd go ask Mama why she was saying that, and we'd both end up with a whippin'. When it come to Del, Mama had her a blind spot a mile wide. After the first few times, I finally smartened up and it never come up no more.

But my sister, she coulda come back for me. She coulda taken me outta that hellhole, but she never did. Never gived me no second thought. I heard about it when she finally run off for good—where I grew up, everybody knew everybody else's business—and she didn't bother to come fetch me afore she upped and gone.

I think maybe it'd been better if she'd just died. That way I'd still've felt abandoned, but it wouldn'ta been her fault. I still coulda loved the memory of her. But the way she done it, it was just plain meanness and there's not one damn thing I love about her. Not then and not now.

Anywise, like I was saying, once I sliced Pinky's knife across the back of Del's knee, everything changed again. Del he didn't make no more midnight visits to my room. He was hobbling around for months, playing the brave soldier, done protected his sister and the house and all. Jimmie and Robbie could see he was cautious of me, and that made them keep their own distance. There wasn't much to the pair a them, the one dumber than the next, but they had a dog's sense about the lay of the land. Knew when to back off and when they could follow the bullying ways they learned from Del.

The old man didn't seem to notice any change, but Mama sure did. 'Cept I wouldn't take crap from her anymore'n I'd take it from anyone else.

Oh, we was wild in those days, me and Pinky, but I learned from my sister's mistakes. I didn't run off so that the cops could bring me home again. I didn't skip school, though I just sat there like some old tree stump from the time I got there in the morning until the bell rang at the end of the day. I didn't get in trouble, in or outta school—or at least I didn't get caught, which works out to be about the same thing.

I wasn't going to end up in juvie, find myself in some girls' home with a buncha dykes and a broom handle up my hole, and I wasn't going into no foster home neither. I wanted my freedom, so I played dumb, but I lived smart.

Like the time Pinky decides she's gonna get back at Mr. Haven, our algebra teacher. It's not that he's flunking us, which he is, like we care. It's that Pinky finds out he's been boning her cousin, Sherry. Has her come by his house for extra tutoring and puts it to her, twice a week. Lets her know that if she squeals, they're gonna come and take her away from her parents, stick her sorry ass in jail till she's old and gray, because there's laws against little girls seducing their teachers.

I know, I know. Sherry's a sweet kid, but not exactly the sharpest pencil in the box, believing that line of crap. She's got the face of a little angel, the body of a woman, and the brains of a squirrel. Sorta runs in the Miller line some, I guess, her being kin to Pinky and all. And the real trouble is, while she developed too soon, like me, she don't got her the spine I do. Ain't her fault. Took Pinky and her knife to give me mine. And you know, there's no reason a kid should need that kinda hardness sitting inside her, 'cept there's freaks out there just a-waiting to take advantage of all them little girls that don't.

What Haven's done to her's the same difference as what Del done to me. Somebody what's supposed to be looking out for you—your family, your teacher—they ain't supposed to break that trust. But it happens all the same. Happens all the goddamn time and there's nothing we can do about it 'cept make the freaks pay when we can.

How this all come out is Haven don't have no use for rubbers, so Sherry finds herself fourteen and pregnant, her old man right ready to kill her, she don't tell who she's been catting 'round with. Sherry, she's too damned scared of what Haven told her to say a word. More scared of going to jail than she is of the lickins her old man gives her. Just starts in on crying anytime anybody asks her anything.

But sooner or later, every dam's gotta spring a leak, and Sherry's leak sprung one night when Pinky were visiting with her, just the two of them in that ugly old double-wide her family's living in.

"You got to promise you won't tell nobody," Sherry says.

"I promise," Pinky lies, 'cause she told me, didn't she?

And that's what brings us to me and Pinky sitting on a picnic table out behind the donut shop the next day. I seen Pinky mad afore, but not like this. Usually there's a lotta hollering going on. She's gonna cut this and bust that. But she's real quiet today. All that mad she's carrying is just a-sittin' there in her eyes, burning and smoldering. I was Haven, I'd be worrying 'bout now.

"I'm gonna say he raped me," Pinky says. "Sherry ain't never gonna step up and talk her own self, so I'll just say it was me he done it to."

At least she isn't talking 'bout going by his house with a baseball bat and breaking his legs, or sticking a knife in his gut like she done with Russell Henderson, but this ain't a whole lot better.

"You can't be doing that," I tell her.

Don't get me wrong, I'm all for cutting the freak down my own self, the piece of work that he is, but there's a right way and a wrong to go about things. The right way is, you get what you want, but no one even knows you was anywheres near where it went down.

"Like hell, I cain't," Pinky says. "You just watch me."

But I shake my head. "I ain't saying, let it go. I'm saying that show-boating ain't our only option here."

We been friends a long time, but this past year, Pinky's got herself a whole new respect for the way I can worry at a trouble, figure a way out that keeps us on top.

"So what're you saying?" she asks.

"Hold your horses," I tell her. "Let me think on it a minute."

The trick to any damn thing is keeping it simple, but I guess I couldn't help but want to showboat some, even if it was only me and Pinky what knowed how it went down.

'Round then there was this hillbilly Mafia up north of Tyson that pretty much run the bootlegging trade. The Morgan family, they was called, and they had them a place in Freakwater Hollow, up off of 'Shine Road. You'd see 'em in town from time to time, clannish and mean-look-ing and all of a kind, tall and lean with their silvery blond hair and dark eyes. Time was they had them a hundred stills up in the backwoods, but then they turned to growing fields of marijuana and nobody but nobody stepped on their toes.

That left the hard drugs to the local chapter of the Devil's Dragon. I guess they was as mean in their own way, but they were bikers and they liked to have them some fun, too. The Morgans didn't mix, but you get the Dragons in the right mood, and they'd party with anybody. They had them a clubhouse just off the Ramble where you could get your heroin and your crack, and the drug of choice, in them days, you had the money: coke. But you didn't mess with 'em neither, and poor old Mr. Haven, well, I guess he didn't learn him that lesson in time.

It was kinda fun, at the start. The most dangerous part was stealing that bag of dope from the Dragon. We knowed they kept the drugs locked up in the back of this old Chevy sedan when they was making their delivery rounds. So one night we took to following them. Pinky was driving one of her brothers' Ford pickups that we'd borrowed without his knowing, and we'd stayed way back, watching as a couple of the Dragon made their deliveries. They'd stop at a place, one of 'em'd get out and pop the trunk, grab something and go inside, the other'd wait in the car.

After a couple a hours of this I pretty much figured this was a bust, 'cept right about then that Chevy stopped around back of Cinders, this strip club on Division Street, and after getting their delivery, both them boys went inside. Now either this was their last stop, or the guy doing the waiting got tired of sitting in the car. Or maybe he just wanted himself an eyeful a what was going on inside. Same difference right now, I suppose, since they was both gone inside and this was my first chance to pop that trunk my own self and have a look-see what might still be there.

Pinky watched the door, ready to run interference if they come out too soon. I don't know what she woulda done. Probably just pulled down her tube top—that's the kinda thing them boys would find impossible to ignore. Be a little chilly tonight, but while they were counting her goose bumps, I'd be gone.

The trunk weren't no big problem. I been learning my way around locks this past summer. Part hobby, I suppose, and part nosiness. I like to know what people got locked up.

"Holy shit," I said when I get me that trunk open.

"What? What?" Pinky called back to me in a loud whisper.

I just shook my head. There was about twenty little plastic bags sitting there in rows, each as big as my hand, and they weren't full of flour. I grabbed me a half dozen, dropped that trunk lid, and we took off.

Course Pinky had to sample the stuff, just to make sure it was what it was. Me, I don't do dope. Don't drink neither, 'cept for beer, and never enough to get me drunk. I don't like the feeling of being out of control of myself. 'Cause the plain truth—I know this for a fact, and my sister rubbed it in with her leaving—is you only got yourself to depend on. I got me Pinky, I know, and she loves me and I love her, but come down to the wire, I don't know which way she'd turn. Least, I didn't then.

Anywise, we had the dope, and got us the Dragon riled up. Can you see where this is going?

Next stop was Haven's place, but that was going to have to wait for another night. We went to school the next day like the good students we were. In algebra, Pinky stopped by the desk to ask Haven a question, bending down real low so that them bug eyes of his was locked tight on her cleavage. Meanwhile, I sidled over and slipped a little folded-paper packet of dope in the front chest pocket of his jacket which was hanging on the back of his chair. There was a chance he'd up and find it, throw it out afore it had a chance to do us any good—'less he had him some other urges we didn't know about—but it was worth a try. How often does a guy look in that pocket, anyways?

That night we snuck 'round his house, but he was playing hard-to-get and never went out. The same thing happened Thursday. But Friday, hell, even cradle-robbing sons a bitches got to have them some fun, and he drove off, all spruced up like he had him a hot date. I had to smile, seeing's how he was wearing that same sports jacket that I left my little surprise in.

I went in through the back. He had him a summer kitchen that he was using as a shed and the door weren't even locked. The one inside it, leading into the house, was, but it was a cheap lock and I made short work of it. I didn't have me the tools of the burglar's trade, but you'd be surprised what you can do with a couple of stiff wires.

Inside, I made straight for the crapper and taped three of them bags of dope to the back of the toilet. I had me another handful of paper packets like I left in his jacket, and them I put in the drawer of the night table by his bed, along with a nice little mirror and some cut-down straws that Pinky had used the night before. She sure enough was enjoying that crap.

After that it was just a matter of waiting till he got home. When he did, Pinky drove off to the closest pay phone and called the Dragons' clubhouse with a little hot tip 'cause she could fake a man's voice better'n me. She got back and we waited some more till them motorcycles showed up. When they was pounding on his door, we went back to that phone booth and called the cops.

Either the bikers'd get him, or the cops. We didn't much nevermind which it was. We heard later that the cops showed up while the Dragons was beating the crap outta him. The bikers took off and the cops went in. I woulda liked to have been there, seeing Haven's relief turn on him when the cops beelined for that dope we pointed 'em to.

Just to finish everything off, make it all nice and tidy, I put the word out—soft and easylike, mind, so it wouldn't come back on me— how it was Bobby Marshall who'd been putting the bone to Sherry. I was just trying to confuse matters, but it shows you how stupid some people can be. That rumor got 'round to Bobby and he'd just wink and grin, like it was all true. Which was funny, I guess, until Sherry's old man come up to him outside the donut shop and gut shot him with his squirrel gun.

I woulda felt bad, but it weren't like Bobby was some choir boy. He maybe didn't do Sherry, but there's a lotta other meanness could be laid at his door. I just wished I'd knowed what Sherry's old man had planned. I woulda give up Del's name if I had.

"Raylene," Pinky told me. "You got yourself an evil mind in that pretty little head of yours."

"Evil?" I said, pretending to be hurt.

"I mean that in the best possible way."

When it was all over, Haven got off on some technicality, but he lost his job and then moved away. The Dragon never recovered their dope. I heard they tracked Haven down, but not the details of what they done to him. Still, I got me a good imagination. Sherry's old man went to the pen. Bobby had him a nice funeral. Sherry had her a baby girl that she and her mama raised in that double-wide. And me and Pinky? Well, we kept up our wicked ways.

Autumn turned into winter. Spring followed on its heels. And then we was both seventeen, finished school, and ready to make our own way in the world. That summer of '72, we got us a room in a rundown boarding-house off of Jefferson Street, right on the edge of Stokesville—a move up in the world for a couple of gals from Hillbilly Holler—and figured we was set until our rent come due. Neither of us was much willing to work, but it ain't anybody's idea of a party without any cash.

We get the landlady to give us a couple of days and put our heads together, see what we can come up with.

Naw, that ain't true. Pinky sits on the front porch, drinking the last of our beer, and I'm the one figures things out.

We could find us jobs, but who wants to work? Trouble is, pretty much everything else needs a stake. Deal dope? First you needed some product and that blow of Pinky's was long gone by now. Get us a gun and we could hold up a liquor store or one of them gas bars out on the highway, but I don't like the idea of putting my ass on the line, though I do like the thought of that gun. Still they cost money, too, and they don't come cheap.

"We could always peddle our asses," Pinky offers.

I shook my head. "I'm drawing the line at certain things," I tell her.

"Like what?"

"Like whoring. Or stripping. Or lap-dancing."

"It comes to that," she says, "I'll do it. I ain't 'shamed of my body."

"It ain't a matter of being 'shamed or not."

She just laughs. Ever since I stopped Del's nighttime visits, I'm a lot more choosy who I do it with. And it's got to be when I'm in the mood. Pinky's not near' so discriminating.

"Maybe we should move out west," Pinky says. "Get ourselves to L.A. It's always warm there." She has another swig a beer and grins at me. "We can become movie stars."

"I ain't gonna be in no porn flick, neither," I tell her.

"So when are you gonna have some fun?" she asks.

I ignore that. "We go anywhere," I say, "we need us a stake. But first we got to make it through the week."

"So we're back to peddling our asses," she says.

I shake my head, firm. I won't be swayed on this. "No one's doing any whoring," I tell her.

But she's got me thinking. There's ways to make money in the sex trade without ever putting out. That's the beauty of a scam. It ain't what you actually give, it's what the mark thinks he's gonna get. You manage to rip him off, what's he gonna do? Once he's offered you cash for favors, he's gone and broke the law his own self, so he won't be crying to the cops. The only real consideration you got at that point is he don't beat the crap out a you.

"Go make yourself sexy," I tell Pinky. "But classy, mind you. Not cheap. You and me is going downtown."

Now, downtown Tyler ain't exactly a social whirl, but we got us a convention center and a buncha hotels, and we got the out-a-towners hitting the bars and making their way down to the Ramble, looking for action. Most of 'em are married and married's best for what I got in mind.

Pinky's done a bang-up job on our makeup. She coulda been a beautician, and she was somewhat seriously thinking on it till she found out it meant more schooling and you were spending most of your day trying to make old bags look halfways reasonable, which was a lost cause in the first place. But she had quality goods to work with when it come to us. She was done and I didn't much recognize either of us, we was so gussied up. We coulda been a pair of models, 'cept for me being so short, or movie stars, and I ain't saying we looked old, but we didn't look like no jailbait neither.

We took us to a bar cozied up near the convention center and ordered some drinks. Pinky woulda had a wallbanger, and probably more'n one, but I convinced her to have a ginger ale like me. I had no thoughts on how this was going to go, or how long it'd take, but quicker'n you can spit, we had us a couple of middle-aged men asking could they sit at our table and next thing you know, we're going up to their rooms. I'm a little awkward on the dollar amount, so I let him do the talking, make the offer. We settle on a yard for the night, no rough stuff.

The whole thing's easier'n you'd think. He's already half-cut afore we go up and first thing I do we get to his room, I open the little wet bar under the TV and fix us a couple of drinks. He's so busy fondling my tits, he don't see me filling his glass with three a them little bottles of vodka afore I top it off with some orange juice. Me, I'm just having the juice, but he don't know that.

"Whew," I say when I slug it back, all in one go. Like the liquor's going right to my head.

I stand up and pretend the room's going all dizzy on me while I try to get my dress off. He just sits there, smiling big and watching the show, tosses back his own drink. I hide a grin when I see his eyes tear up and he starts to cough.

I got the top of my dress down, hanging at my waist, the bra off. I figure I'm going to have to fix him another drink, but when I walk over to the bed to get his glass, I see his eyes're glazing over.

"What's the matter, honey?" I ask.

I give him a little push, playfullike, and he just falls back onto the bed. Out like a light. I study him a moment, sit beside him on the bed, and run my hands over his chest, but he's gone.

I don't horse around none then. I get dressed, then go around the room and collect all his clothes, stuff 'em in his suitcase. It's harder rolling him around on the bed, but I get them clothes, too, and I don't forget the complimentary terry-cloth robes provided by the hotel. He's got him 'near three hundred dollars in his wallet which goes direct in my purse, along with his credit cards. Then I heft that suitcase and get me outta there. See, the thing is, I don't want them clothes. I just want it to be a little hard on him, case he comes 'round quicker'n I'd like and tries to follow.

I bring the suitcase into the elevator and take it down to the lobby. I thought this might be the tricky part, walking across the lobby with that suitcase of his and all. What if the hotel gets it into their heads that I'm one of their clients, trying to skip out on paying for my room? But no one pays me no mind and I'm out a side door and walking along the alley till I get to the Dumpster. I fling that case up over the side and I keep on a-walking straight on to the train station where me and Pinky planned to meet up.

After a while, I start to get me worried. It's been over an hour I'm waiting here on her, and I'm thinking the worst, when in she comes a-sauntering, smiling easy as can be.

"Where the hell were you?" I ask.

She gives me a confused look. "With Beau."

"Who's Beau?"

"The guy who asked me up to his room."

I never even asked mine what his name was.

"Did you take his clothes and stuff?" I ask.

"Sure did. Tossed the case up the Dumpster like you told me to."

"So what took you so long?" I ask. "We was supposed to be in and out."

"Well, come on, Raylene," she says. "I had to give him a little fun for all that money."

"You didn't get him drunk?"

"Well, he was pretty near' drunk anyways," she says, "but I just wore him out instead. It was fun and he was still sleeping when I left."

All I can do is shake my head.

"How much did you get?" I ask.

"A hundred and thirty and change. I took his cards, too, but what're we gonna do with 'em? I sure as hell don't look like no cornfed shoes salesman from Iowa so I cain't use 'em."

"I'm gonna swap 'em for a gun," I tell her.

There's places on the Ramble where you can pretty much trade anything.

Pinky gives me a look of pure admiration. "That's what I like about you, Raylene," she says. "You're always thinking."

Tyler, Early Spring, 1973

First couple of times we do it, I'm a little uneasy. It ain't that I'm scared, exactly. Hell, I got me a little .38 straight off, swapped them credit cards for it in a pawnshop on Division Street that I knew was willing to turn a blind eye, the goods were right. Them cards was so fresh, Fat Jack was extra pleased and threw in a box of cartridges for free. It ain't the best or the newest pistol in the world, but it fits right snug in my handbag, case anything goes wrong.

I don't want to be remembered neither and soon as we can, I get us wigs and such, but that come later. Cash we got that first day went to our rent, some food, and a case of beer.

But by the time winter's done and the spring melt's turning the hills outside of town all green, we got us a routine worked out and afore you know it, we've moved outta that boardinghouse and into a proper apartment closer to downtown, but not too close. I like to keep our real lives separate from our wicked ways. That was just coming up on the ass end of January.

When we're working, we leave the apartment looking pretty much the way we always do, which is Ts and jeans for me, tube tops and halters with her jeans for Pinky. Once we get downtown, we go into the Devary

Hotel on Church Street, carrying a couple of bags. We like the Devary
'cause the washroom there's got it two doors, one on either side of the
building. We go in one door, gussy ourselves up with our wigs and working clothes, and come out the other looking like a pair of ladies, and I
don't mean no cheap hookers. We look classy.

We leave our bags at a locker in the train station and then we go
to work.

I'm careful 'bout where we run our scam. We don't go to the same
bar more'n once a month. We don't work more'n once or twice a week,
depending how many conventions they got in town. We change our wigs
and dresses regular as rain so we're always looking different. Sometimes
we have a good score, sometimes you got to wonder what them boys
thought they was gonna pay us with, but it all works out. I make a point
of skimming a percentage to build us a traveling stake. I leave it up to
Pinky and we'd never have us no money.

And after the first few times, it ain't just the grab and run anymore.
We polish it up some, work different angles. Like Pinky'd let the guy take
her up to his room and once they're hot and heavy at it, I'd come in with
a Polaroid and we start talking about how much the guy's willing to keep
his wife from knowing. Or Pinky takes the picture and, surprise, when I
show the guy some fake ID, I'm fourteen and jailbait and he's in serious
shit unless he comes up with some folding money. The gun makes sure
none of these cowboys get out a hand. Most of 'em take their medicine,
go all quiet and nervous, but need comes, I'm willing to pull that .38 out.

I learned later they call this the badger game, but usually you got you
a man playing the role of the pimp, or the husband, or the vice squad
dick—whatever you went and figured out aforehand. We didn't want to
bring no one else in on it, so we played it solo. Worked fine, and better
the more we got it refined.

Course the problem with a good thing is, it don't last. Tyler's just too
small. Got a population of maybe three hundred thousand on a good day.
The marks we take in, they ain't going to the cops, and we stick to out-a-
towners, but I guess eventually the word gets out that somebody's making a dishonest dollar and the boys in the cop shop ain't getting their cut.
Guess we shoulda looked into who to pay off. And probably paid attention to the fact it was election time and nothing looks so good on a D.A.'s
record than he's cleaning up sex crimes.

Only reason we didn't get took in was pure dumb luck.

And the luck started with me being the one in the bar that evening in early April, 'cause I can think quick on my feet.

"Buy you a drink?" the guy asks, standing by my table.

I think I knew right then, knew something was off, but not what. Later I figured it was his voice, he's hiding a hillbilly accent same as me when I'm in those bars. Or maybe he was just too good-looking to be some loser, fixing to pay for a woman. I'm not saying he was straight-out handsome, but he weren't so bad neither.

"Depends," I say, "on what you think that drink will get you."

He shrugs. "Some conversation."

"A glass of white wine, then," I tell him because I hate the stuff and can not drink it for hours. "Thanks."

I watch him walk to the bar, get us each a glass of the house white. He comes back and we make us some small talk, then finally he leans across the table, giving me this look I can't read, 'cept I know he thinks something's funny.

"What?" I say.

"Well, here we are, the two of us, each of us waiting for the other to bring up the business."

"What business would that be?"

He leans back now, hands behind his head. "You being a hooker and running a badger game on some poor dumb fuck who just wants to get laid."

I don't have time to play innocent.

"Oh, I know what you're thinking," he goes on. "Vice can't do a thing until you incriminate yourself. But I've got news for you, girlie. I can say any damn thing I want. I tell the judge you offered to go down under the table here and blow me, who you think he's going to believe when you say different?"

"I don't know what you're talking about."

"That a fact. Funny. It's not what your partner says."

Just like that, I feel it all go to hell. They got Pinky and we're the both of us heading for jail time. My fingers start in on a-twitching. I want to pull out my switchblade and gut him where he sits. I want to take the .38 out a my purse and blow that smirk off his face. Hell, I got to do time, I might as well do some serious time. But then he screws up.

"Yeah, he laid it all out for us," the cop goes on. "Dates, how much you pulled in, where you're hocking the cards."

"That sonovabitch," I say.

He grins. "You can't trust a pimp. When are you girlies going to figure that out? First thing he does is roll over."

"So I'm fucked."

Another grin. Bigger. "Not yet."

"You offering me an out?" I ask.

I'm playing up the scared and hopeful, not big time, but enough. Easy, like hooking a catfish.

"Well," he says, drawling on the word. "Maybe we could get us a room, talk some. You willing to cut a deal?"

"If it takes that sonovabitch down."

"I'll be wanting more than what you've got on him," the cop tells me. "You'll need to give me the names of the rest of his string. Tell me who's buying the paperwork and credit cards. And then, if you show me the right kind of appreciation, well, I'll see what I can do to make sure you're kept out of all of this when the shit hits the fan."

"Oh, I'll show you appreciation you'll never forget," I tell him, adding eager to the scared and hopeful. "Whatever you want."

"Come on, then," he says.

I want to hurt him so bad. It ain't even so much that we're busted—I mean, that comes with the territory. It's the chance we took coming in on all of this. I don't like it, but what do you do? No, what's got me so pissed is he's as big a crook as we are, 'cept he gets to hide behind a badge while we do the time.

But I don't let none of that show on my face. I just follow him meekly outta the bar and let him lead me to the elevators. He doesn't seem to notice that I left my purse hanging from the back of my chair. I spot Pinky in the lobby, pretending to read some glamour magazine—I swear she gets the same nourishment from them as I do a sandwich. I give her the finger signs we worked out for "big trouble," followed by "cop," my hand held down at my side where he can't see it.

"So what should I call you?" I ask as we get into the elevator.

"Mister sir," he says.

I start to laugh, but then I see that he isn't joking. So that's what he's into.

"I like that," I tell him, still playing up the meek.

He gives me a scornful look. "Bullshit. Truth is, you'll pretend you like anything I say or do, if you think it'll get you off."

I just give him a blank look, like I'm too dumb to get what he's saying. He shakes his head. I don't know whether he's buying my act, or he just don't care. I look at Pinky after we get in the elevator and the doors start to close. She's all gussied up like some tourist, sitting there in a pants suit, cheap camera lying there on the sofa aside her purse.

Luckily the cop and I have the elevator to ourselves. Pinky'll mark the floor where it stops, get my purse from the bar, then follow us on up, quicklike. I just hope the cop hasn't got a few of his buddies waiting for us up in his room. I wouldn't put a gang-bang past him.

The elevator stops at the fifteenth floor and we get out.

"Still scared?" he asks, giving me a little shove down the hall.

I nod, act like I can't look him in the eye.

"You should be," he says.

Shit. I'll bet he does have some buddies waiting for us.

The room's empty but it don't take me long to work out what I'm supposed to be scared of. As soon as we're inside, he just ups and smacks me across the side of my head with the open palm of his hand. I wasn't expecting it and go reeling, trip over the corner of his bed.

"On your knees," he tells me and unzips his pants.

Outside the door, afore we come in, I dropped a wadded-up napkin from the bar. I hope it's enough for Pinky.

The cop's got his dick out now. He grabs my head and mashes my face against his groin. I'm just glad the wig don't come off in his hand, but Pinky knows how to set 'em on, snug and tight.

"Don't even think of biting," he says.

I wouldn't dream of it. I do just what he wants, waiting for the door to open. When we first got into this business, we made a point of ripping off pass keys in all the major hotels, so I know Pinky won't have no trouble getting in. I just got to hope that nobody picked up my marker, but who's gonna grab a wadded-up napkin from the floor 'cept for the cleaning staff and they finished their work hours ago.

I hear the door open afore he does 'cause I'm expecting it and then I bite down hard to distract him. It works real fine.

"Jesus, fuck!" he cries and belts me hard with a closed fist.

I let go with my teeth and allow the force of that blow to knock me away. We both hear the click when Pinky cocks the gun. I scuttle out of his reach, but he's already turning, looking into the muzzle of the .38. Funny how fast that dick of his goes limp again.

"So do I shoot him or what?" Pinky asks.

But the cop, he still thinks he's in control.

"Girlie," he tells her, talking like the arrogant old redneck cop he is. "You are in deep shit. Now you just put that gun down and—"

"Shoot him," I say.

And Pinky does.

Christ, it's loud.

And the mess. Pinky had to get all fancy, went for a head shot, and now there's blood and brains and crap all over the place. But none of it got on me. I didn't touch nothing in the room 'cept his dick, so we ain't leaving no sign. I go to lift his wallet from his inside jacket pocket, find a fat envelope in there instead. It's got a bunch a names written on the side—Jackson, Macy, Brown, and others I don't recognize. Most of 'em got a line run through 'em. The envelope's stuffed with cash, mostly hundreds.

"Guess it was collection day," Pinky says.

I nod and get up and we walk out, wiping down the door handle as we leave. Pinky puts the gun back in my purse and holds it in her hand as we make for the stairs, moving purposeful, but not rushing. She's got her own purse slung from her shoulder.

"How long we got, you think?" Pinky asks as we go down the stairs.

"Beats me," I tell her.

I work at the blonde wig, finally get it off and stuff it in my purse. Comb my own hair with my fingers to fluff it up some. Pinky gives me the jacket she's wearing and I button it up to cover my cleavage. It's not much, but the jacket and my natural hair might be enough to throw anybody off while we're going through the lobby. I just hope anybody who noticed me going up with the cop was too busy looking at my tits to remember my face.

"You scared?" Pinky asks.

I shake my head. Funny thing is, I got me this wild buzz that makes me feel like I'm ten feet tall and made of solid steel. I'm ready to take on anybody wants a piece of us, one at a time, or all in a bunch. Don't matter I got a bruise starting up that takes up most of the side of my face, or that it'll take the better part of a couple of weeks to disappear.

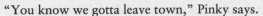

"You know we gotta leave town," Pinky says.

"What for? Nobody knows we was there. There's nothing to connect us to him."

"He was a *cop*," Pinky says.

"A dirty cop."

"Who cares? You know what they're like when it's one of their own. They're gonna tear this town inside out lookin' for us."

"And I'm telling you, they got nothing to find."

She don't like it, but she follows my lead.

We get through the lobby fine, make it to the Devary where we change back into our own clothes.

"There's almost four thousand dollars here," I tell Pinky while she's standing at the mirror, putting on her lipstick.

"You're shittin' me."

"God's truth."

Pinky dabs her lips with a tissue. The Devary's so classy they got fancy tissues set out, hand cream, all kinds of stuff.

"Didn't know you could make that much bein' a crooked cop," she says.

I think about how we left him lying dead in the hotel room.

"I'm guessing it's got its down side," I tell her.

Pinky stares at me for a long minute and then the both of us are laughing. Anybody come in just then and they'd think we was a couple of no-account Hillbilly Holler girls, got us drunk in the big city. Which we was, 'cept for the drinking part.

The more we laughed, the more my jaw hurt. I took me a good hit from that dead cop's fist. I could see the skin getting all discolored, the whole side of my face.

"You're startin' to look a little ugly," Pinky says.

I give her a grin. "Yeah? You should see the other guy."

And that just sets us off again.

That night was when I first started in a-dreaming about wolves. This weren't no fancy New Age crap like got popular later on—you know, animal spirit guides and Indian totems and shit like that. I wasn't getting me no advice in these dreams as to how I could better my life. I was just dreaming I was a wolf. Running wild out in the bush somewheres, ain't got me a care in the world, ain't got me any baggage. Life's just simple, is what it is. You hunt some, you sleep it off, hunt some more.

I tell Pinky 'bout it next morning when we get up and she just shakes her head and laughs.

"I don't know who you are sometimes," she tells me.

I know it's peculiar, but I like them dreams. And the funny thing is, I know who I am in 'em. I mean, I know I'm Raylene Carter, asleep in my bed and a-dreaming, but at the same time I'm that wolf, too. It ain't the least bit confusing. All the stuff that makes my life such a complication, it's gone. And when I wake up, I'm feeling pure and refreshed.

Them dreams, they're the only time I ever feel so strong and free. Like I matter.

Pinky was nervous for a few days, but she oughtn'ta worried. Sure, the cop's death made the papers big time and all, but they had nothing to go on, that was plain to see. They went into enough detail you coulda filled a book with it all, you were so inclined. I noticed there was no mention of his dick hanging out of his pants, but maybe that's 'cause *The Tyler Standard*'s a family paper. The guy from the D.A.'s office that made all the official statements made him out to be some kinda hero cop, closing in on these big-time drug dealers. Hell, maybe they even believed it.

I guess it was 'cause they got them a ballistics report on the bullet what killed him and turns out it matched up with some other drug-related deaths over in Cooperstown and on the rez and such. That pissed me off. Fat Jack had swore to me that .38 was clean, but there ain't much you can do once the horse is outta the barn. Anywise, we got rid of that gun, wiped it down good, and buried it way back in the woods, deep in a holler. Same place we burned that wig and clothes I was wearing.

Things didn't change much for us 'cept we laid low and made plans to head on outta there. I figure we needed us a bigger city. Pinky was all set for L.A. and this movie career she figured was waiting on us out there, but I got her to settle on something closer by where we could build us up a decent stake first. I weren't gonna be one more deadbeat wanna-be arriving in L.A., looking for a handout, though I swear

Pinky sounded like she was looking forward to getting cozy with them movie men.

"I just like the sound of it," she'd say. "You know. Casting couches. Admit it, Raylene. Don't that have a ring to your ear?"

Guess we was both peculiar in our own way.

We waited us a few months till the story got old, living off of the cop's dirty money, and keeping a low profile. But life went on.

That was a busy spring. Papa up and died in March, but I never went to the funeral. He didn't much notice me when he was alive, I didn't see things being any different now that he was dead.

Jimmy and Robbie had got in with a bad crowd 'bout then. Started dealing crack, till Jimmy picked a fight with one of the Dragon, right there on the Ramble and got himself killed for his trouble not two weeks after they put Papa in the ground. Robbie showed his true colors that day and run like a scared rabbit while that biker was beating his brother to death.

I didn't go to that funeral neither.

I lost track of Robbie by the time Pinky and I was looking to leave town. Somebody told me he'd took to working for the Morgans, up in Freakwater Holler, but I didn't buy that. What would they want with a loser like him? The story I liked was that he ended up in Boystown, blowing dicks to pay for the habit he picked up when he and Jimmie was these big-shot crack dealers.

More likely he's just dead, and that's still another funeral I wouldn'ta gone to if I'd knowed about it.

I woulda gone to Del's, just to make sure the sonovabitch was really dead, but he didn't have the good manners to die. He did go to prison for running down some poor little girl while he was blind drunk—the sentencing was in April, just a few days after we killed the cop. Reason he got so much time was he took off and left her to die in the ditch. Word was she coulda made it, if somebody'd got her to a hospital in time.

Knowing he was in prison made it all the sweeter for me when Pinky and me left town—him locked up and me running wild and free. I hoped he was learning what it felt like to be somebody's special midnight girl-friend.

I heard Mama moved outta the old house to a trailer park near the prison where I figure she divided her time between visiting with Del and making life miserable for anybody she happened to meet.

Just afore we took off for the city, I remember me and Pinky made a run out to that place where I growed up—guess that was in May. We just stood there looking at it for a whiles. Nobody's renting it since Mama moved out and it ain't no wonder. The wonder is it's still standing at all.

"What're you thinkin'?" Pinky asks.

I shrug. "Nothing much."

But I'm thinking of my sister, what she done to me, leaving me behind. I'm thinking of Del and how I still got a score to settle with him and Mama. But that's all got to wait its turn.

We went home and went to bed. When we woke up in the morning, we packed up all we had—and it wasn't much—and headed on down to the bus station in downtown Tyler. That's how a couple of hillbilly girls found themselves in Newford.

NEWFORD, END OF THE SUMMER, 1975

You can take the woman outta the trash, but you can't take the trash out a the woman. That's what Pinky says. Hell, she's got her a saying for every no-account thing we get into and every excuse we need to explain why we'd go and do some of the things we done.

That's as maybe, but we was a class act all the same. Me, I'm just a natural con, I guess, but it got so's Pinky was doing such a good job, I considered maybe she really could become an actress, and I don't mean in no porn flick, though I don't doubt she'd shine there, too, given the opportunity. She sure does have her an itch she likes to scratch when it comes to men.

There's quick and easy ways to make a little spending money, slower ones where you can make a whole lot more, and we pretty much done 'em all, without having to sell our asses, neither. City's so damn big, we coulda worked us every night of the week and still not worry about showing up in any one place often enough for it to be a problem.

Nobody much gives a damn about each other and that just makes our job easier.

But after a time we got us itchy feet. I've been working a big score on this widower who lives down the street, been playing the old guy along for months now. I go over and I'm so sweet. He's what, eighty-five, but still horny as some old toad. I'm always bending over him with my blouse falling open, picking something up off of the floor or reaching to a top shelf in my little short skirts. I never touch him, he never touches me, but I could ask him for anything and he'd give it to me.

"I have to go," I tell him one day. "The only thing that keeps me here is you, but things just aren't going well for me right now."

"What do you need?" he asks.

I laugh. "Thirty thousand dollars," I say, "and neither one of us has that kind of money."

"What do you need it for, Susie?"

That's what he thinks my name is. Susie Davis.

I tell him how I'm going to lose my house because I'm three months behind on the mortgage. How my office's moved clean across town and I need a car if I'm going to get to work. How my mother's in the hospital, got no insurance, and I'm the only one can bail her out. I give him a list of trials and troubles that'd almost make me blush, but he's hearing me out, nodding, taking it all seriouslike.

"I can get you that money," he says.

"Oh, please," I tell him. "How could you possibly do that?"

But I already know. He's got ten times that stashed away in bonds and securities and crap. I been through his mail when he's sleeping, seen the statements that come every few months.

"You don't have to worry about that," he says.

I give him a smile like honey fresh from the hive.

"That's really sweet of you," I say, "but there's no way I could accept that much money from you."

I talk nicer around him, like a city girl who could have a career, who could make something of herself, given half a chance.

"What do I need it for?" he says. "I could be dead tomorrow."

"Don't even joke about that," I tell him, sitting on the arm of his chair.

My skirt's already short and the movement hikes it up, grabbing and holding his gaze.

"Only thing that makes me happy is knowing you're alive and well," I add.

"I want to do it," he says, finally pulling his gaze up to my face.

But I shake my head again.

"Think of it as a loan, then."

He's got no family. He's got no friends. He hires a woman to clean his house. Someone else comes in and makes his meals, unless I'm there to do it. He watches TV all day long when he's not playing with his stamp collection. The poor old sap. His only friend is Susie Davis, who don't even exist.

I let him wear me down.

The next time I come over, he's got the money. In cash. I told him I didn't have a bank account anymore since the bank cleaned it out for my mortgage arrears and took back all its credit cards.

I still act like I can't take it, but he presses it into my hands. Insists.

If I was Pinky, I'd give him a kiss 'bout now. A deep French kiss. Sit on his lap and give him a last thrill.

But I just give him a hug. Tell him I can't believe what a good friend he is.

When I walk out that door later, it's the last time he ever sees me.

Pinky and me, we buy plane tickets to L.A. and we're finally heading out west to meet fame and fortune, head-on, on our terms. The Hillbilly Holler gals do Hollywood. That was the summer of '75 when we got us there and let me tell ya, we had us a time.

But the high times never last. Truth of the matter is, all we ever were afore we come here was small-time crooks. We find that out after we're in L.A. awhiles. Everybody there's on the take or got their own con going. It takes a handful of years, but eventually all our tried-and-trues are worth squat and our money runs out so fast you'd think it was made of water.

So Pinky's dream finally comes true and she gets to be in the movies. You know the kind. Straight to video. They sell to the guys with the remote in one hand, their dick in the other.

I can't do it.

"Don't you worry, Raylene," she tells me. "You carried us a long whiles and now it's my turn. 'Sides, it ain't like I don't like it or nothin'."

Everything I try goes sour. It's like I used up all my luck and smarts in Tyler and Newford. Or maybe I was just never ready to play against the big guns. Maybe I never will be.

Finally I get arrested on a soliciting charge—I hadn't got far enough into the con to make it armed robbery or extortion—and pull six months in county. That's in '81. It's also when Pinky starts her career.

When I get out, I can't seem to focus anymore. All I do is sit in this seedy little apartment we got in Westwood Village and watch crap TV and the free copies of Pinky's movies that she brings home. She looks to be having the time of her life in them—hell, she *tells* me, over and over, how she's having the goddamn time of her life—but it breaks my heart all the same.

I only ever feel all right at night. Late, late at night.

When I'm dreaming.

When I'm a wolf.

When I'm leading my pack.

Interview

Extract from an interview with Jilly Coppercorn, conducted by Torrane Dunbar-Burns for *The Crowsea Arts Review*, at Ms. Coppercorn's Yoors Street studio, on Wednesday, April 17, 1991.

Something I've always been curious about: why don't we see your work on the covers of fantasy books?

I did one once—but that was a long time ago. My friend Alan Grant put me in contact with this paperback publisher and I was very conscientious with that first job. I read the manuscript all the way through and made all kinds of notes before I went in for my meeting with the art director and that's when reality came up and gave me a bang on the ear. She loved my ideas, but said they weren't right, then talked about how she thought it should be, could I do it? I did a bunch of sketches in her office while we talked and she said, "That's it. That's perfect."

So I went back to the studio I was sharing with Isabelle at the time and did the painting, dropped it off, and never looked for a job in that line of work again.

Because it compromised your artistic values?

Not at all. The concepts I came up with for that book were very true to what the author had intended to convey to her readers. They were my reaction to that—a response, as though we were having a conversation, which is what I think all good art does. It creates a dialogue. It asks questions, but also answers them—which always opens one up to more questions.

But it's not the sort of art that will necessarily sell a book. I just don't think along those lines, I guess. And the one thing I didn't want to do was simply be a conduit for other people's ideas. The art director's ideas were exactly right for commercial purposes. It's my brain that's the round peg in the square hole.

And yet, you're best known for your fantasy paintings.
I don't paint anything that isn't real.

Literally?
Well, I'm painting what I see is there. But Faerie is so ephemeral, isn't it?

But . . .
Oh, I know what you mean. Still, I'm not simply posturing. Nobody likes to be categorized, but if you want to know the truth, in some ways I embrace the way I've become known as a "faerie painter."

"In person, Ms. Coppercorn is as enchanting and whimsical a gamine as the little creatures she chooses to paint. She could as easily inhabit one of her paintings, as render them."
You've been doing your research. What was that in again?

The In the City *review of your first solo show at the Green Man Gallery. That's the first mention I could find of you being described as "The Faerie Painter."*

But getting back to what you said a moment ago—
How I don't paint anything that isn't real?

Exactly. How can you say that? Surely you don't literally believe the city is overrun with diminutive faeries and such?
Why is it so preposterous?

You're kidding . . . aren't you?

Maybe. [Laughs.] But not entirely. I don't want to get all esoteric on you, but what do you know about quantum phenomenon?

Not a lot.
It's the idea that certain things don't happen unless they're observed by a conscious entity.

That sounds like that business about conceptual reality I've heard you discuss before, how everything is the way it is because we've all agreed that's the way it is.
The "World As It Is," as my friend the professor would say.
    Yes, the two go hand in hand. Faerie—mysterious phenomena in whatever jacket they happen to be wearing, really—have always fallen between the cracks of how most people expect the world to be. It takes a certain innocence of heart to remain open to the Otherworld, to the things that stray out of those lands that lie beyond the Fields We Know. And by that I don't mean naïveté so much as a lack of cynicism.

Have you believed this all your life?
It's not a matter of belief. More something I've come to understand and appreciate over time.

So you weren't a little girl chasing faeries at the bottom of the garden?
I was never a little girl. Or maybe a better way to put it would be that I had to grow up before I was finally able to become one.

You never talk about your family.
What do you mean? I talk about them all the time. Sophie, Wendy, the Riddell brothers, Sue, Isabelle, Mona . . .

You're speaking of your family of choice, if that's the correct way to put it.
Doesn't make them any less my family.

Of course not. But I meant the family you were born into, that you grew up in.
I never had that kind of a family.

So you had a troubled childhood?

Because of the things that happened to me I don't think I ever had a childhood. Until I grew up.

It seems that many people with an artistic bent—musicians, writers, as well as artists—have had a less than wonderful childhood. Any thoughts on that?

I can't speak for anybody else, but maybe it's because so many of us are outsiders. You know, we just don't conform well.

Have you ever thought of tackling these issues with your art?

It's funny you should ask. Normally when I paint, what I want to do is put some beauty back into the world. I'm not a big fan of confrontational art, though I certainly realize it has its place. But I've recently gotten together with some other women to prepare a show that deals with just that sort of thing.

Jilly

The past scampers like an alley cat through the present, leaving the paw prints of memories scattered helter-skelter—here ink is smeared on a page, there lies an old photograph with a chewed corner, elsewhere still, a nest has been made of old newspapers, headlines running one into the other to make strange declarations. There is no order to what we recall, the wheel of time follows no straight line as it turns in our heads. In the dark attics of our minds, all times mingle, sometimes literally.

I get so confused. I've been so many people; some I didn't like at all. I wonder that anyone could. Victim, hooker, junkie, liar, thief. But without them, I wouldn't be who I am today. I'm no one special, but I like who I am, lost childhood and all.

Did I have to be all those people to become the person I am today? Are they still living inside me, lurking in some dark corner of my mind, waiting for me to slip and stumble and fall and give them life again?

I tell myself not to remember, but that's wrong, too. Not remembering makes them stronger.

2

The morning sun came in through the window of Jilly's loft, playing across the features of her guest. The girl was still asleep on the Murphy bed, sheets all tangled around her skinny limbs, pulled tight and smooth over the rounded swell of her abdomen. Sleep had gentled her features. Her hair clouded the pillow around her head. The soft morning sunlight gave her a Madonna quality, a nimbus of Botticelli purity that the harsher light of the later day would steal away once she woke.

She was fifteen years old. And eight months pregnant.

Jilly sat in the window seat, feet propped up on the sill, sketchpad on her lap. She caught the scene in charcoal, smudging the lines with the pad of her middle finger to soften them. On the fire escape outside, a stray cat climbed up the last few metal steps until it was level with where she was sitting and gave a plaintive meow.

Jilly had been expecting the black and white tabby. She reached under her knees and picked up a small plastic margarine container filled with dried kibbles that she set down on the fire escape in front of the cat. As the tabby contentedly crunched its breakfast, Jilly returned to her portrait.

"My name's Annie," her guest had told her last night when she stopped Jilly on Yoors Street just a few blocks south of the loft. "Could you spare some change? I really need to get some decent food. It's not so much for me . . ."

She put her hand on the swell of her stomach as she spoke. Jilly had looked at her, taking in the stringy hair, the ragged clothes, the unhealthy color of her complexion, the too-thin body that seemed barely capable of sustaining the girl herself, little say nourishing the child she carried.

"Are you all on your own?" Jilly asked.

The girl nodded.

Jilly put her arm around the girl's shoulder and steered her back to the loft. She let her take a shower while she cooked a meal, gave her a clean smock to wear, and tried not to be patronizing while she did it all.

The girl had lost enough dignity as it was and Jilly knew that dignity was almost as hard to recover as innocence. She knew all too well.

3

Stolen Childhood, by Sophie Etoile. Copperplate engraving. Five Coyotes Singing Studio, Newford, 1988.

A child in a ragged dress stands in front of a ramshackle farmhouse. In one hand she holds a doll—a stick with a ball stuck in one end and a skirt on the other. She wears a lost expression, holding the doll as though she doesn't quite know what to do with it.

A shadowed figure stands behind the screen door, watching her.

I guess I was around three years old when my oldest brother started molesting me. That'd make him eleven. He used to touch me down between my legs while my parents were out drinking or sobering up down in the kitchen. I tried to fight him off, but I didn't really know that what he was doing was wrong—even when he started to put his cock inside me.

I was eight when my mother walked in on one his rapes and you know what she did? She walked right out again until my brother was finished and we both had our clothes on again. She waited until he'd left the room, then she came back in and started screaming at me.

"You little slut! Why are you doing this to your own brother?"

Like it was my fault. Like I *wanted* him to rape me. Like the three-year-old I was when he started molesting me had any idea about what he was doing.

I think my other brothers knew what was going on all along, but they never said anything about it—they didn't want to break that macho code-of-honor bullshit. My little sister was just born, too young to know anything. When my dad found out about it, he beat the crap out of my brother, but in some ways it just got worse after that.

My brother didn't stop molesting me; when he wasn't coming to my room, he just had this smirk for me, like he was daring me to do something about it. My mother and my other brothers, every time I'd come into a room, they'd all just stop talking and look at me like I was some kind of bug. The only time my mother talked to me was when there was something she wanted me to do and then she'd just give the order. If I didn't jump to it, I'd get a licking.

I think at first my dad wanted to do something to help me, but in the end he really wasn't any better than my mother. I could see it in his eyes: he blamed me for it, too. He kept me at a distance, never came close to me anymore, never let me feel like I was normal.

He's the one who had me see a psychiatrist. I'd have to go and sit in his office all alone, just a little kid in this big leather chair. The psychiatrist would lean across his desk, all smiles and smarmy understanding, and try to get me to talk, but I never told him a thing. I didn't trust him. I'd already learned that I couldn't trust men. Couldn't trust women either, thanks to my mother. Her idea of working things out was to send me to confession, like the same God who let my brother rape me was now going to make everything okay so long as I owned up to seducing him in the first place.

What kind of a way is that for a kid to grow up?

4

"Forgive me, Father, for I have sinned. I let my brother . . ."

5

Jilly laid her sketchpad aside when her guest began to stir. She swung her legs down so that they dangled from the windowsill, heels banging lightly against the wall, toes almost touching the ground. She pushed an unruly lock of hair from her brow, leaving behind a charcoal smudge on her temple.

Small and slender, with pixie features and a mass of curly dark hair, she looked almost as young as the girl on her bed. Jeans and sneakers, a dark T-shirt and an oversized peach-colored smock, only added to her air of slightness and youth. But she was halfway through her thirties, her own teenage years long gone; she could have been Annie's mother.

"What were you doing?" Annie asked as she sat up, tugging the sheets up around herself.

"Sketching you while you slept. I hope you don't mind."

"Can I see?"

Jilly passed the sketchpad over and watched Annie study it. On the fire escape behind Jilly, two more cats had joined the black and white tabby at the margarine container. One was an old alley cat, its left ear ragged and torn, ribs showing like so many hills and valleys against the matted landscape of its fur. The other belonged to an upstairs neighbor; it was making its usual morning rounds.

"You made me look a lot better than I really am," Annie said finally.

Jilly shook her head. "I only drew what was there."

"Yeah, right."

Jilly didn't bother to contradict her. The self-worth speech would keep.

"So is this how you make your living?" Annie asked.

"Pretty much. I do a little waitressing on the side."

"Beats being a hooker, I guess."

She gave Jilly a challenging look as she spoke, obviously anticipating a reaction.

Jilly only shrugged. "Tell me about it," she said.

Annie didn't say anything for a long moment. She looked down at the rough portrait with an unreadable expression, then finally met Jilly's gaze again.

"I've heard about you," she said. "On the street. Seems like everybody knows you. They say . . ."

Her voice trailed off.

Jilly smiled. "What do they say?"

"Oh, all kinds of stuff." She shrugged. "You know. That you used to live on the street, that you're kind of like a one-woman social service, but you don't lecture. And that you're"—she hesitated, looked away for a moment—"you know, a witch."

Jilly laughed. "A witch?"

That was a new one on her.

Annie waved a hand toward the wall across from the window where Jilly was sitting. Paintings leaned up against each other in untidy stacks. Above them, the wall held more, a careless gallery hung frame to frame to save space. They were part of Jilly's ongoing "Urban Faerie" series, realistic city scenes and characters to which were added the curious little denizens of lands which never were. Hobs and faerie, little elf men and goblins.

"They say you think all that stuff's real," Annie said.

"What do you think?"

When Annie gave her a "give me a break" look, Jilly just smiled again.

"How about some breakfast?" she asked to change the subject.

"Look," Annie said. "I really appreciate your taking me in and feeding me and everything last night, but I don't want to be a freeloader."

"One more meal's not freeloading."

Jilly pretended to pay no attention as Annie's pride fought with her baby's need.

"Well, if you're sure it's okay," Annie said hesitantly.

"I wouldn't have offered if it wasn't," Jilly told her.

She dropped down from the windowsill and went across the loft to the kitchen corner. She normally didn't eat a big breakfast, but twenty minutes later they were both sitting down to fried eggs and bacon, home fries and toast, coffee for Jilly and herb tea for Annie.

"Got any plans for today?" Jilly asked as they were finishing up.

"Why?" Annie replied, immediately suspicious.

"I thought you might want to come visit a friend of mine."

"A social worker, right?"

The tone in her voice was the same as though she were talking about a cockroach or maggot.

Jilly shook her head. "More like a storefront counselor. Her name's Angelina Marceau. She runs that drop-in center on Grasso Street. It's privately funded, no political connections."

"I've heard of her. The Grasso Street Angel."

"You don't have to come," Jilly said, "but I know she'd like to meet you."

"I'm sure."

Jilly shrugged. When she started to clean up, Annie stopped her.

"Please," she said. "Let me do it."

Jilly retrieved her sketchpad from the bed and returned to the window seat while Annie washed up. She was just adding the finishing touches to the rough portrait she'd started earlier when Annie came to sit on the edge of the Murphy bed.

"That painting on the easel," Annie said. "Is that something new you're working on?"

Jilly nodded.

"It's not like your other stuff at all."

"I'm part of an artist's group that calls itself the Five Coyotes Singing Studio," Jilly explained. "The actual studio's owned by a friend of mine named Sophie Etoile, but we all work in it from time to time. There's five of us, all women, and we're doing a group show with a theme of child abuse at the Green Man Gallery next month."

"And that painting's going to be in it?" Annie asked.

"It's one of three I'm doing for the show."

"What's that one called?"

" 'I Don't Know How to Laugh Anymore.' "

Annie put her hands on top of her swollen stomach.

"Me, neither," she said.

6

I Don't Know How to Laugh Anymore, by Jilly Coppercorn. Oils and mixed media. Yoors Street Studio, Newford, 1991.

A life-sized female subject leans against an inner city wall in the classic pose of a prostitute waiting for a customer. She wears high heels, a micro miniskirt, tube top, and short jacket, with a purse slung over one shoulder, hanging against her hip from a narrow strap. Her hands are thrust into the pockets of her jacket. Her features are tired, the lost look of a junkie in her eyes undermining her attempt to appear sultry.

Near her feet, a condom is attached to the painting, stiffened with gesso.

The subject is thirteen years old.

I started running away from home when I was ten. The summer I turned eleven I managed to make it to Newford and lived on its streets for six months. I ate what I could find in the Dumpsters behind the McDonald's and other fast-food places on Williamson Street—there was nothing wrong with the food. It was just dried out from having been under the heating lamps for too long.

I spent those six months walking the streets all night. I was afraid to sleep when it was dark because I was just a kid and who knows what could've happened to me. At least being awake I could hide whenever I saw something that made me nervous. In the daytime I slept where I could—in parks, in the backseats of abandoned cars, wherever I didn't think I'd get caught. I tried to keep myself clean, washed up in restaurant bathrooms and at this gas bar on Yoors Street where the guy running the pumps took a liking to me. Paydays he'd spot me for lunch at the grill down the street.

I started drawing again around that time and for a while I tried to hawk my pictures to the tourists down by the Pier, but the stuff wasn't all that good and I was drawing with pencils on foolscap or pages torn out of old school notebooks—not exactly the kind of art that looks good in a frame, if you know what I mean. I did a lot better panhandling and shoplifting.

I finally got busted trying to boost a tape deck from Kreiger's Stereo—it used to be where Gypsy Records is. Now it's out on the strip past the Tombs. I've always been small for my age, which didn't help when I tried to convince the cops that I was older than I really was. I figured juvie would be better than going back to my parents' place, but it didn't work. My parents had a missing persons out on me, God knows why. It's not like they could've missed me.

After running away and getting brought back a few times, finally they didn't take me home. My mother didn't want me and my dad didn't argue, so I guess he didn't either. I figured that was great until I started making the rounds of foster homes, bouncing back and forth between them and the Home for Wayward Girls. It's just juvie with an old-fashioned name.

I guess there must be some good foster parents, but I never saw any. All mine ever wanted was to collect their check and treat me like I was a piece of shit unless my case worker was coming by for a visit. Then I got moved up from the mattress in the basement to one of their kids' rooms. The first time I tried to tell the worker what was going down, she didn't believe me and then my foster parents beat the crap out of me once she was gone. I didn't make that mistake again.

I was thirteen and in my fourth or fifth foster home when I got molested again. This time I didn't take any crap. I booted the old pervert in the balls and just took off out of there, back to Newford.

I was older and knew better now. Girls I talked to in juvie told me how to get around, who to trust and who was just out to peddle your ass.

See, I never planned on being a hooker. I don't know what I thought I'd do when I got to the city—I wasn't exactly thinking straight. Anyway, I ended up with this guy—Robert Carson. He was fifteen.

I met him in back of the Convention Center on the beach where all the kids used to all hang out in the summer and we ended up getting a room together on Grasso Street, near the high school. I was still pretty fucked up about getting physical with a guy but we ended up doing so many drugs—acid, MDA, coke, smack, you name it—that half the time I didn't know when he was putting it to me.

We ran out of money one day, rent was due, no food in the place, no dope, both of us too fucked up to panhandle, when Rob gets the big idea of me selling my ass to bring in a little money. Well, I was screwed up, but not that screwed up. But then he got some guy to front him some smack and next thing I know I'm in this car with some guy I never saw before and he's expecting a blow job and I'm crying and all fucked up from the dope and then I'm doing it and standing out on the street corner where he's dumped me some ten minutes later with forty bucks in my hand and Rob's laughing, saying how we got it made, and all I can do is crouch down on the sidewalk and puke, trying to get the taste of that guy's come out of my mouth.

So Rob thinks I'm being, like, so fucking weird—I mean, it's easy money, he tells me. Easy for him maybe. We have this big fight and then he hits me. Tells me if I don't get my ass out on the street and make some more money, he's going to do worse, like cut me.

My luck, I guess. Of all the guys to hang out with, I've got to pick one who suddenly realizes it's his ambition in life to be a pimp. Three years later he's running a string of five girls, but he lets me pay my respect—two grand which I got by skimming what I was paying him—and I'm out of that scene.

Except I'm not, because I'm still a junkie and I'm too fucked up to work, I've got no ID, I've got no skills except I can draw a little when I'm not zoned on smack which is just about all the time. I start muling for a couple of dealers in Fitzhenry Park, just to get my fixes, and then one night I'm so out of it, I just collapse in a doorway of a pawnshop up on Perry Street.

I haven't eaten in, like, three days. I'm shaking because I need a fix so bad I can't see straight. I haven't washed in Christ knows how long, so I smell and the clothes I'm wearing are worse. I'm at the end of the line and I know it, when I hear footsteps coming down the street and I know it's the local cop on his beat, doing his rounds.

I try to crawl deeper into the shadows but the doorway's only so deep and the cop's coming closer and then he's standing there, blocking what little light the streetlamps were throwing and I know I'm screwed. But there's no way I'm going back into juvie or a foster home. I'm thinking of offering him a blow job to let me go—so far as the cops're concerned, hookers're just scum, but they'll take a freebie all the same—but I see something in this guy's face, when he turns his head and the streetlight touches it, that tells me he's a family man, walking the straight and narrow. A rookie, true blue, probably his first week on the beat and full of wanting to help everybody and I know for sure I'm screwed. With my luck running true, he's going to be the kind of guy who thinks social workers really want to help someone like me instead of playing bureaucratic mind-fuck games with my head.

I don't think I can take any more.

I find myself wishing I had Rob's switchblade—the one he liked to push up against my face when he didn't think I was bringing in enough. I just want to cut something. The cop. Myself. I don't really give a fuck. I just want out.

He crouches down so he's kind of level with me, lying there scrunched up against the door, and says, "How bad is it?"

I just look at him like he's from another planet. How bad is it? Can it get any worse? I wonder.

"I . . . I'm doing fine," I tell him.

He nods like we're discussing the weather. "What's your name?"

"Jilly," I say.

"Jilly what?"

"Uh . . ."

I think of my parents, who've turned their backs on me. I think of juvie and foster homes. I look over his shoulder and there's a pair of billboards on the building behind me. One's advertising a suntan lotion—you know the one with the dog pulling the kid's pants down? I'll bet some old pervert thought that one up. The other's got the Jolly Green

Giant himself selling vegetables. I pull a word from each ad and give it to the cop.

"Jilly Coppercorn."

"Think you can stand, Jilly?"

I'm thinking, if I could stand, would I be lying here? But I give it a try. He helps me the rest of the way up, supports me when I start to sway.

"So . . . so am I busted?" I ask him.

"Have you committed a crime?"

I don't know where the laugh comes from, but it falls out of my mouth all the same. There's no humor in it.

"Sure," I tell him. "I was born."

He sees my bag still lying on the ground. He picks it up while I lean against the wall and a bunch of my drawings fall out. He looks at them as he stuffs them back in the bag.

"Did you do those?"

I want to sneer at him, ask him why the fuck should he care, but I've got nothing left in me. It's all I can do to stand. So I tell him, yeah, they're mine.

"They're very good."

Right. I'm actually this fucking brilliant artist, slumming just to get material for my art.

"Do you have a place to stay?" he asks.

Whoops, did I read him wrong? Maybe he's planning to get me home, clean me up, and then put it to me.

"Jilly?" he asks when I don't answer.

Sure, I want to tell him. I've got my pick of the city's alleyways and doorways. I'm welcome wherever I go. World treats me like a fucking princess. But all I do is shake my head.

"I want to take you to see a friend of mine," he says.

I wonder how he can stand to touch me. I can't stand myself. I'm like a walking sewer. And now he wants to bring me to meet a friend?

"Am I busted?" I ask him again.

He shakes his head. I think of where I am, what I got ahead of me, then I just shrug. If I'm not busted, then whatever he's got planned for me's got to be better than what I've got right now. Who knows, maybe his friend'll front me with a fix to get me through the night.

"Okay," I tell him. "Whatever."

"C'mon," he says.

He puts an arm around my shoulder and steers me off down the street and that's how I met Lou Fucceri and his girlfriend, the Grasso Street Angel.

7

Jilly sat on the stoop of Angel's office on Grasso Street, watching the passersby. She had her sketchpad on her knee, but she hadn't opened it yet. Instead, she was amusing herself with one of her favorite pastimes: making up stories about the people walking by. The young woman with the child in a stroller, she was a princess in exile, disguising herself as a nanny in a far distant land until she could regain her rightful station in some suitably romantic dukedom in Europe. The old black man with the cane was a physicist studying the effects of Chaos theory in the Grasso Street traffic. The Hispanic girl on her skateboard was actually a mermaid, having exchanged the waves of her ocean for flat concrete and true love.

She didn't turn around when she heard the door open behind her. There was a scuffle of sneakers on the stoop, then the sound of the door closing again. After a moment, Annie sat down beside her.

"How're you doing?" Jilly asked.

"It was weird."

"Good weird, or bad?" Jilly asked when Annie didn't go on. "Or just uncomfortable?"

"Good weird, I guess. She played the tape you did for her book. She said you knew, that you'd said it was okay."

Jilly nodded.

"I couldn't believe it was you. I mean, I recognized your voice and everything, but you sounded so different."

"I was just a kid," Jilly said. "A punky street kid."

"But look at you now."

"I'm nothing special," Jilly said, suddenly feeling self-conscious. She ran a hand through her hair. "Did Angel tell you about the sponsorship program?"

Annie nodded. "Sort of. She said you'd tell me more."

"What Angel does is coordinate a relationship between kids that need help and people who want to help. It's different every time, because everybody's different. I didn't meet my sponsor for the longest time; he just put up the money while Angel was my contact. My lifeline, if you want to know the truth. I can't remember how many times I'd show up at her door and spend the night crying on her shoulder."

"How did you get, you know, cleaned up?" Annie asked. Her voice was shy.

"The first thing is I went into detox. When I finally got out, my sponsor paid for my room and board at the Chelsea Arms while I went through an accelerated high school program. I told Angel I wanted to go on to college, so he co-signed my student loan and helped me out with my books and supplies and stuff. I was working by that point. I had part-time jobs at a couple of stores and with the post office, and then I started waitressing, but that kind of money doesn't go far—not when you're carrying a full course load."

"When did you find out who your sponsor was?"

"When I graduated. He was at the ceremony."

"Was it weird finally meeting him?"

Jilly laughed. "Yes and no. I'd already known him for years—he was my art history professor. We got along really well and he used to let me use the sunroom at the back of his house for a studio. Angel and Lou had shown him some of that bad art I'd been doing when I was still on the street and that's why he sponsored me—because he thought I had a lot of talent, he told me later. But he didn't want me to know it was him putting up the money because he thought it might affect our relationship at Butler U." She shook her head. "He said he *knew* I'd be going the first time Angel and Lou showed him the stuff I was doing."

"It's sort of like a fairy tale, isn't it?" Annie said.

"I guess it is. I never thought of it that way."

"And it really works, doesn't it?"

"If you want it to," Jilly said. "I'm not saying it's easy. There's ups and downs—lots more downs at the start."

"How many kids make it?"

"This hasn't got anything to do with statistics," Jilly said. "You can only look at it on a person-to-person basis. But Angel's been doing this for a long, long time. You can trust her to do her best for you. She takes a lot of flak for what she does. Parents get mad at her because she won't tell them where their kids are. Social services says she's undermining their authority. She's been to jail twice on contempt of court charges because she wouldn't tell where some kid was."

"Even with her boyfriend being a cop?"

"That was a long time ago," Jilly said. "And it didn't work out. They're still friends but—Angel went through an awful bad time when she was a kid. That changes a person, no matter how much they learn to take control of their life. Angel's great with people, especially kids, and she's got a million friends, but she's not good at maintaining a personal relationship with a guy. When it comes down to the crunch, she just can't learn to trust them. As friends, sure, but not as lovers."

"She said something along the same lines about you," Annie said. "She said you were full of love, but it wasn't sexual or romantic so much as a general kindness toward everything and everybody."

"Yeah, well . . . I guess both Angel and I talk too much."

Annie hesitated for a few heartbeats, then said, "She also told me that you want to sponsor me."

Jilly nodded. "I'd like to."

"I don't get it."

"What's to get?"

"Well, I'm not like you or your professor friend. I'm not, you know, all that creative. I couldn't make something beautiful if my life depended on it. I'm not much good at anything."

Jilly shook her head. "That's not what it's about. Beauty isn't what you see on TV or in magazine ads or even necessarily in art galleries. It's a lot deeper and a lot simpler than that. It's realizing the goodness of things, it's leaving the world a little better than it was before you got here. It's appreciating the inspiration of the world around you and trying to inspire others.

"Sculptors, poets, painters, musicians—they're the traditional purveyors of Beauty. But it can as easily be created by a gardener, a farmer, a plumber, a careworker. It's the intent you put into your work, the pride you take in it—whatever it is."

"But still . . . I really don't have anything to offer."

Annie's statement was all the more painful for Jilly because it held no self-pity, it was just a laying out of facts as Annie saw them.

"Giving birth is an act of Beauty," Jilly said.

"I don't even know if I want a kid. I . . . I don't know what I want. I don't know who I am."

She turned to Jilly. There seemed to be years of pain and confusion in her eyes, far more years than she had lived in the world. When had that pain begun? Jilly thought. Who could have done it to her, beautiful child that she must have been? Father, brother, uncle, family friend?

Jilly wanted to just reach out and hold her, but knew too well how the physical contact of comfort could too easily be misconstrued as an invasion of the private space an abused victim sometimes so desperately needed to maintain.

"I need help," Annie said softly. "I know that. But I don't want charity."

"Don't think of this sponsorship program as charity," Jilly said. "What Angel does is simply what we all should be doing all of the time—taking care of each other."

Annie sighed, but fell silent. Jilly didn't push it any further. They sat for a while longer on the stoop while the world bustled by on Grasso Street.

"What was the hardest part?" Annie asked. "You know, when you first came off the street."

"Thinking of myself as normal."

8

Daddy's Home, by Isabelle Copley. Painted wood. Adjani Farm, Wren Island, 1990.

The sculpture is three feet high, a flat rectangle of solid wood, standing on end with a child's face, upper torso and hands protruding from one side, as though the wood is gauze against which the subject is pressing.

The child wears a look of terror.

Annie's sleeping again. She needs the rest as much as she needs regular meals and the knowledge that she's got a safe place to stay. I took my Walkman out onto the fire escape and listened to a copy of the tape that Angel played for her today. I don't much recognize that kid either, but I know it's me.

It's funny, me talking about Angel, Angel talking about me, both of us knowing what the other needs, but neither able to help herself. I like to see my friends as couples. I like to see them in love with each other. But it's not the same for me.

Except who am I kidding? I want the same thing, but I just choke when a man gets too close to me. I can't let down that final barrier, I can't even tell them why.

Sophie says I expect them to just instinctively know. That I'm waiting for them to be understanding and caring without ever opening up to them. If I want them to follow the script I've got written out in my head, she says I have to let them in on it.

I know she's right, but I can't do anything about it.

I see a dog slink into the alleyway beside the building. He's skinny as a whippet, but he's just a mongrel that no one's taken care of for a while. He's got dried blood on his shoulders, so I guess someone's been beating him.

I go down with some cat food in a bowl, but he won't come near me, no matter how soothingly I call to him. I know he can smell the food, but he's more scared of me than he's hungry. Finally I just leave the bowl and go back up the fire escape. He waits until I'm sitting outside my window again before he goes up to the bowl. He wolfs the food down and then he takes off like he's done something wrong.

I guess that's the way I am when I meet a man I like. I'm really happy with him until he's nice to me, until he wants to kiss me and hold me, and then I just run off like I've done something wrong.

9

Annie woke while Jilly was starting dinner. She helped chop up vegetables for the vegetarian stew Jilly was making, then drifted over to the long worktable that ran along the back wall near Jilly's easel. She found a brochure for the Five Coyotes Singing Studio show in amongst the litter of paper, magazines, sketches, and old paintbrushes and brought it over to the kitchen table where she leafed through while Jilly finished up the dinner preparations.

"Do you really think something like this is going to make a difference?" Annie asked after she'd read through the brochure.

"Depends on how big a difference you're talking about," Jilly said.

"Sophie's arranged for a series of lectures to run in association with the show and she's also organized a couple of discussion evenings at the gallery where people who come to the show can talk to us—about their reactions to the show, about their feelings, maybe even share their own experiences if that's something that feels right to them at the time."

"Yeah, but what about the kids that this is all about?" Annie asked.

Jilly turned from the stove. Annie didn't look at all like a young expectant mother, glowing with her pregnancy. She just looked like a hurt and confused kid with a distended stomach, a kind of Ralph Steadman aura of frantic anxiety splattered around her.

"The way we see it," Jilly said, "is if only one kid gets spared the kind of hell we all went through, then the show'll be worth it."

"Yeah, but the only kind of people who are going to go to this kind of thing are those who already know about it. You're preaching to the converted."

"Maybe. But there'll be media coverage—in the papers for sure, maybe a spot on the news. That's where—if we're going to reach out and wake someone up—that's where it's going to happen."

"I suppose."

Annie flipped over the brochure and looked at the four photographs on the back.

"How come there isn't a picture of Sophie?" she asked.

"Cameras don't seem to work all that well around her," Jilly said. "It's like"—she smiled—"an enchantment."

The corner of Annie's mouth twitched in response.

"Tell me about, you know . . ." She pointed to Jilly's Urban Faerie paintings. "Magic. Enchanted stuff."

Jilly put the stew on low to simmer, then fetched a sketchbook that held some of the preliminary pencil drawings for the finished paintings that were leaning up against the wall. The urban settings were barely realized—just rough outlines and shapes—but the faerie ones were painstakingly detailed.

As they flipped through the sketchbook, Jilly talked about where she'd done the sketches, what she'd seen, or more properly glimpsed, that led her to make the drawings she had.

"You've really seen all these . . . little magic people?" Annie asked.

Her tone of voice was incredulous, but Jilly could tell that she wanted to believe.

"Not all of them," Jilly said. "Some I've only imagined, but others . . . like this one." She pointed to a sketch that had been done in the Tombs where a number of fey figures were hanging out around an abandoned car, pre-Raphaelite features at odds with their raggedy clothing and setting. "They're real."

"But they could just be people. It's not like they're tiny or have wings like some of the others."

Jilly shrugged. "Maybe, but they weren't just people."

"Do you have to be magic yourself to see them?"

Jilly shook her head. "You just have to pay attention. If you don't, you'll miss them, or see something else—something you expected to see rather than what was really there. Faerie voices become just the wind, a bodach, like this little man here"—she flipped to another page and pointed out a small gnomish figure the size of a cat, darting off a sidewalk—"scurrying across the street becomes just a piece of litter caught in the backwash of a bus."

"Pay attention," Annie repeated dubiously.

Jilly nodded. "Just like we have to pay attention to each other, or we miss the important things that are going on there as well."

Annie turned another page, but she didn't look at the drawing. Instead she studied Jilly's pixie features.

"You really, really believe in magic, don't you?" she said.

"I really, really do," Jilly told her. "But it's not something I just take on faith. For me, art is an act of magic. I pass on the spirits that I see—of people, of places, mysteries."

"So what if you're not an artist? Where's the magic then?"

"Life's an act of magic, too. Claire Hamill sings a line in one of her songs that really sums it up for me: 'If there's no magic, there's no meaning.' Without magic—or call it wonder, mystery, natural wisdom—nothing has any depth. It's all just surface. You know: what you see is what you get. I honestly believe there's more to everything than that, whether it's a Monet hanging in a gallery or some old vagrant sleeping in an alley."

"I don't know," Annie said. "I understand what you're saying, about people and things, but this other stuff—it sounds more like the kinds of things you see when you're tripping."

Jilly shook her head. "I've done drugs and I've seen faerie. They're not the same."

She got up to stir the stew. When she sat down again, Annie had closed the sketchbook and was sitting with her hands flat against her stomach.

"Can you feel the baby?" Jilly asked.

Annie nodded.

"Have you thought about what you want to do?"

"I guess. I'm just not sure I even want to keep the baby."

"That's your decision," Jilly said. "Whatever you want to do, we'll stand by you. Either way we'll get you a place to stay. If you keep the baby and want to work, we'll see about arranging day care. If you want to stay home with the baby, we'll work something out for that as well. That's what this sponsorship's all about. It's not us telling you what to do; we just want to help you be the person you were meant to be."

"I don't know if that's such a good person," Annie said.

"Don't think like that. It's not true."

Annie shrugged. "I guess I'm scared I'll do the same thing to my baby that my mother did to me. That's how it happens, doesn't it? My mom used to beat the crap out of me all the time, didn't matter if I did something wrong or not, and I'm just going to end up doing the same thing to my kid."

"You're only hurting yourself with that kind of thinking," Jilly said.

"But it *can* happen, can't it? Jesus, I. . . . You know I've been gone from her for two years now, but I still feel like she's standing right next to me half the time, or waiting around the corner for me. It's like I'll never escape. When I lived at home, it was like I was living in the house of an enemy. But running away didn't change that. I still feel like that, except now it's like everybody's my enemy."

Jilly reached over and laid a hand on hers.

"Not everybody," she said. "You've got to believe that."

"It's hard not to."

"I know."

10

This Is Where We Dump Them, by Meg Mullally. Tinted photograph. The Tombs, Newford, 1991.

Two children sit on the stoop of one of the abandoned buildings in the Tombs. Their hair is matted, faces smudged, clothing dirty and ill-fitting. They look like turn-of-the-century Irish tinkers. There's litter all around them: torn garbage bags spewing their contents on the sidewalk, broken bottles, a rotting mattress on the street, half-crushed pop cans, soggy newspapers, used condoms.

The children are seven and thirteen, a boy and a girl. They have no home, no family. They only have each other.

The next month went by awfully fast. Annie stayed with me—it was what she wanted. Angel and I did get her a place, a one-bedroom on Landis that she's going to move into after she's had the baby. It's right behind the loft—you can see her back window from mine. But for now she's going to stay here with me.

She's really a great kid. No artistic leanings, but really bright. She could be anything she wants to be if she can just learn to deal with all the baggage her parents dumped on her.

She's kind of shy around Angel and some of my other friends—I guess they're all too old for her or something—but she gets along really well with Sophie and me. Probably because whenever you put Sophie and me together in the same room for more than two minutes, we just start giggling and acting about half our respective ages, which would make us, mentally at least, just a few years Annie's senior.

"You two could be sisters," Annie told me one day when we got back from Sophie's studio. "Her hair's lighter, and she's a little chestier, and she's *definitely* more organized than you are, but I get a real sense of family when I'm with the two of you. The way families are supposed to be."

"Even though Sophie's got faerie blood?" I asked her.

She thought I was joking.

"If she's got magic in her," Annie said, "then so do you. Maybe that's what makes you seem so much like sisters."

"I just pay attention to things," I told her. "That's all."

"Yeah, right."

The baby came right on schedule—three-thirty, Sunday morning. I probably would've panicked if Annie hadn't been doing enough of that for both of us. Instead I got on the phone, called Angel, and then saw about helping Annie get dressed.

The contractions were really close by the time Angel arrived with the car. But everything worked out fine. Jillian Sophia Mackle was born two hours and forty-five minutes later at the Newford General Hospital. Six pounds and five ounces of red-faced wonder. There were no complications.

Those came later.

11

The last week before the show was simple chaos. There seemed to be a hundred and one things that none of them had thought of, all of which had to be done at the last moment. And to make matters worse, Jilly still had one unfinished canvas haunting her by Friday night.

It stood on her easel, untitled, barely sketched in images, still in monochrome. The colors eluded her. She knew what she wanted, but every time she stood before her easel, her mind went blank. She seemed to forget everything she'd ever known about art. The inner essence of the canvas rose up inside her like a ghost, so close she could almost touch it, but then fled daily, like a dream lost upon waking. The outside world intruded. A knock on the door. The ringing of the phone.

The show opened in exactly seven days.

Annie's baby was almost two weeks old. She was a happy, satisfied infant, the kind of baby that was forever making contented little gurgling sounds, as though talking to herself; she never cried. Annie herself was a nervous wreck.

"I'm scared," she told Jilly when she came over to the loft that afternoon. "Everything's going too well. I don't deserve it."

They were sitting at the kitchen table, the baby propped up on the Murphy bed between two pillows. Annie kept fidgeting. Finally she picked up a pencil and started drawing stick figures on pieces of paper.

"Don't say that," Jilly said. "Don't even think it."

"But it's true. Look at me. I'm not like you or Sophie. I'm not like Angel. What have I got to offer my baby? What's she going to have to look up to when she looks at me?"

"A kind, caring mother."

Annie shook her head. "I don't feel like that. I feel like everything's sort of fuzzy and it's like pushing through cobwebs just to make it through the day."

"We'd better make an appointment with you to see a doctor."

"Make it a shrink," Annie said. She continued to doodle, then looked down at what she was doing. "Look at this. It's just crap."

Before Jilly could see, Annie swept the sheaf of papers to the floor.

"Oh, jeez," she said as they went fluttering all over the place. "I'm sorry. I didn't mean to do that."

She got up before Jilly could and tossed the lot of them in the garbage container beside the stove. She stood there for a long moment, taking deep breaths, holding them, slowly letting them out.

"Annie . . . ?"

She turned as Jilly approached her. The glow of motherhood that had seemed to revitalize her in the month before the baby was born had slowly worn away. She was pale again. Wan. She looked so lost that all Jilly could do was put her arms around her and offer a wordless comfort.

"I'm sorry," Annie said against Jilly's hair. "I don't know what's going on. I just . . . I know I should be really happy, but I just feel scared and confused." She rubbed at her eyes with a knuckle. "God, listen to me. All it seems I can do is complain about my life."

"It's not like you've had a great one," Jilly said.

"Yeah, but when I compare it to what it was like before I met you, it's like I moved up into heaven."

"Why don't you stay here tonight?" Jilly said.

Annie stepped back out of her arms. "Maybe I will—if you really don't mind . . . ?"

"I really don't mind."

"Thanks."

Annie glanced toward the bed, her gaze pausing on the clock on the wall above the stove.

"You're going to be late for work," she said.

"That's all right. I don't think I'll go in tonight."

Annie shook her head. "No, go on. You've told me how busy it gets on a Friday night."

Jilly still worked part-time at Kathryn's Café on Battersfield Road.

She could just imagine what Wendy would say if she called in sick. There was no one else in town this weekend to take her shift, so that would leave Wendy working all the tables on her own.

"If you're sure," Jilly said.

"We'll be okay," Annie said. "Honestly."

She went over to the bed and picked up the baby, cradling her gently in her arms.

"Look at her," she said, almost to herself. "It's hard to believe something so beautiful came out of me." She turned to Jilly, adding before Jilly could speak, "That's a kind of magic all by itself, isn't it?"

"Maybe one of the best we can make," Jilly said.

12

How Can You Call This Love? by Claudia Feder. Oils. Old Market Studio, Newford, 1990.

A fat man sits on a bed in a cheap hotel room. He's removing his shirt. Through the ajar door of the bathroom behind him, a thin girl in bra and panties can be seen sitting on the toilet, shooting up.

She appears to be about fourteen.

I just pay attention to things, I told her. I guess that's why, when I got off my shift and came back to the loft, Annie was gone. Because I pay such good attention. The baby was still on the bed, lying between the pillows, sleeping. There was a note on the kitchen table:

I don't know what's wrong with me. I just keep wanting to hit something. I look at little Jilly and I think about my mother and I get so scared. Take care of her for me. Teach her magic.
Please don't hate me.

I don't know how long I sat and stared at those sad, piteous words, tears streaming from my eyes.

I should never have gone to work. I should never have left her alone. She really thought she was just going to replay her own childhood. She

told me, I don't know how many times she told me, but I just wasn't paying attention, was I?

Finally I got on the phone. I called Angel. I called Sophie. I called Lou
Fucceri. I called everybody I could think of to go out and look for Annie.
Angel was at the loft with me when we finally heard. I was the one who
picked up the phone.

I heard what Lou said: "A patrolman brought her into the General
not fifteen minutes ago, ODing on Christ knows what. She was just trying to self-destruct, is what he said. I'm sorry, Jilly. But she died before I
got here."

I didn't say anything. I just passed the phone to Angel and went to sit
on the bed. I held little Jillian in my arms and then I cried some more.

I was never joking about Sophie. She really does have faerie blood. It's
something I can't explain, something we don't talk much about, something I just know and she denies. But she did promise me that she'd bless
Annie's baby, just the way fairy godmothers would do it in all those old
stories.

"I gave her the gift of a happy life," she told me later. "I never
dreamed it wouldn't include Annie."

But that's the way it works in fairy tales, too, isn't it? Something
always goes wrong, or there wouldn't be a story. You have to be strong,
you have to earn your happily ever after.

Annie was strong enough to go away from her baby when she felt like
all she could do was just lash out, but she wasn't strong enough to help
herself. That was the awful gift her parents gave her.

I never finished that last painting in time for the show, but I found something to take its place. Something that said more to me in just a few rough
lines than anything I've ever done.

I was about to throw out my garbage when I saw those crude little
drawings that Annie had been doodling on my kitchen table the night she
died. They were like the work of a child.

I framed one of them and hung it in the show.

"I guess we're five coyotes and one coyote ghost now," was all
Sophie said when she saw what I had done.

13

In the House of My Enemy, by Annie Mackle. Pencils. Yoors Street Studio, Newford, 1991.

The images are crudely rendered. In a house that is merely a square with a triangle on top are three stick figures, one plain, two with small "skirt" triangles to represent their gender. The two larger figures are beating the smaller one with what might be crooked sticks, or might be belts.

The small figure is cringing away.

14

In the visitors' book set out at the show, someone wrote: "I can never forgive those responsible for what's been done to us. I don't even want to try."

"Neither do I," Jilly said when she read it. "God help me, neither do I."

Raylene

It's easy to be nobody in this city. At eight million plus, it's twice the size of Newford. Hell, I don't even want to think about how much bigger'n Tyson it is. All I know for sure is, you want to get lost, this is the place for it. You can just disappear yourself into the woodwork and nobody gives a good goddamn.

I look back now and I understand I was fighting me a big-time depression once I done my time and got outta the county jail. Aw, who'm I kidding? I wasn't fighting it none. I was just three years or so a-laying in bed most of the time, when I weren't laying on the sofa. I watched me more soaps and talk shows and game shows, not to mention those damned videos of Pinky's than you'd think it'd be humanly possible.

I don't know why I watched them videos of Pinky's. All they'd do is make me want to cry, 'cept I couldn't cry. I'd get me a burning up behind my eyes, and my chest'd feel like it was damn near gonna crush me, it was so tight. But the tears wouldn't come, not nary a one. I hadn't cried me none since my sister left me and after that I swore I'd never cry again. I tried to take it back during them years of being depressed, 'cause I had the feeling that crying'd help, but something deep inside me went and took that oath seriously. Whatever that piece of me was, there weren't no give to it. Which is more'n I can say 'bout the rest of me.

So I couldn't cry and I couldn't barely get up offa my ass and when I worried on it, I didn't know what to do. On the talk shows, they was forever talking about this therapy and that drug, but you need money to buy you your Prozac, and I just couldn't see myself paying anybody to listen to my troubles. When Pinky went to work, I had me the four walls of our apartment to do that. But I didn't lay none of my troubles on her.

Where'd it all go wrong? Damned if I know. It just did. Karma, I guess, if you want to use fancy words that belong to some foreign religion. Payback's what they'd call it back home in Tyson. It's like whoever's in the big upstairs of the sky is making sure I get my due for all them folks I robbed and hurt. Funny how there was no one looking out for me when it was me that was being hurt, back when I was just this little kid.

I can't imagine it now, but I must've been innocent at some time in my life. A baby don't just get itself born bad, do it?

But it's the same difference now, I guess. Born bad, grew up bad— who cares how it happened? It's all gone now anyways. I got no spine, got no skill, got nothing of worth to nobody, leastways my own self.

Sometimes I think back on that night in my bedroom when I took the knife to Del. I never did nothing like that again. Never had to. Or maybe I just never got me into another situation where I had to. I pulled a knife on more'n one fella, pulled a gun, too, but I never used neither.

Time was, I'd consider that night with Del and I'd know this as sure as anything: the darkness that woke in me then, it weren't never going away. I always knew that I could do it again, do even worse, if I had to. The capacity I had in me for violence was this dark secret that only Pinky shared and I thought for sure I'd carry it to the grave. But in those days of my depression . . .

Hell, I was lucky I was able to kill me a 'roach when it went skittering 'cross the floor.

Pinky, she worried something awful over me and that just made me feel worse. But there weren't nothing I could do. I just went a-moping around. I didn't put on no weight, though. If anything, I just got scrawnier, 'cept for my chest and that was getting an old lady's hang to it—on account of there being no meat on my bones no more, I guess.

When we first come to L.A. I thought the bigness'd work for us. We could run our scams all we wanted and then just fade back into the crowds. But it weren't the same as back in Tyler, or even in Newford. Everybody's hustling here and if you ain't in the know, you're never gonna connect with the high rollers. No point in ripping anybody off they ain't got much more'n you, but it got so's I was even doing that.

When I was in the county lockup for that six months is when Pinky up and took charge. Got her turn on the casting couch and I guess she must've impressed 'em, 'cause for a long time there she never run outta work.

I think what she liked best about the adult film industry was the trade shows. They'd set her up at a table and she'd just sit there a-smiling and meeting her fans, signing posters for 'em, or the covers of her videos that they'd bring clutched in their fists. I didn't want know where them hands'd been or what they'd been doing, but I could make me an educated guess.

They'd get their picture took with her, too. That was my job at them shows. I'd stand 'round behind of where she's sitting at the table. I got me this old Polaroid and I'd snap away. We didn't charge none—it was all promotion—but it got me thinking that there was money in there somewheres, you look hard enough. I just didn't like the idea of it being Pinky's ass we'd be exploiting, don't matter she loved the work.

Or maybe it was just the attention she liked so much. Hell, we'd finish up at one of them shows and she'd be grinning from ear to ear like some old coon hound, treed himself a critter. I guess it was 'cause that was the closest she was ever gonna come to living her dream—being a movie star, I mean—and we both knowed it.

She was after me all the time to give it a shot my own self. I wouldn't even have to do some guy, she'd tell me, we'd just do each other. But it weren't anything I allowed I could do. I mean, we did it a time or two with each other, but it was only when we was drunk or bored and there weren't no men around.

Don't get me wrong, here. I ain't no prude. I'd have me fellers whenever I wanted 'em afore my time in the county lockup. I just didn't want no strings attached. Nothing complicated. If I was going to put out, it'd be for fun, not for profit. I can't explain why. It's all tied up in the business with Del, being told what to do and when and how and no never mind how you feel your own self.

Anywise, this depression of mine went on a couple of years, I guess, till finally I knew I had to do something or I might as well just lie in the bath, cut my damn wrists, and be done with it. Since I was no good at scamming no more, and I sure as hell wasn't ready to peddle my ass, on film or on the street, I went and got me a job.

You shoulda seen the look on Pinky's face when I told her.

"You're doin' what?" she says.

"I'm working in a print shop."

"What do you know about printin'?"

"What's to know?" I say. "They got these big ol' machines do all the work. Only thing I gotta do is feed in the paper and collect the copies when they're done."

"You like this?" she asks.

"I dunno. I just got to be doing something."

But I kinda did like it. Place I worked was open twenty-four hours and I was on the midnight shift, twelve to eight in the morning, Wednesday through Sunday. I wore me some baggy cargo pants and sneakers, big floppy Ts or sweatshirts. Didn't have no makeup. Didn't do nothing with my hair 'cept tie it back. I looked like some little ol' mole gal, all small and dark and quiet. People didn't pay me no never mind. Hell, in the City of Angels where there's more pretty people per square inch, nobody saw me at all, and that suited me fine.

I was there maybe seven years when this guy named Hector Rivera come in and started in on a-working that late shift with me. He was like the boy version of me, all small and dark and baggy-clothed and all, 'cept he was smarter'n hell, especially when it come to computers. I liked to listen to him when he'd talk about these programs he was writing and what the future was gonna be like when everything had it a little machine brain giving it orders. Toasters, washing machines, TVs, hell, you name it. 'Spect they'll come a time when they'll just be sticking chips in the heads of the newborns, soon's they pop out.

I hear people calling Hector a spic and shit like that and I'd get pissed, but never enough to do nothing. What was I gonna do? I was just going through the motions of being alive my own self, wasn't like I could take on the trouble a someone else, too.

But we got along, him and me. He grew up dirt poor, too, 'cept it was in the barrios here. I asked him how he got to know so much about computers and he told me 'bout how it was in this school of his. The way he'd stay outta the way of the gangbangers and all was by hiding out in the computer labs. He spent him so many hours in there, wasn't much he didn't know about them machines in the end.

Part of his job at the copy shop was working at the computer, making people's newsletters and résumés and the like look like they was made of gold. But whenever he had the time—and let me tell you, we had us a lotta free time most nights, 'specially on the weekends—he'd work on his own stuff. He had him this little computer no bigger'n a hardcover book when you folded it closed. He'd have that sucker plugged in and running first thing he did when he come in and every spare chance he'd be doing his own work on it. He had everything on there, all his files and the programs he was working on.

I thought it was like magic at first, but then he started in on showing me a thing or two and I got me pretty good with it, too, though for a long time I was like some old hen on the keyboard, hunt and pecking the letters with two fingers. But I got better and I liked the logic of the machines. They do what you told 'em to, and that's all they do. Sure them machines is smart and fast and all, but they're dumber'n fenceposts, too, 'cause you forget you just one little period or letter, and that program you're writing don't come out right. Weren't like people. People, you never know what they're gonna do, one moment to the next. Machines don't take advantage of you like Del done, and they don't go all to pieces like I done, neither. They just do what they're told. And when I learned me about going online, well, a whole new world of possibilities opened up for me and I started to get some of that old Raylene Carter confidence back again.

It was Hector helped me set up Pinky's Web site, a year or so after we started working together. We was cutting edge, let me tell you. Took a few years afore the rest of the world caught on. But porn's always driven technology—that's what Hector told me. Weren't for porn, there wouldn't be a VCR in most every house. Was gonna be the same thing with the Internet.

When we started, that site of Pinky's was pretty primitive compared to what you can get you now. Weren't much to see there, just teasers, but they did the job. We'd print up glossy eight-by-tens on the color photocopier, using quality paper, and mail 'em out to all these losers thought they was getting a piece of Pinky for their five or ten bucks. They could get 'em signed, too, 'cept it was usually me or Hector putting her name on 'em. We tried doing T-shirts, but they didn't pan out the same. Most of them customers of ours just liked something they could hold in one hand while they kept busy with the other. We was gonna sell videos, too, but them sleazebag companies Pinky was working for wouldn't give us a break on the wholesale price. The plan was we'd make some of our own—fake outtakes and bloopers and crap like that—and we was also setting up distribution for these programs Hector was writing, but then reality up and kicked me in the face again.

After my sister run off, I promised I'd never get that close to no one again—'cept for Pinky, I guess, but we was more joined at the hip than anything else. I mean, Pinky was always there, right from when we was knee high to a minute, and I figured she always would be. I just wasn't letting nobody new into my life again.

Wrong on both counts.

I don't know how it happened with Hector. He weren't nothing like them cowboys I'm usually attracted to, and in those days, it's hard to believe anybody'd be liking me none. I remember thinking I'd have to gussy myself up—to get him to like me enough to teach me stuff on the computers, I mean. I figured computer nerds just didn't get none at all, and he'd be grateful enough for some flirting, but I wasn't looking forward none to the cleavage and short skirts. Don't ask me why. I still felt I was white trash, pure and simple—inside, like—but I couldn't look the part no more. Didn't know if I could act the part.

Turned out I didn't have to.

Hector he liked me just like I was, go figure. And the damnedest thing was, I took to liking him back. No, the damnedest thing was, I was all shy and holding back with him. Not on purpose, mind. It's just how it happened. But we got along fine. Talked lots, something I never did with no man afore.

We talked about every fool thing you can imagine, I guess, but mostly we talked about computers, seeing's how he plumb loved them machines. I was interested anyways, so I didn't mind. He showed me stuff on that computer, taught me the inner workings so that I'd find myself under-standing these programs he was writing. Hell, it come to that, I even started in on writing a few my own self.

Mostly it was just these little utilities, ways of making things work a little quicker, a little smoother, fixing bugs in programs that already existed. We'd work on that, late at night when only the odd damn fool'd be coming in for any photocopying. After a time of this, we took to neck-ing in the back. We'd be kissing and stuff for hours. I can't remember ever being with a guy afore that where we wasn't having sex of some kind within an hour or two of meeting. But with Hector it was a good year and a half afore we got down to it, right there behind the counter, the door not even locked or nothing.

That first time he pretty much come as soon as I got his dick outta his pants, but he learned quick how to make me happy, too. I swear I never knowed it could be so . . . guess tender's the word I'm looking for here. We had us maybe eight months of that, best times of my life, bar none, so I guess I shoulda knowed something bad was on its way, but it took me by surprise all the same.

No, I just never seen it coming, his leaving me like he did.

Happened one Sunday night, the hour hand creeping up on 4:00 A.M. I wasn't gone more'n three, four minutes. Just long enough to slip 'round the corner to the 7-Eleven and get us some coffee. Just long enough for some strung-out junkie to come into the copy shop with a pistol in his fist.

I didn't know that when I run into him in the doorway. He banged right into me on the way out, knocking the coffee outta my hands. Them foam cups exploded when they hit the pavement and I was already yelling at the guy. But then I seen the mitt full of money in the one hand, the gun in the other.

He was set to give me a whipping with that pistol of his. I could see that plain, no doubt in my mind. Everything slowed down and sped up, like I was drowning in molasses, but sliding down this steep slope at the same time. I saw the hand with the gun go up, setting to hit me, and was already backpedaling outta the way when I hear Hector cry out from inside.

"No!" he yells and comes clean over the counter like some old coon hound jumping a stump.

The gun in the junkie's hand stops coming at my head. It points at Hector. It goes off.

The bullet hits Hector square in the chest and he goes flying back over the counter. It seems to take forever for him to land. The junkie's halfway down the block while I'm just staring at Hector. Watching him fall. He hits the counter, slides off. There's this look of surprise on his face that woulda been funny any other time. He disappears behind the counter and then there's just this big red smear left on the top.

I can't hear a damn thing as I go tearing into the copy shop. My ears are ringing fit to bust from that gunshot, fired so close to my head. I come skidding around the side of the counter, but I'm way too late. Hector's already up and gone and all I got left of him is this limp, bloody body that looks like him, but don't feel like much of nothing. Nothing that's alive, leastways.

I'm still holding his head on my lap when the cops arrive.

I don't go to that funeral neither.

Everybody at work don't know what to make of me when I show up the next night for my shift, but what am I supposed to do? It ain't me done nothing wrong. And I sure wasn't gonna lose my job just because Hector took off on me. And 'sides, with him gone, there was no one else to do the work on the computer like he did. 'Cept me, of course.

Look, I know I'm sounding like some psycho, but I ain't stupid. Some junkie shot my boyfriend, I'm not pretending any different. But Hector, he didn't have to go and die on me, now did he? He didn't have to leave me behind, all on my own, 'cept for Pinky.

All that kindness of his was just setting me up for this deep dark fall.

And then Pinky left me, too.

I don't know how many hundreds of films Pinky made, but it were a lot. Not like she starred in 'em all or nothing. In the beginning she just got the bit parts, but then she started getting what she called the ingenue roles. She'd be the innocent little cornpone gal who'd get pulled into all that debauchery, which was kinda funny to me, knowing her like I did. If they wasn't already using the term "sex bomb," somebody woulda had to invent it for her.

But the thing is, she surprised me. She was pretty good at the acting part of it, so maybe, if she'd got her a decent break of some kind, she coulda been a real actress. Hard to tell, though, seeing's how she let herself be seduced by all the attention she was getting on the porn scene and all. I guess in the end she was happy enough being a big fish in a little pond.

'Cept after a whiles they just wasn't calling so much no more. Now when she got offered a part, it was playing the mama—once it was even a grandma—or in some scene where they got them a dozen or more folks going at it and she'd just be one more face in the crowd. And it just kept going on downhill from there.

It was her own damn fault. She lived too hard and all them drugs and the booze took their toll on her good looks. She got this hardness to her and I swear she started in looking twice her age. She could still perform, but the porn industry's just like the rest of the world. They want their sweet young things. Want 'em pretty and built like only surgery can build 'em. 'Specially in this damn town.

Get to looking like Pinky and the work just dries up on you.

She still had her die-hard fans, but let me tell you, after seeing some of them at them trade shows, they weren't nothing to be proud of. I seen hounds drag home better'n them, gophers and squirrels and crap, two, three days dead.

Even the Web site was a-floundering and eventually I just shut her down. To make any money she was gonna have to start doing animals or kids or something, and there was no way I was gonna let her do that. And to give Pinky her due, she drew the line her own self.

But I knew she was hurting. She missed the sex some, but mostly she missed the attention. She always was the kinda gal who liked to drop her panties in public, just for a laugh, but where that's maybe kinda cute and sexy on a younger gal, it don't seem near so endearing when you're looking as haggard and burned-out as poor 'ol Pinky come to be.

The day she got offered the job of a fluffer—you know, the gal who gets the men hard for their scenes with the women on camera—well, she just lost it. I think the casting director was feeling sorry for her—being nice, you know, giving her some work—but Pinky didn't see it that a-way. She went after that woman with a knife and cut her bad. Cut her and a couple of others on the set till somebody brought her down and then the cops come and took her away.

That was in '95 and after we got done with the courts and all, she pulled six years in the pen.

We couldn't afford no decent lawyer so we had to go with the one the court appointed for us, but I can't even really blame him. See, we couldn't post Pinky's bail so she had to stay in jail all through the trial. That had its good and bad points. Being in there was like going through detox, and it weaned her off the dope and booze, but she ended up looking so rough and haggard I'm surprised she didn't get more time just on account of looking the way she did, this being L.A. and all.

I thought the time I done in county was the worst point of my life, but the years Pinky spent in the penitentiary put a lie to that. And the curious thing is, I finally come to understand my mama moving close to the prison to be near Del like she did back when, 'cause I done the same thing now with Pinky.

'Stead of walking to work, I had to commute now. It was 'bout an hour on the bus. They say nobody walks in L.A., well, yeah, maybe, but there's a lotta us can't afford no car, not even some old piece a crap held together with tape and baling wire. And you know who we are. The blacks and the Mexicans, the immigrants and the white trash like me. Man, you get you a car and already you're living high. Can't afford an apartment? Hell, you can live in your car.

But I didn't mind the long ride. I had me Hector's notebook computer—it was in the copy shop when he died and nobody was paying any attention when I just kinda acquired it for my own. Tell you the truth, I think that's pretty much the way he got it, "found" it somewheres. I'd bring it back and forth on the bus with me, sit in my seat and work on the programs, do my E-mail and stuff like that. Made the time fly by.

Occasionally some asshole'd try to rip me off—I mean, think about it. I'm just this little-bitty thing, riding public transport with a computer on my lap. You can hock one of them suckers for a week's worth of fixes. But the first bunch tried to rob me, that switchblade of mine was in my fist and they knowed from the look in my eyes I wasn't above cutting however many's it took. After that I took to carrying a gun. A few times of waving it in their faces and word got out, I guess, 'cause I didn't get bothered no more.

I kept working at the copy shop, but I didn't make no more friends and nobody much liked working with me on that late shift. Maybe they was scared, on account of what happened to Hector, but mostly I think they just didn't take a liking to me. I wasn't making no effort to be sociable no more. What was the point? Look where it got me the last time.

Lotsa times they'd blow me off and I'd be in there all on my own-some, but it didn't trouble me none. I had the shareware programs to keep me busy. I kept it up so I wouldn't get bored, but all them little five- and ten-dollar checks from my satisfied customers that come trickling in let me save up for some new equipment, too. It let me go out and pay honest money for my upgrades and the like.

I visited Pinky once a week, that was all I had to look forward to.

And I had my dreams.

The whole time me and Hector was seeing each other, I never had me no more of them wolf dreams. And even after he up and left me, I didn't have me nothing that I'd be remembering come morning. But once they took Pinky away, them dreams come back again.

I call 'em dreams but they always felt like more. It was liking being alive, only in a different place. I'd be running through the woods and fields, all my senses big and intense, the unfamiliar body of the wolf like an old friend. You see different when you're an animal, hear different, and lordy lordy, do you use your nose different. There's whole stories written on every smell you take in.

And then there's the hunt: the chase and the kill. I guess it answered to the hunger in me, to that piece of darkness I found inside me the night I cut my brother Del and set myself free. I couldn't go around killing things in my day-to-day life—though there were customers in the copy shop that sore tried my patience a time or two—so I killed 'em here, in my wolf dreams.

I wasn't much good at the hunting at first. Partly it was me fighting the wolf's nature—it knew what to do, but I had my own ideas, 'cept the wolf knew its limitations and I had to learn them. I couldn't hunt the big game. For that you needed a pack. And those damn field mice and voles and the like weren't easy to catch. But I got me the hang of it. I liked the crunch of all them little bones, but it weren't satisfying in the long run. I knew I needed me some serious meat.

So I needed a pack. Hell, not just for the hunting, but 'cause I was lonely, too. Not for friends, and talking and going out and the like, but for the idea that I wasn't the only thing like me in the world.

I don't rightly know where they come from, but I called and they showed up, five or six of 'em, all bitches, ready to hunt. At first I didn't know if they was like me, dreaming 'bout being a wolf here, or if they belonged to this place and I just called 'em to me from wherever they'd been running afore.

I know what you're thinking. Where'd I ever get the idea them dreams could be taking place in some other place that's just as real as what's right here in front of us? A body went and told me that and I'd think somebody put a stop payment on their reality checks. But I'll tell you this: I knew that place was real. Just someplace else. And the way I come to figure that for certain was when I realized one of them wolf bitches had Pinky's eyes.

So whiles I can't rightly say where the others come from, I can pretty much guess how I got Pinky. It was just me missing her so bad. I must've pulled her out of her own dreams and into my own. Into this place that sometimes feels more real than the world where my boyfriend's dead and my best friend's in prison and I ain't nothing but a nobody. Thing was, I didn't know if Pinky knew and it wasn't something I was prepared to go asking her. It wasn't that I was scared of looking foolish in front of her. I been foolish and a lot worse in front of her. It was that she might look at me and not know what I was talking about. That all these nights we's a-running in the dreamwoods together are just something I'm making up in my sleep.

But maybe six months after they put her away, I come visiting Pinky like I always do. I'm regular as clockwork, there whenever she's allowed a visit. It's hard looking at her through the window, the glass all dirty and scratched, talking on a damn phone, but what's the option? Not being able to look at her at all? Not being able to talk to her and let her know somebody on the outside cares for her?

"You 'member those dreams you used to have?" she asks after we been through the how-dos and all. " 'Bout wolves and such?"

I get a funny feeling. Nothing bad, just a kind a itch, deep in my stomach.

"Sure," I say.

"Well, I been having 'em, too."

I don't say anything for a long moment. I look at her through the glass. There's a moment when I see the wolf in her face, then it's gone like it never was.

"I know," I tell her. "They're real, them dreams. Don't ask me why or how, 'cause I can't say. But nights when we're sleeping, you and me, somehow we're out running them woods at the same time."

Now it's her turn to just be a-looking at me awhiles, not saying a thing.

"You ain't shittin' me?" she finally says.

"I ever lied to you afore?"

"You held out a time or two."

"Well, I ain't holding out now," I tell her.

She sits back in her chair and that old shit-kicking grin I remember from afore we growed up and learned too much about the world, damned if it ain't just a-sitting there on her lips. It's the first time I seen her smile in longer'n I can remember, and I grin back, but it makes my heart hurt all the same. Seeing that ghost of the old Pinky just 'minds me how many years they're gonna keep her locked up in this place.

"Well, if that ain't the damnedest thing," she says. "Last night we was hunting . . ."

She lets her voice trail off, a question sitting there in her eyes.

"Some kinda deer," I say, "but its pelt was dark as a crow's wing."

She nods, satisfied. "But the blood was sweet when we took it down."

I have to laugh.

"You testing me?" I ask.

"Hell, Raylene," she says. "What do you think? If this don't sound like the craziest damn thing you ever heard of, then what is? Course I'm testing you. Testing myself, when it come to that."

"It's real," I tell her.

"I'm beginnin' to get the picture," she says. "So who are the others we're running with?"

I shrug. "Don't likely know. Either they come from that place, or they're women like you and me: miserable and looking for something more'n what they got, 'cause what they got ain't worth squat."

"And it don't matter noways," she says.

"That's right. So long's you and me are there together."

There's more we coulda said, but the screw come by then, telling us that our time was up. I say good-bye and lay the palm of my hand on that dirty glass. Pinky does the same on her side and it's like we're touching each other's palms. Then she lets them take her back to her cell and I take myself on home.

The dreams are better after that. We don't get all gooshy about the other wolf bitches we's running with, but we make time to goof off with each other, banging shoulders, nipping at each other, fighting these little mock battles, just generally carrying on. Stuff we can't do through the glass of the prison waiting room.

The next time I visit, she says, "Do you ever get the feelin' there's more to that place than them woods we're a-running?"

"What do you mean?"

"Like there's better things to hunt," she says. "Sometimes when we're chasing one of them deer I get a whiff of something that makes every bit a me curl up inside and just start in a-vibratin'."

"Yeah," I tell her. "I know just what you mean. Something old and . . . special."

I don't say "magic," 'cause that takes me too close to memories of my sister, but it's what I'm thinking.

"So next time we catch that scent . . ." Pinky says.

"We'll give it a whirl," I tell her.

It's not that night or the next. It's not for a couple a weeks. But we finally do catch that scent again and we leave off the deer we're running and follow that new smell. We track it a long time, track it till we're in someplace we ain't never been before. I don't mean to let on like we know everything about these dreamlands, since it ain't like we been everywhere or nothing. It's just different here. You can feel it straightaway—a warning prickle in the back of your neck, like when you step across the invisible border of Stokesville back home and suddenly you're the only white face on the streets. Ain't nobody threatening you, outright, but the potential for trouble's lying thick any which way you turn.

It's like that here, 'cept it ain't exactly trouble you can feel, or not necessarily trouble. More like the hush that comes over you when you walk into a great big ol' church. Don't matter if you believe or not, you still feel the press of some big unseen presence weighing down on you. Here it starts with the trees. They just get bigger and older, the woods darker and deeper. Makes the deep ol' woods back home seem like no more'n an echo. The air tastes like it's been flavored with a shot of whiskey, smoky and wild, and the light's subdued, got the feel of late evening about it. I get the sense it's always like that here.

We never do catch what we're chasing. We never even grab us a peek of it. But we know we're on to something, so the next night, and every night after that, we head straight for them twilight woods and cast for that critter's scent. Some nights there's nothing. Some nights the scent's too old to be worth the bother of tracking it. But every once in a while we get us a fresh noseful and we're hot on the trail. When we finally lose it, it ain't like what we're chasing doubled back or turned out to be wilier'n us or nothing. Instead the scent just kinda fades away, like that critter just up and wished itself someplace else.

We don't give up altogether on our other hunting. We bring down them deer and such, but always in the back of our minds—leastwise it's in the back of Pinky's and mine—is that wild scent and how one day we're actually gonna grab us a peek at whatever it is we're chasing, see what it is and take it down.

"How come we're always wolves in that place?" Pinky asks one of the next times I'm visiting her in the prison. "You'd suppose, it bein' a dream'n all, we could be any damn thing we'd want."

I shrug. "It ain't something I ever chose. Just how it turned out, I reckon."

"Gimme a choice," she says, "and I'd want to be just like we are. People."

"It'd be harder to hunt then."

"Not if we had us some guns."

"I suppose," I say.

But that don't seem right to me. It ain't like I'm soft on the animals we're chasing in that place, thinking that it wouldn't be fair or something. It's that the running and the tracking, and then finally tearing at 'em with tooth and claw, that's what makes me feel so alive over there. Just up and shooting something don't have near' the same appeal.

"So do you think them deer are dreamers, too?" Pinky asks.

"I never thought about it," I tell her. "I suppose they could be."

She gives a slow nod. "So I wonder if'n you were to die there, do you die for real? I mean, do you just not wake up in your bed some mornin' or what?"

"Don't matter to me," I say. "I'd rather take that chance than not have them dreams at all."

She gives me another of them slow nods, like she's doing some deep thinking and she's not altogether right here in the moment with me.

"I wonder if we should feel bad for them," she says. "The deer, I mean. If they're dreamers like us."

"Do you?"

"Naw. Leastways, not when we're bringin' 'em down. But thinking 'bout it now, I ain't so sure how I feel. I mean, if they're dyin' for real and all, maybe what we're doin' ain't right."

I shrug. "They shoulda chose a tougher body."

"But we didn't choose. What makes you think they did?"

"So what are you saying? We should stop a-hunting?"

She shakes her head. "No, I'm just thinkin' is all. You do a lotta thinkin' in a place like this."

"Prison's done made you all philosophical," I tell her, aiming to make her smile.

It don't come close to working. She gets this odd look, part hangdog, part I don't know what. Sad, but fearless, I guess.

"Prison does a lot a things to you," she says finally.

I think about my six months in county, while here she is, doing her years, and I find I don't have nothing much to say 'bout nothing no more.

Then one night we catch a glimpse of a white flank and the scent's so fresh it tastes hot when we draw it in. We been hunting this one for hours now, getting closer all the time. It's taking us so deep into this other place that the land's changing around us again, the forest thinning and the ground rising underfoot, getting craggy and steep, granite outcrops pushing up outta the ground like some ol' monster's bones. We get another glimpse—some kinda horse, standing there high on a crag, looking back at us—and then it's off again.

One of the pack barks, a high, sharp sound, and we go swarming up that mountainside.

It's been months since we started in on hunting whatever this critter is and tonight the air's thick with promise. We get a fourth or fifth wind—I've lost track by this point—and we're just flying up that steep ground, a pack of ghost wolves, driven by the wind.

Way up on that mountainside, it turns into a canyon that cuts between two cliff faces. By now we're crazy with the heat of its scent, all blood and fire, and go pouring in after it. The canyon twists and turns and suddenly there it is, boxed up against a dead end, the cliffs too steep for it to go mountain-goating up them, and it don't fade away neither. But this ain't no goat, and it ain't no horse neither. It's something out of a storybook. White as a sheet in the moonlight, with that long spiraling horn rising up outta its brow.

The pack fans out, pauses, savoring the moment.

I don't know 'bout the others, but I'm pinned by the sight of that horn. For one long moment, I can't move, I can't think, I can't do nothing at all.

The unicorn grabs its chance to try and bolt past us, but it's too late and then we're all over it.

We lose one of the pack to its hooves, another gets gutted by the horn. This ain't nothing like the deer we've been hunting, but we don't even consider backing off. And then our teeth are snapping at its neck and the tendons in the back of its legs. We're tearing at its throat.

The first taste of its blood and it's all over.

That blood's like nothing you can imagine. It burns, but it fills you up like you're in some cathedral and God's stopped by for a visit or something. The next time I see her at the prison, Pinky says it's like the best high she ever had with the added bonus that you don't crash when you're coming down. I don't know 'bout that, but I'll tell you this. Taste it once and you're always yearning for more.

We take that critter down and we're on it like hounds on a coon, just a-tearing it to pieces. We're rolling in its carcass, bathing in the blood, chewing the hot meat from its flanks and throat. Something fills us like the heart of a star and we feel big as the mountains around us. Like we could take one step and it'd cover a hundred miles. When the frenzy finally dies down, we're looking at each other, grinning, eyes laughing.

We don't even consider the two of the pack we lost in the fight. We're just thinking, where can we get us more of this?

Meanwhiles, in the real world, where Pinky's in prison and Hector's still dead, I go through the motions of being normal, leastwise as normal as I ever been, and the years drag on by. I go to work. I go to the prison on visiting days. I ride the bus. I sit in my apartment. I keep up them little shareware programs, always working on new upgrades, new ideas.

At one point I see the future in domain names for the Web, but a hundred folks was there afore me by the time I try and register me some and all the good ones—the ones someone'd pay decent cash for, I mean—well, they're long gone. I try a few start-up companies, but I don't really have the capital to make a go of them and I sure don't have the luck of your Netscapes or Winamps and the like.

Mostly, I make it through my days so I can go hunting at night.

We're always on the lookout for them unicorns now, but there's a big gap and a far between in looking for something and finding it. I lose count how many we bring down, but I do notice how they get harder to track, and even harder to kill.

We keep getting new bitch wolves to replace the ones we lose in them hunts, but neither of us much care, so long as we got each other. And we take a licking or two our own selves. Pinky almost buys it one time, the horn of one a them critters going right into her chest. It's only plain old damn fool good luck it don't pierce an organ and kill her. For a long time after that, she's recovering and we have to take it easy.

Another time I take me a kick in the head and it plumb knocks me ass over paws and I'm out like a light. Pinky's sure I'm dead, but by then the pack's took down that critter we been chasing. She drags me over to the body, warns off them other bitches, and laps that blood up, from the unicorn's throat into mine, though mine ain't got no big holes torn in it.

I come 'round real quick, like I wasn't even hurt, and then we're all rolling in the body, turning our gray pelts red.

Oh, we have us a time in the dreamworld. Outside of it, not too much stands out over the years 'cept this one Thursday night, when I'm on my ownsome in the copy shop and I come across the piece on my sister. Somebody's brought this magazine in, wanting some other article copied, but when I'm turning to the pages it's on, I see her face looking out at me and I near tear the damn magazines to pieces.

It's like someone turned on a switch in my head. One minute I'm standing there at the copier, flipping through the pages, thinking 'bout some changes I'm gonna make in one of the shareware programs, the next I'm gone into that red killing haze that comes over me when I'm dreaming, just afore the pack's taking down some critter we been running through the bush for most of the night. If she'd've been standing in front of me right then, I'd been happy to go at her throat with nothing but my teeth.

But she ain't here, and I guess it's a good thing or I'd be sharing a cell with Pinky in the pen.

I take a breath, steady myself. Look closer. She's older and she's gone and changed her name, but I know her. The Carter blood ain't hard to miss. Hell, I could be looking in a mirror 'stead of some picture in a magazine.

The article's not long. It ain't even just 'bout her. It's 'bout the art scene back in Newford and it talks 'bout a whole mess of these up-and-comers they got making waves there, and how their work relates to that of the more established artists like my sister. There's other pictures, too, of some of the other artists, but all I see is the one of her, these damn fairy paintings hanging on a wall in back of her.

I can't explain my reaction, not in no way that'd make sense to anybody but me.

It's like this black hole inside me suddenly filled up with something even darker.

I guess what I had me right then was what the preachers back home'd call an epiphany. I realized how all the crap in my life could be laid at her feet. The road that brought me here, that's made my life what it is, that let Hector die and put Pinky in prison, it all started the day she walked outta my life and left me to fend for myself. A little girl, dropped straight into hell with no never you mind.

I don't know how long I'm standing there like that, but then I realize the customer's looking at me like maybe I sprouted me an extra tit or something. I turn to the pages I was looking for and do the copies for him, but afore I give him that magazine back, I make me a copy of that article, too.

He leaves, shortchanging me, and I don't even notice at first, and when I do, I don't care. All of this, it's got me thinking. What, I don't rightly know. But I figure there's got to be some justice in this world. None that nobody'd ever give me, mind—hell, I ain't stupid. The world don't work like that. But maybe there's some justice I can take for my own self. Some way I can grab hold of that power I feel in me when I'm dreaming, bottle it up and bring it back here with me.

And then, look out.

It's the ass end of winter, February 1999, the day Pinky finally gets released from prison. We had us a slate-gray sky that morning that put me in mind of winter in Tyson, but it weren't nowheres near as cold. I kinda got to missing that cold my own self, the change of seasons and all. Gives you a sense of time moving, sets you in your place. Here it's sixty degrees and sunny, there's no snow, and the plum trees and acacias are all in bloom. It ain't my idea of winter.

Pinky coulda got out earlier, but she wasn't gonna take no parole and be beholding to anyone. She just did her time, paid her debt to society. I figure now it's time for society to pay something back to us, but I ain't quite figured exactly what yet.

I took most of the money I'd been saving over the years Pinky was in prison and I bought us a vintage Caddy convertible and had it painted pink. So you can guess who particularly appreciated that gesture when I showed up at the prison gates to pick her up. She stood there looking at that long cool stretch of candy-floss car and she couldn't stop grinning.

"Raylene Carter," she says, "where in hell did you get this beauty of a machine? I sure hope to hell you ain't stole' it or nothin'."

"No, ma'am," I tell her, grinning right back. "Hector bought this for us."

In a way it was true. All them little five- and ten-dollar checks add up to something over the years, you collect enough of them and stash 'em away, 'stead of spending it all.

Pinky looks like she's got something to say—'bout Hector, I guess, and his being dead all these years—but then she just shrugs, tosses her bag in the backseat where it joins a couple of suitcases and the case with my notebook computer in it. The trunk's filled with the rest of our stuff that I thought was worth keeping. There weren't all that much. Everything else I just chucked out.

Pinky slides in on the passenger side. She lights up a smoke.

"So where we goin'?" she asks.

"We're going home," I tell her.

" 'Bout time," she says.

She's giving the prison walls the finger when I pull out a the parking lot. The freeways are bumper to bumper like they always are, but neither of us much give a damn. I got a few thousand left over after buying the Caddy and the paint job, so we can travel in style. It don't much matter if we go fast or slow, 'cause we're together now, like we're supposed to be, and we're heading home.

Jilly

They moved me into rehab at the end of April. It's a smaller, older building, west of the main hospital complex. The view isn't as spectacular as it was from my window on the ward, but I'm on the first floor and my window looks out onto a kind of park. The beds of tulips and all the green of the lawns and the budding trees out there do wonders for my spirit. When I'm not in therapy, I get them to put me in my wheelchair and roll me over to the window so that I can look out and paint pictures in my head.

I've been here for a couple of weeks now, keeping my promise to Joe and doing everything they tell me to do, building my strength, exercising, and trying not to get too discouraged. But it's hard. The improvements, if you can call them that, are so minuscule that they're hardly worth mentioning.

I still get headaches—along with the paralysis, they're a leftover of my concussion—but my hair's starting to grow back where they had to shave it. I've got a little field of dark stubble growing up beside the tangled forest on the rest of my head. The bruises and swelling on the left side of my face are all gone. I've still got casts on my right leg and left arm, but they're going to remove the plaster one from my arm in a week or so because the bones are healing so well.

When I was a kid, I was kind of ambidextrous. I preferred writing and drawing with my left hand, but I threw a ball and automatically used a fork or spoon with my right. In school they made me do everything with my right hand and I went along with them to fit in and because it wasn't super hard for me. But I wish now I hadn't. If I'd used my left hand all along, I could be drawing again in a week or so. I guess I'll just have to teach myself how to do it.

My right side is still paralyzed but I've got feeling again in my face. I hated the numbness. It was like the freezing from a visit to a dentist's office, only it never wore off. But the muscles are starting to work properly now so I don't have that slack look on that side of my face anymore. I've got some feeling in my torso, too, and I'm starting to get some pins-and-needles tingles in my fingers and toes, though I can't move them yet. That's supposed to be a good sign—the tingles, I mean—but they're really uncomfortable and painful.

Other than that, I can still freely move my left leg—maybe I should learn how to hold a pencil with my toes—and my cracked ribs still ache when I laugh, or when they're moving me from the bed to the wheelchair. So the Broken Girl's mending, but it's taking forever.

I'm thinking I should give up my loft, but I hate the idea because I've been there forever. I moved into it back when that whole part of Crowsea was pretty seedy and the rent was dirt cheap. Now, block by block, building by building, they're gentrifying the whole area. Forget being a student and living there these days.

But it'll be months before I can move back in, if ever. It makes no sense to keep it, except as storage space, and that's expensive storage space now. I haven't talked about it with anybody because packing everything up and moving it into storage will be just one more burden I'll be putting on my friends.

I find myself missing Daniel, my nurse from the ICU. He worked me hard, and I know I've said his chatty good humor used to drive me crazy sometimes, but I'm guilty of the same thing in normal circumstances. The nurses are really nice here, too, but it's not quite the same. When I left he gave me a brooch that he said used to belong to his mother—"What? I'm supposed to wear it?" he said when I told him he should keep it. It was just costume jewelry, one of those oval miniatures of an English cottage with a frame of fake pearls and a kind of brassy metal, but I like it. I keep it pinned to my pillow.

Maybe Sophie was right and he really did like me. As if. It's not like he's been by to see me since I got transferred to rehab.

But I can't believe the parade of visitors I've had since I was first admitted into the hospital. I didn't know I even knew that many people. Christy's always joking that the only reason I don't know everyone in Newford is that I haven't met the last few stragglers yet and after the past few weeks, I'm starting to believe it's true. Once I got moved out of the intensive care unit, I had so many flowers in my room at one point that my bed felt like it was nested in the middle of a garden. I liked it, but after a while it began to feel a bit like overkill, so I got Daniel to spread them out to some of the other rooms on the floor to share in the bounty. Hopefully nobody minded—the people who brought the flowers, I mean. I know the other patients appreciated them.

The cards I kept. I had them pasted all over my room in the hospital, and now that I'm in rehab, they're decorating the walls here. But the sheer numbers makes me feel pretty humble.

You rely on your friends at a time like this and mine have been supportive above and beyond the call of duty—especially Sophie and Wendy and Angel. But then if any of them were ever in the hospital, I'd have moved into their room myself, so their coming by as often as they do isn't really a surprise.

It's all the others, people I just didn't expect. Coworkers from Kathryn's Café where I still work part-time. Fellow volunteers from the food bank and the soup kitchen, from Angel's Outreach program and St. Vincent's Home for the Aged. Teachers and students from the Newford School of Art and kids from the Memorial Arts Court that Isabelle founded a few years ago in memory of her writer friend, Katharine Mully. I'm there at least one afternoon a week—at least I used to be—talking to the street kids about art.

Actually, I guess I do volunteer work in a lot of places. Sometimes I wonder if I'm really trying to help, if it's payback for how I was helped, or if I'm trying to atone for the kind of person I was before Angel and Lou got me off the streets. I wasn't necessarily a bad person; I just wasn't very thoughtful or considerate of anybody else. Sometimes what you don't do is just as bad or worse than what you do.

So anyway, there's all of those people, and then there's all the others, the ones I just sort of know, from the guys at my local fire station to my city councilor, and people I hardly ever see anymore. Little Jillian's adoptive parents brought her by—I think it's so cool that they let Sophie and me still be Jillian's godparents. Katy Bean, the red-haired storyteller who took over Jack Daw's bus on the edge of the Tombs, visited with her sister Kerry. Zeffy and Max dropped in and played a few new songs— they're really sounding good as a duo. Geordie's old musical partner Amy came by as well, though she didn't bring her Uillean pipes, which is probably just as well. While they aren't as loud as Highland pipes, they're still an acquired taste and I don't know if the other people on the ward would have taken to them.

I've even been visited by a few of Isabelle's numena, those secret spirit people that her paintings brought into the World As It Is from someplace even more distant and mysterious than the dreamlands. Paddyjack and Cosette. Rosalind, John Sweetgrass, and the strangest pair of all, younger versions of Isabelle herself and the dead Kathy, ghosts from the past looking just as I remember them from all those years ago.

The numena sneak off Isabelle's farm on Wren Island, late at night when there's less chance of anyone seeing them, and slip into my hospital room to offer comfort and companionship. Sometimes, when they're with me, I feel like I'm dreaming, that my room in the hospital, and now the rehab, has been transported to some part of the dreamlands, because how else could such wonderful creatures exist? It's not that they look different from you or me—except for Paddyjack, of course, a thin little scarecrow man who seems to be made as much of twigs and leaves as he is flesh and bone. But he's a sweet little fellow and has that same large presence that the others do, the sense that their spirits are so big, they can't quite fit into their bodies. You can feel them before they come into a room, a pressure in the air, a presence that makes your pulse quicken and a smile come to your face without them having to say a word.

After they leave, I always think of Isabelle and what it must be like for her, having to be so careful of what she paints, because her paintings can literally bring her subjects to life. With that kind of responsibility, it's no wonder that these days she's still mostly painting abstracts.

Maisie Flood and her adopted brother Tommy have been by a few times, with their little terrier Rexy hidden in Maisie's knapsack. That dog just becomes a nervous wreck if he's separated from her too long. I love Tommy. He's simpleminded—Maisie found him abandoned in the Tombs and took him in like she did the little pack of dogs that make up the rest of their family—but he's one of the sweetest guys I know. Whenever he visits he brings all these little figures of people that Maisie cuts out of magazines and sticks on cardboard backings for him. He spreads them out on the bed and tells me all their stories.

More cards and letters arrive all the time, too. I hope people understand that I can't actually reply to them. There was even a card from Natty Newlyn in Ireland, a crazy drawing of her and her beau Ally breaking me out of the hospital like we're escaping from some dark and dismal dungeon. If I close my eyes, I can see that cheeky grin of hers when she's pulled some prank or another, and then I hear her innocent, "Don't go all serious on me now. I was only messin'."

I guess the best and worst visit was when Geordie flew in from L.A. on the weekend before I got transferred to the rehab center.

It's nothing Geordie says or does. I love seeing him, but it hurts so much, too. That's never happened before. I've always been able to deal with our friendship being just that, but having lost the other most important thing in my life—my art—it's just too hard having lost him as well. The Broken Girl's needy and she just wants to steal him away from Tanya. He's not in the room with me for more than five minutes and I know he has to leave the city and get back to her as soon as possible before I say or do something stupid. That would just complicate everybody's life and it wouldn't be fair. Which isn't to say I think he'd drop Tanya to be with me—Geordie's not built like that. He's way too loyal and besides, he really cares about her.

And even if he wasn't involved with Tanya, what would I have to offer him? The Broken Girl's no bargain as she is, and that's not even counting all the other issues I have with intimacy. Though, of course, I have to ask, I have to know, how he and Tanya are doing. I was the one who sent him to L.A. to be with her in the first place, but it doesn't mean I wanted to, or that I don't have this curiosity about their relationship that's part wanting things to go well for them because they're my friends, and part my own morbid fascination with what I can't have.

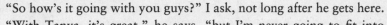

"So how's it going with you guys?" I ask, not long after he gets here.

"With Tanya, it's great," he says, "but I'm never going to fit into that city."

"How can it be so bad? There's movie stars and sun twelve months of the year."

"The sun I like," he says with a smile, "but the rest I could do without. Mostly it's all these people we have to make nice to because of Tanya's career."

He launches into a couple of the worst movie-business specimens he's run into lately and I just want to say, so leave that place. Come back here. Come back and be with me.

"But your music's going well, isn't it?" I say instead.

He's been doing a lot of studio work since he got there, playing on soundtracks and at various recording sessions.

"I suppose. But it's not the same. All my gigs are so structured and you always have this clock running in your head telling you that time's money, so get it right the first time. I really miss just playing on a street corner, but that'd look bad for Tanya if some tabloid snapped a picture of me doing it."

Geordie's the only musician I know who actually prefers busking. "It keeps me honest," he likes to say. "If people like what you're doing, they stop and listen, maybe throw you a few coins. If they don't, they just walk on by. Where else can you get such an honest reaction to your music?"

There's no real analogy for art, but I know what he means all the same. It's the reason I've never lost touch with my street roots. Sure, it's not always pretty out there. Actually, it can be downright heartbreaking. But it does keep you honest as a person. As soon as we forget that those are people, living there on the street, I think we start to lose our humanity. The way the world works now, any one of us could wake up one morning and find they have nothing. Look what happened to me. It's only by the grace of the professor's having kept up an insurance plan for me that means I won't come out of here one day and have nothing left because everything I owned went to pay for my medical bills.

It's not like you can plan getting hit by a car, or any of the thousand and one other catastrophes that are potentially waiting out there for us.

"You shouldn't have to give up being yourself," I tell Geordie, and this is me as his friend talking, not me trying to get Tanya and him to break up.

"I know," he says. "But I promised I'd give it a shot and if I quit now, I won't have done that, will I?"

"I guess not."

He gives me a wan smile. "At least I've still got my music."

We've talked about this before, the way you do late at night when you're sitting in each other's apartment, or in a café somewhere, and feeling, not exactly melancholy, but taking a kind of stock as to who you are and what you're doing with your life. You bring up weird what-ifs. Like if you had to lose one of your senses, which would it be? Or if you had to lose a limb. Pointless conversations, really, but they did reiterate how important his music is to him, my art to me. Neither of us could imagine life without it, so he knows exactly how I'm feeling right now.

At least about my art. I hope he can't read my heart. But then Geordie's always been a little obtuse about whether or not a woman's taken a liking to him. So I have that going for me. To keep my secret safe, I mean.

There's a point where we run out of words for a while and just sit there, enjoying each other's company. That's something else I've missed since he moved. Just this being together with him. But then I realize he's studying me.

"What?" I say. "Did the nurse forget to wipe my lunch from my face?"

He shakes his head. "No. There's just something different about you."

"Hello? I can't get up out of this bed. I can't paint. I can't even scratch my own nose."

"It's not that," he says. You can tell what old friends we are because he hasn't once gotten that awkward look most people do when they realize just how broken I am. "It's something else."

I guess I was wrong and he's not so obtuse, because I know what he's feeling. It's me, reaching for him. Wanting him to crawl up onto the bed beside me and just hold me until everything's better. How could he not feel it? But I can't even begin to tell him that. So I talk about the dreamlands instead.

Time was, a conversation like this would have driven him crazy. Back when we first met at the post office—filling in as part-timers during the Christmas rush one year—I'd deliberately tell him the most outlandish stories, just to get a rise out of him. He was Mr. Pragmatic in those days. A lovely boy, but give him what he could see with his own two eyes, what he could touch with his hands, or don't bother. I think a lot of that came from how his brother Christy had plunged so wholeheartedly into an exploration of the weird and the wacky and in those days they weren't getting along nearly as well as they do now. My flights of fancy just reminded him too much of Christy.

But he's seen and experienced an odd thing or two in the years since. Right now I find him listening with interest, and dare I say it, even belief in what I'm telling him about the Greatwood and Mabon and the people I've met there.

"It would have to take something like this happening to let you get across," he says. "Trust you not to take the easy route."

"Oh, Geordie, me lad," I tell him. "Haven't you discovered by now that there's never an easy route to the things that matter."

He nods, that sad look when he talks about his life in L.A. coming back into his eyes.

"Isn't that the truth," he says.

I send him home that Monday, back to Tanya. Maybe the music scene in L.A. isn't everything he's looking for in terms of his career, but he and Tanya have a potentially great thing happening between them, and we both knew he needed to give it a real shot.

I take comfort from the pain of his departure by retreating into the dreamlands whenever I'm not needed to be present in my body for therapy sessions.

2

Sophie was having a bad day. After a couple of weeks of relative quiet, Jinx had started acting up something fierce this morning. Her TV had been showing British game shows since she first woke up and no matter how often she shut it off, the set came back on its own. More aggravating were the collect calls she kept being asked to accept from places like Hong Kong, Melbourne, and Bogotá—the South American one, not the one in New Jersey. Not to mention her door buzzer, which sounded every fifteen minutes or so. She'd long since stopped going to answer the door, so when Wendy dropped by later in the day she had to bang on the door with the heel of her hand for ages before Sophie finally came down the hall to let her in.

Wendy gave her a considering look, then asked, "Jinx?"

Sophie gave a weary nod and led the way back into the living room where she'd been watching a snooker game that was being broadcast from Wales with all the commentary in Welsh.

"I kind of thought so," Wendy said as she settled in a chair. "I tried calling from work before I came, but your phone's out of order."

"I had to unplug it."

"Electronic telemarketers?"

"Not this time," Sophie said. "This time it was collect calls from all over the world."

Wendy smiled. "But you didn't take any."

"I'm not Jilly."

They both laughed. Jilly would have happily chatted to whoever was on the other end of the line, never mind if she understood their language or not.

"Speaking of Jilly," Wendy said. "Isabelle was out walking on Yoors Street and swore she saw Jilly across the street. But when she called out to her, Jilly ducked into a convenience store. Isabelle said she was so sure it actually was Jilly that she crossed the street and went inside herself, but there were no customers in there at all and she felt weird asking the proprietor if anyone had just come in and then slipped out the back door, so she just left."

"Except Jilly's in rehab," Sophie said.

"Of course she is. Whoever Isabelle saw just really *looked* like Jilly. But don't you think it's weird?"

Sophie nodded. Except she'd seen that doppelgänger herself, not two days ago outside of Jilly's loft. She'd been up early and after doing some grocery shopping, she'd gone by the loft to bring the mail in, put out a bowl of cat kibbles on the fire escape for the strays that Jilly fed, and check to make sure that everything was undisturbed, just as she'd been doing every day since the break-in. Halfway down the block from the loft, she'd seen the impossible: Jilly coming out of the door of her building and turning up the street, away from her.

She'd been so startled that she'd dropped the bag of groceries she was carrying. Her gaze was pulled down to the fallen bag, then followed a tin of peas rolling off into the gutter. By the time she looked up again, whoever it was that she'd mistaken for Jilly was gone. But the whole incident had left her shaken in a way she couldn't explain, as though a piece of her dreaming night world had strayed into the World As It Is. She'd found herself shivering then, and felt the same chill now.

"What's the matter?" Wendy asked.

For a moment, Sophie had trouble focusing on her friend and could only manage a distracted, "Mmm?"

"You've gone all pale," Wendy said.

Sophie remembered to breathe, then gave a wan smile.

"I had that same experience a couple of days ago," she finally said. "When I went by the loft."

"And you never *told* me?" Wendy said after Sophie had described what she'd seen that day.

"This is the first time I've seen you since then and I kind of forgot about it."

Which was odd in itself.

"Oh, this is too spooky," Wendy told her. "Remember what Cassie was saying when she went by the loft after the break-in?"

Sophie nodded. Cassie was something of a sensitive and had dropped in at the studio to see if she could pick up any psychic traces of whoever it was that had broken in and destroyed all of Jilly's faerie paintings. She said she'd found traces, if you were the sort to give credence to that kind of thing, but they all pointed to Jilly. Only not the Jilly they knew. Instead, Cassie had described it as though some shadow Jilly had come in and vandalized the paintings.

"I keep wondering about that," Wendy said. "I mean, if that's the reason she doesn't seem to care about having lost all of those paintings."

Sophie gave her a blank look.

"You know," Wendy went on. "If her spirit came back to the loft while she was in the coma and destroyed all those paintings."

"Wendy."

"Stranger things have happened."

Sophie sighed. When it came to Jilly, she supposed that wasn't all that far off the mark. Though she herself wasn't entirely comfortable with the whole concept of the dreamlands intruding into the World As It Is, the odd and the peculiar seemed to be attracted to Jilly like burrs were to the cuffs of your jeans when you went tramping through an autumn field.

"She loved those paintings too much to destroy them," Sophie said.

"But if she has this dark side . . ."

"We all have a dark side, but it doesn't go off wandering about on its own. Especially not when we're in a coma, or laid up in the hospital."

"I suppose," Wendy said. "But I'm worried about her reaction. Or maybe I should say, her lack of reaction."

Sophie shrugged. "It probably hasn't really sunk in yet. It's not like she doesn't have other things on her mind."

But she could tell that Wendy wasn't ready to let this go.

"I don't know," Wendy said. "It's not that I'm wishing some great depression on her—Lord knows she's got enough to worry about as it is—but she's lost a lifetime of work. Those are all the paintings she really cared about, the ones that she'd hang in shows with the 'Not for Sale' tags on them."

Sophie thought how she'd feel if she'd had this kind of loss. It was hard to imagine. She'd probably react the way Isabelle had when her studio burned down—totally, completely displaced from everything. Especially from her art. She remembered how Isabelle said it hurt just to walk into a studio or gallery, to even think of starting to paint again.

"I suppose Jilly's reaction is odd," she said.

"It's more than odd," Wendy said. "It's taking relentless good cheer to a new and really scary height."

"That's just Jilly's way of dealing with it."

Wendy nodded. "But you know what scares me the most? That maybe she sees it as a sign. Like she's being told that now it's okay to go off into fairyland forever, because one by one, all the things she cares about are being stripped away from her."

"She can't go to fairyland forever," Sophie told her.

"Oh? And why's that?"

"Because it's not real. It's just dreams and fancies."

"And if she just lets herself drift away into a coma and dreams away forever?"

Sophie shook her head. "That's not happening. She's been working hard at the rehab, strengthening muscles, exercising. A week or so ago, maybe I'd have agreed with you. But it's obvious now that she's determined to get better."

"It still worries me," Wendy said. "There's something going on here that she's not telling us."

"What's to tell?"

"Her visits to the dreamlands, for one thing. A couple of weeks ago, that's all she wanted to talk about. Now she barely mentions it, and if you ask, she just shrugs it off and wants to be brought up-to-date on what's going on with everybody."

Sophie gave a slow nod. That much was true. Jilly had been so excited about being able to dream herself into the spiritworld, and with Jilly, excitement equaled enthusiastic, blow-by-blow descriptions and discussions. But now she hardly talked about it at all. Sophie had thought it was just because she herself wouldn't allow that dreams were anything but dreams and rather than argue about it anymore, Jilly had just stopped talking about it with her.

"What can we do?" she said.

It was more a rhetorical question, but Wendy leaned forward in her chair. "We have to keep watch over her."

"I suppose . . ."

"And maybe you could check in on her in the dreamlands."

"I can't do that," Sophie said.

"Why not?"

"I don't know. Whenever I go to Mabon I run into people she's met, but there seems to be some kind of veil between where she goes and I do." She smiled. "We're just never in the same dream, I guess."

"But the dreamlands . . ." Wendy began.

"I don't know what they are," Sophie told her. "Maybe it's a place where our collective unconscious can gather and experience things together, and maybe it's something else again. I just don't see how it can affect the real world—beyond influencing our art, say, or just making for good stories we can share with each other."

"But you've met people from the World As It Is in Mabon."

Sophie had to give a reluctant nod. "Except I don't know what that proves, if anything. I just know that I can't seem to find Jilly when I'm dreaming."

"There's got to be something we can do to make sure she's okay. I mean, mentally."

Sophie had to smile. "That could be a loaded question."

"I'm being serious," Wendy said, but she smiled as well.

"I know you are," Sophie told her. "I'll have another talk with Jilly when I go see her tonight."

Wendy wanted to know more then about this mysterious twin that both she and Isabelle had seen and Sophie was happy to oblige, though she didn't have many more details to share than those she'd already given.

"But I guess the oddest thing," she said, "was—you know how you sometimes mistake a stranger for someone you know, but when you look again, or more closely, the resemblance is so superficial that you have to wonder what it was that made you feel so sure about it in the first place?"

Wendy nodded.

"It wasn't like that with the woman I saw outside of the loft. Yes, I only got that one brief glimpse of her, but there was no question in my mind that if it wasn't Jilly I'd just seen, then she's got a twin we don't know about."

And that was probably what had bothered her the most about the incident. That she was so sure it had been Jilly she'd seen, impossible though that was. She'd almost told Jilly about it when she went to the rehab later that morning, but when she walked into the room and saw her lying there, the casts on her arm and leg, the paralyzed arm lying limply on the sheet beside her on the bed, the idea that Jilly could have been up and about anywhere was so ludicrous that she hadn't said a word.

But the question had returned to nag her since. Sophie had a good eye. She might have to contend with Jinx playing havoc on all things electrical and mechanical in her general vicinity when it decided to show up for a visit, but she also was a keen observer who could render a fairly recognizable sketch of a person after only a cursory glance.

Maybe she'd talk to Jilly about that tonight as well.

3

Once upon a time . . .

All forests have their own personality. I don't just mean the obvious differences, like how an English woodland is different from a Central American rain forest, or comparing tracts of West Coast redwoods to the saguaro forests of the American Southwest. Or even the more subtle differences, like how the piney wood hills that back up onto the rez north of Newford are nothing like the cedar and birch forests around Tyler where I grew up, and there's less than a hundred miles between the two.

But even when they seem to be the same—two stretches of hemlock woods, a seemingly similar pair of tamarack and scrub tree forests—they each have their own gossip, their own sound, their own rustling whispers and smells. A voice speaks up when you enter their acres that can't be mistaken for one you'd hear anyplace else, a voice true to those particular trees, individual rather than of their species.

So it's no surprise that the Greatwood is so singular. What is surprising is how it also seems to be the sum of all forests at the same time. Never mind the towering heights of its trees, some of them with girths as wide as a Crowsea tenement building. When you step under the shadow of the Greatwood's twilight reaches, you hear a voice you immediately recognize as the deep rumbling murmur that you've heard whispering up from under the individual voices of any forest you've ever been in.

I guess this is what Joe means about the Greatwood being such a close echo of the First Forest, the vast woodland that covered everything when Raven first made the world. When you're standing under this enormous canopy, it's easy to imagine that you've been transported back to the beginnings of time.

These days I spend most of my dreamlands time here in the Greatwood, sticking close to where I first arrived and met Joe. Like the hospital, I have lots of visitors when I'm under its canopy, but they haven't come to say hello to the Broken Girl, studiously looking away from the bandaged shape of her body under the sheets. It's just people passing by, stopping to say hello, standing to look over my shoulder when I'm drawing, happy to share a few quiet moments before they travel on.

I'm meeting most of them for the first time, and don't see them again, but there are a few regulars. These ones are mostly friends of Joe's, or related to him in some way, like Jolene, and this guy who calls himself Nanabozho, who could have been Joe's twin brother with that same canid head on his human shoulders, except his coloring runs more to wolf grays than Joe's chestnut fur and he's got these mismatched eyes: the right one's brown, the left one's a steel-blue gray. Nanabozho's like

Toby, always wanting me to draw him. I don't mind. There's something wonderfully strange about those lupine features looking out at me from under the flat-brimmed hat he wears, the startling juxtapositioning of animal head on a human body, with the long dark braids framing either side of his face.

I keep hoping the crow girls will drop by, but the only corbæ I meet are a couple of Jack Daw's cousins, dark-haired siblings with a Kickaha cast to their broad features. They introduce themselves as Candace and Matt, the one ganglier than the other, but handsome in a way Jack never was. While they're chatty, and certainly as friendly as Jack used to be, they're full of gossip instead of the wonderful stories he used to tell. I guess Katy Bean, the red-haired girl who took over Jack's school bus on the edge of the Tombs, inherited his storytelling gift as well as that old bus.

Once, watching me from a distance, I see a woman with a white buffalo's head on her shoulders. The whole forest goes still while she's here. Even the Greatwood's rumbling voice quiets to a barely discernible murmur. I want to talk to her so badly, but my throat goes all dry, and I can barely breathe, never mind get up and go over to where she's standing.

The hush holds even after she slips away, then it's as though the Greatwood lets out a breath it's been holding. I hear squirrels chattering again. A jay scolding in the distance. The deep whoosh of a raven's wings as he passes overhead, followed by a hoarse croak when he's out of sight.

I ask Nanabozho about her the next time I see him and he just smiles. "That was only Nokomis," he tells me, "doing her mysterious earth mother thing."

"Well, it worked for me."

"Works for everybody," he says. "No surprise, when you think about it."

I lift my brows in a question.

"Well, maybe Raven made the world," he says, "but Nokomis has been taking care of it ever since."

"You mean she really is . . . ?"

Nanabozho grins, laughter filling his blue-gray eyes. "You bet. Hey, somebody's got to do it, and nobody else wants the job."

"I think we should all help her. I sure would."

He looks serious then. "Next time you see her, you tell her that. She could sure use an extra pair of hands or two."

There are others that don't approach, but I figure it's mostly because they're shy. Deer women stepping daintily between the trees, bolting when I call out to them, but coming back cautiously once they think I'm not looking at them anymore. A few times I've seen a small, quick-footed man with a hare's long ears hanging across his shoulders like braids. He always gives me a quick, nervous smile, but keeps his distance as he goes along his way. More recently I've seen a regular gang of little twig people that look like they've stepped out of an Ellen Wentworth painting. She illustrated my favorite book of fairy tales when I was a kid and now I know for sure she was rendering from life. It's hard to figure what keeps them together—no more than moss and vines, it seems, from the glimpses I get of them. They have high sweet voices and giggle a lot, waving to me and smiling, but they keep their distance, too, which is too bad. I'd love to do some serious studies of them, rather than the quick gesture drawings that're all they give me time to do as they go trooping by.

And then there's Toby. I don't see him for a while after that day when he ran off at Jolene's approach, but one afternoon I'm sketching after a long day in the rehab and suddenly he's there.

"Hey!" Toby cries.

I take a step back, startled. He appears to have simply stepped out of nowhere.

"Where did you come from?" I ask.

He gives me a mischievous grin.

"Maybe I came right out of that tree," he says.

I smile as he collapses beside me, leaning over my arm to look at my sketchbook. I've been drawing fungi again today and I've already filled a half-dozen pages. Next trip to Mabon, I'm going to pick up some colors—pastels or colored pencils, or maybe just a stick of red chalk.

"I didn't know that you lived in a tree," I say.

He leans back against the root and shrugs.

"There's a lot about me that you don't know."

"This is true," I say.

I turn to look at him lounging beside me, enjoying his merry features and the curious whisper of something wise and knowing that occasionally crosses his mischievous gaze.

"In fact," I add, "I don't really know anything about you at all."

"Ask me anything," he says, as magnanimously as might some ancient king, granting a boon.

"Okay. What's the deal with you and Jolene? Why did you take off the way you did when she arrived?"

He gets a funny look and I get the feeling he doesn't want to answer.

"It's okay," I tell him. "I guess that was prying. I'm too nosy for my own good. It's just this gift I have, you see—being curious, I mean—and it's not one of my more endearing ones."

"It's not that," he says.

I can't help myself. "Then what is it?" I have to ask.

Still he hesitates. He looks away and won't meet my gaze and I realize that I'm still, howsoever inadvertently, venturing into some private place. I try to back out again before I make him too uncomfortable. I know what it's like to have secrets you're not ready to share.

"Never mind," I tell him. "You don't have to talk about it if you don't want to."

"It's because I'm not real," he says suddenly.

He turns to me, gaze searching my face for a reaction. I'm guessing all he finds is confusion, because that's what I'm feeling.

"What do you mean you're not real?"

He shrugs. "You wouldn't understand."

"Try me."

"You're real. Somewhere out there"—he waves his hand vaguely in the air in a gesture that encompasses pretty much everything, but I know what he means—"you have a body that's sleeping while you go gallivanting about here. You're real. You have a life. A spirit."

"You seem to have plenty of spirit to me," I tell him.

But he doesn't crack even a small smile.

"Somebody made me up," he says.

"Who?"

"I don't know. A lonely child. A writer. An artist. Somebody. And then when they grew up, or the story was done, or the painting was finished, they let me go. They forgot about me and here I am. Not real. With nothing to call my own, no place to be my home, and who knows how long I have before I just fade away."

"Are you saying you were somebody's imaginary friend?"

"I don't know," he repeats. "I don't remember."

What he's saying reminds me of Isabelle's numena, those spirits she called up from someplace else with her paintings. The paintings were like a door that opened up into our world and let them in, and then they could live forever, unchanged, unless something happened to their painting.

"I've heard of them," he says when I tell him about the numena, "but I don't think it's the same."

"But why does this make you run away from someone like Jolene?" I ask.

"Because she's one of the People and they're too real," he tells me.

"You're losing me again."

"You know about the animal people, the ones who were here first at the beginning of the world?"

"Sure. Like the crow girls. Or Lucius."

He nods. "When someone like me is near them, the sheer potency of their presence makes me even less real. If I spent enough time in the company of one of the People, I'd fade away completely."

"Really?"

He gives me another nod. "I'll fade anyway, but they'll just make it happen quicker."

"Do they know that?" I ask.

He shrugs. "Why should they care about something like me?"

I can't imagine Jolene or Lucius, and certainly not Joe, being so callous and say as much.

"Your friend Joe's something else again," Toby says.

"I thought he was one of the People."

Toby nods. "Second generation. I heard that his father was a crow and his mother a canid. She was related to the Red Dog clan that welcomed the spirits of the corn and squash and first introduced them to you humans."

Crow and dog, I'm thinking. That explains the features he sometimes wears in the dreamlands. I try to imagine how his parents got together. You've got this bird and you've got this dog . . .

"But how—?" I begin.

He laughs, the first bit of his old humor I've seen since we started this discussion.

"They made him when they were in human shape," he says, still grinning.

"Of course."

"But that's a rare thing," he goes on. "Two of the People from such different clans having a child, I mean."

"I thought at least a third of the animals and people living in the world right now had some mixed blood in them."

He nods. "But his parents were pure bloods, and that's different. The clans of the People are pretty insular. They mate with humans, or cousins to their clan when they're in animal form, but hardly ever so directly outside of the clan."

"So would you fade around Joe?" I ask.

"Probably."

"If he knew, he wouldn't put you at risk."

Toby just gives me another of those shrugs of his. He's good at them. Very cool and casual.

"We just run when we see them," he says.

I focus on the "we."

"Are there a lot of you?" I ask.

"More than there are heart homes in the spiritworld. Any one person can make hundreds of us. All they need is imagination. But it requires belief to sustain us, and with that people aren't quite so generous."

Again like Isabelle's numena, I think. Though not quite the same. Once created, her numena live forever, unchanged.

"But do the people who make you even know?" I ask.

"They should know the stories."

I know what he's talking about, all those old folk tales about faerie fading away because we stopped believing in them.

"But they don't necessarily know the stories are real, do they?"

"And there's the irony," he says. "For we're dependent on their belief all the same. And most of us are ephemeral—fading soon after we're made. It's very sad."

"Well, I guess," I say. "But I still don't understand why the—what should I call it?—the hyper-reality of the animal people diminishes you. How would something like that even work?"

"I think it's like believing in Faerie."

"I thought this was Faerie."

He nods. "Except the truth is, this place is whatever you call it. Faerie. The spiritworld. *Manidò-akì*. People find what they expect to find here. In many places it *becomes* what you expect it to be."

I give him a slow nod. "Joe's told me about some of that."

"But the other Faerie," he goes on, "is the one in which people like me live. The one that exists because people believe in it. When they lose their belief, we just fade away."

"Like the stories about the old gods," I say, thinking aloud. We're back to those old folk tales again. "Or how every time a child says she doesn't believe in faerie, a faerie dies."

He nods.

I realize that for all my penchant in believing that there's more to the world than what we can see, that folk tales and fairy tales are based on real, if forgotten events, I never accepted that part of it as being real.

"But that's horrible," I tell him.

"Yet it's the life we've been given," he says. "And since it's the only one we can have, we've learned to take what we can get."

I study him for a long moment, then lift a hand and trail my fingers from the curly hair at his brow, down the length of his cheek.

"I don't believe it," I tell him.

"It's not a matter of believing or not. It simply is."

But I shake my head, firm on this.

"One's origins don't matter," I say. "Once you exist, you are. If a tree, a stone, a house, can have a spirit, then so do you."

Now he shakes his head.

"Maybe it'd help if *you* tried to believe," I say.

That wakes a laugh. "Maybe you're right."

"I know I am. It would be so unfair otherwise."

"That's not the best of arguments. We don't live in a fair world."

"Maybe not," I say. "But isn't that all the more reason for us to work at making it one?"

"You argue well."

"It's not something I'm debating," I tell him, and repeat, "it's what I believe."

We fall quiet then. Toby seems more relaxed since we started this conversation, as though this was something he had to get out of the way before our friendship could continue. Or maybe it's simply his mercurial nature. He doesn't seem able to focus on any one thing for too long a period of time. I've been accused of that myself, but it's never bothered me. You could have a lot worse said about you.

As for me, I'm mulling what I've just learned. It explains a lot, about a great many things, but it also sends my brain off on a hundred other tangents, each of them filled with an ever-expanding tangle of questions. I settle on the simplest one to ask first.

"So what are you called?" I ask him. "You and these other so-called ephemeral people?"

"We are the Eadar. Creatures of Meadhon, the middleworld."

"I don't understand."

"You know that *geasan* wakes in between places?"

"*Geasan*?"

"Magic."

I nod. Both Sophie and Joe have explained this to me. Magic lies in between things, between the day and the night, between yellow and blue, between any two things.

"Meadhon is the grandmother of between," he explains. "The half-world or middleworld one needs to pass through from your world to reach this one. Thin as gauze in some places, wide as the Great Plains of Nydian in others. Some think that all the *geasan* called up in either this world or yours is drawn from Meadhon. Without passing through the middleworld, you could never be sitting here talking to me."

"You mean dreams? But I thought all of this"—I lift a hand—"was the dream."

He smiles. "No. The dream is what carries you here. The spiritworld is as real as your own world, only someplace else. It's the middleworld that provides all the doors between, but it's a chancy place with no real boundaries and not a great deal to commend it, except for its service as a passageway. The difference between the middleworld and the worlds it joins is like the difference between the People and the Eadar. Except it has a purpose, as do the People, while we are merely whims, long-lived only if we capture the fancy of enough believers."

His voice has been changing throughout this conversation, having transformed from the somewhat innocent and happy little fellow I first met to someone with the same merry face, but the sound of an old man, full of a knowledge that has brought him only a resigned sadness, rather than any understanding or even intellectual pleasure. The whisper of wisdom I've noticed in his eyes from time to time has come to the fore.

"Who are you really?" I find myself asking.

"The face under the bark," he says. "The child that the Green Woman abandoned to follow the ghost of Grian Eun, the sun bird." He lifts the hand with the tattoo of the thunderbolt on its back. "This is the sign of her luck medicine," he adds. "Borrowed from the Grandfather Thunders. And this"—he lifts the other with the thunderbolt encircled—"is that luck swallowed by the earth—the way it looked before Raven pulled the rounded turtle shell that is the world out of the darkness. Though some say it's the moon that is Nokomis's heart, and that luck is a twisting snake, not a thunderbolt."

His dark brown eyes study me for a long moment before he asks, "And who are you, really?"

"Just who I said I am. A painter. A visitor here. A stranger, really, nothing more."

"And the light burns so bright in you because . . . ?"

I shake my head. "I don't know anything about that."

He nods gravely. Then it's as though someone has passed a hand over his features, transforming them once more. He grins and points upward.

"Do you want to climb a tree?" he asks. "The twigs at the very top are fat with magic. We could gather up a handful each and become wizards."

I start to comment on this abrupt change, but then decide it's not my place to say who he should be, how he should act. It's not like who he sees in me is the whole story either. He knows nothing of the Broken Girl I really am. If I'm going to wear a mask, I have to let others wear their own, and not comment when they decide to trade one for another, and then back again.

But it serves as a healthy reminder that nothing is necessarily what it seems, not here, not in the world where the Broken Girl is sleeping, dreaming she's able to walk and paint and live a normal life.

"Come on, come on," he's saying.

He's on his feet now patting the tree bark.

I give that enormous tree trunk a dubious look. The bark's rough and there are plenty of hand- and toeholds, but the first branches seem to be miles away, and I don't think I have the courage to clamber up into its heights.

"I don't think so," I tell him.

"Oh, it's easy. It's fun."

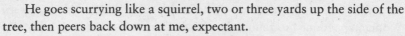

He goes scurrying like a squirrel, two or three yards up the side of the tree, then peers back down at me, expectant.

"Not today, anyway," I say. "I have to go now."

Before he can argue me out of it, I wake myself up.

But we keep talking about it on other visits and finally I put my sketch-book in its plastic shopping bag, put the loops of its handle through my belt so that it's hanging behind me, and I follow him up one of the trees. It's not as bad as I thought it would be. In fact, although I'm climbing straight up, fingers and toes finding easy purchase in the bumps and crevices of the rough bark, I don't feel perpendicular to the ground at all. It's more as if I'm going up a gentle slope. And I've already decided that if I fall, I'll just wake myself up before I hit the ground, so what's the worry?

I don't fall. Don't even come close. I just follow Toby, up and up. We're like a pair of Jacks climbing a beanstalk, because when we finally reach the immense first branches, there's another world up there. The dreamworld's an amazing place, no question, but this might be the most amazing part of it I've found to date. I don't know how many times I looked up into the heights of these giant trees, never guessing there was all of this up here.

The branches are as broad as a two-lane highway and slightly flat on top, so that we can walk along them, side by side, going higher and higher, pulling ourselves up onto the next levels of branches by way of tangled nests of vines that hang here and there like clusters of ropes. As we rise from branch to higher branch, the twilight gives way to a deep yellow light and then we find actual patches of grass growing on those broad branches, swaths of wildflowers, little pools of clear water from which we can take a drink, other pools where the water's sat too long and is thick with algae. Frogs peer up at us out of the slimy green, invisible except for their eyes and the triangular tops of their heads.

It really is a whole other world up here, and much livelier than the quiet, stately cathedral feel that I get below on the forest floor. I see more wildlife than I saw below. Here there are songbirds in plenty—finches, sparrows, wrens, bluebirds, cardinals—flitting among the smaller branches, and all sorts of little lizards and butterflies and bugs. We pass sleeping moths that are bigger than my two hands put together, with creamy wings that look like they'd be soft as velvet to the touch. Noisy red and black squirrels arguing with each other and scolding anybody who comes by. Fat rabbits, chewing on clover. I see that one of them has a small set of antlers, like the supposedly mythical jackalope in Texas and the Southwest, before they slip away.

"Why are you smiling?" Toby asks.

Smiling? I think. Surely, I'm grinning like a loon.

"I can't help it," I tell him. "All my life I've read about people who manage to find themselves in some magical otherworld full of marvels and wonder, and now here I am." I wave a hand at the branch/road we're walking along. "Now I'm in the impossible place, and I just love it. I wish I never—"

But I break off before I finish the sentence.

"You never what?" Toby asks.

Have to go back to my broken body, I think.

"Have to wake up," is all I say.

"Why do you have to?"

"The same reason you're an Eadar, I guess. That's where my real life is and until I finish dealing with everything back there, I can't go on to whatever might be waiting for me here."

"I hate rules, don't you?" Toby says.

"Rules?"

"You know, whatever makes our lives have to be one way and not another."

I think about getting run down by a car and having my body left lying there on the side of the street like so much broken china. And I think about older hurts, the ones that twist like scars across my memory and no one but me knows I'm carrying them.

"I suppose I do," I say.

He gives me a considering look, then shrugs. "Come on," he says. "We have to get higher up."

I love this world of trees. The broad boughs overlap one another so that it's possible to continue walking to the top as though following a switchback trail on a steep mountainside. But closer to the trunk there's a veritable nest of vines and tangled branches that Toby leads me up and I feel less like a Jack and more like a monkey as we climb and climb.

Eventually, we don't reach the top, but we do clamber up onto what turns out to be several branches growing snug together, one against the other, forming a huge natural platform. Standing on it feels like being on a raft, the slight sway of the giant tree taking the place of a slow river current. The branches open up here and an incredible vista is revealed. It's soon apparent that large as the trees of the Greatwood are, this one we're climbing dwarfs them, for we're looking out across the tops of the forest, westward, I think. In the far distance I can see where the forest ends and a range of foothills climb up the skirts of a mountain range. On the closest hill is what appears to be a structure of some sort. A castle, or a chateau. I can't tell. It's too small to make out from this distance.

I look up and see that the tree we're in still goes up and up, its heights disappearing from sight. No wonder the topmost twigs are supposed to be magical. It would be a fairy-tale journey into forever just to reach them. My gaze goes back to the structure on those distant hills.

"What's that place?" I ask my companion.

"The Inn of the Star-Crossed. It's a place where gather those who have been ill-treated by the fates. It's not a happy place."

"It's an inn? But it looks so big."

Toby laughs. "So it's a big inn." He tugs my sleeve. "You're not stopping, are you? We still have magics to gather."

I let my gaze go traveling back up the trunk of the tree until it gets lost in the maze of branches.

"How far is the top?" I ask.

"I don't know. I've never been there." He laughs again. "Do I look like a wizard to you?"

"But are there really magic twigs up there?"

"Bushels of them," he assures me.

"Why haven't you gone to the top before?"

"I never had anyone who'd come that far with me," he says. "It's a very long journey. Nobody has time anymore."

"How long a journey?"

"That's a tricky question."

"Hours, days, weeks, months?" I ask.

"It all depends on who you are and how badly you want to get there—at least that's what I've heard."

"What do you mean by that?"

"Well, it's like a lot of things, I suppose. The more you want it or need it, the harder it is to get."

I sigh. There must be something in the air of the dreamlands that makes people particularly oblique. I mean, look at Joe. It's *so* hard to get a straight answer out of him sometimes.

"Can you give me an even remotely more comprehensible answer?" I ask.

He gives me a guilty look. "I need that magic so badly," he says. "So I know I'll never get there on my own. With those twigs in hand I wouldn't have to worry about fading ever again."

"I still don't understand."

"Well, look at you," he says. "You're coming along for the lark of it, aren't you? Doesn't matter if there's magic or not. I thought with you accompanying me we'd just . . . be there so much more quickly."

"Because I'm not desperate for magic."

He nods.

I think about how my life has been, always following the scent and incident of magic, and how my life is now, that of a Broken Girl, waiting for a miracle to save her.

"You don't know how badly I could use some magic," I tell him.

He slumps down onto the branch.

"Then we're doomed," he says. "Doomed to never find it."

"It's not the end of the world," I say.

"But it could be the end of my life."

"I'll never stop believing in you."

"Maybe that won't be enough," he tells me.

He gets up then and abruptly begins to descend down the rat's nest of branches and vines we climbed to reach this odd platform of branches. He's very good at just walking away from a problem and it's starting to annoy me.

"Was that the only reason you hung around with me?" I yell down at him. "Because you saw me as the way to get yourself a piece of some magic?"

He pauses and looks back up at me, puckish good humor vanished. All I see is sorrow now.

"I thought you liked me," I say.

"I did. I do. It's just . . . you wouldn't understand."

And then he looks away and continues his descent, moving so quickly that he's soon out of sight. I study the route down for a long moment before lifting my gaze back up. Up and up. The top of the tree's somewhere high above me, but I'm not going to go looking for it on my own. I'm not going to climb all the way back down again, either. Now that I've been here, I can reappear on this platform the next time I return to the dreamlands. If I want to.

But right now, I've had my fill of giant trees and magic lands, and I just let myself wake up, back in the rehab.

4

Wendy ended up going to visit Cassie by herself to see if Cassie could help them find out anything about this mysterious twin of Jilly's. She'd felt there was no point in trying to get Sophie to come with her since Sophie's reticence to talk about the dreamlands with any seriousness might hinder a useful conversation. And there was no one else she could have asked to accompany her. Jilly hadn't talked about the dreamlands to anyone except for Sophie and herself. She was apparently keeping it secret from everyone else. And if that was the case, Wendy didn't feel it was fair for her to be the one to make public those secrets.

Cassie and Joe lived in the north end of Upper Foxville. It wasn't much of a place, a basement apartment in an old run-down building, but Wendy supposed it was a step up from the squats they used to live in. The surprise came once she got past the front door and stepped into their apartment. While the building might have appeared dilapidated and gloomy from the outside, and the foyer hadn't exactly been ready to win any *Good Housekeeping* awards, Cassie and Joe's apartment itself was cheerful with color and light, though where exactly the light was coming from, Wendy couldn't tell. It was as if the furnishings were casting their own illumination. Or maybe it was simply a reflection of Cassie's personality—the glow she carried about her that seemed to contain some echo of all that was kind and right in the world.

I know some good people, Wendy thought as she followed Cassie into the apartment. And most of them she'd met through Jilly.

"I'm trying to remember," Cassie said. "Are you a tea or a coffee drinker?"

"Actually," Wendy said, "I wouldn't mind a beer if you have any."

Cassie smiled. "A woman after my own heart. Make yourself comfortable, I'll be right back."

Wendy wandered around the room, taking in the contradictory decor. Somehow all the African and Native art and artifacts blended perfectly, if however improbably, with the most commercial kitsch. Pez dispensers based on Star Wars and Disney characters shared a shelf with small fetish carvings from both Africa and the rez. A gold-painted plaster Elvis bust stood on another shelf with a beautiful African print scarf draped around its shoulders. Swanee whistles, kazoos, and a plastic Gene Autry ukulele missing its strings shared the top of a cedar chest with some skin-headed drums from Africa, an Apache wooden flute, and a Kickaha water drum. Moose- and deer-hide medicine bags hung on the wall beside an outdated poster advertising the new fall lineup on one of the local TV stations. On the other side of the poster was an African mask carved from some dark wood. A small throw pillow with Bart Simpson's features on it lay against a stunning Navajo blanket hanging over the back of the sofa.

The room had the charm and curiously harmonizing effect of a crowded junk shop, the sort of place you could lose yourself in for hours, but it wasn't an apartment that Wendy could ever live in herself.

She was standing in front of a small oil painting that Jilly had done a couple of years ago when Cassie returned to the living room with their beers. The painting was a portrait of Cassie and Joe holding hands, the two of them sitting under her own Tree of Tales in Fitzhenry Park. She recognized it as her tree because whenever Jilly painted it, she always put in any number of small colored ribbons among its leaves, so cleverly rendered that they seemed to grow there, a natural phenomenon rather than an intrusion. The ribbons were to represent the stories that fed the tree, Jilly explained the first time Wendy had asked her about them.

"I love that painting," Cassie said as she handed Wendy her beer. They tipped the tops of their bottles against each other. "Joe looks just so . . . Joe."

"I like the way she's captured the affection between the two of you." Cassie smiled. "That, too."

She waved Wendy to a seat on the sofa, then settled on the other end, pulling the Bart Simpson pillow onto her lap.

"I've never been here before," Wendy said, "but I can see why you and Jilly get along so well. You have a similar eclectic taste."

"I met her through Joe, actually. But it's true. We do get along, and have from the day we met." Cassie smiled. "There's not a lot of other women I'd let spend as much time as she does with my partner, but I trust her implicitly. Joe, too, of course."

"It's just this gift she has," Wendy said, paraphrasing one of Jilly's favorite expressions.

Cassie's smile broadened. "But it's interesting how she connects so many of us who might not otherwise seem to have all that much in common. I don't mean you or Sophie so much as people like Sue who's so uptown or . . ." She started to laugh. "The Crowsea Fire Department."

Wendy began to laugh as well. "I *know*. Can you believe that they *all* came to see her?"

"With Jilly I'm ready to believe anything."

"She can be very convincing," Wendy said.

Cassie nodded and Wendy decided that this was the perfect opening to segue into why she'd come here.

"But I'm not so convinced about her new role," Wendy added.

"What do you mean?"

"You know, the dutiful patient, doing what she's told just so that she can get well."

"Now you've completely lost me," Cassie told her.

"Well, it's the main reason I'm here," Wendy said.

She went on to explain her suspicion that Jilly was getting ready to simply disappear into the dreamlands forever, ending with the mystery of this doppelgänger that both Isabelle and Sophie had seen in the vicinity of Jilly's loft recently.

"That's what you sensed in her studio when you went over, wasn't it?" Wendy said. "A kind of twin Jilly, only a bad one."

Cassie hesitated before answering.

"I sensed that the paintings had been destroyed by someone with a similar energy to hers," she said finally. "Not that whoever did it looked like her."

"But a dark energy instead of a bright one, right?"

Cassie nodded.

"And this person *could* look like Jilly, couldn't she?"

"I suppose," Cassie said, obviously reluctant at where all of this was going. "But you make it sound like the plot of some dumb B-movie, where, big surprise, the villain turns out to be the dark side of the hero."

"If we use Jilly's usual logic," Wendy argued, "even bad B-movies have their basis in some kind of truth."

Cassie shook her head. "I don't know. This is something Joe would know more about."

"Where is Joe?"

"On a wild goose chase, looking for Gaea."

"Gaea?" Wendy repeated, certain she'd misheard.

Cassie shrugged. "That's what the Greeks called her—the mother of the world. Or more correctly, 'the Deep-breasted One.' Joe calls her Nokomis."

"But . . . what do you mean he's looking for her? That's like, well, looking for God, isn't it? How would you even start to do something like that, besides entering a seminary?"

"Joe went looking for her in the dreamlands," Cassie said.

The reply was so not what Wendy had been expecting that for a long moment she couldn't speak. She'd accepted—at least most of the time she did—that there was this other world where you could run into faeries and goblins and animal people and who knew what other sorts of magical beings. A place where Sophie, and now Jilly, could have these amazing adventures. It was easier to think of it as the dreamlands, a place you could visit when you were asleep and dreaming, than as the spiritworld, some magical parallel dimension that you could simply step into from this one, but even that she could usually go along with—in theory, at least. But this seemed too much.

"You can meet God there?"

"Gods, plural," Cassie replied. "Apparently. I never have, but Joe's met this one before."

"But it was just someone who called herself that, right? He didn't really meet . . ."

Wendy didn't even know what to call her. The Goddess? Mother Nature? The Earth Mother?

"Joe's an unusual guy," Cassie said, "so it wouldn't surprise me. He's not like you or me. His roots go back a lot further than ours do. In fact, he goes back a lot further than we do. He's older than he looks, you know."

"How much older?"

"I don't know. I never asked."

Wendy took a steadying breath. She looked down at her hand and saw she was still holding her beer, so she took a swallow of the amber liquid. The flavor barely registered.

"Okay," she said, setting the bottle down on the coffee table between a clay sculpture of a turtle and a shot glass with a "Buffy the Vampire Slayer" logo on its side. "I know the world's weirder than I ever think it is, even though I have to be reminded from time to time. So I'll give you all of that."

Cassie shook her head. "I'm not asking you to believe or disbelieve anything."

"I know. It's just that, don't you see? What you're saying is so amazing, right? So if it's possible to actually meet God in the dreamlands, then why shouldn't it be possible for Jilly to have an evil twin?"

Cassie smiled. "Just because you have a tree that is nourished on stories, does that mean Elvis is really still alive?"

"Well, no."

"And Nokomis isn't God," she went on. "At least she's not my conception of what we usually mean by God. She's an elder being, I'll grant you that. Probably been around since the first days, or even before the world was made."

"So what *would* you call that?"

"Like I said, an elder being. They're different from us, powerful in ways we aren't, and certainly longer-lived, but I believe someone like Nokomis embodies *our* perceptions of a deity, not her own. I don't have a name for the life force I perceive making up the fabric of the world and all the beings in it, but I don't think she's it. Or even the more traditional ideas of God. I believe we're all part of this . . . I guess I'll call it the Wheel that is the World, the way that Joe does."

"But even he believes in something called the Grace," Wendy said. "I remember Jilly telling me about it one time."

Cassie nodded. "Except, as I understand it, Grace is a state, like the Kickaha's concept of Beauty, and we all carry a piece of it inside us so long as we don't deny it and push it away."

"I still think it's worth checking out this evil twin business," Wendy said. "First there's the hit-and-run with the car, then Jilly's studio gets trashed. What's she going to do next?"

"She?"

"The evil twin."

Cassie didn't say anything for a long moment. Then she got up and went over to where her jacket was hanging from the back of a chair. She reached into the inside pocket and brought out a deck of cards held together with a rubber band.

"Let's see what the cards can tell us," she said.

She knelt on the floor across the coffee table from where Wendy was sitting and cleared a space between them.

"This won't be an absolute answer," she said as she undid the rubber band and placed the cards in a neat stack on the table. She slid the rubber band onto her wrist where it joined the half-dozen brightly colored plastic bracelets she was already wearing. "But it may give us a better idea as to where we can direct our attention to learn more."

The cards didn't seem to be anything special, but Wendy had seen them in action before and knew there was far more to them than an initial appearance might let on.

"You'll have to turn the cards," Cassie said.

Wendy gave her a surprised look. "Me? Why me?"

"I don't like to use them for myself."

"Why not?"

"Well, for one thing, it would be too easy to get dependent on them and want to use them for every little thing that might come up in my life. You'd be surprised how quickly that sidles up on you. And the other is, I'm too attuned to them and they're more likely to show me what I want to see than what we're actually looking for."

"Everything's got a limitation, doesn't it?"

"I don't think of it as a limitation," Cassie said. "More a protocol. A right way to do things. The world always seems a little brighter when we do things for each other instead of just for ourselves. I don't know that I can explain it better."

"It's okay," Wendy said. "I can do it."

She shuffled the cards, then set them back on the table and turned the topmost card over. An inadvertent gasp escaped her lips as the blank face of the card slowly resolved into an image. She could just never get used to magic.

She and Cassie both leaned closer to make out the image that was taking shape. It was murky at first, showing a small, unlit bedroom, night skies lying beyond its window, starlight shining in on its basic furnishings. They saw figures on the bed and as their eyes adjusted to the bad lighting of the image, they realized what the two figures were doing. It was a teenaged boy, abusing a much younger girl, no more than a child really.

The image was so graphic that Wendy quickly pulled her gaze away from it.

"Did you recognize those people?" Cassie asked.

Wendy swallowed hard. "I think so. Do you know anything about Jilly's childhood?"

"We've talked about it," Cassie said. "And about her life on the streets, after she escaped." She was still studying the card, leaning even closer to it. "It's hard to tell, but the hair, if nothing else, makes me think of Jilly."

"I'm sure that's who it is."

It was such a heartbreaking reminder of how Jilly had begun her life.

"I can't imagine having had to go through that as a kid," Wendy added.

Cassie nodded. "Turn another card."

Wendy didn't want to, but she did. And then she didn't want to look at it, but she did that as well. She'd come here to learn something, to see if she could help, so it would be stupid to turn back now, for all that she wanted to step inside that card, smash that horrible brother of Jilly's, gather the child Jilly had been into her arms and hold her safe from all the hurts in the world.

The next image was innocuous and confusing. It showed a pink Cadillac convertible, parked on a city street that she couldn't recognize.

"Could that be the car that hit Jilly?" Wendy asked.

Cassie shook her head. "Lou said that according to the forensic evidence it was a dark blue. They're still waiting to get the results back to see if they can make a match between the paint flecks that were recovered and a particular manufacturer. The trouble is, it's not exactly a priority. But Lou's pushing."

"So I wonder what the card means?"

"I don't know. Maybe the last card will make it clearer."

"We only do three?"

"This isn't a traditional oracular device," Cassie said.

Wendy had to smile. "No kidding."

"Everything I do with them works on an intuitive level, and threes are what feels right to me—have been since the first time I used them." Her gaze clouded, as though at a painful memory, before they focused on

Wendy again. "Joe's always pushing for four cards—to get the word from each of the four quarters of the world, he says—but that's something that answers to his Kickaha heritage, not mine."

"So what does your intuition tell you about this pink Caddy?"

"Nothing. You?"

"The same."

"Let's do the last card," Cassie said.

Wendy took it from the pack and turned it over, bracing herself for she wasn't sure what. But when the image began to resolve, it didn't make any more sense to her than the pink Caddy. This time the card showed them a couple of wolves, close-ups of their lupine features. Superimposed over the wolf heads were the faces of two very different women. One appeared to be Jilly. The other looked like a trailer park version of Farah Fawcett, a television actress from the seventies. It was the hairstyle that did it.

"Are they supposed to be wolf people?" Wendy asked.

Cassie looked up from the card. "Wolf spirits move in them. That much I can tell." She sighed and sat back on her heels. "This hasn't been much of a help, has it? The same thing happened when I did a reading for Joe, just before he went back into *manidò-akì*."

"Say what?"

"The spiritworld."

"Maybe the card's telling us that the dark Jilly is—" Wendy shrugged. "Oh, I don't know. Some kind of animal person."

"With a friend."

"A friend with badly dated hair."

That called up a smile on Cassie's lips. She left the cards on the table, the three of them laid out in a row beside the rest of the deck, and returned to her seat on the end of the sofa.

"Can I pick them up?" Wendy asked.

"Of course. They won't change until they've been returned to the deck."

Wendy ignored the first card, but picked up the other two.

"I wonder what Jilly would say if she could see these cards," she said. "If they'd mean anything to her."

"The first card . . ."

"Oh, I wouldn't show her that one. Like she needs any reminders of that time in her life. But maybe she'd recognize the other woman in this."

She held up the card with the wolves. "Or can tell us what the pink Caddy means. What time is it, do you know? I'm always forgetting to wear my watch."

Cassie looked at hers. "Almost nine."

"Which means visiting hours are just about over," Wendy said. "Or will be by the time we could get there. Still, we could sneak in. You know how Jilly likes any sort of an intrigue. It'll make her night." She glanced at Cassie. "Will the images hold until then?"

"They should."

"I'll keep these two out," Wendy said, holding the last two cards in her hand, "but I don't want to have to look at that other one ever again."

She began to turn the first card face over, back onto the deck.

"Don't," Cassie started to say.

But it was too late. The card fell into place on the top of the deck. As it did, the images on the pair Wendy was holding faded away. Wendy sighed.

"Well, I screwed that up, didn't I?" she said. "The pictures on those cards were the best clues we've had so far and now they're gone."

"It's not your fault," Cassie said. "You couldn't have known."

Wendy appreciated her kindness, but really. What else was she going to say? The truth was, Wendy had blown it, and she knew it.

"We can still describe them to Jilly," Cassie added.

Wendy gave her a glum nod. Sure, they could. But it wouldn't be the same thing at all. Description couldn't come close to the immediate impact of an image. Showing the cards to Jilly might have surprised something out of her that words couldn't.

"I'll try when I go see her tomorrow," she said.

"I thought you wanted to go tonight."

Wendy sighed. "Without the cards it doesn't seem so pressing anymore."

5

As my dream life becomes more magical, my life in the World As It Is grows all that much more stupifyingly mundane. Being in the rehab is like the Worm Ouroborus, a serpent eating its own tail. You do all this physical therapy, but the end result is this circle leading you to only more of the same. I think the endless routine of it all is what's going to kill me in the end.

I've always been pretty much the least organized person you'd ever know—flighty would probably be the kindest way to put it. It's not that you couldn't count on me. Whatever I'm involved in, I give it all my attention, whether it's a painting, a customer at the restaurant, one of the old folks I'm visiting in St. Vincent's, or just hanging with my friends. But I was always all over the place, flitting from this to that. Here it's the same routine, day in and day out.

They say I'm getting better, and maybe there's been some improvement—the muscles in my face are hardly drooping at all anymore and the feeling's almost completely returned all the way down to my shoulders—but I still can't walk. I can't paint. I can't even eat or go to the bathroom by myself. And that's just the physical side of things. There are other problems that I don't even let on to anyone. I don't know why. Maybe because they're even more scary than the idea of never being able to paint again, to walk or take care of myself. They're things inside me, under my skin, inside my head. Things you can't see. Holes in my memory and something worse: my mind doesn't work the way it used to.

I was ambidextrous as a child, but like I've said, that got whupped out of me pretty early on. It started in school, but my mother took it up with a vengeance. Both my little sister and I were the same, the boys were all right-handed. Just one more thing she had to hold against us, I guess, don't ask me why. There was never any rhyme or reason to why she hated us, me especially. I like to think it got better for my sister when I finally got away, but who am I kidding? I should never have left her there, but what did I know? I was only ten myself when I first started running away, and then out on the street, I was too screwed up to take care of myself, never mind anybody else.

But back then, well, most of the time it was okay. So long as we didn't step out of line, just did what we were told. But if we tried to do anything with our left hand—cut a pork chop, use a pair of scissors, write or throw a ball—that was a sure way to guarantee we'd get a lickin'.

Whupped. Lickin'.

It's funny. I haven't used those words in years. But just thinking about when I was growing up brings the twang back into my thoughts— the twang and all those hillbilly words that even back then I was trying to erase from my vocabulary. I wasn't ashamed of being poor. I was ashamed of the ignorance that surrounded me. The pride that was taken in being ignorant because anything that smacked of manners or learning was considered putting on airs.

I mention this because of those theories that left-handed people are more likely to be drawn toward the arts while right-handed ones are more analytical. Even though I seemed right-handed, I was actually comfortable using either, especially as a child. And my thinking's been the same. I have the spontaneity and intuitiveness that helps create good art, but I've always been good with linear thinking, too. With maths and logical problems.

That's pretty much gone, now. Numbers don't work in my head at all anymore.

I know it doesn't sound like much, but just imagine if you've always been able to do a certain thing, and then it's just taken away from you. That describes my body, too, I suppose, but somehow it's scarier when it's in your head. I suppose it's because no matter what happens to us physically, we hold on to this concept that we're still the same person inside. It can be as simple a thing as aging. You might be forty, but in your head you're forever fifteen. Who you are inside is who you really are. When that starts to change . . .

Today I couldn't make change for a simple bill, never mind figure out a tip. And my thinking's gone way intuitive. Where once I could think things out, figure out a logical path from A to B, now my brain just jumps to a conclusion and I've no idea if it's a logical one or not. It just *feels* right, which is fine for my art—just saying I was able to even pick up a pencil—but not so good for day-to-day life.

Then there's all these gaps I've got in my memory.

The big one's a black hole that contains the week and a half or so before the accident. I can't remember a thing from that period. Up until that time, sure. And the accident itself. But nothing in between.

The accident. God, I still hate thinking about it, and not because of any sort of need for denial on my part. It just . . . hurts to remember. Everything closes up inside me and it all comes back like it's happening to me all over again. It just won't fade. If anything, the memories just get stronger. More intense each time they come back.

The blinding lights that pinned me.

That moment when I knew this huge monstrosity of metal was really going to run me down.

The roaring sound in my ears, layers and layers of sound, each super-imposed upon the next in this bewildering cacophony.

The impact itself is the worst. The wet smack of car against my flesh. The crunch of my bones before I was flung into the air. The pain's like nothing you could ever imagine, not unless you'd gone through something like it yourself.

In the moments before the actual impact, my life didn't flash before my eyes. Instead my brain just short-circuited. The memories that make up who I am just kind of shattered, like one of those screen savers on Christy's computer, where the image falls apart into all its pixilated pieces, except this was a hundred thousand images, all the pieces of my life, all shuffled together in a sharp-edged tangle.

There was a moment then when it all went away. When I was standing over myself, and all I could see was the unnatural splay of my limbs against the pavement and the blood pooling under my body. Or maybe I wasn't standing there. Maybe this memory is just something I imagined, something I called up to free me from the pain.

Because when I looked up from the Broken Girl I'd become, I saw Zinc, this street kid I'd taken under my wing who used to live in a squat with Lucia and Ursula, a couple of performance artists I knew. It was Zinc, standing in the middle of the road, looking at me, except he died back in 1989. He was talking to me, but I couldn't understand what he was saying. But I could see his lips moving, and I could make out that they were shaping my name.

I got the sense that he wanted me to go with him. That he was waiting for me. But I couldn't move. I *wanted* to go, but right at that moment, time seemed to have come to a sudden halt and I was locked in place.

Finally he shook his head and started to walk away. I watched him go to the end of the block. The streetlights were all out on this block, but they shone brightly the next street over. Incredibly brightly. Zinc looked back once, this small dark silhouette against the glare. Then he turned again and walked into the light. And here's the weirdest part. As he stepped into the light, out of all the mouths of all the alleys, up and down the block, these riderless bicycles came wheeling out of the darkness that lay between the buildings, following him until they'd all disappeared into that light.

I stared at them as they went, feeling this huge swell of loss rear up inside me. Then I looked down again and felt myself falling, back into my body . . .

The next clear memory I have of the World As It Is—as opposed to the dreamlands where I've been wandering while in the coma—is waking up in the ICU and Sophie's face, so close to mine.

None of which is particularly odd, apparently, considering the trauma I'd been through, but the other little blackouts really do scare me. See, it's not just that my mind seems to have cut a new channel for itself in how it goes zipping through my brain. I've also got all these little holes to contend with.

I didn't really pay much attention to them at first because I was forever drifting in and out of consciousness during those first few days. I had no strength and I'd just fall asleep right in the middle of a visit with someone. Under those circumstances, it's not something you'd really notice.

But now, here in the rehab, I'm more alert. Broken, sure. My relationship with pain and helplessness is obviously a long-term arrangement and I'm learning to deal with it. But I know I'm not drifting off every few moments now. So those little black holes in my life that used to get buried in drowsiness and sleepy confusion really stand out.

They're not the same as the boxes I learned to build around the bad memories of my childhood and my life on the streets. The boxes keep them at bay, but I always know they're there. I can open those boxes, if I need to. If I'm feeling masochistic. Or if doing so can maybe help somebody else. But these blackouts are just holes. There's nothing there, nothing hidden, nothing to recover. They're pieces cut out of my memory that I can't recover.

I've been hiding them from everybody and I can't really explain why except, I guess, with the helplessness I already feel with everybody poking and prodding at my body, I'm just not ready to deal with having the same thing happen to the inside of my head. I already have an endless parade of people constantly looking in on me. Back in the hospital I had my own little team: neurosurgeon, head nurse, physical therapist, occupational therapist, respiratory therapist, recreation therapist. And each of them seemed to have his or her own aide or tech.

It's not a whole lot different here with all the nurses and therapists, the case counsellor from the state, psychological counsellor from the hospital, the chaplain who keeps stopping by to see if I want some company. There's always someone looking in on me, turning me over in the middle of the night, giving me a pill, asking me how I'm doing.

It's not that I don't appreciate the help. I want out of here and I can't do it on my own. But let's fix the body first and worry about my head later. I think I can live with the lack of linear thinking and a drop in my math ability, and maybe even the black holes, if it means I don't have doctors examining the inside of me as thoroughly as they do the outside.

I think of what Joe said, about me having to fix what's inside, before the Broken Girl can start to mend as well, and now I really don't know what to do. It was bad enough trying to figure out how I'm supposed to deal with childhood traumas that date back almost thirty years. If boxing them up doesn't work, then I don't know what I'm supposed to do next. But with all this other business coming up now as well . . .

I guess I'm really counting on Joe to find a way out of all of this for me.

Joe

It takes me a while to get to Cody's *manidò-tewin*, that big old red rock mountain that serves as his heart home. There's not much grows on it, though the lower canyons and slopes are treed with mountain juniper and pinyon on the north-facing slopes, Douglas fir, limber, and ponderosa pine on the south. I guess that tall lonely mesa top says something about the emptiness in Cody's life—or the emptiness that was there for so many years. Now, according to Whiskey Jack, he's got this magpie cousin in his life.

I try to imagine how something like that could have happened—this is Cody, after all, full of piss and vinegar, and set in his ways—then decide it doesn't matter. All I have to do is think of Cassie and I know that the only thing that matters is that he and his corbæ lady are friends as well as lovers, that they live for each other, as well as with each other. I've got no idea as to how they're making out along those lines, but I do know this. They're not living here.

Truth is, I don't see much of anything. No birds, not even a turkey buzzard. Looking up to the mesa that tops this old mountain from where I'm standing here at the edge of the woods, I get the sense that he hasn't been here for a while. The whole area feels unattended. Makes sense, I guess. With Cody's loneliness swallowed by his newfound happiness, there's not so much need for him to be hiding out in this place anymore. The barrenness of these slopes no longer reflects the state of his heart.

I wonder if he's got him a new *manidò-tewin* somewhere, or if this one's going to adjust to the changes in his life. There's no hard and fast rule as to how it works. But that's the spiritworld for you. There's no hard and fast rule to anything here. Anytime you might think you've got it all figured out, it'll just up and change on you. That's why some folks still call it the Changing Lands.

I leave the woods and start up the lower slopes, picking my way through the pines and dried grass, then across a stretch of loose slides of stone till I get to the canyons. The slope gets steeper here, but after casting around some, I find a switchback path that leads me right up to the mesa.

It's not as flat up here as it looks from down below. Everywhere you turn there are jumbles of rock, big as cars some of them. There's also a handful of bristlecone pines growing up here, gnarled, shrublike trees that are hanging on for dear life to the rock and poor soil. I've seen some in California and Nevada that are over four thousand years old, but the soft song I'm hearing from these tells me they're older still.

On the far side of the mesa top I get a view that takes my breath away. Canyons stretch away for as far as I can see, though maybe canyons isn't the right word. They're more like all these amphitheaters carved into the edge of a high plateau that just shoots into the distance until the shadows cast by the setting sun make the far end fade away. Some combination of wind erosion and freeze-thaw cycles of the water caught in the cracks of the rock has created a wonderland of freestanding spires and towers that put me in mind of the red rock canyons of southern Utah where they call them hoodoos or goblins.

I stand there, drinking in the view until the sun finally goes down, then I turn around again. The seep I'm looking for is just over on the far side of these raggedy bristlecone pines. When twilight descends and the moon rises, I see the moon's reflection in its water, just like in the image on Cassie's card, but there's no sign of Nokomis. Still, somebody's been camping here. I'd say Cody, before he hooked up with that new girl of his, but the signs seem too fresh. There's a bed of juniper and pine boughs gathered from down below, and the remains of a campfire. A little wood-pile tucked away under the lip of some nearby rocks.

I use some of that wood to make a small fire and take a tin mug out of my pack. Filling my mug from the seep, I put it on a rock that I've set right up against the fire. Once the water's bubbling, I drop ground coffee into it, stirring with a stick until it gets good and dark. I use the end of my sleeve to hold the handle until it cools down enough from the night air. It's gotten chilly up here—not real cold, but you'd want a blanket for sleeping, no question.

Funny thing is, I'm not hungry. I've been moving hard and fast all day and I should have worked up an appetite, but right now, all I want is this coffee and a smoke. And the stillness that surrounds me. I need a little downtime from the hectic pace I've been keeping before I start in on considering my next move. I suppose it was a long shot, thinking I'd find Nokomis here, but that's the trouble with those cards of Cassie's and why I'd just as soon never use them. Once you decide what the image means, it makes you forget to consider all the other possibilities that are out there.

Not that I'm blaming Cassie or her cards. I could've stopped her from laying them out for me. But this business with Jilly's just got me too worried and I was making the same mistake everybody does when they're looking for a quick way out of a problem. But that's not the way the world works—not here in *manidò-aki*, and not in the world outside either. There's a thing I learned a long time ago but keep forgetting on a regular basis and that is, if it can get complicated, it will.

Which probably explains my visitor.

The sun's long down and I'm on my second cup of coffee when I hear someone approaching. Boots crunching on the red dirt and stones. I think it's Cody at first and hope he really has taken a liking to corbæ these days, but I don't have to worry. I recognize the shine of my visitor's spirit first, and then the shape of his long lean body and features. It's only Whiskey Jack. He smiles at me as he approaches the fire, moonlight shining in his eyes, and tips a finger against his flat-brimmed hat.

"Are you following me?" I ask.

"Well, if I was," he says, "you weren't doing much to hide your trail."

I don't have a spare mug, so I offer him the one I'm using, still half full. Jack smiles and takes a contented sip.

"You always did make a good cup," he says. "Got any smokes to go with this?"

I've never met anyone who likes a smoke as much as Jack does but never carries any on him.

"What's up?" I ask him as I hand him my tobacco pouch. "That puma girl decide she likes somebody better?"

"Like that'd ever happen," Jack says.

This kind of self-assurance is a canid trait, part of our genetic makeup. We always like to think the world's going to go our way, doesn't matter how much we screw up. I mean, look at Cody. He's the king of denial. He's been behind some of the most horrendous screwups you'd ever want to hear about, but nothing's ever his fault. With my corbæ blood, I've got it twice as bad as a regular canid—you think the dog boys are full of themselves, you should spend a little time with some of my black-winged cousins—but I've also got Cassie to keep me honest.

Jack lights his cigarette with that Zippo of his that he won from Cody and hands me back my pouch.

"So why'd you leave her?" I ask.

"Never hooked up with her," he says.

I raise my eyebrows.

"Once I saw the trouble we've got," Jack tells me, "I knew I didn't have the time to go courting anybody, doesn't matter how pretty she might be."

There's a smile in his voice, but then there's always a smile in Jack's voice. It doesn't matter what the situation.

"What kind of trouble?" I ask.

"That unicorn we put in the ground? It wasn't the first those wolves killed. From what I heard at Harley's, they've taken down maybe twelve, thirteen of them now."

I nod, to show I'm listening.

"You know what that means," Jack says.

"They've taken a liking to killing."

"Exactly."

He looks off into the night, blows a lungful of smoke into the darkness.

"And I guess that answers the old question about the medicine in their blood," he adds after a moment. "Dreamers like that, they'd be looking for more variety in their hunts unless there was something really special about killing you a unicorn."

"Unless they just like a hard run," I say.

We've both heard all the stories, how nothing can lead you on a chase like a unicorn. And then there's this trick they got where they can step onto a spirit road and it's like they just vanished on you. I'm pretty good at spotting those roads myself, but it's something you have to work at and keep up once you do get the knack. Most people can't make the time.

But Jack's shaking his head. "Naw, it's more than that. You know what these dreamers are like. Give 'em a mouthful of any kind of medicine and all they taste is the power, none of the spirit. They'll be growing strong on that unicorn blood. Strong and fearless."

I remember the eyes of that pack leader and nod. The only reason she didn't take us on was that we were unknowns. She was smart enough to want to study us first.

"And that's where it stands," Jack says.

I wait a beat, but when he doesn't go on, I ask, "So what's that got to do with us?"

He takes a last drag from his cigarette and tosses the butt into the fire. When his gaze lifts to settle on my face, I can see he's puzzled.

"Aren't you the one who's always saying we have to be more responsible?" he asks.

"So what are you saying?" I reply. "You want us to watch out for these unicorns and keep them safe?"

"No, I just want to kill those wolves."

"Kill them."

One of my failings, at least so far as most of the other canids are concerned, is that I like to find solutions that aren't quite so final. I can be as hard as need be when push comes to shove, but I figure violence never really solves anything. You kill someone, then maybe you've solved one problem, but you're carrying the burden of that killing around with you for the rest of your days. Kill enough and there's no room left inside for your spirit to grow anymore. All you are is a burden, a stunted spirit, going through the motion of living.

"They're giving us canids a bad name, Joe."

But that's not it at all. I can read it in his eyes. Something about that dead unicorn we buried has put a deep cut in Jack's heart. I know what

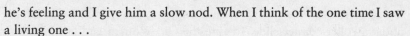

he's feeling and I give him a slow nod. When I think of the one time I saw a living one . . .

"Yeah," I tell him. "We've got to put a stop to it."

"I don't get you," Jack says. "You're the justice dog. You see a wrong, you set it right. But this . . ."

"I've been distracted."

"Because of your sister."

I nod. "I haven't been thinking straight since that car ran her down. And there's no one to help her, except maybe Nokomis."

"Not much chance of that," a new voice says.

For a minute I think it's Cody. Then Jack calls out to him, and I realize it's Nanabozho standing there on the edge of our fire's light. They're both coyotes, so the mistake's easy to make, but Bo's not as tall as Cody and he's got those mismatched eyes: the right one's brown, the left a steel-blue gray. The way he just appeared here without either Jack or me hearing him is what threw me most, but now I realize this *manidò-tewin*'s got an echo in more than one coyote's heart.

That's the thing about a heart home. When it's yours you can just be there, doesn't matter where it is. It's like snapping your fingers. The campsite here's probably so fresh because he's been keeping it up.

"Why do you say that?" Jack asks.

Bo comes and sits by the fire. "I was talking to Jolene," he says, "and she mentioned that Joe here had a friend he wanted us to look in on from time to time."

"Jilly," I say.

He nods. "Sweet girl. So I've been keeping her some company, when I'm in that part of the Greatwood. She's the one who told me that the Old Woman already had a look at her."

"They talked?"

"Not in words," Bo tells me. "And not so's Jilly understood. But I did. She was White Buffalo Woman, Joe, and you know what that means. She's gone back on a buffalo walk for sure and won't one of us be seeing her anytime soon."

"But—"

"You pay any attention to the world outside this place?" Bo asks, interrupting me. "It's gone to hell, no question. You expect her to worry about some hurting girl when she's got a whole world hurting on her?

Dying even. And it's not slow but steady anymore, Joe. We're talking about a roller-coaster slide. I figure the Old Woman had her a look at Jilly and decided there was nothing there the girl couldn't deal with on her own."

I'd been afraid of that. Nokomis has been drifting further and further from individual concerns, for all the reasons Bo just made. With the whole world in trouble, dealing with individual problems is just too overwhelming. Tracking her down had been a long shot and maybe, I had to admit, a way for me to avoid making Jilly do what had to be done. Go down into that hurting place inside her and deal with what was waiting for her there on her own. Her friends could stand beside her, hold her hand and offer their support, but only she could do the work.

"What's so important about her anyway?" Bo asks.

"She's a friend," I tell him. That should say it all, and it does. Except . . .

"I understand that," Bo says. "But there's something else going on there, too. She's got this big burning light in her like I've never seen before."

"I don't know," I say. "But it means something. She's in this world for a reason."

"Everybody's in this world for a reason," Jack says, and for once his voice hasn't got the trace of a smile in it.

I nod. "Except that light tells me that the reason she's here could make a big difference for more people than either you or I could ever touch."

"You've got to see her for yourself," Bo tells Jack. "Then you'll understand."

Jack looks from him to me.

I try to explain. "She's like . . . like . . ."

I can't find the words. I look past the fire and for that moment before my night sight kicks in, all I see is darkness. Then one by one, the stars start to appear. The moon, so big and bright it's almost white.

"She's like those unicorns," I tell Jack finally. "Got a fire in her that just makes you feel good to stand beside, warming your soul."

We fall quiet then. Bo helps himself to my coffee and my tobacco pouch, rolls a smoke for each of us that Jack lights with his Zippo.

"Wasn't that Cody's?" Bo asks.

Jack nods. "I won it from him in a card game." He gives Bo a considering glance. "But since we're talking about Cody, isn't this his *manidò-tewin*?"

"Was," Bo says. "He's got a new place now, all sunshine and flowers. Imagine a desert where the saguaro and other cacti are always in bloom and everywhere you walk, the ground's thick with yellow poppies and pink fairy dusters."

I smile. "So he's really in love."

Bo nods.

"And what about you?" Jack asks.

"Me?" Bo says.

He gets a look, you can tell his gaze has gone inward, found some past time that maybe he doesn't want to remember, but he can't help going back to it, again and again, worrying at it the way you pick at a scab. Keep picking at it and it never gets the chance to heal.

Bo sighs. "Me, I've got a use for a lonely place like this now. I'm like the Old Woman in that way, I guess. The more I walk in the outside world, the more it hurts. Can't get no rest from it except when I'm here."

Jack turns to me. "You see what I'm talking about here? That's why we've got to stop those wolves. Bad enough they do what they do to themselves and their own world. And maybe we can't stop it there. But we can stop them from doing it here."

"Close the dreaming doors on them," I say, "so they can't ever come back."

That's what I'm good at—must be the crow in me. Opening and closing the doors of the spirit.

But Jack's shaking his head. I expected as much. He already told me what he thinks we've got to do.

"No," he says. "That won't be enough for the likes of them. We've just got to put them down."

"Dog gets the sickness," Bo says, "you can't let it live."

I think again about that body we found, the dark glee in the eyes of those wolves, tearing at its flesh, drinking down the hot fire of its blood.

"Yeah, you're right," I say. I can't keep the reluctance from my voice, but I know it's what we've got to do. "She was strong, the one leading that pack. Close a door on her and she'll just find another way to get in." I let my gaze settle on Jack's face. "But how are we going to find them? *Manidò-aki*'s a big old world. We could be chasing them for the rest of our lives."

But Jack's shaking his head again. "We don't have to find them," he says. "They're going to find us. I saw the look in their eyes when we chased them off. They never knew anything like us even existed. I'll bet you even money they'll be looking for us, wanting to know how sweet our blood tastes."

Bo's features shift from the human who was drinking coffee from my tin mug to the feral grin of a coyote.

"And then we take them down," he says.

I'm still thinking about those wolves. There was something that bothered me about them, something familiar, but I still can't place it. I only know it's going to prove that old truism once again: if it can get complicated, it will. Story of my life, lately.

But I give a slow nod in agreement.

"Then we take them down," I say.

I only hope we're not making the mistake that Cody always makes: trying to do what you think is right, but only screwing things up until they're worse than they ever were.

Jilly

Sophie couldn't explain why she invariably went into immediate denial mode the moment the subject of the dreamlands came up. No matter what she might tell anybody else, she knew they were real. She just couldn't talk about them as if they were.

Sometimes she wondered if this inability was pure selfishness on her part, that admitting they were real to anybody else wouldn't make them special for her anymore. Wouldn't make *her* special. In her heart she knew that wasn't true. Other people had access to the dreamlands—a lot of them more so than her. She only had to think of someone like Joe who moved as easily back and forth between the worlds as anybody else might cross a street.

But still she couldn't shake the thought that by admitting they were real rather than simply dreams, she might lose her own connection to them.

It was an awful thing to contemplate. She liked to think of herself as a generous person, especially when it came to Jilly and Wendy. She honestly believed that she was willing to share anything and everything with them, and it would be so much fun to have them with her when she crossed over to Mabon. But every time the subject of the reality of that other world came up, she could feel something close up inside her and denials came swimming up into her side of the conversation.

The rational part of Wendy's mind seemed happy to accept these denials—yes, the world is what we see, no more, no less, and everything else belongs to illusion and dream—but Sophie knew that it drove Jilly a little crazy sometimes. And maybe even hurt her as well, though she never said as much. Still, Jilly rarely talked about anything that really troubled her, not the old hurts or any new ones that might come up, so that wasn't something this could be measured against.

The accident that had put her in the hospital and what had happened to her faerie paintings were perfect examples, Sophie thought as she entered the rehab building and walked down the hall to Jilly's room. It was close to the end of visiting hours and night's quiet was stealing back into the building. Her footsteps echoed on the marble floor and she could smell a faint whiff of incense as she neared the room of the practicing Buddhist who was Jilly's neighbor.

Jilly was sleeping when Sophie stepped into her room, or at least her eyes were closed. Sophie paused for a moment in the doorway, remembering again that odd feeling of the world going a-kilter when she'd thought she'd seen Jilly coming out of her Yoors Street loft the other day. Impossible, of course. It hadn't been Jilly.

"Are you coming in?"

Sophie blinked to find Jilly looking at her, a slightly lopsided smile tugging at her lips. The paralysis had mostly left her face and her speech was now as clear as it had ever been. If only the rest of it would go away.

"I thought you were asleep," she said.

Jilly gave a small shake of her head. "Just resting. I had a busy day."

Sophie came into the room and sat on the side of the bed. Knowing what she did of Jilly's exercise schedule, the comment wasn't an overstatement.

"I half expected to still find a gang of people in here," she said.

"It's been quieting down a little," Jilly told her. "Which is kind of a relief. I mean, I love that everybody's been so supportive and everything, but the broken body's pretty obvious lying here on the bed and it gets in between any chance of relating with people on any kind of a normal level."

"They're looking at you, but not looking."

"Exactly. It's a really weird feeling. And people you wouldn't expect, either. Like Isabelle. The whole time she's visiting, she's just focused on my face."

"I guess it makes some people uncomfortable."

"I suppose. But enough about the trials and tribulations of the bedridden. What brings you back today?"

Sophie had already visited this morning.

"I wanted to talk to you about a couple of things," she said.

Jilly made an exaggerated grimace. "Uh-oh."

"Nothing too serious," Sophie said, then corrected herself. "Well, maybe a little."

"I had nothing to do with it. I was somewhere else. I've never even met whoever it is that claims I did it."

Sophie had to laugh. "You don't even know what it is that I want to talk to you about."

"I know. But I thought I'd get my excuses in first."

"It's nothing you need to be excused for."

"Well, that's a relief."

Sophie shook her head and regarded her friend for a moment. It was nice to see that Jilly had regained a bit of her silly good humor. Sophie had missed that these past few weeks. It made it feel a little bit like old times, except Jilly wasn't bouncing around the room while she was declaiming her innocence, or sitting sideways on some easy chair, limbs dangling over its arms, displaying all the nonchalance of a drowsy cat. The return of her good spirits was more than welcome. That they seemed genuine as well was even better.

"I was wondering about the dreamlands," Sophie said. "You haven't really been talking about them as much lately."

"Ah, the dreamlands," Jilly replied.

Something guarded came into her eyes and Sophie felt a twinge of disappointment that there could be secrets between them where there never had been before.

"Wonderful place," Jilly told her. "Though they're not real, of course."

Sophie's twinge became the point of a knife darting straight for her heart.

"I suppose I deserved that," she said.

Jilly gave her a puzzled look, then smiled. "Oh, I see. You think I'm just saying that because you're always denying them being a real place."

"Aren't you?"

"Maybe a little."

Jilly's gaze went past her, as if looking at something that lay far beyond the wall behind her.

"But it's funny," Jilly went on. "I find that the more time I spend there, the more reluctant I am to talk about them. Or at least talk about how they relate to the World As It Is, or whether or not they're real."

"Because you think, if you do, they might be taken away?"

Jilly's surprise was plain. "Something like that. How did you . . ." Her voice trailed off and then she grinned. "You feel the same way, don't you? That's why you talk about them the way you do . . . or rather don't."

Sophie gave her a reluctant nod. Even that seemed to be too much conversation about them. She could feel a tightening in her chest, but under it was another, almost alien feeling. The sense that she'd stepped up to a door in a locked room only to find that it had opened under her touch and freedom lay just beyond. She took a steadying breath.

"I can't explain it," she told Jilly.

"I don't think you have to," Jilly said. "At least not to me, because I know exactly what you mean."

"Why do you think it's like that?"

Jilly slowly shook her head and Sophie found herself focused for a moment on how wonderful it was that Jilly had that much motion back.

"Who knows?" Jilly said. "Maybe it's some kind of a safety mechanism for the place itself. I imagine that if too many people believed in the dreamlands and realized how they can manipulate what they find there, the place would turn into total chaos."

"It already is in a lot of places."

Jilly smiled. "That's what Joe says when he's in teacher mode. And maybe that's another reason we find ourselves kind of denying the dreamlands. Maybe it's a safety mechanism put in place by our brains. You know how the old stories go—when you come back from fairyland, it's either as a poet or mad. I'd think our brains would be scared about the madness part."

"Left side, of course."

"Of course."

"Though that would mean that Wendy's already been there," Sophie said.

"She probably has—in dreams she can't remember. Joe says everybody spends some time there when they're asleep and dreaming, but most of us just accept it as part of the dreams that our brains come up with to amuse our sleeping minds."

"That's sounds like Joe."

Jilly smiled. "Pretty much a verbatim quote."

Sophie sighed. "But it doesn't answer why we find it hard to talk about our experience there as real. To just come out and say that the dreamlands themselves . . ." She found herself hesitating, still. "Are, you know. Real. Or why we can't find each other when we're there."

"So why do you think that is?" Jilly asked. "And don't you dare say it's because we're having different dreams or I'll smack you. Once I can smack people again, that is."

Sophie felt her heart go out to her friend. She couldn't begin to imagine how someone as active as Jilly was coping with all of this.

"I really don't know," she said. She fiddled with the end of Jilly's sheet, then lifted her gaze to Jilly's face. "I'm supposed to be checking up on you there, you know."

"Wendy?"

Sophie nodded. "Our resident poet is worried about you. She thinks you're just going away into the dreamlands forever."

Jilly looked past her, out the window. Her gaze took on a faraway gleam.

"If I could, I would," she said softly.

"What?"

"Not in dreams," Jilly said, her gaze returning to Sophie. "But like Joe does. Crossing the border in my body—being there in flesh and blood. If I could step across for real, I don't know that I'd ever come back."

"But . . . why? Are you so unhappy here? Or is it the magic thing?"

Jilly was forever talking about how she'd like to be magic. To live inside a story, instead of always standing on the outside of it. To know what magical beings did when they were just hanging out—and did they even hang out? What would it be *like* to be a part of that world?

"A bit of both," Jilly said. "Well, no. That's not really true because

I'm not really unhappy, per se. Or at least I wasn't before the accident. These days, just a smile can be a real challenge sometimes."

Sophie nodded, understanding.

"But I've always had this sense that there's something out there, waiting for me. Not here, in the World As It Is, but in the dreamlands. That there's a place for me in Faerie and I'll be there one day if I can just be good enough, or patient enough, or tenacious enough. Or . . ." She gave a small smile. "It's a place where I'd be home, really home. I want it so badly sometimes that just thinking about it hurts."

Sophie regarded her for a long moment.

"I . . . I never knew," she said finally. "You've never talked about anything like this before."

"And say what?" Jilly asked. "How do you even begin to explain this sort of thing without sounding crazy?"

Sophie gave her a look.

"Okay," Jilly said. "Even crazier than people already think I am."

"I didn't think that mattered to you."

"It doesn't. Not really. But this idea of a home waiting for me, somewhere in Faerie, it's so private and special that I couldn't bear to have anybody laughing about it."

"I'm not laughing."

"No," Jilly said. "And you're not even pretending that it's something that can't be true, either."

Sophie would have started to feel bad all over again, but she knew Jilly hadn't meant that as a recrimination.

"So," Jilly went on. "I've been wanting to compare notes with you."

Sophie could feel what was coming, and already her chest was starting to feel tight, her pulse quickening, but she was determined to fight the urge to close up. She was going to be completely open. Surprisingly, simply deciding that made the tension ease a little.

"Like what?" she asked.

"Well, do you have to actually think about crossing over when you're falling asleep, or do you just go there automatically?"

"I just close my eyes," Sophie said, "and I'm there—usually in the same place I was the night before. You know, wherever I was when I last left. If I want to start off somewhere else, I have to be concentrating on it when I fall asleep. You?"

"Pretty much the same, though it took me a while to get the hang of it. At first I just kept showing up in any random place—well, mostly Mabon and the Greatwood. But I was wondering, can you go to sleep and not cross over?"

Sophie slowly shook her head. "It doesn't seem to be something I choose to do. The only choice I get is where I end up, and even that doesn't work all the time."

"What if you could decide to stop it? To never cross over again. Would you do it?"

Sophie thought of the strange alternate life she had in the dreamlands, starting with the fact that her boyfriend only existed there, in Mabon.

"No," she said. "Of course not."

"But would you like to have the option to choose when you go and when you don't? Don't you ever get tired of always being awake?"

It did feel like that sometimes, Sophie thought. You were always awake. You closed your eyes here, and when you opened them a moment later, you were over there.

"Although it doesn't exactly feel like it," she said. "Does it feel like it to you?"

Jilly shook her head. "But then before the accident I never slept much anyway."

That was true. Before the accident Sophie had sometimes thought that Jilly never slept at all.

"I guess what I'm wondering," Jilly said, "is how we cope without sleeping. People are supposed to need their sleep to stay healthy."

"And dreams," Sophie said. "We're not having dreams, we're going someplace else that's just as real as here, except we're going in our sleep." She smiled. "Or maybe because our dreams are so true, that makes us superhealthy."

"Yeah, right," Jilly said, pointedly looking down at her broken body.

"That's not what I meant."

"I know."

"I thought of going to a sleep clinic once," Sophie said. "To let them measure my brain waves, or whatever it is they do in there, while I'm gone—into the dreamlands."

"I remember you talking about that. But you never went, did you?"

Sophie shook her head. "I got scared. What if they found something weird about me? Or what if they explained it all to me and by doing that, by knowing the physiology of how it works, I couldn't do it anymore?"

"Because of Jeck."

"I know it's pathetic to only have a boyfriend in the dreamlands, but it's better than not having one at all."

"I could have a boyfriend there, too," Jilly said. "Or I could have up until yesterday."

She told about her last trip there and what had happened with Toby while they were climbing the great tree, questing for these wizardly twigs.

"Mind you, he doesn't do it for me in that way," she said.

Sophie didn't say anything and they fell quiet for a time. Sophie had no idea where Jilly's thoughts were taking her, but Sophie's were worrying at that last thing Jilly had said, how this Toby Childers didn't really do it for her. In the long run, no one did it that way for Jilly, except for Geordie, and she often wondered if the feelings Jilly carried for him were able to survive only because they were unrequited. An actual relationship never worked out for Jilly and she'd long since given up on trying to find one. That was the legacy she carried from her old hurts—what had happened to her as a child and then her life on the streets.

Sophie wondered if she was all that much better. Her real world relationships never worked out either, though she didn't have the same issues to deal with. Being abandoned by your mother wasn't the same thing as spending the first decade and a half of your life being abused.

"So was that what you came to talk to me about?" Jilly said.

Sophie blinked, startled out of her reverie.

"How you're supposed to be checking up on me in the dreamlands?" Jilly added.

"Partly," Sophie began, but then she didn't quite know how to go on. This whole business with the doppelgänger was just too weird, if anything could be too weird considering how their conversation had been going so far.

"And then she stopped talking," Jilly said, "and everybody wondered where her mind had gone."

Sophie smiled. "It's just that I don't know how to explain this without sounding crazy."

"You see? It *is* all poets and mad people. No more dreamlands for you, m'dear."

"It's not a dreamlands thing," Sophie told her. "It's something from right here and now, in the World As It Is."

"Oh, do tell."

If Jilly hadn't been bedridden, Sophie knew she'd be leaning forward now, a gleam of anticipation in her eyes. The gleam at least was there.

"We've been seeing your double," Sophie said. "Or at least Isabelle and I have. One time for each of us."

She went on to explain and though it took a little effort, she didn't try to explain it away with any sort of logic. No more secrets between them, she vowed. No more denials.

"You're sure about this?" Jilly asked.

"I can't answer for Isabelle—although she's certainly sure—but I know what I saw. It might have been just a glance, but you know me."

"Ms. Takes-It-All-In."

"But I also know it can't have been you, unless . . . you can't travel back from the otherworld in your dreamland body, can you?"

"I don't think that's even possible," Jilly said. "I mean, then there'd be two of me, wouldn't there? And I certainly don't *remember* walking around on Yoors Street."

"Weird."

Jilly gave a tiny nod. "And kind of creepy."

They fell silent again. This time it was Sophie who spoke first.

"I think I know a way we can be together in the dreamlands," she said.

"How's that?"

"If we go to sleep together. Lying here on your bed, holding hands."

The gleam of anticipation was back in Jilly's eye.

"I'm game," she said.

Sophie laughed. "You're always game for anything."

"This is true. It's one of my many gifts. Even as the Broken Girl, I'm always ready and willing to go forth and be dazzled."

"It might not work," Sophie warned her.

"Oh, pooh. What have we got to lose?"

"Absolutely nothing."

With that she stretched out on the bed beside Jilly. They lay shoulder to shoulder. When Sophie took Jilly's hand in her own, Jilly gave her fingers a weak squeeze.

"Will you be able to go to sleep?" Sophie asked. "I mean, just like that?"

"It's the one thing I'm good at these days," Jilly told her.

Sophie wanted to argue that point, but instead she simply closed her eyes. She listened to Jilly's breathing even out and timed her own breathing to the same rhythm. A moment later she could feel the room fade away around her.

2

Once upon a time . . .

I guess I'm not really expecting it to work. After all these weeks of looking for Sophie in the dreamlands, this falling asleep together seems, I don't know, too obvious a solution. But it does work. I fall asleep in my room in the rehab and when I open my eyes, I'm in the dreamlands, lying on a bed of moss with Sophie, still holding hands. We turn our faces to each other, grinning. I laugh and give her a kiss on the nose, then bounce to my feet and dance around.

"We did it!" I sing. "We diddly-diddly-did it! Ain't life grand."

I try to do a little soft-shoe, but the moss soaks up the impact of my sneakers and they don't make a sound. Doesn't matter. I don't know how to tap dance anyway. So I do a spin instead, like I did when I was a little girl, before my life turned horrible, arms spread out wide, head thrown back.

But then I realize that Sophie's still lying there. And when I look at her, I see she's crying. I drop down to my knees on the moss beside her.

"What's the matter, Soph'? We're supposed to be in happy mode."

"It . . . it's just you're so you again."

For a long moment, I don't understand what she means. She sits up and lifts a hand to my cheek. But then I get it. I'm so used to being my old self, here in the dreamlands, I don't even think twice about it. But it's a shock for Sophie, who's only had the Broken Girl to relate to for all this time.

"And look at you," she says. "You look like you did when we first met in university."

I smile. "When we were uppity arts students who knew it all."

"You were never uppity," she says.

"Neither were you."

I remember Joe telling me once that when you dream yourself into the spiritworld, you come looking like you think you are—the way you see yourself—not necessarily the way you look back in the World As It Is. But I never really thought about it until now. No wonder Toby was coming on to me before he suddenly went walkabout away on me—he thought I was some spry little twenty-year-old. Which is what I am, I guess, when I'm here.

A lot of people talk about how they always feel—inside, I mean—like they're still a teenager, doesn't matter how old they really are, or how responsible they are in their lives. But my teenage years are closed up in that bad memories box, along with my years as a child, so it makes sense that my self-image is from my university years. That was the first time I felt that I could actually be someone. Be my own person. Act, instead of reacting.

Sophie looks younger, too, even younger than me. Eighteen, maybe, or nineteen.

"Have you ever looked in a mirror when you're over here?" I ask.

She smiles and nods. Her eyes are still glistening. Forget about the Broken Girl, I want to tell her. When we're here, she doesn't matter. But I don't have to. I think she's already doing it on her own. I think it's easier for her to just connect with the me that she knew before the accident, because she's known that me for so long, the Broken Girl only for a few weeks. Though she never looks away when she visits me.

"It's a kick, isn't it?" she says. "If we could bottle this and bring it back, we'd make a fortune."

"I can't tell what I look like," I say, running my hands through my hair. I did notice, right away, the first time I came, that when I'm here my hair's all grown back where it's only stubble on the Broken Girl. Then I never thought about it again.

"I need a mirror, I guess," I say.

"You look wonderful," Sophie assures me.

I hold out my hands, fingers spread. Though I haven't been near a paintbrush in weeks, I have bits of paint all over my hands.

"It's in your hair, too," Sophie tells me. "Just like always. Must be just—" She grins. "This gift you have."

"It's cheaper than nail polish."

"And ever so much more colorful."

I laugh with her.

"We *have* to get Wendy here, too," I say.

Sophie nods. "Wherever here is."

We stand up and look around ourselves. I don't recognize the place at all. It's a little like the Greatwood, but it feels older, even if the trees aren't as big. There's more undergrowth, too. The light's dimmer, the night side of twilight, and the air smells deep-wood mysterious. It's so quiet that I hear our breathing and I'm beginning to regret my little impromptu song-and-dance when we first arrived. There are a lot of dangerous places in the dreamlands, as Joe never gets tired of telling me. This place doesn't feel particularly dangerous as it stands. It's more like walking on the far side of some mystery, something old and resonant. But there's still the potential of danger in the air. My shenanigans might have brought us to the attention of who knows what kinds of nasties.

"Do you have any idea where we are?" I ask Sophie.

She shakes her head, which isn't exactly the reaction I was hoping for.

"It's no place I remember being before," she says. "I guess we should have been concentrating on where we wanted to end up before we went to sleep."

I can't explain my sudden uneasiness. I've never felt like this in all the times I've crossed over since the accident. But something definitely feels a-kilter here.

"Maybe we're on the outer reaches of the Greatwood," I say. "This place has that kind of feel to it—you know, like it's full of magic. Old."

"It reminds me a little of the fairy-tale world where I first met Jeck," Sophie says.

That's not encouraging to hear. Except for Jeck, the fairy-tale world is full of nasty haunts and quicks and goblins, not to mention the mercurial Granny Weather with her pet Baba Yaga shed that walks around on chicken legs. According to Sophie, Granny Weather can be your friend or turn you into a toad. It just depends on the mood she's in when you meet her.

"You don't think that's where we are, do you?" I say.

"Could be," Sophie says. "But don't be too worried. I mean, think of all the times you've told me you wanted to be in a story. Can't get more storyish than the fairy-tale world. Stories are all its made up of."

It takes me a moment to realize she's teasing.

But then I think of the professor's theory about how people need to be storied to get over their fears. Which I suppose includes those boxes of bad memories that I have stored in my head like an attic full of half-remembered shadows. Maybe being in the fairy-tale world wouldn't be such a bad thing. Maybe that's exactly what I need, to be re-storied, and not just from hearing a fairy tale, but from being in one.

"You've gone all serious," Sophie says. "You know I was joking, right? I really have no idea where we are."

I nod. "But I was just thinking how the fairy-tale world might not be such a bad place for me right now."

She gives me a quizzical look.

"You know," I say. "Because of what Joe was saying about how I need to deal with all my old hurts before I can really get past the new ones."

She gets it immediately. "You're thinking of all that stuff that the professor used to talk about—using fairy tales as templates for moral structure and dealing with problems and whatnot."

"Can you think of a better place to put them into practice?"

"Oh, please," Sophie says. "He meant it metaphorically. He believed that reading fairy tales lets you connect with the stories in your own life and can help you deal with problems you might be having. The operative word being 'reading.' He didn't mean that you had to literally be in a fairy tale."

"Except I'm such a literal girl," I say.

"You're a literal something," she tells me with a smile.

We might have gone on along those lines except we both hear it at the same time. What exactly, I'm not sure at first, but it's enough to make us stop and hold our breath, listening. Then we hear it again. There's something running through the undergrowth, the noise of its movement rising and falling. I can picture some largish animal, pushing through thickets, then across a soft carpet of moss and pine needles that swallows the sound of its passage, then the noise arising once more as it enters another stretch of undergrowth.

Faster than I would have thought possible, a small russet shape suddenly appears in front of us. We have a moment to register the human face—long and pointed features, but still human—on a fox's body, then the creature's gone again, the sound of its passage diminishing as quickly as it arose from its approach.

Sophie puts a hand on my arm. I look at her and we both have the same thought: something's chasing that man-faced fox and right now we're between the hunter and its prey.

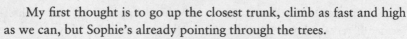

My first thought is to go up the closest trunk, climb as fast and high as we can, but Sophie's already pointing through the trees.

Wolves.

The lean gray shapes are almost invisible in the dim light, loping toward us, their own passage soundless for all that they're each at least four times the size of the little man-faced fox they're chasing. I count four, no five, no six of them. They become aware of us only moments after we spot them. I guess the wind's blowing from them to us and we've been standing here so silently that they simply didn't notice us until now, when they're almost upon us.

They stop in a half circle maybe twenty paces away. We're too late to try to escape by climbing a tree. I don't much relish the thought of turning my back to them while I try to scramble up. They'd be pulling us down before we got to the first branches which are far lower than those on the giants in the Greatwood.

"Maybe they won't attack us," Sophie says, her voice a whisper.

I nod, but I don't believe it and I doubt she does either. There's something very feral about these wolves and all I have to do is think about the terrified look on that little man-faced fox's face to understand that the pack means business.

One of the wolves breaks away from the others to approach us, stiff-legged, hackles rising. The pack leader, I decide from the way the others give way to her. I think it odd that the leader is a female, but as the others draw nearer, I see that they're all female. I look in the wolf's eyes and I'm shocked at the raw rage I see burning there. What's even more troubling is that I see a human mind behind those eyes. Someone's wearing that wolfskin and she hates me. Not me in a general sense, a member of the human race or whatever, but me personally, and that makes no bloody sense at all.

"I . . . I thought wolves didn't go after people," Sophie says from beside me, her voice still pitched low. I hear the quaver in it, recognize the fear because I'm tasting it, too. "Isn't that what all the environmental groups are always telling us?"

I have to clear my throat before I can speak, my gaze never leaving the wolf's.

"These aren't normal wolves," I say.

"Right. They're dreamland wolves."

"No," I say. "Look at them. There are people behind their eyes."

"So you're saying they're animal people—like out of Jack's stories? What does that mean for us?"

I almost don't hear her. I'm mesmerized by the pack leader. There's something about this wolf that's both familiar and scary all at the same time.

"We are so screwed," Sophie says.

I glance at her, return my gaze to the wolf's. "No, we're not. You always forget the most important thing when you're having your dream-land adventures."

"And that is . . . ?"

"We can always just wake up."

And as the pack starts to move closer, joining the leader, that's what we do. Or at least, I get Sophie to.

3

Sophie woke with a jerk, disoriented, her heart beating wildly in her chest. It took her a long, frightening moment to realize that the wolves were gone, that they'd left them behind in the dreamlands and they were safe now, here on Jilly's bed in the rehab.

"I do always forget that I can just wake up," she said as she turned to look at her friend.

Her voice trailed off. Jilly was still lying there, eyes closed. Asleep.

"Jilly!" she called, pitching her voice firm, but low enough to not attract attention from the nurses' station out in the hall.

She put her hand on the shoulder closest to her, the one that wasn't paralyzed, and gave Jilly a little shake.

"Jilly," she repeated. "Wake up!"

But there was no response.

4

I mean to go with Sophie, but there's something about that lead wolf that won't let me go. I need to understand it.

"You know me, don't you?" I tell the gray-furred creature with the human mind behind its eyes. "You know me and you really don't like me much."

The wolf makes no response, but it doesn't need to. That hatred's plain in its eyes.

Great, I think. Someone hates me enough in the World As It is to destroy all my faerie paintings—maybe they were even the same person who ran me down with their car. Maybe the accident was anything but. And now I've got someone in the body of a wolf, hating me here.

I guess I should be more scared than I am. But a kind of fatalistic indifference to danger has come over me. I don't just *want* to know who this is, what they've got against me. Why the mind behind those eyes seems so familiar. I *need* to know.

But then the wolf lunges at me and self-preservation takes over. I wake up and instantly I'm back in the rehab, in the body of the Broken Girl, with Sophie leaning over me, shaking me.

"Why didn't you come back with me?" Sophie is asking. "You had me scared to death."

I give a small nod, the most I can do here, in the World As It Is with the limitations of the Broken Girl's body.

"Jilly?" she says.

I finally focus on her.

"What happened back there? What kept you?"

"It was that wolf," I say finally. "She was so familiar."

Sophie gives me a blank look.

"She reminded me of my sister," I explain.

I realize it's true the moment the words come out of my mouth although this is the first time I've actually stopped to consider that. It's like some deep part of my subconscious has spit the information out between my lips and my brain's only catching up with it now.

"Your sister? But you haven't seen her . . ."

Sophie's voice trails off and she gets this awkward look. Not a whole lot of people know that whole story. What I did, the guilt I carry. But Sophie does. She probably knows all my secrets—even the ones I've never told her. It's her faerie blood, though she'd never admit to that. At least she wouldn't have before tonight. Who knows how she'd deal with it now that she's decided not to hide from the truth anymore.

"I know," I say. "It doesn't make any sense. What would she be doing in the dreamlands, running around like a wolf?"

"What even got you thinking about her?" Sophie asks.

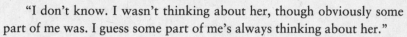

"I don't know. I wasn't thinking about her, though obviously some part of me was. I guess some part of me's always thinking about her."

"You were just a kid yourself," Sophie says. "There's nothing you could have done."

"Maybe."

It's true. I was just a kid. And then there was all that time I lived on the streets—a whole lifetime compressed into a few short years. It wasn't until I came out of the far side of all that pain and misery that I could even start to think about what I'd left behind in an old farmhouse in Tyson.

"But it would make sense," I say. "For her to still hate me after all these years."

Sophie just looks at me. I can see she's still struggling with the very idea of someone hating me. It's good to have such loyal friends. But she has no idea how bad it was in that house of my childhood, how leaving my sister behind was the most awful thing I could ever have done.

"You know," I add. "She looked just like me when I was her age."

"You mean . . . ?"

I nod. "My sister."

I can see it when understanding dawns for Sophie. This doesn't necessarily explain the wolf part, out there in the dreamlands, but it makes a good argument for what's been happening closer to home, here in the World As It Is. The hit-and-run. All those faerie paintings destroyed. Even the doppelgänger.

"We have to tell Lou," Sophie says, but I'm already shaking my head.

"I've been responsible for enough pain in her life," I say. "I won't add any more."

"You didn't hurt her."

I don't say anything. I've heard all the arguments before. From Angel. From Wendy and Sophie. From Geordie. They're very logical, and it all makes perfect sense, but it doesn't change what I did. Nothing can. Nothing ever will.

Interview

Extract from an interview with Jilly Coppercorn, conducted by Torrane Dunbar-Burns for *The Crowsea Arts Review*, at her Yoors Street studio, on Wednesday, April 17, 1991.

Any regrets? Anything you'd do over again, given the opportunity?
Not really. We are who we are because of our life experiences and I'm comfortable with who I am. I wish I'd never hurt anyone, but I never did so deliberately—which isn't an excuse, really, because we're responsible for all our actions, even the thoughtless ones—but at least it was never my intention to hurt anyone.

Can you give me an example?
I started running away from home when I was ten years old because life there wasn't just unbearable, but dangerous.

So what is it you regret about that?
I left my little sister behind. I was pretty messed up for years after running away. When I finally got my life back on track, I went back to make sure she was okay, but they'd moved, the house was empty, no forwarding address.

Over the years I've tried to find out what happened to her, but I've never had any luck. [Long pause.] Or maybe I just never tried hard enough.

Jilly

There's nothing worse than the things we leave undone. No matter how long ago it was we deserted those obligations, they find ways to return, again and again, nagging at us like intermittent toothaches, fermenting a bitter and depressing brew in the shadows of our minds that's one part guilt, one part shame. They sour pleasures and sow a discontent inside us that seems so far removed from its true source, we end up finding other things to blame, creating new problems to stack upon the old. And so we end up with this midden in our heads, hot coals smoldering deep inside the refuse, invisible, but no less dangerous for that. At any moment they could burst into flame, the subsequent conflagration utterly consuming the safe little world we've been pretending to live in for all this time.

And all our kindnesses would come undone . . .

ON THE ROAD NORTH OF NEWFORD, JUNE 1973

We've no money to speak of and we've borrowed this ratty old car of Christy's that doesn't look like it'll take us out of Crowsea, little say the city, but here we are anyway, Geordie and me, setting out for Tyson like newlyweds on their honeymoon; except we're not even a couple and what's waiting for us at the end of the trip is anything but fun.

We're still learning about each other as we head off on our road trip. We only met a few months ago, two part-timers hired at the post office to help deal with the Christmas rush. That doesn't happen now. Now the union's too strong and they don't bring in casual labor. Their members get the extra hours at time and a half, leaving the art students and street buskers like us to find other ways to augment their meager winter income.

I'm not even sure how Angel got me the job. Even back then there must have been some kind of security check and here's me, not even using my real name. Except Jilly Coppercorn is my real name now. I even have the documents to prove it and I have no idea where Angel got those either. I have a birth certificate and a social security number. I'm on the voter rolls.

"Don't ask," Angel told me when she handed me the envelope full of documents.

When I looked inside, I understood. And I didn't.

I guess that's another reason she and Lou must have broken up. The true-blue cop he is would never have been able to stand by while she was providing new identities for kids like me. He wouldn't understand how we couldn't bear the idea of ever being tracked down by our old families again. His solution would be by the book. If someone hassled you, call the police. That's what the police were for.

Except all of that just adds to the old pain. Better to be invisible. Better to disappear completely from who you were and be reinvented as a stranger that nobody from your past has ever known. Technically, it's breaking the law, yes. But ask any Children of the Secret, ask the abused wife in hiding, and they'll all tell you the same thing: better to break the law like this than be hurt again. Who knows what'll happen to you the next time? Who knows if you'll even survive? Too many don't.

But anyway, there I am at the post office last November. It's my first day and I stand in the doorway of the cafeteria with my bagged lunch in hand because there's no way I can actually afford to buy a lunch. I look around at all these people—good, solid, hardworking people, most of them—and all my own attempts at fitting in and making a new life for myself just disappear.

I feel like I'm this runaway junkie hooker again. That they'll look at me and see through the lie of what I'm pretending to be, see right through it to the truth of who I really am. Angel warned me when I first got off the street: the hardest thing would be trying to feel normal again. For some of us, it never happens.

I've been doing pretty good. Finished high school through an adult education program and I'm halfway through my first year at Butler U. as an arts major. I'm off the streets—living in a boardinghouse, it's true, but I'm paying my own way now, not scrounging a living from the goodwill of others. Angel's found me a sponsor to pay for my courses and books and art supplies. Everything else I pay for with waitressing, modeling for artists, and part-time jobs like this.

I'm saving up to get myself one of those run-down lofts on Lee Street, or Yoors. It'll be a studio and place to live, two in one. My own place. My own space. No more sharing bathrooms and kitchen facilities. No more coming downstairs in the morning to find that the small bag of groceries you managed to buy the day before has been used by somebody else. No more creeping in late at night, shoes in hand and holding your breath, hoping you don't wake the other boarders, because then the landlady will be on your case. Instead, I'll have a place where I can stretch and breathe, leave a work-in-progress on the easel, and if I don't feel like doing my dishes for three days, I don't have to. A place where I can play my music as loud as I want and actually have friends in for a visit or a party, anytime of the night or day.

These are the things that hundreds of other students are thinking about, right now, right across the country. It's normal. I can be normal, too.

Except the past still comes rearing up inside me—unbidden and certainly unwanted. Usually at times like this, when I'm facing a room full of strangers. You should have seen me in my first class at the beginning of the year. If it hadn't been for Sophie making friends with me while I was sitting on the floor in the hall outside the lecture hall, too scared to step through the door, I might never have gone in at all.

And the weirdest thing is, it catches me off guard. It always catches me off guard. The fear that somebody in this room could've been one of my johns. One of the women might have dropped a quarter in my grubby hand when I was panhandling. They might have seen me huddled in a doorway, shaking with the need for a fix, or stumbling down the street, high on some cocktail mix of alcohol and pills.

So I turn away and bump right into the only other person who looks as out of place here as I'm feeling. Geordie.

Let me describe Geordie Riddell at the time: he's all arms and legs, tall and gangly, with long, long brown hair and kind brown eyes and a big hurt inside him walled off from the world the same as I have, though that last thing I don't know yet. Or maybe I do, maybe I recognize a kindred spirit beyond the outward scruffiness we share, only the recognition is still working on a cellular, unconscious level. He's wearing raggedy bell-bottom blue jeans, a collarless, plain cotton Indian shirt with a tweed vest overtop, and desert boots that have salt rings from the slush outside.

Of course I'm no fashion plate myself. I've always been somewhat of a rake, albeit a small one, and baggy is my usual style choice. Today it's cotton trousers with ties at the ankles and tights underneath for the warmth. A long-sleeved jersey and a shapeless sweater that hangs down almost to my knees. Black cotton Chinese slippers, though I did wear boots for the walk to work, which are now stored in my locker along with a dark brown duffel coat.

We're like bag people in training. All we need is the shopping carts.

I've got my own reasons for wanting to look shapeless. As for Geordie, well, this was the early seventies, after all, so he was pretty much in style for the time. The sixties, really. When most people talk about the sixties, they really mean from about 1966 through to 1974. The early sixties had the Beats, but otherwise it was all ducktails and bobby-soxers.

But the one thing is, no matter how raggedy we look, our clothes are clean and so are we. After all those years of living on the street with grimy skin and crusty clothes, I've promised myself that I'll never have to live like that again. When I can't afford to go to the laundromat now, I wash my stuff in the bathtub at the boardinghouse and hang it up to dry on the backs of chairs and the like. Mind you, I can't seem to keep paint off my hands, or out of my hair for that matter, but at least it's clean paint.

Anyway, I bump into him and we do that fumble people do when they're both off balance, but being polite and not trying to grab at each other. Neither of us manages to fall, though I do drop my sandwich in its brown bag. Ever the gallant, Geordie picks it up and offers it to me.

"Thanks," I say.

I find myself considering his features. Now that I'm studying art and have started drawing and painting for real, I see everything in how it will translate into art. How the light falls, how lines and shading can define character. Geordie's features are strong rather than handsome, but I like that better than a pretty choirboy look. There's a shyness in his face, as well. When I meet his brother Christy later, I see it's a family trait, or at least one that the two of them share, though with Christy it comes off more as this distance he puts between himself and everything else.

With Geordie the shyness is coupled with this feeling of kindness and a good heart that draws people to him. I'm sure it's why he does so well when he's busking. People hear it in his music, stop to listen, see it in his eyes. He rarely comes away with an empty fiddlecase.

But I don't know any of that right now. All I know is that he seems safe. That the kindness I sense draws me to him. I find myself asking his name and after work we go for a coffee together.

We end up becoming pretty much inseparable, certainly during lunch breaks, but away from work as well. He becomes an honorary member of the close sisterhood I share with Sophie and Wendy—"our boy mascot," as Wendy put it once when he wasn't around.

I suppose people think we're a couple, but it isn't really like that. We never kiss, or even hold hands. We just hang together, and talk forever, about every and any thing. I realize now that he was simply too shy to make a romantic move—those Riddell boys are seriously bad at initiating an intimate relationship, or at least they were back then. But that suits me well because I don't want a boyfriend, though I do like having a friend that's a boy.

It's a novelty for me. Being with a guy I actually like, I mean. And being relaxed in his company because there's no pressure, no worry about things going any further, or getting complicated, or anything really. Until that day we borrow Christy's old clunker of a Chevrolet and start our trip to Tyson.

Geordie knows about my past, just as I know about his—in a general way, not all of the exact specifics. We didn't go through exactly the same thing by any means, but his wasn't even remotely a happy childhood either. The only thing he took away from his family was his father's old Czech fiddle and this awkward relationship with Christy that they were both determined to maintain.

The fiddle had been their grandfather's and once their father knew Geordie was interested in it, he'd locked it up in his tool chest, down in the basement of their house, just for meanness' sake. Geordie learned to play on a sixty-five-dollar fiddle he bought with money he'd earned doing chores for their neighbors. The day he left home for good, he broke into the tool chest and took his grandfather's fiddle with him. He was fifteen at the time and lived on the street for a lot of years before we met. He has an apartment up on Lees now, but he still spends more time on the street, busking, than he does at a regular job.

As for his relationship with his brother Christy, that's a kind of complication I don't understand. They like each other, anyone can tell, but they are forever pushing each other's buttons. The thing that drives Geordie craziest is how his brother has escaped into fairy tales, the way Geordie has into music. Christy collects the strange and odd things he hears on the street and weaves them into stories that are sometimes simply anecdotal, sometimes containing braids of traditional folklore and fairy tales as well. He isn't really selling them these days, but they appear from time to time in the Crowsea community newspaper and he's always happy to let you read the ones that haven't yet been published.

Naturally I'm delighted with these stories of his and I like him, too. That quirky way he has of looking at the world coincides perfectly with my own little worldview. But as I said, it drives Geordie crazy. Not the fact that Christy writes these stories, but that he believes in them. Utterly and completely.

I do, too, of course, though back then it's more wishful thinking on my part. It's another six years before I find the stone drum down in Old Town and find out for sure that magic is real. But I like to tease Geordie about magic and ghosts and faeries living in those places you can only see out of the corner of your eye. For some reason, he takes it better from me than he does his brother. Maybe it's because I don't push other buttons as well.

But that's where we are when he comes by the boardinghouse to pick me up, that old Chev coughing a blue cloud of exhaust as we pull away from the curb. It's a half day's drive to Tyson by the highway, but we have to go by the back roads since the Chev won't go over forty and with a missing headlight and no rear bumper, we'd just be asking to get stopped by the police if we took a busier road. That's saying we make it out of the city without getting stopped.

But we do.

Soon we're putt-putting along back roads, raising a cloud of dust, side panels flapping, feeling every bump on the road, our teeth chattering when we come to one of those washboard sections. After two hours of these country roads, we top a rise and the engine splutters, coughs, and then it just dies. The silence is almost a relief. Geordie gets out and pops the hood and then we both stare down at the greasy engine with its fine coating of dust.

"Do you know anything about cars?" I ask.

Geordie shakes his head. "No. Do you?"

"I can't even drive."

When we asked to borrow the car, Christy warned us that it might not even make it. "If it dies on you," he told us, "just take the plates off and leave it where it is."

That seems too strange. And besides, we're out in the middle of nowhere. I can't remember how far back the last farm we passed is and all that's ahead of us are the Kickaha Mountains, which, in this part of the country, are mostly wild and all reservation land, except for Tyson and the farms around it, though that's still a-ways off and to the east. The road we're on points straight north.

Geordie tries jiggling wires, cleaning the battery posts, wiping out the distributor cap, but nothing helps.

"I guess we walk," he says.

I grin at him. "Good thing we packed light."

We'd planned to stay overnight in Tyson at the very least, so we each have a little backpack with a change of clothes and some toiletries. Mine also has a sketchbook and some pencils and paints stuffed into it. Geordie has his fiddle with him. We have no food except for a bag of chips and some candy bars. Nothing to drink except for half a bottle of apple juice.

Borrowing my penknife, Geordie works loose the screws that hold the license plates and takes them off. The plates go into his pack and that's it. We're ready to go. We take a last look inside the car and in the trunk. There's a ratty old blanket in the back that I roll up and put under my arm. Geordie pats the hood of the car and then we set off, walking down the road.

"This is kind of nice," I say. "It's a beautiful day."

And it is. Blue skies, the June sun shining. Everything's in that in-between spring and deep summer stage—lots of fresh green pushing up through the old dead grass and weeds, whole squadrons of dandelions and other wildflowers adding splashes of color. Compared to the city, the air tastes like it's supercharged with oxygen and everything smells as fresh as a sweet Sunday morning, to quote a line from a song in the repertoire of one of Geordie's pickup bands. The temperature's balmy and there aren't even any bugs. It's still too early for deer flies and happily just past the black fly season, though if we're still out walking this evening, we'll certainly have mosquitoes to contend with.

Turns out mosquitoes are the least of our worries.

By the time the poor old abandoned Chev is two hills behind us and well out of sight, our brisk walk has slowed to an amble and threatens to simply come to a halt. It just feels like too nice a day to do anything more than laze about. All I want to do is lie on my back in one of the fields on either side of the road and stare up at the blue. Sketch, maybe, while Geordie plays a few tunes. I could sketch Geordie *playing* a tune.

I suggest we do just that as we reach the crest of yet another hill. Geordie shrugs. I guess he figures it's my road trip, so I can decide the agenda. He's just along for the ride. While we had a ride, that is.

I look ahead. The road drops into a valley below us before it starts to climb up the next hill once more. The forest is closer to the road here. The fields are spotted with scrub trees, outriders that will get swallowed by the forest as it marches a little closer to the road every year. I guess we're finally running out of old pastureland and getting into the reservation proper. The Indians only got militant about farmers running cows on their land a few years ago, so you still see sights like this all along the southern ranges of the rez—pastures returning to scrubland, then going completely wild.

"How much farther do you think it is?" Geordie asks.

"To what?" I say. "Tyson?"

He smiles. "Sure. Though I'm thinking more of a restaurant where we can grab something to eat. Or a motel for later. We're not exactly geared for overnight camping."

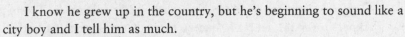

I know he grew up in the country, but he's beginning to sound like a city boy and I tell him as much.

"I know we can rough it if we have to," he starts to say, "but I'd rather sleep in a bed than a field, and eat in a restaurant instead of foraging for edible roots and . . ."

His voice trails off. I look to see what's distracted him and spy a plume of dust coming down the next hill. Squinting, I can see it's being kicked up by the wheels of a red pickup truck. Geordie perks up beside me.

"Hey, maybe we can catch a ride," he says. "They're going the wrong way, but if we can get back to the highway we can—"

But I'm grabbing his arm and pulling him toward the ditch. He follows a couple of steps, then stops and that makes me stop, too.

"Jilly," he starts, but I interrupt him.

"Come *on*," I tell him, tugging on his arm. "We don't want anybody to see us on this road before we've checked them out first."

I don't know if the occupants of the pickup have spotted us yet. All I know is I want to be gone before they do. Geordie didn't grow up in these hills, but I did. I know all the stories. Guys like my older brother liked nothing better than to go cruising along the edge of the rez, looking for Indians to harass. And if they couldn't find any Indians, a couple of hippies'd do just fine.

Now maybe that pickup's carrying no more than some old farmer or an Indian taking a back roads shortcut. But it's just as likely to be full of the kind of white trash I grew up with who'll want to have their idea of fun with us. A longhair like Geordie, they'll just beat up. Me, well, they won't beat me up. Or at least not right away. They'll have other things in mind first.

I could be wrong. I've been wrong before. But I'm not as trusting as people think I am. Sure, I see the best in people, but that doesn't mean it's really there.

"We have to *go*," I say.

And this time I give his arm a yank that pulls him off balance so that he has to take a few steps in my direction or fall down.

I hear the pickup's engine revving louder. Could be it's just to make the steeper grade. More likely, they've spotted us.

"Run!" I tell Geordie.

I scramble down into the ditch, then back up the other side. Tossing my backpack over the fence, I squeeze through the strands of barbed wire. Geordie hesitates a moment longer, still not understanding, but when he sees I'm serious, he follows. I grab his fiddle and lift the wire when he reaches me, making it easier for him to get through the fence.

"It's not hunting season," I say, "so they probably won't have serious hunting rifles with them. But you can die just as easily from a .22."

Geordie gives me a shocked look. "Oh, come on."

"Let's talk about it later, okay?"

"But—"

I ignore him and take off at a run through the field, dodging around the scrub trees. Glancing over my shoulder, I see he's following. I also see the pickup come to a skidding stop. Dust clouds around it, but I get a glimpse of a young hard face looking at us through the driver's side window. I have to look away or I'll run smack into some little tree, but I keep glancing back. Geordie's almost caught up to me. I look again and I see someone standing on the hood of the pickup. There's a glint of metal.

"Start weaving," I tell Geordie.

"What?"

But then he hears the crack of the rifle. Something goes whistling by us, far to the right. Now Geordie knows this is serious. He almost passes me.

"Puh . . . pace. Your. Self," I tell him, the words coming out in gasps.

I drop the blanket but don't go back to get it. There's another shot, also wide. This time it's on the left.

I don't think they're really trying to hit us. This is just a laugh for them, scare the shit out of a couple of hippies. But it's frightening all the same. Maybe they're not aiming right for us, but that doesn't mean they won't hit us. Doesn't mean they won't come over that barbed wire fence themselves and do a little hunting. And if they do catch up with us . . .

My friends complain that I'm fearless—the way I'll walk around by myself at night or won't back down from bullies—but that's not true at all. I get just as scared as anybody else in a situation like this. The difference, I guess, is that I no longer let my fear paralyze me. I've already been to the bottom, thanks to my brother, to my boyfriend-turned-pimp Rob, to the johns that got mean or violent, to the creeps on the street getting a laugh at beating up some screwed-up little junkie, to all those people who like to power-trip on those more helpless than them.

I'll stand up and face them now, because what else can they do to me that hasn't already been done? Kill me, I suppose, but I'm not afraid of dying. There were times in my life when death seemed a sweet promise, not something to fear.

No, I stand up to them all now, each and every one of them, because to do otherwise is to start the long spiral back down to the bottom and I'm never going there again. My panic attacks only really come from having to deal with ordinary people and they're centered around the shame of who and what I once was. It's something I can't quite shed, no matter how I try.

I guess the scariest thing is knowing that it could have gone either way. If Lou hadn't found me. If Angel hadn't sweet-talked me into one of her programs. If the professor hadn't been my sponsor. If Wendy hadn't rescued me from the crowds on frosh week and walked me through registration. If Sophie hadn't come to my rescue again on my first day of classes.

I made a choice to be where I am today, but I wouldn't have been able to do it without people like them.

When Lou first found me, I no longer even knew there was a choice anymore. But I got lucky. I got helped out of the darkness. And I did make the choice not to go back. And that led to the other choices by which I live my life: Not to back down. To help anybody I can. To find beauty in the unlikeliest places and show it to the rest of the world. That's why I paint what I do. Why I do the volunteer work that I do. Why I look for the best in people.

I'm not trying to build myself up here. I'm just trying to explain why I can seem fearless. Why I go out of my way to help others. I said that I made these choices, but the truth is I don't have any choice in those matters. To do or be otherwise would make me no better than the freaks and monsters who tried their damnedest to cut me down and keep me there. Every day I live—offering a smile, a kindness, a helping hand, a painting—is a day I've stolen from them. It's a day they can't have.

But there are times to stand up and there are times to cut and run. Out here, in the middle of nowhere like we are, there's no percentage in standing up against a bunch of yahoos, probably drunk, certainly armed, definitely with a mean streak running through them.

It's different here, in the hills. There isn't a cop on every corner. There's nobody you can turn to. Everything depends on your reputation.

Who you are, who you know. If you're from a certain family, a certain part of town, a certain holler, no one will mess with you. If you don't have the connection, then you become fair game. By the time the law gets called in—and it'll have to be you that does the calling, if you're even in enough shape to pick up a phone—it's all over, one way or another.

I'm not saying everyone's like that. Far from it. But if you get caught alone somewhere by the ones that are . . .

We're almost to the forest now. Once we get there, we'll be able to lose them if they decide to come chasing after us. But the forest presents its own set of problems. It's easy to get lost there—easier than you'd think.

They're still shooting at us. I can hear more than one rifle, but I can't tell if there's two or three. Some of the bullets are coming closer than I'd like. That's a laugh. Any bullet coming in your direction is too close for comfort.

Then we're in under the trees. A bullet hits a pine tree to my left, right between Geordie and I. It skids off the trunk, spraying bark over us. A wood chip catches me in the back of the head and for a moment I think I've been hit. By the time I realize I haven't, I've lost my balance and go tumbling to the ground, bumping into a tree trunk as I go down. Geordie turns when I fall and comes back to me, bends down. I've never seen his face so pale. He looks at me, back out to the field, down to me again.

"Are you okay?" he asks. "Were you hit?"

I've got a bruised shoulder from where I banged against the tree and I have to catch my breath, but basically I'm fine and give him a nod.

"Can you . . . see them?" I ask when I get my breath back and sit up.

He looks out between the trees again, starts to shake his head, then freezes. I follow his gaze and see them, in the field still and far enough away, but only for the moment. They seem to be arguing. We can hear the faint sound of their voices, but not what they're saying. I grab a hold of some scrub sapling and start to get up. Geordie helps me the rest of the way.

"If they decide to come after us," I tell him, "we have to go deeper."

He nods. "How did you even know they'd start shooting at us?"

"I didn't."

"But you had us running before we could even see who they were."

"I knew there was a possibility," I tell him. "That's all. I figured better safe than sorry."

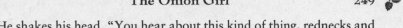

He shakes his head. "You hear about this kind of thing, rednecks and their guns and—"

"Don't call them that," I say. "They're just assholes. Most people you run into around here . . . well, maybe they won't like the length of your hair, but they'll keep their feelings to themselves."

"I was just—"

"I know. But saying 'redneck' is like saying 'blue-collar.' Like there's something wrong with people whose necks get red because they're outside working all day, or who don't wear a nice white shirt and tie because they're a plumber, or a mechanic, or they work in a factory. It bugs me."

"But you're always telling me how you grew up white trash."

I smile. "It's different when I'm talking about myself. And besides. We *were* trash."

He starts to smile back, except we catch movement out in the field. Whoever was arguing to go back to the truck must've lost.

"Come on," I tell Geordie, grabbing his hand. "We've got to go deeper. But stick close. If we're going to get lost, I'd rather get lost together."

He gives me an unhappy look, but I just shrug and start off at a trot, trying my best not to leave too much of a trail. You know, no broken branches, try not to kick the mushrooms or leave scuffs in the grass. I don't know what I'm doing, really. I spent a lot of time in the woods when I was growing up, but I wasn't Daniel Boone or some Indian scout, and I had no reason to hide my presence. I can only hope that those boys out there aren't trackers.

Happily, the land dips and rises so by the time they reach the forest, we're well out of sight, up on the far side of a ridge I spotted when we first stepped under the canopy ourselves. We come across a game trail on the ridge and I get an idea.

"Can you climb a tree?" I ask Geordie.

He gives me a disgusted look. "What do you mean, can I climb? I grew up in the country. Not the country around here like you did, but we did have trees."

"Okay, okay. So start already."

I point to one of the pines up here on the ridge. Because they get better light than the ones on the slopes below, their lower branches are more filled out. If we can get high enough, you'd have to really be looking up to find us. I'm guessing these boys won't do that much.

"My fiddle," Geordie says. "I can't leave my fiddle."

"Loop the handle through your belt," I suggest.

He nods and does, starting up the tree when he's done, the fiddlecase banging against the back of his thigh. I take my sketchbook out of my backpack and stick it down the back of my jeans so that my own hands will be free. My little tin of paints is flat and can fit into my pocket. I toss the pack onto the game trail where it runs down the other side of the ridge. The pack goes rolling down the incline and I check to make sure it's visible before I pull myself up that broken off branch and start to climb as well.

Maybe Geordie can climb, but I soon pass him, sticking out my tongue as I go by. I don't know why, but the tightness is leaving my chest. I just don't feel so scared anymore. I guess it's because we're actually doing something, instead of running like a pair of startled deer.

We're pretty high up and I can't see the ground easily anymore through the thick cover of branches, when I hear them coming. Geordie and I freeze. I hug the trunk, then grimace as I realize I've put my face against a gooey stream of pine sap. When I pull my face away, my hair's still stuck. Great. This is going to take forever to clean out. But that could be the least of our worries.

My fear comes rushing back, a sharp adrenaline rush that makes it hard to breathe again. I look down at Geordie a branch below me. When he lifts his gaze to mine I see my own fear mirrored in his eyes.

"Fer Christ's sake, Roy," says one of the boys.

And they are just boys, I realize from what I can see of them. Nineteen, twenty tops. Greasy-haired, T-shirted trailer trash. I should know. I as much as grew up with their kind.

"You plannin' to tramp right up the mountain after 'em?" he goes on.

"Hell, no," the one called Roy responds. He horks up a wad of phlegm and spits it out. "I'm just havin' me some fun."

"Hey, lookit," a third voice says. "There's somethin' down on that game trail."

I hear them move off the ridge and almost lose my grip and fall out of the tree when they start shooting again. It takes me a heart-stopping moment to realize that they're not shooting at us, but my knapsack. When the gunfire stops, the three of them start to laugh.

"Well, that's one backpack ain't gonna cause us no more trouble," one of them says.

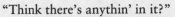

"Think there's anythin' in it?"

"It's all shot to hell if'n there was. 'Sides, who wants to touch that shit an' get hippie cooties?"

"Fuckin' hippies. You cain't tell the boys from the girls."

"Sure you can. The girls got their titties all floppin' loose under their shirts."

"Well, I ain't haulin' my ass after them boys."

"Maybe they're girls."

"Naw. Girls cain't run like that pair done. They'd just fall down an' start in a-cryin'."

"Man, they was like rabbits, the way they went tearin' across that field."

"Bet they pissed their pants."

More laughter. So witty. Just like my brothers were. You wonder how they ever survive to grow up to be men when they start off with such little brains.

Their voices have been getting louder as they come back up the ridge. They stop to light cigarettes and the smell of the tobacco comes drifting up to where we're hidden.

"What the hell do you think they was doin' out here?"

"Who knows? Who the fuck cares?"

"Bet they was gettin' back to the land."

"Or blowin' each other."

"I'd like to see 'em blow the end of my rifle."

"Your rifle gets more 'n you."

"Fuck you, Thompson."

"Fuck yourself."

The voices begin to fade as they wander back to the field. Geordie looks up at me, but I shake my head. Not yet, I mouth. I want them to be good and far away before we start back down and maybe make some noise that would bring them back again. So we wait, butts getting sore from our awkward perches, arms and legs cramping. We don't start back down until we hear the pickup starting up, a dull coughing engine sound that carries clearly in the still air.

We're all wobbly when we're finally on the ground—as much from the adrenaline rush leaving us as from cramping muscles.

"When they started shooting," Geordie says, "I almost did pee my pants."

"Me, too."

Once my legs stop feeling so wobbly, I go over to my knapsack, but it's pretty much beyond salvage. So much for a change of clothes and my toiletries. I manage to scavenge my toothbrush and some underwear that have bullet holes in them, but otherwise are wearable.

"So now what?" Geordie asks.

I look down the game trail, picking at the pine sap that's gumming up my hair. All I manage to do is make my fingers sticky. I wipe them off on my jeans without a whole lot of success.

"I don't think we should go back to the road," I tell him. "At least not for a while."

"You think they'll wait around?"

I shake my head. "But it's a long stretch of road and they'll probably cruise up and down it for a while. I think we should try going cross-country. How's your sense of direction?"

"Not as good as Christy's. You can put him down anywhere and it's like he has this compass in his head."

"Mine's pretty good, too," I tell him. "I know we're southwest of Tyson right now, so it's just a matter of keeping track of the sun and steering ourselves in the right direction."

Geordie gives me a dubious look.

"Do you want to chance another encounter with Roy and Thompson and whatever that other idiot's name was?"

"When you put it like that . . ."

This tramp through the woods would be much more pleasant if we hadn't been driven to it by that bunch of yahoos. Although I know they're long gone, I can't help starting every time a squirrel runs through some dry leaves, or a jay gives us a sudden scolding. Geordie still has trouble believing it even happened and can't stop talking about those three morons—". . . just shooting at us like that. Maybe they were only kidding around, but they could kill someone . . ."

Like it'd matter to them, I think, but all I do is nod in agreement as he goes on. Just because I grew up with guys like that doesn't mean the bizarre makeup of what passes for their brains makes any sense to me either.

We've finished the apple juice and eaten one of the chocolate bars by the time we reach the stream. I rinse out the juice container and fill it up with water.

"Are you sure that'll be drinkable?" Geordie asks.

"No, but what's our choice? Besides, it's coming down from the mountains. The most we'll have to worry about is squirrel poop."

I take a long drink, then pretend to retch. Geordie steps forward, features full of concern, then he whacks me on my shoulder when I grin at him. He finishes the water in the juice container and then we fill it again.

Neither of us have a watch, but by the height of the sun I figure it must be past six. It'll start to get dark soon. I don't say anything as we keep walking along the trail, but I'm not planning to keep walking once it gets dark. It's easy enough to get turned around in these hills in the daytime. There's no way I'll take the chance at night.

The mosquitoes come as the light starts to leak from the sky. They don't bother me, but they're driving Geordie crazy.

"Stop swatting at them," I tell him. "That just eggs them on."

"If I stop swatting them, they'll suck every drop of blood out of me," he says, squishing another that was on his temple. He gives the bloody goop between his fingers a disgusted look. "How come they don't bite you?"

"It's just this gift I have. My blood's not appealing to either biting bugs or creatures of the night."

"Right."

"Actually," I tell him. "That's not entirely true. My real gift is that whenever I'm around bugs, I always manage to be with someone who tastes better than I do."

Happily, just as the twilight begins to really deepen, when Geordie's going completely mad from the bugs and I'm seriously looking for a place to camp out, we come up over a ridge and find somebody's hunt camp. It's no more than a one-room cabin, log walls, with a flat tin roof that overhangs a woodpile, but it'll do us just fine. For one thing it's got shutters on the window and a door that closes. We can leave the bugs outside.

Geordie gives it a dubious look.

"What if whoever owns it shows up?" he asks.

I know he's thinking about the yahoos that chased us into the woods in the first place.

"It's not hunting season," I tell him. "And look around. Nobody except for mice have been here in ages."

We sweep it out, find blankets in a tin-lined chest, get a fire started in the cast-iron woodstove. With a candle burning on the windowsill, it's actually cozy. Geordie finds some cans of brown beans, stew, and soup in the cupboard and we make a supper of the beans and some vegetable soup. We leave a couple of dollars on the shelf to pay for what we've used. In the morning I plan to go out and scavenge some kindling to replenish the box beside the woodpile. It's just common politeness.

I guess this is the night that something romantic could have started between us, but we get to telling war stories about our family life, going into more detail than we ever have before about how we ended up on the streets and the kinds of things we had to do to survive, and I guess that kind of puts a damper on any ardor the situation might have otherwise generated. I mean, it's about as intimate as you can get, sitting together on the bed, heads leaning against each other's on the backboard as we talk, and it certainly cements the fact that we're going to be best friends pretty much forever, but when we've finally dismantled those walls we've both got there inside us to keep the rest of the world at bay, there's not a whole lot left over to start thinking about boyfriend/girlfriend stuff.

The truth is, I'm years from actually being able to have a physical relationship with a guy, and I still can't maintain one. And I guess Geordie sensed that. Or maybe I'm just not his type. As the years go by I see that whenever he does fall for someone, she's usually tall and gorgeous. Though at one point my looks come into the conversation, I can't remember quite how, and he just shakes his head at how I feel about the way I look.

"I don't know where you get that idea," he says. "You're beautiful."

"Right. In a scare-the-children kind of way."

"You can't tell me a guy's never told you that before."

"Sure," I say. "Just before they come. They only ever want one thing."

Geordie sighs. "Maybe a lot of guys do," he says. "But not all of them. Some want the rest of the package, too."

"Well, I've never met one of them."

I'm not looking at him, and with just the candle across the room on the windowsill, there's not much light to judge reactions anyway. But years later I find myself coming back to this conversation, wondering if there was hurt in his eyes. Wondering if he'd have said more if he wasn't carrying around his own baggage. Sophie once told me that the only reason he goes for girls who are so different from me is that he can't have me.

"I'm sure," I told her.

"Oh, it's nothing he'd even know himself," she said. "It's a subconscious thing. But I can tell."

"Because of your faerie blood."

She pulled a face. "No. Because I have eyes to see and I know the both of you so well."

But I didn't consider it then, and since I'm the Broken Girl and he's got a whole other life with Tanya, it's too late for it now.

In the morning, we have the rest of the beans for breakfast, spooning them up with our chips. Too late we realize that now we might not have anything to eat later in the day. We don't have anything to open the cans with and it really wouldn't be right to take the can opener from this hunt camp. My penknife hasn't got a strong enough blade to work as a makeshift one, and Geordie doesn't even have a pocketknife, but we end up taking a can of stew and another one of the brown beans anyway, figuring we'll worry about how to open them when the time comes.

We leave more money for the food we're taking and put in a good load of kindling before we go. When we're out looking for the kindling, we find another stream in back of the cabin and use it to wash up and rinse out the cans we used. I'm able to get the worst of the pine sap out of my hair, though it could still use a good shampooing. And then we're tramping through the woods again.

It's overcast today and a little cooler, but the temperature's still pleasant and it makes the hike more comfortable, except that there are still mosquitoes here under the trees—I guess the cloudy skies make them think it's dinnertime. Though there aren't as many as there were last night and walking briskly keeps them from being too much of a bother, Geordie's still flapping his hand around his head. It's a good thing they weren't in the trees yesterday. He'd probably have fallen off his branch while swatting at them.

The trail leaving the hunt camp is more defined than the one we took to get to it, and after an hour or so the tall pines start to give way to cedars, aspen, birch, and other less easily recognized scrub trees. When we come to what must be a parking spot for whoever owns the hunt camp—a rough rectangle of cleared ground—the trail becomes a track, two ruts with a grassy hump in the middle that runs off in the distance.

We follow it for another twenty minutes, finally coming to a gate, with a gravel road on the other side of it. Geordie grins at me.

"We're not lost," he says.

"At least not in the bush."

"Well, I'm impressed. If I'd been leading the way, we'd still be wandering in circles. You weren't kidding when you said you had a great sense of direction."

I give him a little curtsy. "It's just this gift I have, kind sir."

I climb over the gate, then take Geordie's fiddlecase from him so he can follow. We look up and down the road. The skies have gotten more overcast, making it impossible to place the sun, but I can feel a tug pulling me to the right. I really do have this gift when it comes to finding my way around, even if I've never been somewhere before.

"That way," I say.

Geordie smiles. "That's what I was going to say."

"Yeah, right," I tell him, handing back his fiddlecase. "Are you hungry?"

"A little."

"Enough to try to hammer our way into one of those cans?"

"Not yet."

I lead us down the road to the left.

"Now if we hear an engine—" I start.

"I'll be over that fence and into the bush before you can say 'The De'il's Run Away wi' the Excise Man.' "

I laugh. "I'll *never* be saying that. I can't even remember it."

A misting rain starts up an hour or so later, but it doesn't wreck our mood. We were already friends before the walls came down and we let each other all the way into our heads. The closeness we're feeling now doesn't feel like it'll ever go away. When we get back to Newford, I insist to Sophie and Wendy that we make him an honorary member of our gang of small fierce women instead of our token boy mascot.

Geordie pulls a jersey and a jacket out of his knapsack and offers me my choice. I take the jersey and he puts on the jacket. With moisture clouding our hair and leaving a cool damp layer on our faces, we continue to follow the road until, topping another rise, we see the outskirts of Tyson below us. Five hundred yards ahead, the gravel road joins an asphalt one, but we don't have to follow it down. I know where we are now. Right below us is Hillbilly Holler, the white trash part of Tyson where I grew up. I know how to get down to it through the fields and woods.

"You okay?" Geordie asks.

I turn to him, then look back down the hillside. I can't begin to describe the conflicting emotions that are coursing through me, but okay doesn't describe any of them.

"Not really," I admit, where I wouldn't have before. "But we've come this far, so we might as well finish it."

He doesn't say anything, just reaches out and lays a hand on my shoulder, gives it a squeeze. I offer him a little smile in return and then we set off again.

Tyson, June

I'm not really sure what I was expecting. That everything would be the same, I guess. But of course nothing is, and how could it have been?

The first inkling I get is when we come up through the fields behind the house and I see that my old tree's gone. All that's left of that huge old friendly monster is a blackened and charred stump. What wood remains is rotted and covered in fungus and ants. I remember how, even as a little kid, I used to sneak out of the house, day or night, whenever I needed to escape, and I'd just lie under that tree, staring up through its boughs.

I knew everybody who lived in its branches. The moths sleeping away the day, almost invisible against the bark, and the line of ants that were always marching up or down the trunk. The constant rivalry between the red squirrels and chipmunks. The old crow that used to visit it every afternoon and the jays that would scold me when I approached. Wrens and sparrows were constantly flitting from branch to branch. Sometimes there would be a raccoon, watching me from the lower branches.

I'd follow their various adventures the way other people follow soap operas, making up stories about why they did the things they did. And at night I'd find the stars through its branches and pretend they were faerie, or at least faerie lights.

A long time ago, some farmer cleared all this land for pasture. But he spared that tree. Probably it was already big at that time, had lived a communal life with all its brothers and sisters in the forest for decades. Then it had this new life, overlooking the pasture, providing shade for the cattle and something for them to rub up against to ease an itch. The cows went, the farmer probably lost his land to the bank, and slowly the forest started to reclaim the cleared land, which is how things were when the lost little girl I was came out to find comfort under the spread of its branches. I don't know if I could have survived my childhood without the friendship of that tree.

All gone now. Tree. Little girl.

I guess I've been standing here forever, looking at the blackened stump. I hear Geordie clear his throat and the sound makes me blink. I feel like I've come out of a dream.

"You okay?" he asks.

I figure this is going to be the echoing question of the day.

"This was my friend," I tell him, pointing at the stump. "Probably the only real friend I had when I was growing up."

Stuff goes on behind his eyes, it's hard to tell exactly what. Sympathy for the kid I was. His own unhappy memories. Probably both. He nods but doesn't say anything.

The misting rain has eased off, but it's still overcast. I look past the stump and feel my chest go tight when I see the back of the house. It hasn't changed at all, except it looks a little more worn-out than I remember it. I can see my window—there still aren't any curtains on it. As we get closer, I realize it's not because whoever's living here now is as poor as we were, but because the place is deserted. The lawn in the back-yard is overgrown—if you can call that tangle of weeds a lawn—and everything has an abandoned look about it.

We walk by the outhouse. The door's on an angle, hanging off one hinge.

"Did you really have to use that?" Geordie asks.

I nod. "We didn't have indoor plumbing except for a hand pump in the kitchen. Of course the outhouse was in better shape when I was living here."

But not by much.

I realize that, in many ways, the house and yard haven't changed much at all. This was always a shabby, unkempt place, with junked cars in the front yard, an old fridge, machinery debris and other rubbish in the back. Inside there was cheap, hand-me-down furniture. What we weren't given, we got out of the trash.

My parents never believed in more than the most basic upkeep, and that was done by us kids under their vague direction, and usually as a punishment—at least for the boys. I cleaned inside the house and did yardwork because I couldn't stand to live the way we would if I didn't. But mostly, it was a way for me to forget my terrors—burying them under fierce bouts of sweeping and cleaning and weeding.

The real difference I sense here now is a lack of menace, and isn't that a sad thing to realize?

"How could I have left her here?" I say, my voice a bare mumble.

Geordie touches my arm but I hardly feel the contact. I'm overwhelmed by despair for my little sister. That I left her in this place of horror. That I fled for safety with no thought as to what would happen to her, left behind and abandoned by her only protector. I'm as much of a monster as my oldest brother Del.

Where is she now?

I'm not going to find the answer here. I don't know what ever made me think I would. This place has obviously been deserted for months, even years perhaps. Maybe as soon as I ran away that last time, they just upped and moved themselves. Certainly no one lives here now.

But we proceed anyway, step onto the lawn and wind our way in between the hulks of rusting machinery until we get to the back of the house, the tall wet grass and weeds making our pants wet up to our knees. The screening's all torn out and hanging loose. The window in the back door is broken.

"Do you want to go in?" Geordie asks.

I shake my head, not trusting myself to speak. I know the place has been abandoned, and I don't sense the menace that was a part of my daily life here when I was growing up, but I'm terrified all the same. Of what, I can't exactly explain. Ghosts, I suppose. Not of people dead, but of the people we were. My family. Myself. I'm eight years old again, coming home, scared that there'll be no one there except for my brother.

It doesn't matter that I'm not alone or eight years old anymore. Or that the house is empty. My brain knows all of that. But my heart doesn't.

Instead of going in, I lead the way around to the front. Once upon a time somebody loved this house. I know that because of the remains of flower beds and gardens that I could find when I was a child. I tried to nourish them, but there's not much left now. Raggedy tulip foliage topped by dead flower heads that should have been cut off back in May after they'd bloomed. A few hardy perennials are still present, but obviously losing their struggle with the weeds. Irises and lilies. Some lavender. And then there's the rosebush that used to grow alongside the porch by the front door. It was already a feral tangle of thorns and small blossoms when I was living here. Now it's spread across the top of the porch and growing up the whole side of the house, a Sleeping Beauty thicket that might one day swallow the house like kudzu.

I look across the Old Grange Road to Margaret Sweeney's house. She's always hated my family. I guess it was because we were the most direct representation of the white trash that moved into these houses that got built on what used to be her family farm. Her home was the original farmhouse, pretty much as run-down now as any of the other structures in what the local people call Hillbilly Holler, except, for all its worn and frayed edges, you can tell that it's a house somebody still loves. The yard's tidy, the lawn is cut, the garden beds are weeded and full of flowers. The house might need paint and repairs, but the windows gleam, showing the pretty curtains hanging on the other side of the glass. And there aren't junked cars and trash all over the front yard.

When I look at how she's struggled to keep up the place, I can understand her animosity without even trying. I guess I always did.

Her husband died working in the fields. She tried to raise the family on her own, but had to sell off almost all the land to be able to just keep the house. Her children all moved away as soon as they were old enough to leave. What must it have been like to lose her family, her farm, to watch it all get taken over by trailer trash and the like?

I don't want to talk to her. I don't want to see the look in her eyes when she realizes who I am, because that'll just bring the past back all that much stronger. The last thing I need to feel right now is that I never changed, that I'm always going to be the kid whose brother abused her, who lived in a house full of losers, who was only ever really loved by one person, her little sister, but she went and abandoned her.

But I don't see that I have any other choice. If we go to the other houses, either no one's going to talk to us, or they're going to have them some fun like those boys back in the woods tried to have.

"I'm going to ask Mrs. Sweeney if she knows where they all went," I tell Geordie. "She lives just across the street."

"You don't sound too happy about talking to her."

Right now, I don't even know what happy means. It feels like the last time I was happy was the last time I shot up, but I know that isn't true. Junk doesn't bring happiness. All it brings is temporary oblivion. It just seems like happiness because the sick feeling that sits inside your gut has been eased.

"She never much liked any of us," I say.

"I've had neighbors like that."

"Except they were probably just pills. Mrs. Sweeney's a wonderful woman. We were the ones that brought down the neighborhood."

"She's got an Irish name," Geordie says. "Maybe we can sweeten her mood with a couple of tunes on the fiddle."

I think about Mrs. Sweeney, trying to remember if I ever noticed anything that gave her any pleasure.

"I'll give you the nod if it seems like a good idea," I tell him.

As we cross the dirt road separating the two houses, I can feel a weight lifting from my shoulders and I start to breathe normally again. I'm still nervous about meeting Mrs. Sweeney after all these years, but even that isn't enough to take away the relief I feel at leaving the old house behind. I start to lose my nerve again once we're up on her porch, but Geordie's a half step ahead of me and just presses the bell. I find myself holding my breath again as we hear movement inside. And then Mrs. Sweeney's there, looking older than I remember—but of course she is older. It's been over ten years since I ran away from my last foster home, longer since I've been here.

She's got a hill woman's strong features—character they used to call it. The skin's pulled tight against her bones, gray hair up in a loose bun, dark eyes not hiding their suspicion as she looks us over. She comes from stock that farmed these rocky slopes for generations, a woman who withstood heartbreak and sorrow and still carries on.

I never realized it until this moment, but I think maybe she was an inspiration to me, however subconsciously, when I finally came crawling out of my own dark years. No matter what the darkness threw at her, she never gave in.

She comes out onto the porch and looks us over, silent and formidable, and any words I might have had dry right up inside me. Geordie glances at me, then back at her, gives her a bright smile.

"Sorry to trouble you, ma'am," he says. "We were just wondering if you could tell us what happened to the family that used to live across the road."

"Why?" she asks. "Are you kin?"

Geordie pauses for a moment and I finally manage to speak up.

"I am," I tell her.

That earns me a sharper look. She studies me for a long moment, before finally nodding. Her eyes soften a little.

"You've got the Carter blood all right," she says. "You'll be the older girl—Jillian May."

I nod.

"I remember you at least tried to keep the place up before you got the good common sense to run away."

That surprises me. Her voice almost seems to hold some respect for me.

"So what brings you back to this sorry place?" she adds.

"I'm looking for my little sister."

"Took your time, didn't you?"

I almost lose it, right there and then, but I swallow, and nod again.

"I know," I tell her. "But my own life was a mess and . . . I've just been thinking about her a lot lately."

She considers that for a moment, then glances at Geordie.

"This your boyfriend?" she asks.

He could have been, I think, except after last night we moved to a different kind of closeness and I don't know if the one excludes the other. It's too early to tell how it will all work out.

"He's my friend," I say and I introduce him to her. "About my sister . . . ?"

"You look a little worn-down," she says. "The pair of you. Come in and have some iced tea and we'll talk."

Opening the screen door, she ushers us inside.

For an old woman who distanced herself from her trashy neighbors the way Mrs. Sweeney always did, she turns out to know an awful lot about our private lives. Sitting in her kitchen, drinking iced tea and eating the cheese sandwiches she makes for us, we hear the whole sorry story of my family—or at least up until the last of them moved away.

It's funny how, when you leave home, you expect everything to stand still while you're gone. Not when you think about it, of course, but sub-consciously that idea's still sitting there in the back of your head. Or at least it was in mine. But life goes on for those you left behind, the same as it does for you, and it's only when you return that the shock of it hits you. Everything's changed.

I already knew from the empty house we found sitting cross the road from Mrs. Sweeney's place that things had changed, but it isn't until she starts to tell me what happened to my family that the truth of it hits home. I listen to what she has to say with a growing numbness.

There's the litany of my brothers' arrests—it turns out Del wasn't the only bad apple in the family. His was only the most bitter fruit in our sorry little orchard.

Raylene left home, but instead of following in my footsteps, she waited until school was done. No one knew where she'd gone, just that she was with Pinky Miller. "I heard they moved into a boardinghouse in Stokesville," Mrs. Sweeney says when I ask for more, "but that didn't last. Those girls always wanted more. Then the word was they moved into Tyson proper, but I've no idea how they were making a living. Could be they followed your lead and upped and gone themselves.

"It wouldn't surprise me none if they ended up on one or the other of the coasts—New York City or Hollywood. They had those stars in their eyes, leastwise Pinky Miller always did. Hard to tell what your sister ever wanted, or what she was thinking."

"So you don't know where she is?"

Mrs. Sweeney shook her head. "The last time I saw her was 'bout a month ago, standing there in the middle of the road with her friend Pinky, just looking at that old house for a time. Like she was saying good-bye, maybe."

Our father was dead. Of a stroke. He died in March, just three months ago.

Jimmy was dead, too, gunned down in a fight only a week or so after our father had died.

No one knew what had happened to Robbie.

Del ended up in prison—no surprise there—and our mother moved near the penitentiary to be close to him.

"Is he still in jail?" I ask.

Mrs. Sweeney gives me a nod.

"But he won't be troubling you for a whiles," she says.

I look at her, wondering how much she knows about what went on in that house across the road from hers. And if she did know, why didn't she do something? Would an anonymous call to the police have been that hard to make? But I realize I'm being unfair. There's no such thing as anonymity, not in a community this small and when you're on a party line as we all were. She had her own family's safety to keep in mind. Considering what she knew about my brother, she would have been afraid that he'd burn her house down, with her in it.

"What put him in prison?" I ask.

"Drunk driving. He killed a little girl out walking along the highway one evening, then just took off without a never-you-mind. Left her to die in the ditch like some old 'possum or fox. Only reason they caught him is Butch Stiles—you remember him?"

I nod. Butch Stiles was a war vet who lived back in the woods with a Korean woman he'd brought back with him when the war was done.

"Well, he was out with his dogs that night and saw the whole thing. Told me he pretty near put a bullet through the head of that brother of yours, but he went to see to the girl instead. He was too late to help that poor child, but not too late to make sure some kind of justice was done."

"He's no brother of mine," I say.

Mrs. Sweeney studies me for a long moment. I glance at Geordie to see what he thinks of all of this, but he just gives me a sympathetic look. Then I remember his own brother—Paddy, the oldest one, not Christy—ended up in prison, too. Unhappiness can run through a family like a fever that won't quit.

"You know," Mrs. Sweeney finally says, "I've kin back in Virginia and Tennessee."

I nod to show I'm listening. Right then I don't quite know where she's going with this.

"Lot of Carters out that way," she says.

"I don't understand."

"I just want you to know that every family's got its bad apples. Most Carters I've met, they're good, decent folk."

"I'm not a Carter anymore."

She shakes her head. "Changing your name doesn't change where you come from, Jillian May Carter. You've got to know that your branch of the family tree took it a wrong turn is all. Wasn't your fault. But now I figure maybe it's your job to set it right again."

I don't know if something like that can ever be set right, but I don't say anything. It's not an argument I want to get into. What Del did to me isn't something that gets mended with words or good intentions. And I sure don't have a warm spot in my heart for the rest of my family, standing by on the sidelines the way they did when all I knew was hurt. There was only Raylene, and she didn't know what was going on. Sweet little Raylene.

"I'm not trying to tell you what to do," Mrs. Sweeney says. "I just want you to think on it some, is all."

"I will," I tell her, thinking it's a lie.

Though I suppose it's not. She's given me lots to think about. I just won't be thinking about it the way she'd like me to.

We finish our tea, then we thank Mrs. Sweeney and say good-bye to her. Outside, the skies have cleared a little. It's not raining, or even drizzling anymore, but there are still more clouds than sun. Geordie turns to me.

"Hard things to hear," he says.

I nod. "Like the bit about forgiveness and clearing the family name."

"That's asking a lot," he says, but I can't tell from the way he says it if he's agreeing with me or Mrs. Sweeney, or just being sympathetic in general.

"I don't know if it's even possible," I tell him.

"It's not something you have to think about today," Geordie says. "Or even ever, if you don't want to."

I give him a small smile. I see he's on my side and I don't feel quite so alone. I guess that's the moment when I get my first real taste of the Riddell loyalty. That loyalty is pretty much black and white, but when it's on your side, all you feel is comfort.

"How far do you think it is to the nearest bus stop?" he asks.

"Depends on how much things have changed," I say, "but we'll probably have to hike into Stokesville before we can find a bus line. They never ran out this far when I was a kid."

He switches his fiddlecase from one hand to the other.

"Then we'd better start walking," he says.

As we reach Stokesville, I start to get depressed again. Everything's unfamiliar, but nothing seems to have changed either. Shacks and little clapboard houses with tin roofs and walls covered with tarpaper or black joe give way to nicer places with tended lawns and little gardens. The dirt road turns to asphalt and finally acquires a sidewalk on either side, and then it goes downhill again. Now it's two- and three-story tenements and small businesses and then finally we're in the Ramble, Tyson's wrong side of the tracks with all of its bars and diners, pawnshops and poolrooms, dance halls and strip clubs.

For a long time, we're the only white faces—pretty much until we get to Division Street where the Ramble starts—but no one bothers us unless you count the dogs that took to following us for a while when we first reached Stokesville. They made Geordie nervous—after what we went through yesterday, I think pretty much anything around here would make him nervous—but I wasn't. I've never met the dog, doesn't matter how mean its reputation, that I can't make friends with. These ones wouldn't come for a pat, but after I called out to them a few times, they stopped growling and finally faded away down alleyways and side streets.

I'd never been to this part of town—at least not by myself, on foot like this. We drove through it lots of times on the way into Tyson, but it's not the sort of place you bring a kid. I could never understand why, but now that I'm grown up, now that I've lived through my own years as a junkie and hooker, I don't have any trouble seeing plenty of reasons. These last few blocks, all we keep walking by are these poor messed-up druggies, scrawny prostitutes, and tough-looking men who wear tattoos with the casual indifference that uptown men wear a cologne. I find myself offering up a prayer of thanks to whoever or whatever was responsible for Lou finding me and taking me in the way he did.

Everybody looks so rough, Indians, blacks, and whites, all mixed now. In this part of town, the only differences that are noted are who's got the money and who doesn't. We're strangers, and it's pretty obvious we don't have anything anybody'd want, but I still find myself wishing we'd waited for the bus back a-ways, instead of deciding to walk to the station like we are. Nobody's threatening us, but the potential for violence lies thick in the air, as does the hopelessness and despair.

I will us to be invisible, or at least not worth anybody's attention, and that works for a while. But then this guy pushes away from the wall of a poolroom where he's been leaning with some friends and comes walking over to us and my heart sinks. First impression: he's as wide as he is tall. His chest strains his T-shirt, biceps bulging, arms covered in tattoos. His eyes are dark, unreadable, hair slicked back. His jeans grease-stained.

"Ray Baby," he says. "I thought you blew town." But then his gaze drops to my chest, comes back up to my face. "You ain't Raylene."

"I . . . I'm her sister," I say, guessing Raylene's much better endowed than I am.

"No shit. I didn't know she had her a sister."

"Jillian May," I tell him. But I don't offer him my hand.

He glances at Geordie, then back at me. Pops a pack of cigarettes out from where it was wedged in the sleeve of his T-shirt and shakes one out. Geordie and I both decline when he offers it to us.

"You said she left town?" I say.

He nods, lights his cigarette. I note the prison tattoos on the back of his hands—they're primitive, self-made, not like the ones on his arms, which were obviously done by a professional. There's a Harley logo on his right forearm, a naked woman on the left. There are others, higher on the arm, but they disappear under his shirt sleeves and I can't make them out.

"I wasn't talkin' to her, my ownself," he says, "but that's the word. Her an' Pinky are headin' off to make it big somewheres."

"But you don't know where?"

His eyes narrow slightly.

"We're family," I remind him. "I haven't seen her in years and thought I'd come look her up."

"Where ya been?" he asks.

I hesitate for a moment, then fall into a role.

"Hallsworth," I tell him. Hallsworth Prison is the women's penitentiary just outside of Newford. "I just got out a couple of weeks ago. Fucked the wrong cop."

I don't even look at Geordie as I'm saying this. I just hope he knows enough to play along.

"There ain't no right cop," our new friend says.

"Well, I guess I know that now."

He laughs. "I guess you do. You heard about Del?"

"Del's my brother," I say, "but he's not exactly on my list of favorite people."

"Yeah, he's a mean fuck, no question. Him an' me've had words a time or two. Ain't right what he did to that girl, leavin' her to die like that."

"Being Del, it doesn't surprise me."

"Nothing he'd do could surprise anybody."

I nod. "So you don't know where Raylene went?"

He takes a drag and shakes his head. "Just off to make her fortune."

"But she was happy?" I ask. "She was looking good?"

He laughs. "Oh, that sister of yours, she was always lookin' good. Not much for the sharin' of them good looks, mind. Not like Pinky. Man, she's the original party gal . . ."

His voice trails off and he actually looks a little embarrassed with where he was going. I can't even place who Pinky would be. I remember some Millers who lived a little farther down the Old Grange Road, but I thought they were all boys.

"You don't worry none about your little sister," he tells me. "She can take care of herself."

"Well, if you see her . . ."

"I'll tell her you dropped by to say how-do."

I nod. "Thanks."

"You need anythin'?" he asks. "I know what it's like, gettin' outta the joint an' there's nobody much interested in even givin' you the time of day."

"I'm good," I tell him. I start to turn away, then stop and ask, "What's your name?"

"Frankie," he says. "Frankie Bennett."

"I liked talking to you, Frankie," I say.

Then I take Geordie's hand and we start walking away. The back of my neck prickles for a moment.

"You be good, Jillian May," Frankie calls after me.

I can feel myself relax then. I turn, give him a smile and a wave, but we keep walking.

"What was all that about?" Geordie asks when we're out of Frankie's hearing.

I shrug. We're crossing the tracks that separate the Ramble from Tyson proper, leaving that other world behind. The bars, the junkies, and the whores. Farther back, Stokesville. Farther still, Hillbilly Holler where I grew up. Or at least where I put in some years. I don't think I really started to grow up until after Lou found me.

"I was just fitting in," I say. "I could tell he'd done time. I knew he'd be friendlier if he thought I had, too."

"But Hallsworth?"

"So I exaggerated. You're still locked up when you're in juvie."

"But you haven't really been in prison, have you?"

"I've been a lot of places where a person shouldn't have to be, but that's not one of them."

"You don't think prison's the answer? I mean, if you screw up, you've got to pay."

I guess he's thinking of his brother, Paddy.

"That's not it," I tell him. "It's just there are a lot of people inside who don't deserve to be in there, and a lot of people walking free who should be locked up tight and the key thrown away. They just never seem to get the balance right."

Geordie nods. "Well, Paddy's no angel, that's for sure."

"You think he'll go straight when he gets out?"

"I'd like to say yes," Geordie says, "but I doubt it."

There's nothing I can say to ease the hurt in Geordie's eyes. I give his hand a squeeze.

"Let's find that bus station," I say.

He nods. "I guess this was all pretty much a waste of time."

I think about the friend I've made in him and shake my head.

"Not for a moment," I tell him. "Not even for a moment."

Raylene

Pinky and me, I guess we cleaned up some since our original cowboy days in Tyson. We don't talk a whole lot prettier, and we still don't take no shit from no one, but you could say we mellowed some. Had us a whole bunch of adventures, didn't we just? But like the pair of bad pennies we was, we finally turned up back home again in the April of '99.

I suppose everybody comes back sooner or later—isn't that a hoot? All us no accounts can't run away fast enough, but then we come crawling back again, 'cause the rest of the world don't want no part of us neither.

But me and Pinky, we wasn't so much crawling back as just catching our breath, stopping by for old times' sake. We never had us no plan on staying. We got to town in late March, took us a room in the Slumber Inn Motel on Division Street, and just walked around, remembering. Most of our time we spent in the Ramble, that three-block strip of bars, strip joints, and honky-tonks that still serves up the entertainment for folks from either side of the tracks. Every which way we turned, we was tripping over the memories.

We walk by the old place off Division Street where we used to live.

We try to find the bars and billiards halls and all where we used to spend our social time, though most of them is shut down, or got them new names.

We stop and have us a look at that street corner where Jimmy got himself beat to death by one of the Devil's Dragon. And that only puts me in mind of the rest of my sorry family. Del and Mama. Robbie. My sister.

I figure my sister's still living the good life in Newford. If that article I saw back in L.A. was anything to go by, she's doing so well there'd be no need to change her ways. But the others . . .

One afternoon I leave Pinky in our hotel room, smoking cigarettes and watching her soaps—she got herself hooked on them in prison. Me, I don't watch much TV no more and when I do, I don't really see what's on the screen. I use it like a white noise machine and just go away in my head, thinking—mostly about being a wolf, about that world we're running through and where it is and how come we can hunt there the way we do.

I get on the Division Street bus at a stop near our motel and stay on it as the street takes its long curve into downtown Tyson, a slow stop-and-start trip that 'minds me of all them times I went to visit Pinky in prison. I get off at one of our old haunts, the Devary Hotel, but I'm not planning on running no scams today. I'm not even scouting. I just needed to get away on my own for a time.

I can't get over how everything's changed. The Devary's a Hilton now, all spruced up and shiny like some strollop out for an evening stroll, trying to impress the locals. But the locals all have them new duds, too, when they haven't been torn down and rebuilt into something different themselves. There's more fancy office towers and indoor malls and high-end boutiques and galleries than a body'd know what to do with. The longer I go ambling about, the more I realize that Tyson's not just some hick county seat no more. The developers have done pulled it into the ass end of the twentieth century like they done pretty much every other place else they got their hands on. Makes me wonder 'bout some of the outlying towns like Hazard and Cooperstown. They's probably your picturesque little tourist traps now, 'stead of the run-down old mining and lumber towns they been for the past hundred years or so.

Well, it's not like it's any of my concern.

I buy myself a bag of sour jelly candies and check things out. As I walk around for a while, I begin to feel like I'm in any one of the cities me and Pinky come through on our drive back from L.A. I guess I come to understand that it's not a matter of everything changing, really. It's that everything's becoming the same.

After a time I come upon a Radio Shack and go in to pick up a longer phone cord for my notebook computer. Our hotel room's not really set up for Internet access and I keep having to move the computer from the coffee table where I use it, over to the bed so that my cord can reach the phone jack when I actually want to go on-line.

I can help myself just fine, but naturally a sales clerk comes sidling over as soon's I come in through the door. I start to tell him I don't need no one holding my hand, but he's just grinning like some old coon hound, caught himself a mighty fine smell.

"Raylene Carter," he says. "It's been forever."

His using my name takes me by surprise and I find my hand going for my pocket and that switchblade Pinky give me all them years ago that I still carry. I'm used to being invisible. Someone knows my name, it usually means trouble.

"You don't look like you've aged a year since high school," the clerk's saying. "How do you do it?"

And then I place him and let myself relax. This here's Benmont Looney, and, man, didn't he take some ribbing over that name in school. Like Tyson, he's changed, too, but it weren't any improvement. He was always this pudgy, moon-faced kind a kid, clothes never fit quite right on account of they had nothing solid to hang from. He's bigger now and the suit he's wearing still hangs like a sack. Face is broader and if the zits are gone, so's most of his hair.

"How're you doing, Ben?" I say with a smile I don't mean.

"Pretty good, pretty good. I'm managing this store now."

All it takes is an encouraging "uh-huh" to start him in on telling me about his wife and his kids and how he's living in Mountainview, one of the new suburbs outside of Tyson which "is a long step up from the Old Grange Road where we grew up."

Funny hearing that stretch of the Holler referred to by its proper name. I can't remember the last time I did, though it's only been me and Pinky all these years, so I guess that's no surprise.

I let Looney run on for a while, then finally steer the conversation to the remnants of my family since a guy like him'd keep up on all the kinds of things I want to know. I'm not being mean-spirited here. It's just that there's always going to be those who like to keep up on other people's business and Looney was one of them, no question. Even when we was growing up, he was like that. I remember Pinky was always wanting to thump him, just to get him to stop talking. I never cared much one way or the other and right now I'm happy to let him ramble on about the sorrowful affairs of the Carter clan.

"I guess you heard about Del going to prison," he says.

I nod. "Nothing he didn't deserve. That was a long time ago—before I left town."

"That's right. He did seven years, all told, and once he got out he took up with the Morgans."

"Whatever for?"

I'm thinking of Del, always wanting to be the top man on the totem pole. It don't make a whole lotta sense, him taking up with them Morgans where he's just going to be one more stoop-an'-fetch-it boy.

"Well, the thing is," Looney tells me, "seems he fell in love with one of their girls and I guess they took him in on account of her."

"I thought they were all inbred."

He gives me that old Looney grin, you'd really think he was short the full load of bricks. He ain't half dumb, really—I remember that from school—but that grin and his name pretty much sealed his fate when we was kids.

"You'd think that, from the look of them," he says, "but I've got it on good account that your brother's not the first to marry into the Morgan clan."

"Then how come they all still look the same?"

"Stronger genes, I guess, than those they take in."

See, that's what I mean. Looney might look like some dumb old yokel, but there's plenty of thinking going on inside his head.

"I guess our mama wasn't too pleased," I say.

He gets that look folks do when they know bad news you don't.

"I'm sorry to tell you this, Raylene," he says, "but your mama's dead. I would have thought someone might have told you."

Then why do you think I'm asking you all of this? I think. But I only tell him how I've been pretty much outta touch all these years.

"Well, I'm sorry to have had to be the one to give you the bad news," he says.

What bad news would that be? I'm wondering. That's just one more no-account Carter for me not to have to think on.

"How'd she die?" I ask.

Hard, I'm hoping. She didn't deserve nothing less.

"Well, there's the irony, I guess," he says. "All those years she was fighting against the stiff penalties for drunk driving and what does she do but get killed herself—head-on collision with Dewie Mackery who was so full of whiskey and beer that night you could've stuck a spout in him and opened a bar."

That sounds like my mama, I guess. Del got jail time for drunk driving and killing someone, so she'd be up in arms against that, never you mind all the poor innocent folk getting themselves killed with all of them drunks on the road. She never did look no further than her damn own self and her favorite boy.

"Quite the turnout at her funeral, though."

"People just wanted to make sure she was really dead," I say.

He gives me a look, then nods. "You're probably right. She wasn't exactly well liked. Never did her cause much good, what with her own drinking and strident ways."

"And Robbie?" I ask. "Is he dead, too?"

"Got on that road not long after Jimmy was killed—but I guess you were already out of town by then. They fished him out of Pine Creek, dead of an overdose."

All them Carters dead. Makes the world just a little bit sweeter, I figure.

"What about Del?" I ask, hopefully.

"You didn't hear about the Morgans? I figured that was big news everywhere."

"I don't follow the news much," I tell him. "It's all bad anyways."

"Well, this was bad all right. The official story is they had some falling out with a bunch of colored boys and the whole clan got wiped out."

"That can't be true."

He nods, pleased he's found someone who don't know a thing about such a big event.

"Oh, it's true, all right," he says. "They only caught one of the killers and he was executed back in '83 or '84."

"You said official story—what's the unofficial one?"

"That the man they killed did it all on his own. But that's not possible. There must've been forty, fifty Morgans died that day and you know how mean they could be. They'd cut a man for giving them a sideways look. There was no give to those Morgans, not an inch."

I give a nod. Plenty of folks found that out the hard way.

"Who's saying that one man killed 'em all?"

"That's the talk on the rez. Story is he was some kind of hoodoo man, maybe a ghost or a spirit. But that's just talk. You know how people like a good story."

I think about me and Pinky and our pack of wolves, running through the dreamlands. I guess I know firsthand how what you see in this world ain't necessarily all there is. But I don't see no reason to enlighten Looney on that account.

"So did Del die with the rest of them?" I ask.

"No, but he was pretty broke up about losing his family and all."

He lost us a long time ago, I'm thinking, but I know that isn't what Looney means.

"He still around?" I say.

Looney nods. "He's on welfare and living in that trailer park at the end of Indiana Road."

A place to avoid, then, though I got to admit to a certain curiosity. The thing is, he still troubles me. I don't know what kind of loser he's grown into, but the Del that terrorized me as a kid still stands tall in my head. I'd like to get him in the dreamlands, see how well he stands up to a pack of wolves.

"How about you?" Looney asks. "What've you been up to? You ever see Pinky anymore?"

"Oh, sure," I tell him. "We moved down to Florida where we've been working as secretaries all this time. Thought we'd take a holiday this year and come back to the old hometown. Look around, see how things've changed."

"Whereabouts in Florida?"

He's got the nose, all right, but I'm not up to adding to his storehouse of gossip. I can just see him, next time he runs into one of the old crowd. "You'll never guess who I ran into the other day . . ."

"Tell you the truth, Ben," I say. "I'm kind of pressed for time here. Why don't you sell me one of those phone cord extensions and we'll do us some more catching up a little later on. Maybe get together with the old crowd and have us some laughs."

He likes that idea, but after he's rung me through the cash and starts in asking where we're staying, I just take his card from the little holder by the register and tell him I'll give him a call.

He smiles and I smile and we both know we're never going to see each other again, unless it's like this, by accident.

Pinky caught up on her own family not long after we arrived. She didn't go looking for them, which was just as well, I reckon, since when she did run into her brother Elmer on the street one day, there wasn't even a how-do. He just up and slapped her openhanded across the face and told her not to be calling on their mother as she weren't welcome in that house no more.

"Always figured you'd end up to no good," he says, "but even I never thought you'd sink so low as to be making the kinda movies you done."

Pinky'd used her a fake name in her porn days, but you ain't exactly hiding much when the name you're going by is Pinky Sugah and everybody back home knows what you look like anyways. Though now that I think on it, seems strange that old Looney, so on top of everything else, didn't have something to say about it. Maybe he was just being polite.

But them Baptist boys like Pinky's brothers was always walking the high road, and I guess politeness don't enter into the story with them. Course it makes you wonder what they was doing watching them porn movies in the first place. But then I was raised Catholic my own self and I sure as hell know Catholics 'round here don't have much integrity neither—not if my own family's any kind of example.

When Elmer hit her like that, I half expected Pinky to knife him, or at least take a swing at him her own self, but she didn't do neither. Guess the time she spent in prison taught her something—when to fight and when to walk away, if nothing else.

I asked her later if she felt bad about how things turned out.

"You and me," she says, "is all the family either of us need."

I knowed it was true for me, but I guess I never stopped to question how it was for her, what made her so hard and able to stand up for her own self with no never mind for nobody else. I'd always thought she got along fine with her folks and her brothers and she never said nothing to make me think different.

"It wasn't like that," she tells me. "They taught me how to be tough, yeah, but it wasn't outta any kind a love for me. I had to go learn that on my own, just so's I could stand up to 'em. They never done nothin' like Del done to you, but they're so dumb, it wouldn't surprise me none that it just didn't never occur to 'em. Lord knows they had the morals of dogs, though that ain't bein' fair to dogs. And as for my momma and poppa—they wasn't quite in the drinkin' league of your old lady, but they wouldn't've shamed her much neither."

"It don't seem right, us growing up like that."

Pinky laughs. "When you going to figure it out, Ray? The world don't turn on right and wrong. It's just what it is and you and me, we got to make the best of it how we can."

"Seems to me, we got us a choice," Pinky says one day.

We're sitting in the Pearl, a diner on the Ramble, early of a weekday morning, drinking bad coffee and smoking—or at least Pinky is. The Pearl hasn't changed much. It's still no better'n one step up from a pigsty. We don't actually recognize nobody, but it's really only the faces that've changed. The waitress who slops our coffee on the table could be the daughter of the old bag serving us fifteen years ago. A drunk sits at the counter, nursing a hangover. A couple of hookers are in one of the back booths, counting money. In the booth behind us some guy's snorting blow through a cut-down straw, the coke laid out in lines right on the table.

"Either we clean up our act," Pinky says, stubbing out her smoke, "or we take it right to the bone, badasses all the way."

I just look at her. She's lounging there on the other side of the booth, all relaxed, smiling. Her black pedal pushers are back in style and her pink tube top's never gone out, at least not anywheres we find ourselves. Pinky's still always wearing something to match her name. It was going to be her trademark, she used to say when she first started up the habit.

Like anybody was taking fashion notes. But it's the reason I had that pink Caddy convertible waiting for her the day she got outta prison.

"You leaning any particular way?" I ask.

Pinky shrugs and gives her dyed-blonde bangs a fluff. She'd first gotten her that Farah Fawcett haircut back when the Angels was still running in prime-time and she's stuck with it ever since. "You don't change what works," she told me when I asked once. Me, I used to be as fickle as an alley cat when it come to my hair. I'd wear it any which way it might happen to occur to me. But the last few years I just let it grow and tie it back.

Pinky's looking a sight better these days—pretty much like she did when she first started in on making them porn movies way back when. Her skin's soft, she's firm in all the right places, the lines are gone from her face. I'm looking pretty good, too, though I don't spend near' as much time in front of the mirror as she does. But sometimes I catch a glimpse a myself when I'm getting in or outta the shower, and it takes me by surprise. I ain't sagging neither. The lines are gone from my face. I had some gray in my hair, but it's all gone, too.

I made mention of it to Pinky one day and she just looked at me for a long moment, then stripped down and went and stood in front a the full-length mirror in our room.

"I'll be damned," she said. "It just never occurred to me." She turned to look at me. "What's going on here, Ray?"

I felt pretty much the same way Pinky was feeling when the realization come to me. But I had me an answer and I gave it to her then.

"It's that unicorn blood," I told her.

"But we're only killing them in our dreams."

"It's like I been telling you," I said. "Maybe we're dreaming, but someplace that forest is real."

Pinky nodded, but she'd turned back to the mirror and was just standing there, running her hands on her stomach, hefting her breasts.

"I'd like me some serious foldin' green," Pinky says to me now, "but I don't much feel like earnin' it."

I smile. Like that's news.

"But not here in Tyson," I say.

"Naw, I was thinkin' of Newford."

"Think anybody'd remember us in the city?" I ask.

It's been a long run of years since we played out any of our scams in Newford.

"We're unforgettable," Pinky tells me. "That's just the cross that you and me, we got to bear. But it's a big city."

I nod. I've been looking through the paper while we're talking and something stops me dead. I have this moment when everything just goes cold and hot at the same time. I want to tear that paper up and scatter the pieces. I want to grab somebody by the hair and just ram their head against a wall until there ain't nothing left of their face. But I force myself to breathe. To calm down.

When I'm feeling more myself, I look up at Pinky, but she hasn't noticed nothing.

"Do you believe in fate?" I ask her, surprised at how calm my voice sounds.

She shrugs, likes it's no never mind to her, one way or the other.

"Look at this," I tell her.

I turn around the entertainment section of *The Tyson Times* where it talks about a Newford artist being hit by a car and show it to her. Pinky studies the picture of the woman they're talking about.

"That's your sister?" she asks.

"There sure as hell ain't two of her."

"She went and changed her name."

"Yeah," I say. "She tried to change a lot a things, I guess, but she's still gonna be Hillbilly Holler trash when it's all said and done. How we all growed up, that's something that never goes away, don't matter how slick we try and make ourselves out to be."

It's the reason that, in the end, I let everything pretty much ride. What's the point of fighting who you are, or how the world's going to look at you? I coulda had me a million dollars and people'd still know I was just a Carter from the other side of the tracks.

"She looks a lot like you," Pinky says. "I mean, give her some tits and you could be sisters."

I let out a sigh. "We *are* sisters."

"I meant twins."

"I guess we do share a resemblance."

It's funny. I hear Del's living in that Indiana Road trailer park and it touches me some, but only with curiosity and a scraping of my old fears. He could die tomorrow—hell, he could die this minute—and it wouldn't worry me none. But that sister of mine, I just got to think on her and I'm in a rage.

I guess it's that Del was always bad, so anything he ever done to me never come as no surprise. But she, she betrayed me, and that cuts the heart deeper than anything I can imagine, and I can imagine plenty. It's a hurt that just don't go away.

"I'm thinking maybe I should pay her a visit," I say.

Pinky gives me a look. "You ain't thinkin' of doin' nothin' foolish, now are you? 'Cause let me tell you from personal experience, prison ain't worth it."

"That's only if you get caught."

Pinky just keeps on a-studying me, then finally she nods.

"I guess if there's anyone can get away with it, it'd be you," she says. "You always was too smart for your own good."

"I'm not planning on hurting her," I say. At least not yet. " 'Sides, read what it says. She's in some goddamn coma."

Pinky nods. "Sure. Time we was doin' somethin' new. Tyson was gettin' old anyways."

NEWFORD, APRIL

So that's how we find ourselves parking the pink Caddy just off of Yoors Street and walking back down the block to where my sister's apartment is, one of them studio lofts across the street from a Chinese groceteria. There's three other apartments in her building and I guess there was some stores on the ground floor, but they're all boarded up now, the windows papered up, and I can't tell what they was selling. But there's a coffee shop coming in on one side, according to the "Opening Soon!" sign, and something called Whispering, which could sell just about anything, having a name like that. The door to her place has a couple of bells with names beside them. Hers is number two.

I gave the hospital a call afore we come out here, but my sister's still flat out in her coma—two and a half days now and counting. As we turn down the alleyway beside her building, I'm trying to decide whether I want her to ever wake up again, or maybe go ahead and stay that way until she just kinda wastes away into nothing. I want to tell her to her face what I think about what she's done, but one more funeral I'm not going to attend'd probably suit me just as well.

"If her place is on the second floor," Pinky says, pointing, "that window's lookin' into her place. The fire escape can take us right up to it."

I nod. "Here, put these on."

I pull out a couple a pairs of surgical gloves I picked up at a drugstore earlier in the day and hand one over to her. Pinky gives them a look.

"What're these for?" she asks.

"We don't want to leave no prints, what with the both of us being on record and all."

"I thought we wasn't goin' to do nothin'."

"We're breaking in, ain't we?"

"There's that."

I can tell she don't know why we're doing this and I'm not so sure I do neither. I guess I just have a need to be in this place where she's been living all these years, see what was so important that she could abandon me to Del and just take off on me like she did.

It's midafternoon as we go climbing up that fire escape, but I'm not worried. All I can see is the rear of buildings and maybe they're gentrifying the front of the street, but back here it's still catch-as-catch-can. Nobody going to be paying a whole lotta attention to a couple of women going up a fire escape. Still, I take a good look around afore I break the window. We wait a breath after the glass breaks, listening in the silence that follows the shards as they fall inside and drop to the asphalt below. No one appears to be paying us any attention, so we clear away the rest of the glass and step over the window frame, inside.

And then I know why I'm here.

It's those damn paintings. All them fairies of hers, transplanted from the woods around the holler and put here in the city.

"She's kinda messy," Pinky says, looking around.

I suppose Pinky's right. It's one big room that's a jumble of art gear and scattered clothes and things piled up in stacks every which way you happen to look, but I'm not really paying much attention to any of it and I hardly hear Pinky. I'm just focused on this dark place inside me, thinking of all them fairy tales my sister told me and how they come true for her, maybe, but she sure didn't leave me living in no fairy tale. Where was my happy ending with Del coming into my room, night after night, and me just a little girl?

"Ray?" Pinky says.

I got no time for words. All I got is a red haze over my eyes making everything look like it's got a film of blood covering it. I pull that switchblade outta my pocket and walk across the room to where this big painting's sitting on the shelf in front of a half dozen others. I keep the blade of that knife honed sharp as a razor, just like Pinky taught me to all them years ago, and it cuts through the first painting like it was hot and the canvas is butter. The smiling fairy looking at me splits in two and then three and then I got the damn thing shredded and I'm on to the next one.

It's a long time later, after I've cut me every damn one of them fairy paintings, broken most of the frames, knocked over a few things, that I finally start to see normal again. I find Pinky sitting on a battered couch, just a-looking at me. There's a sharp smell in the air—from one a them jars of turpentine I broke, I guess.

"You about done now?" Pinky asks.

I give her a slow nod.

"Are you feeling any better?"

I take a long slow breath. I look at the ruin surrounding me and slowly fold the blade of my knife into its handle and stick it back in my pocket.

"Some," I tell her.

"Time we was goin' then."

That night we take us a room at the Sleep Comfort Motel up on Highway 14 and once we get to sleep, we're a-hunting, fierce and wild, full of piss and vinegar and just a-spoiling for a fight, but we don't catch us one decent scent. I wake up in the early hours of the morning and stare at the ceiling of the motel room above our bed, feeling lost and hurt. The only thing that makes it bearable is the idea of my sister coming back to that apartment of hers and seeing all her dreams ripped to shreds the way mine was when she left me behind.

Things is kinda funny after that, like what I did stirred up something inside me instead of easing it away. Turned me into a stalker. We got us some money left, but I can tell Pinky's fretting about how I can't concentrate on much of anything these days. I go back to my sister's apartment pretty much every day, mostly looking the way I always do, sometimes playing with wigs and outfits and makeup, like we used to do when we run our scams, so that it's a complete stranger going there.

Her friends have cleaned the place up, but I got back in easy enough. The first time I go up the front stairs and use me a couple a wires, kinda brushing up on my old lock-picking skills, though the lock on her door's not much of a challenge. Poking around in her things, I find a junk drawer with keys in it and try 'em all until I got me one that works and after that I don't need to play the cat burglar no more.

Twice I hear someone at the door while I'm still inside and I have to scoot under the Murphy bed and wait there while whoever it is dumps off some mail, does a slow walk around the apartment. I can tell by the feet it's a woman. The second time she sits on the sofa a whiles and I hear her crying.

I been by the hospital, too, and later the rehab, all dressed up like I'm someone else. I walk by her room, pause in the doorway sometimes, get me a good look. I don't know what I'm thinking, what I want to do. I just know that there's still a world of unfinished business lying there between us.

Then one night we have us an encounter in the dreamlands like we never had before, something that changes everything. We take us down another of them unicorns—the first one in a long time—and hardly get a decent wallow in its blood afore we're chased off.

Pinky and me, we wake up at the same time in that big king-size bed we're sharing in the Sleep Comfort Motel.

"That can't have been real," Pinky says. "I mean, what the hell *were* them things?"

I'm still reeling myself. They had the bodies of men, but the heads of wolves or coyotes or something. A couple of dog boys, dressed up casual in jeans and all.

"Some kinda . . . animal people," I say.

And then it hits me. The clothes they were wearing, the way they talked . . .

"You notice anything unusual about them?" I ask Pinky.

She gives me this look like all my brains done gone and drained outta my head. "Well, yeah. You mean like how they had dog heads on the bodies of men?"

"No," I say. "That one guy was wearing a T-shirt with 'Don't! Buy!

Thai!' written on it. Who the hell's going to advertise a boycott in the dreamlands?"

"What're you talkin' about?"

"And he *knew* we weren't real wolves."

"You didn't need to be no brain scientist to pick up on that," Pinky says. "But I still don't get the deal."

"They come from this world," I tell her, slapping my hand on the bedspread. "Just like you and me, 'cept I got the sense they was solid. That they can cross over without the need to go to sleep and dream first."

Pinky takes the time to light a cigarette and gives a slow nod. "You think?"

"Oh, yeah. I ain't got no question in my mind."

"But you'd think we'd've heard about guys walking around with dog heads—if they come from here, I mean."

"They're not going to look like that here," I say, wishing that just for once Pinky'd try and exercise them few brains god give her. "I'll bet they can decide how they want to look any old time they please."

"Well, they scared the crap right outta me," Pinky says.

I know what she means. It's the reason I backed off sudden as I done. There was some powerful mojo working in them dog boys. I got the feeling, real quick, that they coulda just shut us down without no more'n a word or two.

"You know what this means?" I say.

"That we ain't goin' to have us our fun no more."

I shake my head. "Not a chance."

"Then what does it mean?"

"That we got the chance of going over there our own selves. For real. Think about it. If we can figure it out, we don't got to worry about nothing in this world no more 'cause we'll be able to just walk us back and forth between the two like that pair can."

"We don't know that they can," Pinky says.

But I do. I can't even explain how I know. I just do. And if they can do it, then we should be able to figure out a way to do it, too.

"And why would we even want to?" Pinky adds.

"Well, for one thing, we'd never have to work again."

"Like we ever did."

"I did."

Pinky nods. "I forgot about all them years you was in that copy shop."

"But this works out, we won't have to work, and we won't have to risk our asses running no scams no more, neither."

Pinky leans back against the headboard. "So how you figure that?"

"Say we need us a little money," I tell her. "We just slip outta the dreamlands into a bank vault, say. Help ourselves to whatever we need, and then slip back out the way we come." I grin. "Hell, even if we ever got caught, how're they going to hold us? They put us in a cell and we just up and disappear ourselves back into the dreamlands." I snap my fingers. "Just like that."

In the neon light coming from the sign outside, I can see the understanding dawn on Pinky and she gives me that big old grin of hers.

"How're we gonna learn how to do that?" she asks.

"I dunno. Let me think on it a spell."

Come morning, I get me an idea.

"You remember that old woman, used to live at the head of Copper Creek?" I ask Pinky. "Had that bottle tree in front of her house."

Pinky turns from the mirror above the vanity where she's been putting on her makeup. It's pretty clear from the look on her face that she don't like where this is going.

"You think she's still living there?" I go on. "She had to be a thousand years old, that time we saw her."

We was still in school back then, sneaking out into the woods to have us our little parties. That day there was only the three of us—me, Pinky, and Rolly LeGrand, this fella Pinky had taken a liking to that week. We was smoking cigarettes and drinking beer, wandering off from where we'd parked Rolly's Duster by the rickety little bridge on Early Road where it crosses over Copper Creek, when suddenly we come upon this old log cabin, the bottle tree out front and the old woman just a-setting on the porch.

She was dark-skinned, but you couldn't tell if she was a black or got herself burned brown in the sun, setting out on that porch of hers, day after day like she done. She had dark hair—not a speck of gray in it—hanging down either side of her face in a pair of braids and was wearing a gingham dress, smoking a pipe, and just a-staring at us when we come outta the trees and stumbled on her place. Her eyes were so dark you'd've thought they was all pupil.

I remember a wind come up and shook them bottles on her tree against each other, making this strange hollow clinking sound. Supposed to chase the bad spirits away, is how I heard it. The wind fell off and the bottles stopped moving. We wasn't moving neither, just a-looking at her looking at us. Then she raised her hand and that wind come up again, rattling the bottles. I don't know about spirits, but it sure enough chased us off that day.

"We don't want to go messin' 'round with the likes of Miss Lucinda," Pinky says.

That's what everybody called her. I don't know if anyone ever knew her family name, or if she'd ever had one. I 'spect every small town's got itself some peculiar old woman, people think she's a witch. The difference being in this case, I think Miss Lucinda most likely was.

"You know the kind of stories they tell about her," Pinky tells me. "They don't call her a juju woman for nothin'."

"That's exactly why we need to talk to her."

"Ray. The reason Orry Prescott had that gimpy leg of his was on account of his trying to steal a bottle off'n that tree of hers."

I'd heard that story, too, but I didn't set me much store by it. The Prescotts was as inbred as the Morgans and I'm pretty sure Orry grew up with that gimpy leg of his, though I didn't know for certain. I never saw him 'round until junior high and he already had that leg of his then, walking with a wooden crutch. You never seen shoulders like he had. Most of him was built like some football player, 'cept for that one leg all shriveled and wasted away.

But that didn't mean Miss Lucinda hadn't put some juju on him.

"We ain't going there to steal nothin'," I tell Pinky. "You got my promise on that."

"And if she don't want to talk?"

"Then we say a polite 'Thank you, ma'am,' and we take ourselves away from there."

"I don't know," Pinky says.

"Then how about you just drive me there and let me off and you can wait for me at the bridge. I'll walk back to meet you."

We had some more discussion on the matter, but in the end we made the drive up to Tyson together. It's a beautiful day, the skies clear and blue above us, but not so warm that we have the top down on the Caddy. Once we get outta Tyson, we take the back roads until we find ourselves on Early Road.

Here nothing's changed, 'cept maybe the woods are deeper, trees growing closer to the road. We leave that long pink car of ours where the bridge goes over the crick and follow the path to Miss Lucinda's cabin, the two of us making our way between the trees, Pinky nervous, me feeling a kind of eagerness I ain't known in a long whiles, which is a surprise on a lotta counts, considering how I feel about this kinda thing, hoodoo and magic and all.

Truth is, I'm not even sure the old woman's still going to be alive after all these years. But when we step outta the trees, there she is, still a-setting on her porch like she ain't moved in the thirty or so years since we was last here. That bottle tree of hers is still there, too. Only difference is it's grown somewhat bigger and it's got more bottles on it.

We stop within hailing distance of the cabin. Pinky's eyeing that tree, waiting for the wind to come up and rattle the bottles. But me, I give that old woman a wave.

"Howdy, ma'am," I call over to her. "I was wondering if we could have us a word or two."

A couple of the bottles on the tree clink against each other, but I don't feel no wind. I can tell Pinky's about to bolt so I grab ahold of her arm.

"You mind if we come up there on the porch with you?" I ask. "We brung you something."

There's a long moment of silence and I'm almost beginning to wonder if maybe the old woman's up and died and is just a-setting there, waiting for the undertaker to come and cart her away. But then I make note of them eyes of hers, glittering and dark and alive.

"What do you have?" she asks.

She's got her a strange voice, creaky and hoarse, like she's not used to using it much. But I'm not fooled into thinking it means she's some senile old thing, not no way.

"Whiskey and tobacca," I tell her.

That dark face cracks a smile, white teeth flashing.

"You come on up, girls," she says. "Set with me a spell."

I'm not shy. With a "Thank you, ma'am," I go right on up to that porch, but Pinky's lagging behind.

Miss Lucinda just keeps on grinning. "Don't you be feared now, girl," she tells Pinky. "I ain't a-gonna hurt you."

Pinky gives her a quick nod. "No, ma'am."

"Why don't you go on inside," the old woman says. "You'll find a plate of biscuits on the stove and a pot of tea. Bring 'em on out to us."

There's only one other chair. I leave it for Pinky and set up on the banister, swinging my feet.

"Nice place you've got here," I say.

"Well, it's private."

"Downright off the map."

She laughs. "I don't need for much."

Pinky comes back carrying a tray with the biscuits and tea.

"Help yourself, girls," Miss Lucinda says.

When Pinky sets the tray down on the floor of the porch, I jump down and pour a tea for the old woman, add in a dollop of whiskey from the flask I take out of my jacket pocket. I leave the whiskey flask by the foot of her chair, along with the pouch of pipe tobacco I brought along with me, and hand her the mug. The pattern's pretty much wore away and the china's cracked some, but it still holds up fine.

"I like a considerate girl," Miss Lucinda says.

"My name's Raylene," I tell her, "and this here's my best friend Pinky."

"Pleased to meet you."

"Likewise," I say.

Pinky manages a quick smile.

I pour myself a tea, black and steaming, and help myself to one of the biscuits. It just melts in my mouth. I haven't tasted biscuits like this since my sister run off and the cooking in the Carter household became a more haphazard affair 'cause no one else'd take it on, regularlike. But then I find myself thinking about these biscuits and the tea, all waiting and ready for us.

"Were you expecting company?" I ask.

"I'm always expecting something," Miss Lucinda says. "You don't get to be my age without being ready for pretty much anything the world's gonna throw at you. The one thing I'm not overly fond of is a surprise."

I consider how we come here, outta the blue, my bringing the whiskey and tobacco. I woulda thought that was a surprise. But all I say is, "I'm not so partial to surprises my own self. Take last night."

I start in talking then about the dreamlands and us being wolves there and the dog boys we met last night. I leave out the part about the unicorns.

Miss Lucinda she sets there, smoking her pipe and sipping at her spiked tea. But I can tell she's listening. She's listening and she's not disbelieving, neither. She can be as cool and collected as she likes, but I can tell. Just like I can tell she's intrigued about what all this's got to do with us being here. But I don't get into that none. I just finish off my story, then compliment her again on her biscuits.

"A story like that," she finally says. "A body'd have to take you two for a pair of crazy women. On drugs, probably."

Pinky shoots her a look from where she's sitting in the other chair, chain-smoking, carefully putting out each butt in the lid of her cigarette package and storing 'em in a little pile by the leg of her chair. As Miss Lucinda starts to look in her direction, Pinky's gaze quickly slides away from the old woman's face and settles on mine.

"I suppose a body would," I say. I let a long breath of time hang between us all afore I add, "Unless she knew about that kind a thing her own self."

Miss Lucinda focuses her attention back on me.

"You're not one bit shy, are you, girl?"

"No, ma'am. Not about some things."

"So what brings you to my cabin? I doubt it was the simple charity of a good heart, though I do appreciate the whiskey and the tobacca."

I shrug. "I just found them dog boys to be a real curiosity and then I got to thinking, who might be able to explain 'em to me?"

"What makes you think I can?"

I figure it's time to be bold.

"Are you saying you can't?" I ask. " 'Cause if'n you can, I'd be beholden to you, no question. That's a plain fact."

She touches the whiskey bottle with her foot. "You think these little offerings of yours can cover the debt?"

"No, ma'am, I don't. I brought them along for politeness sake and nothing else."

"That's a good answer."

"How's that, ma'am?"

She smiles. "Well, there's an old story that the spirits don't like to be tricked into nothing. But a gift, freely given, that's a whole other matter. Makes 'em feel beholden themselves."

As she's talking I get this wave of vertigo, a little dizzy spell that comes snaking along my spine and up into my head and to keep my balance I've got to clutch one of them old wood support poles holding up the roof of the porch. I'm looking at Miss Lucinda and for a moment I don't see no old woman's face looking at me. I see the face of an animal, a muskrat, maybe, or an otter. I can't tell. I hear Pinky gasp, but then the animal face is gone and it's just Miss Lucinda, setting there in her chair, looking at me with them dark eyes of hers.

"Let me tell you a little bit about who you mighta met in them dreamwoods of yours," she says.

My dizzy spell's gone like it never was, but I still hold on to that support pole when she starts in a-talking.

"I can tell the neither of you is much for learning," she says, "leastways not book learning, but this ain't the sort of thing you'll find accounted for in no book anyways.

"We got us an old world here, girls, and it weren't made in no seven days like the Bible-thumpers and such'd have us believe. How do I know that? 'Cause we got us people still walking around today who been here since the world began. Hell, you believe all the stories, some of 'em was sitting around in the dark, just a-waiting on it to start up and get interesting.

"Now back in them early days, none of the People—that's what they called themselves, just the People. None of 'em was locked in to the one shape they was born to—that is, those that *was* born. Like I said, if you believe what some'd say, there's a big handful that've just always been. Was here right from the start and'll probably be here when the lights get turned off and everybody else goes on home.

"But I was talking about shapes—what you look like, how the world sees you. In those days, everything kind a flowed. A crow becomes a little black-haired gal, then sprouts her feather wings again and flies away. Or maybe an otter steps up from a mud slide and sheds his skin, walks outta the water like a man. It was a wonderful magical place, by all accounts, everything's like soft rubber, changing its shape depending on the pressure of the world around it, not to mention the world inside it.

"Trouble is, somewhere along the line, folks got to putting names to things. Cataloguing and defining. And once you start in on defining what things is—saying a wolf's a wolf, for instance, and that's all it is—they start getting locked in to that shape. They set like a pudding and the only way you can shift 'em is you got to stir 'em up. You following me so far?"

We both nod, though I'm thinking it might make a little more sense to me than Pinky. She never was the one for any kind of philosophical thinking.

"Anyways," Miss Lucinda says, "as time moves on, everything gets more and more set into what everybody agrees it is. Only the People stay outside of all this fixing of limits and the reason they can is 'cause they're only half living in this world. They got their other foot in that place you girls are visiting in your dreams.

"Now you might call it a dreamworld, and there's others do that, too. Hell, they got all kinds of names for it. Spiritworld. Otherworld. Over on the rez, the Indians call it *manidò-aki*. Everybody visits it some—when they're sleeping—but most of 'em don't really remember much about it when they wake up. And they sure don't know it's as real as this world you girls and me are sitting in right at this moment.

"But those ones that call themselves the People that I'm telling you about, reason they're still shapechangers is that they're walking in both worlds. That old blood of theirs is what lets 'em cross back and forth when they're awake, and it's something in the air of the dreamworld that allows them to have them more'n the one shape."

"So that's who them dog boys were?" I ask.

Miss Lucinda shrugs. "Maybe. But if they're not of the People, then they're closely related to 'em. The thicker the spill of old blood running in you, the less tied you are to the rules that say this is this and that's impossible. So those dog boys, could be they're first People, could be they're just close kin. Either way, they're something a bit more special than anything you're gonna meet on a normal kind of day."

"So it's not something you can learn," I say.

"No," Miss Lucinda says. "But it's a trick a body can acquire."

I lean away from the banister, a little closer to her.

"Could we learn that trick?" I ask. "Cross over between these worlds looking the way we want, 'steada dreaming we're wolves?"

"Everybody's got the potential," Miss Lucinda tells us. "It's locked in to what they call the junk DNA, all them genetic strands that don't seem to have them no practical use. I ain't saying everybody's got the animal blood in 'em, but everybody's got their own mess of juju inside 'em, just a-waiting to be woke up."

Listening to her, I realize that she's playing up the backwoods in her, same as me. You don't get no hillbilly grandma talking 'bout DNA and genetics without her having got some learning you won't be finding in these hills. I give a look to Pinky, but she's just looking confused.

"Why do you live out here like this?" I ask Miss Lucinda.

I want to know more about this shapechanging trick'n all, but she's got me distracted now with this learning I wasn't expecting she'd have.

She just smiles. "Listen, girls. You live long enough like I done and you start to appreciate how the simple life's got it over everything else."

"Yeah," Pinky says, speaking up for the first time. "Folks're always sayin' that. I guess it makes 'em feel a whole lot better 'bout just being ignorant and poor."

I shoot Pinky a dirty look.

"Don't mind her," I tell Miss Lucinda. "She ain't talking 'bout you."

"Oh, I know that," Miss Lucinda says. "I know all about wanting what it don't seem you can have."

"And speaking of that," I say, "any chance you'd share this trick you were talking about?"

Miss Lucinda doesn't say anything for a long moment and I'm getting feared that Pinky up and pissed her off. That she's not going to talk to us no more and we might end up walking outta here with gimpy legs our own selves. She's looking off into the forest, a thin trail a smoke rising up from her pipe to the rafters of the porch. But finally she brings her gaze back to me.

"There's two ways you can wake up that junk DNA in you," she says. "The first is you catch yourself one of the People, or one of their close kin, and you drink their blood."

I think about a lot of movies I seen—at the drive-in and on the late-night movie.

"That where all them vampire stories come from?" I ask.

"Could be. Drinking the blood's mighty effective, but somewhat frowned upon among the People—as you might expect. And don't go kidding yourself. They *know* when someone's been feeding on one of them."

"You said there's another way?"

Miss Lucinda nods. "You got to make you up a potion and drink it down. It takes a little longer to work, but it's got the benefit of not making you any enemies among the cousins."

Before I can ask what the potion's made of, she starts in a rhyming off the ingredients, one by one, emphasizing that you got to collect 'em all your own self:

Dried 'sang root flakes, gathered from a patch that's only ever been harvested during the full of the autumn moon.

A toad skin, smoked over a hickory fire, then dried and powdered.

Corn pollen, brushed from the plant onto a red oak leaf with the shredded end of a sycamore twig.

Rattlesnake venom, milked at high noon.

A mescal button, chopped in four, each piece dried in the sun on a separate day.

A tincture made from boiling down pinecones till all you got left is a kind of sticky sap jelly.

Baked dog bones, powdered.

Shredded bits of fresh morning glory vine.

The chopped-up tail feather of an owl.

And lastly, a pinch of the top of the Mexican mushroom from which you make you your psilocybin.

"That's a mess of hard-to-find items," I say.

"But they ain't impossible."

"No, I guess they ain't. Though a body'd be traveling all over hell and creation tracking some of it down."

"I guess a body's really gotta want to do it," she says.

She finishes up, explaining how you got to mix it all together in a measure of corn whiskey and let it set for four days. Then stop it in a vial with a rowan berry and the blood red resin collected from the inner bark of a nutmeg tree, and finally bury it in an unhallowed graveyard for thirteen nights starting on the dark of the moon.

"And then," she says, grinning, "you drink it down and wait for the change to come."

"What do you call it? A death's wish cocktail?"

Miss Lucinda's still grinning. "I like a girl with a sense of humor."

"I'm guessing there's some pain involved," I say.

"Oh, there's a lotta things involved," Miss Lucinda says. "Pain's only a part of it. You're talking about shifting the whole makeup of who your body thinks you are. There'll be fevers and shakes. You'll be seeing things ain't there, and the things that are there are gonna be wearing new skins for a time. But you get through it, I believe you'll find it worth it."

"Not everybody gets through it then?"

She shakes her head. "There's some ain't got the gumption it takes." She looks from me to Pinky. "Course only the one of you's got to go through it. Then the other could just share a bit of her blood with her friend."

"Thought you said these People didn't 'bide that kinda thing?"

"Oh, they can tell when it's a willing gift or if it's been stolen."

We sit another spell then, Pinky and Miss Lucinda smoking, me thinking.

"I know why we come to see you," I say afore we go, "but why're you helping us? I know you're one of these People, or pretty close-related. We could just take your blood, now's we know."

"Could you?"

There's a change in her voice, low and dangerous, and her dark eyes are almost black now. I hear the clink of a glass and know that sudden wind's moving in the branches a the bottle tree again.

"Not that we would," I quickly tell her. "It's just got me wondering, is all."

The eyes are still black when her gaze settles on me.

"People come, time to time," she says, "asking for something. Looking for potions and spells. Had me a girl with a desperate need to fly like a bird, once. But most of them ain't going to make the world any more interesting if I take the time to help them. Just the opposite, in fact. But you, girl—" She's looking right at me. "You're different."

"Different how?"

"There's a light in you," she says, "a dark light so strong it hurts the mind to look on it too long. So you're wondering why I'm helping you? That light tells me you could make things interesting again, if a body were to give it a little direction."

She lifts a hand before either me or Pinky can say a thing.

"Oh, I know what I said," she tells us. "How I like the simple life and all. But there's two kinds of complications. The ones we bring on ourselves, and they ain't nearly so entertaining, and then the ones the world brings on us. The kind that make you feel kinda desperate and alive while you're trying to get through 'em in one piece."

"You feel like that," I say, "why don't you just give me a sip of that blood of yours and I'll see how interesting I can make the world for you."

She shakes her head. "Don't think I ain't already thought've it. But the trouble you bring might not be appreciated by everyone. I don't want none of it coming back on me—that's bringing it on myself, y'see? The cousins aren't so partial to those of us that meddle like you're asking me to, and the one thing you never want is a whole mess of such powerful folks coming down on you all at once. Trust me on that one. I seen it happen afore."

She goes back to smoking then and I get the sense we're all done here.

"Well, we're obliged for all your help," I tell her, hopping down from the banister.

"I'd say be careful," Miss Lucinda says as we leave, "but if you were, that'd just spoil the fun."

She's mocking us now, but there's not much we can do. I don't know exactly what she is, but them bottles start rattling on the tree beside us and there's still no touch of no damn wind at all. So I just lift my hand and give her a smile.

"Looks like we got our work cut out for us," I say as we walk back through the forest to where we left the car.

"You don't believe that old bag, do you?"

"You saw her change—just for a moment there. Some kinda animal face looking at us. I know you did."

"I don't know what I saw," Pinky says, "but none of it makes me feel comfortable."

"This ain't about comfort," I tell her. "It's about being strong and getting stronger."

But Pinky only shrugs.

I know what she's thinking. We got no reason to believe that old woman. She don't owe us a damn thing. But I got me the feeling that she was telling the truth. If nothing else, I think she's looking forward to the idea of me and Pinky stirring up some trouble.

I consider them dog boys that chased us off from our kill and I know I ain't going to let that happen again. But first I got to get me strong. Stronger'n them, that's for damn sure.

· · ·

When we go hunting that night, we're somewhat cautious now as we don't want to run into them dog boys again till we're ready for 'em.

We talk about that potion of Miss Lucinda's, but it just sounds like too much work and we was always the ones to go for the quick'n dirty anyways. So when we cross over tonight, we're looking for only one kind a scent—some kinda mix of human and animal like them dog boys had, 'cept we're planning on finding us a smaller critter. Something not quite so fierce as them.

Tonight's a bust, and that pretty much sums up the next week or so, but I ain't ready to go collecting all them potion ingredients just yet. By day I go haunting around my sister's old neighborhood and apartment, not being too cautious, I guess, since a couple of her little friends spy me once or twice. One of 'em even follows me into a store, but she's easy to lose.

Of an evening afore we go hunting, time to time, I have me a look in on my sister her own self. Once I even stand there over her bed while she's sleeping, wondering what she'd do if I put that pillow over her head and pushed down on it. Just pushed down hard and keep on a-pushing till all them broken bits of her stop moving altogether.

But I don't.

I also take me a ride back up to Tyson one afternoon and park nearby that trailer park on the end of Indiana Road. I just want me a look-see at Del, for old times' sake. There ain't much moving around in the park 'cept a bunch of raggedy dogs and even raggedier-looking kids. But then I finally catch me a glimpse of my old boogeyman. He comes a-shuffling out a his trailer, walking down to the mailboxes, don't even look up at this mighty fine pink Caddy parked 'longside the road.

The years haven't been too kind on him, that's a fact. He's got him some ugly jowls and a bloated gut and he don't look so much scary as pathetic. Still I have me a little dream as I watch him collect his mail. I see me walking up to him, snapping that switchblade open, waiting for the look in his eyes. There gonna be a hint of the old hard Del in 'em, or is he just gonna be scared?

But I don't find out. I let him go back inside his trailer and I sit there awhile longer, not thinking of much of nothing. Finally, I start up the car and make the drive back to Newford.

And then one night we catch that smell we been looking for—part man, part fox—and I know we're in business.

We already determined we ain't sharing this kill with the rest of the pack. We don't know who or what they are and once we got what we want from the blood of this foxman, we ain't gonna need them no mores anyhow. But right now they're a help to us as we run down our prey.

I guess the whole point of the dreamworld is that's it's going to be full of the unexpected, but I got to tell you, what we find tonight comes on us so outta the blue, my mind closes down on me and I pretty much stop thinking for a heartbeat or two. We're hot on the heels of that little foxman, just a-tearing through the woods, he's so close I can already taste his blood. I know we're seconds from taking him down when we break into a clearing and who do we find but my sister and one of her friends.

The wind's coming from behind us, so we had no warning, not no way. We just stop, the pack automatically forming a half circle, waiting for my lead. But me, I can't think. All I can do is stare at them. Then I realize how scared they are, and I know we got 'em. Don't know what the hell we'll do with 'em, but we got 'em all right.

I walk forward on stiff legs. That wash of red rage is flooding my sight. I think I'm going for 'em. The pack's following my lead, edging closer. But then the friend just ups and vanishes. My sister and me, we lock gazes for a long whiles.

"You know me, don't you?" she says suddenly. "You know me and you really don't like me much."

Big surprise there, sister of mine.

I lunge for her, but then she follows her friend's lead and just vanishes and I come up hard against the tree behind her. I lose my balance, fall in a tangle, rise up fast, snarling at the pack as they move closer. I piss on the place my sister was standing, then walk stiff-legged away, snapping at the shoulder of the nearest of the pack. She gets submissive real quick, let me tell you.

I look at Pinky and she looks at me. We both know there's no point in following our little foxman now. He's gonna be long gone. I give Pinky a nod and we wake up, the two of us, lying on our motel bed.

"That was her!" Pinky's saying. "Goddamn, but if'n it wasn't your own sister."

I can't talk yet.

It's not just seeing my sister, it's seeing her over there. In the dream-lands. *My* goddamn dreamlands.

"How'd she get there first?" I finally manage to say. I sit up and look at Pinky. "How the hell did she get there, walking in her own body like she never got hurt?"

"It's a puzzle, all right."

I shake my head. "No," I say, my voice still kinda rasping in my throat. The red veil's still hanging over my eyes. "It's a mistake. She made her a serious mistake 'cause now I got to put her down. No way I'm shar-ing this with her. You hear me, Pinky? She don't get no more chances."

"You think this through," Pinky says. "You don't want to do no more time. Hell, we got us a death penalty still. You kill that girl and you're going to get worse'n time. They're gonna feed you the injection and that'll be all she wrote."

"I can't let this go." I stare at Pinky. "All my life, everything that's gone wrong with my life, it was her doing. I can't let her have the dream-lands, too."

"I ain't saying let it go. I'm saying use them brains of yours to find a cautious way to deal with it."

"I can't think."

"Okay," Pinky says. "You're mad and hurtin'. That's okay. So I'll do your thinkin' for you."

I just look at her.

"First thing we're gonna do," she says, "is stay on track here. Hunt us down one of them critters and get the blood we need. And then—"

"Then we hurt her."

Pinky grins. "Hell, Ray. Then we do any damn thing we want. Ain't that how it's gonna work?"

I stare at her through the red haze, but it's starting to fade now.

"Yeah," I say, my voice still rough. "That's how it's gonna work, all right."

Jilly

Wendy really did plan to wait until the next day to go see Jilly with Cassie. She knew waiting would be the sensible thing to do. Sure, Jilly would like the adventure of Wendy sneaking in to see her after visiting hours, but considering how hard they were working her in the rehab, she'd probably be asleep by now anyway. But the problem for Wendy was that the whole experience with the cards already had a certain dreamlike quality about it. Having screwed up by losing the images on the cards, she now felt an urgency to share what she had seen with Jilly before her own memory of it faded away as completely as the images had.

It would have been better if she was an artist and could simply render the images she'd seen, but her drawing skills didn't go much past stick people, so writing it down would have to do. She'd go home and do just that, then, when she went to see Jilly tomorrow she'd have her notes and Cassie would be there to fill in whatever holes there might be in her memory.

So home it was.

She waited at the bus stop and got on her bus when it arrived. It wasn't until she sat down that she realized how, without even thinking about it, she had gotten onto the bus that would take her to the rehab instead of the one back to her own apartment. Settling in her seat, she decided to allow fate to run its course.

She didn't have notes, or Cassie to help her out, but surely her memory would hold for a few more hours. She'd sneak into Jilly's room, wake her if she had to, and tell her what she and Cassie had learned. But when she got to the rehab and snuck past the nurses' station to Jilly's room, it was to find Sophie sitting on the edge of the bed, the two of them arguing, voices pitched low.

"What's going on?" she asked from the doorway.

Both of her friends started, looking almost guilty when they turned in her direction.

"I'm sure I don't know," Sophie said. "Jilly's gone all wonky on me—as bad as Jinx."

"Okay," Wendy said. "Now I'm way confused." She came into the room and sat on the end of the bed. "Anyone care to enlighten me?"

"But aren't you supposed to reach nirvana on your own merits?" Jilly said.

Sophie gave her a pointed look. "Jilly," she said in her "it's time to be serious" voice.

Jilly sighed. "Okay," she said. "But this doesn't mean I agree with you," she added to Sophie.

"About what?" Wendy asked before they could start to argue again.

Between the two of them, they told her about their evening, how they'd traveled together to the dreamlands, the little man-faced fox they'd seen, the wolves, how the leader of the pack had reminded Jilly of her little sister.

"Oh my god, oh my god," Wendy said. "Now it makes sense."

Two blank faces turned in her direction.

"I was just over at Cassie's," Wendy explained, "and she did a reading for me. Well, for Jilly actually. About this whole problem."

She described the three images that the cards had shown.

"The first was obviously you when . . . when you were a kid," she said.

"Not necessarily," Jilly told her. "Who knows what happened to Raylene after I left home."

For a moment none of them could speak as they considered another child having gone through the same torments that Jilly had.

"Okay," Wendy said, "but the wolves with those faces superimposed on them. The one that looked like you, Jilly. It could have been your sister, right, and not some . . . um . . . ?"

"Evil psycho twin?"

"I didn't say that."

"Did you and your sister resemble each other?" Sophie asked.

Jilly gave a small nod. "The whole time we were growing up, she looked exactly like all the pictures of me at the same ages. So it makes sense that the resemblance continued. There was even this guy, when Geordie and I went back to Tyson in '73, who thought I was her."

"So," Sophie went on. "If it is your sister, which is starting to seem ever more likely now, she's got access to the dreamlands as well. Along with a bunch of her friends."

"There was only one other person on the card," Wendy said.

"There were six or seven in the dreamlands." Sophie gave a slow shake of her head. "And they were hunting this little man-faced fox. That can't be good."

"Well," Wendy said. "If she ran Jilly down with her car and then wrecked all her paintings, we're not exactly talking about a nice person here."

"You don't understand," Jilly told them. "Raylene was just the sweetest little kid you could imagine. There's no way she could do those kinds of things. We don't *know* it was her."

"I saw her on the street outside your apartment," Sophie said. "And so did Isabelle. At least we saw someone who looked *just* like you, Jilly. Who else could it have been? And if she didn't wreck the paintings, then why's she hanging around your street?"

But if Jilly's sister had destroyed the paintings, Wendy thought, why *would* she still be hanging around? But she kept the question to herself, not wanting to interrupt the flow of Sophie's argument.

"And if she doesn't mean you any harm," Sophie went on, "then why hasn't she come to see you?"

"I don't know."

"What about the other card?" Wendy asked. "The pink Cadillac?"

"It doesn't even start to ring any bells," Jilly said.

Sophie started to nod in agreement, but then held up her hand.

"Wait a minute," she said. "I remember that morning I saw the doppelgänger. There'd been a pink car on the street that morning, farther down the block from your place. A long, pink convertible. I remember I started humming that Fred Eaglesmith song when I saw it."

That brought smiles all around—a welcome moment of respite from the intensity of their present conversation.

They'd seen Eaglesmith playing with his band at Your Second Home in January and danced the night away like mad dervishes to the driving sound of surf guitar meets electric bluegrass/country rock, with those gruff but biting vocals of Eaglesmith and the driving delivery of his lyrics cutting above the sound of the band. They'd been utterly enchanted from the first song when they realized that the surf guitar was actually a mandolin treated with electronics. The icing on the cake was the mad percussionist, a fellow called Washboard Hank who'd played a washboard, naturally, but also had a metal fireman's hat with a cymbal on it and all these air horns attached to the washboard. Each of them bought a different one of his CDs after the show and they'd been trading them back and forth ever since.

" 'That's a mighty big car,' " Jilly sang softly.

Sophie nodded. "Maybe it's hers. Your sister's, I mean."

"I suppose."

They all fell silent again.

"So what were you two arguing about when I came in?" Wendy asked.

"Sophie wants me to tell Lou about my sister. But I don't want the police involved. I don't want to get her into trouble."

"But, Jilly—" Sophie began.

"*Especially* not if she had to go through what I did. If I abandoned her to that." Jilly shook her head. "Who'm I kidding? Of course that's what happened. No wonder she'd be messed up."

"But you went through it," Sophie said. "And you're not messed up."

"Oh, please. All that crap's been living inside my head for as long as I can remember."

"But you're not going around hurting people because of it," Sophie said.

"I was just lucky," Jilly told her. "I got help. Like in a fairy tale. But she didn't."

"We don't know that. We don't know anything about her."

But Jilly wasn't listening. "Did you know that after the accident—when I was still in a coma—Joe brought in some magical healers to help me?"

Wendy and Sophie both nodded.

"But they said they couldn't do a thing because first I had to fix that old hurt. Except *how* do you fix something like that? Never mind me dealing with what happened to me. There's also what I did to Raylene. That's not something that can ever be forgotten. Or forgiven."

Sophie started to speak, but then she just bent her head and took Jilly's hand, giving it a squeeze.

Wendy sighed. Of the three of them, she was the only one who didn't have to deal with some horrible trauma left over from her childhood. The rules that made the world turn had all worked for her. She hadn't had a brother who'd abused her, a mother who'd deserted her, or any of the horrible things that seemed to have happened to two out of any three of the women they knew.

"Well, I agree with Sophie," she said, reluctant to keep pushing at it, but knowing that someone had to. "I think you have to tell Lou. And you should tell Joe, too."

But Jilly was already shaking her head.

"Why Joe?" Sophie asked.

"Well, do you know anybody else who knows as much about the dreamlands?" Wendy replied.

Sophie smiled. "Besides me, you mean?"

"He knows different stuff. He doesn't go there just in dreams, right? He'd know how Jilly's sister can be like a wolf over there."

"If it is my sister," Jilly said.

"Right. Maybe he could figure that out, too."

Jilly shook her head. "I don't want her hurt anymore."

"But what if she's hurting other people besides you?" Wendy asked. "Maybe on some cosmic karma chart, you deserve penance for running off on your sister the way you did—though I, for one, don't believe it. God, you were just a kid yourself. Look at all the years you were so messed up."

"That's an excuse?"

"No," Wendy told Jilly. "That's just a fact. But what if she's hurting other people? Innocent people. Are they supposed to pay penance as well?"

"No. Of course not."

"So we have to tell."

"Oh, god, I don't know," Jilly said. "Can we leave it until tomorrow? I just can't think about it right now."

Wendy exchanged a quick glance with Sophie.

"Of course we can," she said.

Jilly studied her for a moment. "Promise me you won't do anything till after we've talked tomorrow." She looked at Sophie as well. "Both of you."

"I won't tell Lou," Wendy said, "but I think Joe should know as soon as possible."

Jilly didn't say anything for a long heartbeat, then finally gave a small nod.

"Sure," she said. "We can tell him. Though how you expect to find him, I don't know. He's gone deep into the dreamlands."

Wendy nodded. "That's what Cassie said. But I'll pass the word on to her—and," she quickly added, "I'll tell her not to talk to anyone else about it."

There was little to say after that, so Sophie and Wendy got ready to leave.

"You'll be okay by yourself?" Sophie asked.

"As okay as I ever am these days."

Wendy's heart broke to hear the resignation in Jilly's voice. After they said their good-byes and were walking down the hall, she turned to Sophie.

"You could look for him, too, couldn't you?" she asked.

Sophie shook her head. "I wouldn't know how to start. But I can certainly put the word out when I go to Mabon tonight."

"We've got to help her through this," Wendy said. "All of this."

Sophie gave a glum nod. She fit her hand into the crook of Wendy's arm and the two of them left the rehab with their heads leaning together, trying to gather what strength and comfort they could from each other.

2

I'm so scared to go to sleep after Sophie and Wendy leave. I'm not even close to being ready to believe that my sister could be trying to kill me—either with a car in the World As It Is, or in the dreamlands as a wolf. I know people change, but that much? It doesn't seem possible that the sweet kid I left behind when I ran away from home could grow up to become some kind of monstrous shapechanging killer. It's too big a stretch and my mind can't accept it.

But whoever occupied the brain behind that wolf's eyes sure hated me. *That* I have no trouble believing. And it makes me nervous about going to sleep. I mean, I know I can just wake up to escape her if I run into her again, but what if she follows me back this time? Is that possible? I know Joe can walk in and out of the dreamlands at will. What if I only surprised her that last time and she wasn't quick enough to follow? Or what if she *is* quick enough, but she just hasn't yet? Or maybe she already knows where to find me, the Broken Girl lying helpless here like some bedridden version of Little Red Riding Hood, and she's just biding her time until she finally decides to come and get me here.

I wish I hadn't thought of that, because now I find myself straining at every odd sound I hear, imagining the click of a wolf's nails on the marble floors. I can't hide. I can't get up out of this bed. I can't even pull the bedclothes up over my head. And there wouldn't be just the one wolf either, but a whole pack of them, making their way down the hall to my room.

And this bugs me, too, because I've always loved wolves and now she's got me scared of them. I know they're predators and all, but I also know they don't attack humans unless they've been provoked.

But what did I ever do to provoke it?

Sophie's arguments come back to me and I'm full circle again, denying it could be my little sister Raylene, but I'm even more tired now than I was when Sophie was actually here for the conversation, my eyelids drooping like leaden weights, but my pulse working double time because of what might be waiting for me on the other side of sleep.

I'm surprised I ever get to sleep at all. But when I do, when I step back into the once upon a time of my dreams . . .

As I feel myself drifting away, I concentrate on that last place I was with Toby—high up in the branches of the biggest of the cathedral trees—because I feel I'll be safe there, far from the reach of any wolf, shapechanger or otherwise. At least it sounds good in theory.

Except what if she can just appear up in those branches the way I hope to?

She has to have been here first, the logical part of my mind argues. That's how it works. You can slip over and end up anywhere—the way people do when they're dreaming, and then they barely remember it anyway—or you can decide where you want to go, but you have to have been there before to do that. And what are the chances she's been there before?

But if she's a shapechanger, what's to stop her from changing into human form and climbing up after me? Or taking the shape of a bird, for that matter.

I fall asleep before my logic can find a way to make me feel better about that and then it becomes a moot point anyway because, instead of finding myself safe in that cathedral tree, I'm on a hilltop with a strange building at my back, looking down at where an enormous forest starts at the distant foot of the slope and runs off into the far horizon. It takes me a moment to realize it's the Greatwood I'm looking at. I've never seen it before from this vantage.

I take my gaze from the panorama and study the slope around me. There's such a jumble of rock and so many little ravines you could hide a dozen packs of wolves down there. When I don't see anything move after long moments, I turn slowly to have a look at the building.

There's not much to see from where I'm standing. There are windows in its stone walls—three tiers of them, one for each story, I guess—but the glass is too dark for me to see in. The fieldstone walls themselves appear to have been raised from material gathered close at hand and there's still plenty more of it to be found there, a quarry's worth of loose rocks and small boulders scattered all the way down the slope of the hill before it disappears into the forest. The roof of the building is thatched and the only opening I can see in the wall is this large arch that appears to lead into a cobblestoned courtyard, though oddly it has no keystone.

I give the slope and the forest a last look, then start for the building. A few minutes later, I step through the archway and into the courtyard. The space inside is large, maybe the size of a baseball diamond. There's another arch directly opposite and large wooden doors in the walls on either side. Wooden benches are set against the walls and there's a well in the center of the cobblestones. Higher up, the walls are studded with more windows, the glass all dark like the ones I saw outside. The lower ones have window boxes under them, overflowing with herbs and flowering plants.

I walk over to the well and look down. I can't see the bottom. The air in the courtyard is crisp and clean, but I can smell beer and things cooking: something spicy and the unmistakable aroma of fresh baked bread. Of the four doors, only two are open. Through the one to my right I can see stalls and bales of hay so I guess it leads to the stables. Through the one on the left I can make out a scattering of wooden tables with chairs set around each. My gaze lifts above the door and finds the sign hanging there:

Inn of the Star-Crossed

Now I know where I am. This is that building I saw from the branch of the huge cathedral tree I climbed when I was with Toby the other day.

There doesn't appear to be anyone around, but someone has to be cooking and baking, and maybe brewing beer. I want to call out, but I'm nervous about bringing the wrong kind of attention to myself. It's all too easy to imagine wolves skulking in the shadows, or watching me from behind the dark panes of all those windows.

I walk toward the door with the sign above it and step inside, blinking as my eyes adjust to the dimmer light. There's a long wooden bar directly to my left. It looks like something out of a cowboy movie with a mirror the length of the bar on the wall behind it and all the bottles and glasses on the shelves in front of the mirror. As my eyes adjust to the light I realize that the liquid in those bottles are all the colors of the rainbow. Weird. I can't imagine turquoise wine. Or blue whiskey.

Farther to the left is a hearth with no fire in it. There are wooden booths like in a diner on either side of the hearth, more along the wall to my right. Paintings and tapestries hang from the walls—landscapes and old-fashioned portraits. Each table and booth has a couple of fat white candles on it, unlit. There's no one sitting at any of the tables. No one behind the bar.

I clear my throat.

"Um . . . is anybody here?"

There's no reply, but I hear the sound of cloth brushing against cloth, as though someone's shifting their position. Then I see that there's a person sitting in one of the booths to the right of the hearth. I hesitate a moment, waiting to see if he or she'll speak. When they don't, I look around myself once more, then cautiously cross over to that booth, winding my way through the empty tables, ready to bolt at the first sign of danger.

The man sitting there watches me approach, but he doesn't say a word. He has a glass filled with a blue liquid in front of him on the table. There are wet blue rings on the wood around the glass. The man is handsome, in a rough sort of way. Bad-boy handsome, Wendy'd say. The kind you see outside of pool halls, but not so much a loser as a bit of a romantic loner. He'd have a motorcycle and he'd smoke, but he'd probably have a paperback of Rimbaud in his back pocket. Or at least something by one of the Beats. Dark hair pushed back from his brow and cleanshaven. Blue-eyed with long dark lashes that most women would kill for. Lean, dressed all in black. The hand resting on the table beside his drink is slender and well formed, but it's not a weak hand.

"Um, hello," I say. "I'm sorry to bother you . . ."

He keeps looking at me, but doesn't give me any indication that he understands what I'm saying.

"Do you speak English?" I try.

He lifts his glass and has a drink, then sets it down to make a new blue circle to join the others.

"Well, well," he finally says. "Look what we have here. The mother of misery herself. Well, you've come to the wrong place, dearheart. Anybody who comes here is already full up on their own unhappinesses. No need for you to come 'round and peddle yours."

He has the kind of voice that immediately makes little catpaws go running up your spine. Low and resonant. Very personable, for all the nasty things he's saying. I don't want to like him, but I can't help but feel drawn to him and that annoys me.

"Do I know you?" I ask.

"Does it matter?"

"Well, if you're going to be unkind, I think you should at least have a reason. Or are you just naturally mean-spirited?"

The blue eyes regard me for a long moment before he says, "Though some might consider otherwise, I save my cruelty for those that deserve it."

Lovely. Mr. Congeniality here isn't exactly a wolf with hate in her eyes, lunging at my throat, but he's obviously not a member of my fan club either. This being immediately disliked by people and creatures I don't even know is a novel and unnerving experience for me. It's not that I'm perfect or think that everybody should like me or anything. But I've never made enemies very well, and whenever I have hurt anybody, however inadvertently, I make a point of apologizing and trying to set things right as soon as I can. Always have.

Except for that one time when I ran away from home . . .

That makes me wonder. Maybe he's mad at her and has the two of us mixed up with each other.

"Do you know my sister?" I ask.

"Heaven help us. There are two of you?"

"Look," I say. "What's your problem? So far as I know, I've never met you before so you don't know anything about me."

"You'd like to think that, wouldn't you?"

"What I think is you've either got me confused with someone else, or you're just a rude person."

"They call me the Tattersnake," he says then. "Does that help jog your memory?"

The name rings a bell, but I can't quite place it. It think it's lost in one of my little memory holes until it suddenly comes to me.

"You're Toby's friend," I say.

Except what had Toby said?

You can't be friends with the Tattersnake. That's like trying to be friends with the stars or the moon—ever so filled with the potential for disappointment. Because they're so bright, and they hang so very high.

"No, not friend," I add before he can make some new nasty comment. "Toby said you weren't the sort of person you can be friends with."

The eyebrows lift and fall and there's a mocking look in those blue eyes of his.

"Is that what he said?" he asks.

There's just a hint of danger in his voice and I start to feel nervous again. I keep myself from looking around, but where *is* everybody? Shouldn't there at least be an innkeeper?

"I'm a friend of Joe's," I tell him, using the name as a talisman, hoping that it will mean something the way it did with the cousins I've met in the Greatwood. "You know." I have to think a moment to retrieve the name Jolene has for Joe. "Animandeg."

"But Joe's not here, is he?"

I don't let my fear show, unless you count the trembling in my legs, but his gaze is locked on my face so I'm guessing he doesn't see the way they're shaking.

"Yeah, well, it's been fun," I tell him.

Before I can start to back away, he makes a negligent wave to the bench on the other side of the booth from where he's sitting.

"But, please," he says "Don't go off pouting now. Have a seat. Share some of your wisdom with me."

"I don't know what you mean."

"Oh, come on. Everyone's talking about you down in the Greatwood: the dreaming girl with the big spirit light burning in her. They're all so sure your arrival means something grand."

He's having fun with this, but his amusement only goes so far as the mockery in his eyes. I don't need to be a mind reader to know that he's got some serious "I hate you" jones that he needs to express. I want to be out of here before it goes from verbal to physical.

"I don't know what you're talking about," I tell him. "I don't know anything."

"And yet you're so very free with your advice and wisdom. Oh, and your help. You're so very helpful as well, aren't you? Or at least for so long as it suits you."

I start to back up. I don't know who he's got me mixed up with—my sister, some complete stranger—but I don't like where this is going. Not at all.

"You're not leaving, are you?"

There's such menace in his voice that it stops me dead in my tracks. "I . . ."

I'm not quite sure what to say.

But before he gets the chance to make some new nasty remark, a voice calls out from behind me.

"Rue! You're not bothering my customers, are you?"

I want to look around but I'm scared of turning my back on Mr. Congeniality here.

The Tattersnake looks past me with a sour expression—all his fun spoiled, I guess. He downs the rest of that weird blue drink and stands up, tall and foreboding.

"We're not finished, you and I," he says as he brushes by me.

I turn now to watch him go, follow to the door after he's stepped out into the courtyard. He turns to the left and walks toward the archway opposite the one I came in by. When he steps under its stone span, there's a flicker of amber light and he's gone, just like that. I stare for a long moment. I'd been wondering what an inn was doing up here on top of a hill in the middle of nowhere and not a road in sight, but I guess if you can just teleport through its door, it could be on the moon and still have a regular clientele.

When I'm sure the Tattersnake's not coming back, I turn back inside to find my benefactor standing over the table the Tattersnake vacated, wiping the blue circles from the smooth wood with a cloth. He looks up at my return.

"Sorry about that," he says. "Ruefayel's not the best company when he's in a mood."

I guess this is the innkeeper. He looks sort of like a jovial biker or construction worker—a large, almost square man in a white muscle shirt that shows off his big arms and the tattoos that run up and down them. They're all of animals—lizard, wolf, lynx, eagle, dragon. He has long brown hair, tied back in a ponytail, and a small goatee. But unlike the Tattersnake—or I guess Ruefayel, as this guy knows him—he exudes friendliness.

"He told me his name was the Tattersnake," I say.

"It's more a description—like I'm an innkeeper. Name's William, by the way. William Kemper."

I remember then that Toby had said pretty much the same thing about the Tattersnake. *It's not a name, it's a title.*

I introduce myself to William and follow him to the bar where he washes out Ruefayel's glass in a stainless-steel sink and then starts to dry it. I'm surprised by the modern sink and running water, but I've got bigger questions on my mind.

"So what's a Tattersnake?" I ask.

William grins and gives me a shrug. "Who knows? He first came in a while back and just introduced himself as Ruefayel Grenn, the Tattersnake. Seemed a little put out that no one recognized him."

"Is . . . is he dangerous?"

"Everybody's dangerous, if you push them hard enough. But—" He nods. "Yeah, Ruefayel's pretty much dangerous all the time. Got a chip on his shoulder the size of a log and he's been in a fight or two. What was he bothering you about?"

"I don't really know. He seems to think he knows me and he *really* doesn't like what he knows."

"You a writer?"

I shake my head.

"Then I haven't a clue. Would you like something to drink?"

I look at all those bottles with their oddly colored contents.

"I wouldn't know what to order," I tell him.

"What do you usually have—at home, I mean."

"Beer. Coffee."

"I've got both."

"Then coffee, I think."

"Cream and sugar?"

When I tell him just black, he takes down one of those bottles and pours steaming coffee from it into a fat china mug and puts it on the bar in front of me. He grins at the look on my face.

"Come on," he says. "This is the dreaming place. Things work differently here."

I smile. "I guess I haven't been around it enough. So far I've only explored some parts of Mabon and the Greatwood."

He nods. "And then you got depressed and ended up here."

"Is that your only clientele—depressed people?"

"No, we get all kinds. You should see it in here on a full moon. But a name like the Inn of the Star-Crossed tends to attract its fair share of unhappy and unlucky people. A lot of first timers come because of the name."

"I'm not really depressed," I tell him. "At least not when I'm over here. Back in the World As It Is, I'm not so happy."

He just gives me another nod, a barman's universal response. I can keep talking, or I can stare into my coffee. Either way, it'll be fine by him. I have a sip of my coffee.

"It's delicious," I tell him, then add, "Why did you ask if I was a writer?"

"Because of Ruefayel. He doesn't like them."

"Why not?"

"Well . . ."

William looks past me for a moment, not really focusing on anything.

"Guys like him I call peripherals," he says, bringing his gaze back to my face. He lifts a hand before the question in my eyes can reach my lips. "You know. They're not native to the dreaming lands, and they don't come through the gates of sleep like you did. Somebody made them up, so they have a limited shelf life, as it were, existing only so long as there's people that believe in them."

"The Eadar," I say, remembering the conversation I had with Toby. "The people that come from the middleworld."

He gives me a curious look. "Yeah. Where'd you hear about them?"

I tell him about Toby.

"I know him—calls himself the Boyce, right? I think the two of them are from the same story. I've seen a few others from it, but they're pretty insubstantial these days."

"So it's true? They really fade away if they're not believed in?"

"Oh, yeah. Talk about your raw deals."

"I still don't understand why Ruefayel was so mad at me."

"That's his way of being remembered," William says. "He pisses people off and they don't forget him."

I shake my head. There seemed to be more to it than that, but I don't know where to go with the idea.

"Well, I could be wrong," William says.

"I wasn't disagreeing," I tell him. "It just seemed more personal than that."

"I wouldn't worry too much about it. Trust me, I've seen him do the nasty more times than I care to remember. I keep threatening to bar him, but . . ." He shrugs. "I guess I feel sorry for him."

"You don't seem very busy," I say to change the subject.

"Well, most of my business is with the peripherals and we had us some of the old cousins in here this morning, kind of scared them away. You've heard about the effect pure bloods have on them?"

I nod. "Do you think it's true?"

"Doesn't really matter. If the peripherals believe it, they're going to take off anyway. But yeah, it's probably true."

"I wonder if the cousins know?"

"Hard to say," William says. "But I kind of doubt it. They keep to themselves pretty much anyway, and since the peripherals take off whenever one of them's around, who's there to tell them?"

You could, I think. But I'm not going to annoy anybody else today if I can help it. I'll just ask Joe about it the next time I see him.

"Do you get any shapechangers in here?" I ask.

"You mean besides the cousins?"

"I guess."

I hadn't even considered that the wolf hating me so much could be one of the People.

"Not really," William says. "Dreamers like yourself usually get themselves a shape when they cross over and stick with it. And the peripherals are pretty much the same—except if whoever made them up added in the ability to shift shape, I suppose. But unless they shifted in front of you, how would you know?"

"So you don't get wolf people in here?"

He smiles. "Oh, we get lots of canids—pure bloods, I mean."

"Besides them."

"Anyone in particular you're looking for?"

Just for one that hates me, I think, but I shake my head.

"No, I'm just curious, is all."

He leans his elbows on the bar, face close to mine.

"Maybe it's none of my business," he says, "but these days, that's something you shouldn't be too curious about. There's a bunch of dreamers crossing over as wolves and they're hunting unicorns and pure bloods."

I can feel my eyes go wide, the flush on my skin.

"Yeah," William goes on. "It's kind of got everybody on edge, as you can well imagine. I hear some of the cousins are trying to track them down and if they think you're involved, you could be looking at a world of trouble."

"I . . . I'm not one of them," I say. "But I think I saw them. They attacked me and a friend earlier tonight."

"But you woke up and got away."

I nod.

"Natives can't do that. They've got no place to wake up to and this pack's been cutting them down. Nobody knows how long it's been going on, but it must have been awhile. The canids are particularly pissed, seeing how these dreamers are wearing one of their shapes."

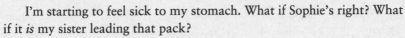

I'm starting to feel sick to my stomach. What if Sophie's right? What if it *is* my sister leading that pack?

"I . . . I better go," I say. "How much do I owe you?"

"It's on the house," William says. His gaze locks on to mine. "You've got quite a glow, sitting there inside you."

I sigh. "Apparently. At least nobody seems to get tired of telling me that."

He holds my gaze a moment longer, then straightens up.

"Watch your back," he says. "That kind of shine's like a beacon."

"I wish it was something a little more useful than this 'Hello, here I am' kind of an advertisement."

"It's useful," William assures me. "But a thing like that, it can take its time letting you know the how and why of its usefulness."

Which is ever so helpful, I think.

I stand up from my stool. "Thanks for the coffee and the conversation," I tell him.

"You be careful."

I give him a small smile. "And for all the advice."

"Hey, I'm only trying to—"

I put a hand on his where it's resting on the bar.

"I wasn't being sarcastic," I tell him. "I am grateful. Honestly."

I give his hand a squeeze and leave the common room. I pause in the courtyard, looking around. I still get the feeling that there are people watching me. Maybe it's some of the Eadar, insubstantial and fading. I walk quickly across the cobblestones and through the archway I came in.

The view sucks me in and for a long time all I can do is stand there and look out on the enormous sweep of the Greatwood. When I think of how big the individual trees are, the vast forest lying out there below me becomes almost impossible to take in. I look for a moment longer, then I let myself wake up again.

3

Sophie hadn't created the dreamlands. She knew that. By all accounts, that otherworld had existed forever, perhaps longer, and was known by as many names as there were beings to name it.

But Mabon, that sprawling dream city, was hers.

Not now, perhaps. Not any longer, or at least not entirely. But it had begun with her.

It wasn't like a painting. She hadn't stretched the canvas, sketched the design upon it, laid in the background with large blocks of color and slowly worked up the details. She hadn't planned it at all.

She'd been a little girl, a latchkey kid, taking refuge after school in the home that she shared with her father, for her mother had left them a long time ago. Sophie could barely remember her. They'd been poor in those days and there was no money for art supplies and books. So she amused herself while she waited for her father to come home by drawing on old shopping bags and reading the stack of books she took out from the library, once a week. She kept the house, made their dinner, did her homework, but there was still plenty of time to read and draw. Too much perhaps. By Tuesday she'd usually already gone through the five books that she took out from the library on Saturday mornings. And so she began to daydream.

It began with Mr. Truepenny and his curious shop in which you could find all the books that authors hadn't gotten around to writing, with a gallery in the back that held the same never-to-be-seen treasures of the great artists.

There, sitting in one of the leather club chairs that dotted the store, she read books like *North Country Stoic* by Emily Brontë. Lord Dunsany's *The Peregrine's Broken Waltz*. The fifth canto of Byron's *Childe Harold's Pilgrimage*. *The Knight in the Shadow* by Alan Garner.

She was able to take in private viewings of sketches Watteau and Dali would have made had they lived to do them. Paintings by Waterhouse and Collier, etchings by Sargent, pastels by Degas—none of which had ever been seen in the World As It Is. But she could see them and more in the little gallery in the back of the bookshop.

She daydreamed the shop and its contents with such clarity that her time spent imagining them was as real to her as the world around her when she was awake. And slowly a city built up around that shop. First it was only the street outside as seen from inside, then the buildings on either side of Mr. Truepenny's establishment and across the street, finally the city blocks that started up on either end of the street. The city grew and spread out, no longer under her control, its existence fueled now by other dreamers who came and stayed and added their own ideas and considerations. It became inhabited by these dreamers and by the Eadar drawn out of the middleworld, whose existence here depended on the belief of those with whom they interacted.

But Sophie was aware of none of that. She grew up, went to university, became an artist herself, and forgot all about the city, the curious little shop, even Mr. Truepenny himself until about eight years ago, when a chance meeting with another of the city's dreamers brought it all back to her. Without her influence—her "faerie blood," as Jilly would have it, which was apparently the glue that held the whole magical construct together—the city was coming apart at the seams, tattered and worn, its inhabitants fading as they rattled about empty buildings and increasingly deserted streets.

Her return brought the city back to life.

The downside was that was about the time that Jinx came back into her life, as well. As soon as she started what Jilly called her "true dreaming," electrical and mechanical items began their jittering arbitrary dance of going awry around her on a regular basis, just as they had when she was a kid. It was something she'd managed to forget until Jinx's return.

But at least Jinx stayed behind in the World As It Is when she crossed over into the dreamlands. However it was connected to her dreaming or her faerie blood, once she stepped between the worlds any problems that came up were ones that she had usually generated on her own. It was nice to be able to wear a watch that worked, to play with an art program on a computer and not have the machine crash, to stick in a videotape and see the movie that was supposed to be there instead of something she wasn't even close to being interested in watching.

That was the part of it that drove Jilly particularly crazy: how Sophie could be in a magical dreamworld, where surely anything was possible, but spent her time in a city not so different from Newford, doing the same things she'd do if she were at home.

"Well," Sophie would respond to Jilly's suggestion that she should be doing more with her gift than simply spending the evening doing nothing with her boyfriend Jeck. "I guess I just don't have much of an imagination."

"But you're magic—simply brimful of faerie blood."

"As if."

"You could be living a fairy-tale life."

"Having Jeck for my boyfriend and not being under attack by any errant toaster or telephone I happen to come across *is* a fairy-tale life so far as I'm concerned."

"You know what I mean."

"I suppose I do," Sophie would say. "But I wouldn't know how to change."

Jilly's usual response at that point would be a shake of her head, accompanied by a theatrical sigh, and then she'd satisfy her curiosity by poring over the sketches and drawings Sophie did from memory of the interesting places and people she'd seen in Mabon.

She was particularly fascinated with Jeck, as much because of his crow blood as the fact that when Sophie did have adventures in the dreamlands, it was usually in his company. To this day neither of them could decide if he was a native to the dreamlands, a dreamer such as Sophie herself, or one of the Eadar, drawn up out of the middleworld by someone's story. Sophie herself had never asked, and Jeck didn't volunteer, and just because Sophie had found a story in Mr. Truepenny's shop that seemed to coincide with some of the incidents in Jeck's family history—a lovely little chapbook called "The Seven Crow Brothers" by Hans Christian Andersen, illustrated by Ernest Shepard, unavailable in the World As It Is, of course—it didn't mean he was an Eadar.

But whatever his origin, he knew far more about the dreamlands than Sophie did herself. He had a confident knowledge, that of a native, or someone who had spent much of his life here. The sort of knowledge that was simply part of one's makeup and background, as opposed to the haphazard information that Sophie had acquired over the years.

So when she met up with him in their apartment that evening, after first filling him in on all the odd occurrences that had been scattered through what felt like a very long day since she'd seen him the night before, she asked his advice on how to track down Joe. Because if anyone here would know, it would be him.

"I don't know any canids," he said, "but they'd be the ones to ask."

"These are like the original animal people, right?" Sophie asked. She never paid nearly as much attention to this sort of thing as Jilly could and did. "The ones that can be wolves or dogs?"

Jeck nodded. "Or foxes or coyotes. They say the clans of the People can find those of their own clan much more quickly than others might."

Joe had canid blood, Sophie knew. He also had crow blood, but it wasn't the same as the crow blood that ran through her boyfriend's veins. Jeck's shapeshifting could only take place in the fairy-tale world where she'd first met him; it wasn't bred into his blood and bones like it was for the People.

"So we need to find one of these canids," she said.

"Easier said than done. It's not like the cousins have an office on Main Street where we can just call up and make an appointment. We'd probably have as much luck finding Joe on our own as we would one of the canids—at least in time for it to be of any use to your friend Jilly."

"But we must know someone who knows one of them," Sophie said. "Like Kerry."

"Kerry?"

"You know. She has that herb shop down the street from Mr. Truepenny's . . ."

Sophie's voice trailed off.

For all Jilly's complaints, and Sophie's protests to the contrary, Sophie didn't spend all her time in Mabon. She'd had adventures—though none she'd precipitated. Most of them were in what she called the fairy-tale world, a part of the dreamlands where magics were more obvious than in Mabon. Where there were goblins and bogles and witches like Granny Weather. Where she'd met her Jeck—first as a crow, then as the handsome man who'd become her boyfriend. But once, she'd gotten trapped in another place, a desert dreamland that echoed the American Southwest, and for the longest time, whenever she fell asleep, she'd returned to it, instead of to Mabon.

"What is it?" Jeck asked.

"*I* know a coyote," she said. "That time I went through the back door of Mr. Truepenny's shop . . ."

"And were gone forever."

She leaned across the table and gave him a kiss. "It just felt like that, but it's sweet of you to say it all the same."

"You got trapped in that world."

Sophie nodded. "But I wouldn't now. I found the way out."

"Coyotes can't be trusted."

"They say the same thing about crows."

Jeck sighed. "How would you even call him to you once you were there?"

"With my famous faerie blood, I guess."

Jeck stared at her for a long moment, surprise in those violet eyes of his. Finally he leaned forward.

"Where's my Sophie," he said, "and what have you done with her?"

For a moment Sophie didn't know what he was talking about. But then she realized.

"I know it seems odd," she said, "but I think I'm coming to accept that it might be true. Or at least that there's something odd about me that has machines malfunction back home and allowed me to do whatever it is I did to help make all of this—" She waved a hand to encompass all of the city, not just the apartment where they were sitting. "Real."

Jeck slowly shook his head. "What brought this on?"

"I'm not sure. Talking to Jilly, I suppose. Are you all shocked?"

"No. Happy, actually."

Sophie gave him a curious look.

"Why?" she asked. "Does it make a difference in our relationship?"

"Only in how you might become more comfortable with yourself," he told her.

Sophie thought about that for a moment and realized he might be right. There was always this tug-of-war going on inside her, a struggle between what she believed was real and what she thought wasn't. With all this business with Jilly and the wolves and everything, she hadn't had the time to stop and be still for a moment. But now that she was, she found that the inner struggle had gone silent. It was an odd feeling, actually. Like a favorite tight T-shirt suddenly gone loose.

"You might even find," Jeck said, "that when you return to your homeworld, Jinx will be gone."

"You think my problem with machines was because of my denying this whatever it is I have—this faerie blood?"

"It's possible. You don't have that kind of trouble here, but here you're much more accepting of marvels and magics. Here it's all a dream for you. The stress of having to believe in it doesn't come over you until you leave. Until you return home."

Sophie looked at him for a long moment. "I always believed in you," she said. "You know that, don't you?"

He nodded.

"I don't know why," she added, "but that was just never a question for me."

When she reached a hand across the table, he covered it with his own and they sat like that for a time, looking at each other, and smiling.

"I'm coming with you," he said after a time.

"I'm glad."

Mr. Truepenny's Book Emporium and Gallery was only a few blocks from their apartment so it didn't take them long to get there. Although it was after store hours, when they looked through the window, Mr. Truepenny was still sitting at his desk, his long Don Quixote body folded up to fit in the small space because of the clutter of hardcovers and paperbacks and magazines stacked around him. He was studying a book that was open on the desk, absentmindedly fussing with that pipe of his that he never lit.

When Jeck tapped on the window to get his attention, Mr. Truepenny started, almost dropping the pipe. Turning, he pushed his round spectacles up his nose and broke into a smile when he recognized the pair of them.

"Come in, come in," he said after he disentangled himself from his cramped position behind the desk and came around to unlock the door. "To what do I owe this late-night pleasure?"

"We need to use your back door," Sophie told him.

He gave her a puzzled look.

"You know," she said. "The one that leads out into a desert world sometimes."

She saw understanding come to him then. That last time she'd used the door, Jeck had driven Mr. Truepenny half mad trying to find out what had happened to her, so she was surprised he hadn't twigged immediately to what she was asking him.

"You understand that it doesn't only open out into the desert?" Mr. Truepenny said.

Sophie nodded. "I know. Most of the time it just leads out to the alleyway . . ."

Her voice trailed off as Mr. Truepenny shook his head.

"The problem with that door," he said, "and others like it, is that they lead to anywhere and anywhen."

Sophie sighed. "Is this one of those 'you have to really keep your mind focused on what you're doing' kind of things?"

Mr. Truepenny nodded. "Either something will lead you to where you need to go—"

"Like that sound of the flute did the last time."

"—or you have to be very certain of where you mean to arrive."

"We can do that," Sophie assured him. "Can't we, Jeck?"

"We can try," Jeck said.

"I mean, crow blood and faerie blood—we've got the mojo, right?"

Mr. Truepenny pushed his glasses up again and regarded her through their round rims.

"You sound as though you're trying to convince yourself more than me," he said.

Why did people always see through her so easily? Sophie wondered.

"I suppose I am," she said aloud.

Mr. Truepenny gave a thoughtful nod.

"I know it's none of my concern," he said, "but might you be able to tell me why it is that you need to access the desert world?"

"It's no secret," Sophie told him, "but it is kind of a longish story."

"I'll put some tea on," Mr. Truepenny said.

While he was getting the tea, Sophie and Jeck returned to the front of the store where they made room for themselves by shifting aside stacks of recent arrivals. Sophie smiled at the top book of the first stack she moved: *Country Car Interiors* by Martha Stewart. Now there was a book that wouldn't be appearing anytime soon in the World As It Is. Another stack had *Coyote Cowgirl Hitches a Ride* by Kim Antieau on top of it. That one she put aside to have Mr. Truepenny hold for her after he'd priced it.

Later, when Sophie was done with her story, Jeck poured them all another cup of tea from the big brown betty that Mr. Truepenny had used for as long as Sophie had been coming to the shop. Dodger, the marmalade store cat, chose that moment to come out from under Mr. Truepenny's desk and jump up onto Sophie's lap, bumping her hand with his head until she started to scratch him under his chin.

"So it would be specifically Joseph you need to contact," Mr. Truepenny said. "Rather than your coyote friend—or a canid in general, for that matter."

Sophie supposed she shouldn't have been all that surprised when Mr. Truepenny had told them he knew Joe. Joe was like Jilly in that way, except where Jilly only seemed to know every third person in Newford,

Joe's circle of acquaintances and friends encompassed a good part of the dreamlands as well.

"Do you have some way that we can contact him?" she asked.

"Not I, personally," Mr. Truepenny said. Before Sophie's hopes could sink, he added, "However, it would be a simple matter to acquire the services of Longfoot & Quick and have a message sent to him."

Sophie and Jeck exchanged glances.

"Longfoot & Quick?" Sophie asked.

Mr. Truepenny paused with a spoon of sugar halfway between the pot and his cup of tea and looked at her from above his glasses.

"The courier people," he said and gave their address, which was a few blocks over from his shop. He put the sugar in his tea and reached for the milk. "They've been the talk of the town since they set up shop last year—I'm surprised you're unaware of their services."

Both Sophie and Jeck shook their heads.

"They claim a two-day turnaround, anywhere in the dreamlands," Mr. Truepenny continued, "or offer a complete refund."

Considering the bewildering quiltwork of timelines and pocket worlds that made up the dreamlands, Sophie couldn't begin to imagine a service such as this, especially one with such a guarantee.

"How can they possibly do that?" Sophie asked.

Mr. Truepenny shrugged. "I have no idea. How does the Pixie Wood Bakery make their breads and pastries out of sawdust?"

"I didn't know they did."

"They do it with magic," Mr. Truepenny said.

He stirred his tea, adjusted his glasses yet one more time, and then took a sip. Smiling with satisfaction, he put the cup on his desk and began to fuss with his pipe.

"It always comes down to magic," he went on. "We never seem to be privy to the inner workings of it, but then it's always struck me that mystery is one of its prime ingredients."

"Is Longfoot & Quick open at this time of night?" Jeck asked.

"They provide a twenty-four-hour service," Mr. Truepenny said. "I'm really quite surprised that you've never availed yourself of their services before. I find them terribly useful for sending out special orders." He looked down into his empty teacup and sighed. "I wish I hadn't thought of the Pixie Wood," he added. "It's made me come over all peckish. For something sweet, rather than savory, mind you, and I ate my last hazel-nut cookie this morning."

Sophie collected herself. Setting Dodger down on the floor, she stood up. She ignored the cat's grumpy look at being dislodged.

"We've got sticky buns at home," she said. "We could bring some by after we've sent our message."

"With raisins?" Mr. Truepenny asked hopefully.

"Chock-full of them," Sophie assured him.

4

If Cassie was surprised by Wendy's reappearance at her apartment later that night, she showed no sign of it. She only smiled and ushered Wendy through the door without a comment. Inside, only one large fat candle lit the living room and the air was redolent with the scent of cedar incense.

"Can I get you anything?" she asked.

Wendy shook her head. "I don't want to be a bother."

"I've got a pot of green tea already made."

"Tea'd be lovely."

Cassie had answered the door wearing silk pajamas that were such a bright pink they had banished any sleepiness Wendy might have been feeling and made her forget for a moment why she was here. Still smil-ing, Cassie steered her to a seat on the sofa and went to fetch another raku teacup. Like her own, it had a blue-green glaze that caught the can-dlelight and made Wendy feel like she was looking at a jewel from underwater.

"I love the incense," she said as Cassie poured her tea for her.

"I was thinking about Joe," Cassie explained. "The smell of cedar always makes me feel closer to him."

Wendy was about to ask why, but now that she thought about it, there was often the faint hint of cedar about him, rather than the smell of tobacco. Odd, really, when you considered how much he smoked. But he never smelled like cigarettes.

"Actually, I'm here because of Joe," she said.

"You've heard from him?"

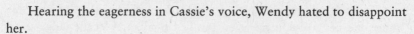

Hearing the eagerness in Cassie's voice, Wendy hated to disappoint her.

"No," she said. "I just need to get a message to him and I thought you'd know how."

Cassie shook her head. "Once he's in the otherworld, he's pretty much out of contact. Why do you need to reach him?"

"Well, I went by the rehab," Wendy said, "and Sophie was there with Jilly, the two of them arguing . . ."

She filled Cassie in on the latest developments.

"That would explain the residual presence I felt in Jilly's apartment," Cassie said when she was done. "Jilly, but not Jilly. Or rather the same strong presence, but much, much darker."

Wendy remembered Jilly's comment, made in jest.

"Her psycho evil twin," she said.

"Did Jilly say that?"

"She was kidding. Actually, she's way protective of this sister she hasn't seen in, what? Twenty years? She just won't believe that she could have changed that much. But people do change. I've seen them change overnight."

Cassie nodded. "I have, too—when the circumstances are right."

"And we don't know any of this sister's circumstances."

"Maybe Jilly just doesn't want to believe," Cassie said. "It's got to be hard to have suspicions like that about someone in your own family."

Wendy shook her head. "I don't know about that. For as long as I've known her, she's said she doesn't have a blood family. Only the one she chose."

"I know that feeling," Cassie said.

"Yeah, I'm probably the only one in our circle of friends who actually enjoys a family get-together. But then I'm lucky—in my family, we all get along."

Wendy had finished her tea and was happy to hold out her cup when Cassie offered her a refill. There was something about tea that she found so comforting. They all drank it, though for Jilly the real comfort drink was coffee. Sophie's was a glass of red Bordeaux.

"Has Jilly told Lou?" Cassie asked.

Wendy shook her head. "She doesn't want the police involved."

"Lou's not like other cops. He's a friend."

"But he's still a cop and he's so by the book that he'd never let it slide either. It'd be, arrest Jilly's sister, put her in jail, and let the judge sort it out later."

Cassie nodded. "I guess that's Lou all right. I wish Joe were here. He's always been better dealing with this kind of thing."

"Can't your cards tell us where he is?"

"They'd only tell us what we already know: he's in the spiritworld. How far, how deep, is anybody's guess. I wouldn't begin to know where to go look for him."

Wendy gave her a curious look.

"So you can cross over as well?" she asked.

Cassie nodded. "Though I almost always go with Joe. My sense of direction's awful over there and if I was left to my own devices, I'd probably never find my way back."

"So you can really go over. You don't go in a dream like Sophie and Jilly."

"I wish I could go in a dream," Cassie said. "Then whenever I got lost, I could just wake up."

Wendy sighed and slouched back in the sofa.

"Are you all right?" Cassie asked.

Wendy nodded. "Just tired, I guess."

Cassie regarded her for a long moment but said nothing.

"I guess I feel kind of stupid," Wendy added.

"About what?"

"I don't know. The spiritworld. All this traveling around in dreams. I didn't really think about it when it was just Sophie—or even when Jilly was able to do it, too. It was just the way it was. But now . . . I guess it really hit me tonight when I realized that they're going to be hanging out together in the dreamlands without me. Before this we've always done everything together. Well, not everything, but you know what I mean."

Cassie nodded. "The important things."

"Exactly. The dreamlands is something I'm never going to be able to share with them and I hate feeling this way—you know, how I'm going to be more and more on the outside of things." She shook her head. "I told you it was stupid. I mean, I'm used to Sophie being able to do it and it's what Jilly's always wanted, so I should be happy for her, right? And I *am* happy for her. But I can't help feeling left out, and I guess a little hurt at the same time."

"That's not stupid," Cassie told her.

"Maybe. But it's not helping matters either. And 1 hate feeling jealous."

"You have to tell them how you feel," Cassie said.

"And that'll solve what?"

"I don't know. You won't find that out until they know how you're feeling about all of this."

"I don't want them to stop going on my account," Wendy said.

"But you'd like to join them."

Wendy nodded. "Except that's not going to happen because I don't have this big shiny light in me like Jilly and Sophie do." She sat up from the couch and looked at Cassie. "I don't, do I?"

"Not that I can see."

Wendy slumped back in the sofa again. "So it's all hopeless."

"Not necessarily," Cassie told her. "I don't have that shine, either. Or the blood of the cousins like Joe does. But I can still cross over."

"Can you show me how?"

Cassie nodded. "I can take you over, but it'll depend on you whether or not you'll be able to do it on your own."

"So it still comes down to being special."

"Not exactly. But it does take a certain way of observing the world, an ability to look sideways and find those places where the borders are thin enough to slip through from one world to the other. That's how we do it," she explained before Wendy could ask. "Those of us who don't have magic of one kind or another in our blood."

"Can we try it now?"

Cassie laughed. "Hardly. We're both tired and we have other commitments we need to deal with first."

"Helping Jilly," Wendy said. "Finding Joe."

Cassie nodded. "And it might be a good idea if Joe was the one to show you how to cross over."

"I thought you said you could."

"I can, and I will, if need be. But Joe's got a better eye for how you'll do on the other side. He'll be able to prepare you better."

"Prepare me for what?"

"The spiritworld's a confusing place," Cassie told her. "Time runs differently there and it's all too easy to get lost in otherwhens. You know the old story: those who cross over return either mad or as a poet."

"I thought that was from fairyland."

"Which is just another name for the dreamlands."

"Well, I'm already a poet," Wendy said.

Cassie smiled. "There's that." She finished her tea and stood up. "I think you should stay here tonight. I can make up a bed for you on the sofa."

"I don't want to be a bother."

"You won't be. Besides, I could use the company."

"What about contacting Joe?"

Cassie shrugged. "Like I said earlier. I wouldn't know where to begin. I'm going to do what I usually do when I need him to come back from the dreamlands and that's think really hard about him while I'm going to sleep."

"Does it work?"

"It seems to. He usually shows up within a day or two whenever I've done it before."

"I don't know if we have a day or two."

"Let's worry about that in the morning when we're more awake. Now I'm just going to get some bedding and a pillow."

Wendy brought their teacups and the pot back into the kitchen when Cassie left. On her return, they took the back cushions off the sofa and made up a bed on the seat cushions.

"I'm going to think about him, too," Wendy said.

Cassie smiled. "Let's just hope he's listening tonight."

5

I still don't know what to do when I wake up the next morning. Wendy comes by on the way to work and tells me that Cassie's sending a message to Joe, but that there's no guarantee that he'll get it anytime soon, deep as he is in the dreamlands. She doesn't stay long.

"I can't be late again this week," she says before she hurries off.

It's not until she's gone that I realize there was something different about her—a vague feeling of reticence in her manner, like there's a distance growing up between us. Then it's too late. I'm trapped in my bed and I can't follow after her to ask about it. I wonder if I've done something to annoy her, but nothing comes to mind. If I have, I guess it's lost in one of my little memory black holes.

Sophie's by next and tells me about this new messenger service in Mabon and that, at least, gives me a smile. I love the idea of all these punk elfin sprites, dressed up like bicycle couriers as they flit about the dreamlands, delivering messages. She also insists again that we can't wait to hear from Joe; that we have to tell Lou before something even worse happens.

"Those wolves tried to kill us," she says.

"We don't know it was my sister leading them," I argue, but without a lot of conviction. I'm pretty sure it was, and Sophie knows it. "And besides, what do we tell Lou? Well, we were sharing this dream and then these wolves jumped us. How'd we get away? Oh, we woke up."

"What if they can cross over?" Sophie asks.

That's treading too close to my own fears.

"We don't know that they can," I tell her, but I can't even convince myself, never mind her, and Sophie picks right up on that as well.

"Someone trashed your studio," she says. "That was physical, here and now. Not in the dreamlands."

"But they did it with a knife, you said. A very sharp knife. Not wolf's teeth and claws."

Sophie nods. "And if she comes for you here with that knife? You can't wake up and escape her from here, Jilly."

I know. The Broken Girl can't do anything.

"Okay," I say. Finally. Reluctantly. "But don't tell him you know it's her for sure. Just that maybe it could be."

"We can't tell him about the dreams anyway," she says. "But I can make a case for her being mad at you for abandoning her all those years ago."

"How could she not be?"

Sophie sighs. "You're probably right. But if we're wrong . . . I mean, if Lou does manage to track her down and it's not her, maybe you'll at least get the chance to talk to her."

"And I'll *really* have endeared myself to her, then, siccing the police on her and all."

"It won't be easy," Sophie agrees.

"Nothing ever is."

"But at least you'll get to explain yourself."

I think about the look in that wolf's eyes.

"What makes you think she'd even listen?" I ask.

Sophie doesn't have a response for that.

After she leaves, I don't want to think about this anymore. I do my therapy and all my exercises and purposely focus on anything but my sister and wolves and the dreamlands and all. Angel comes by for a visit while I'm having lunch and she takes over from the nurse that's helping me eat. Angel doesn't know about all these weird things that have crept into my life—it's not the kind of thing I'd ever talk to her about anyway; Angel's too intent on what's happening in this world with her charges to even consider anything that might exist on the periphery. So it's easy to stay on safe topics.

But once she goes, when I'm alone and resting, it's pretty much impossible. I stare at the ceiling and see those wolves. I turn my head to look at the wall and there's my sister, waiting for me, accusation plain in her eyes. I close my own eyes and jerk awake with a start as I begin to drift off. Finally a nurse comes to take me for another rehab session and I can forget for minutes at a time.

It's strange. I forget things I don't want to forget. But the things I do want to forget just stay with me, wrapping me in onion layers that get so tight sometimes I can hardly breathe. And then I get a completely unexpected visitor and my life acquires another layer of complication.

"Well, look at you," I say when Daniel comes into my room that afternoon.

I've just gotten back from an intensive rehab session and my muscles are all limp and weary—the ones that I can actually feel, at least. It takes me a moment to figure out what's different about him, then I realize it's that he's in civvies. A pair of faded jeans, an old Hawaiian shirt, and sandals have replaced the pale green scrubs and soft-soled shoes which is all I've ever seen him in before today.

He smiles when he sees the brooch he gave me, still pinned to my pillow, and the room kind of lights up a notch or two.

"How're you doing, Jilly?" he asks.

"I've been better," I tell him, then before he can jump on me about my attitude like he used to do when I was under his care, I quickly add, "but I've been worse, too."

He pulls a chair over so that he can sit near the head of the bed and we talk a little about how things are going, some of the old patients that were on the ward when I was there, that sort of thing. Then he surprises me.

"So maybe you'll think this is inappropriate," he says, "seeing how you were under my care and all, but I was wondering if you'd maybe want to go out with me sometime."

Go figure. It looks as though Sophie was right about him after all. Except he's so nice and so handsome, there's got to be some catch.

He sits there waiting for my answer, but I don't know what to say.

"Why'd you become a nurse?" I finally ask.

He doesn't respond, doesn't say anything for a long moment.

"I'm sorry," I tell him. "I guess I'm prying. And all you wanted to do was ask me out."

"No, it's okay," he says. "You just surprised me and it's not something I've thought about for a long time." He pauses for a long heartbeat before going on. "My dad died of cancer— when I was a kid. I used to go to the hospital to sit with him every day after school and it just, I don't know, really made an impression on me, I guess, the way the nurses would take care of all these dying people. By the time my dad died, I knew that was what I wanted to be: a caregiver. To help people when they're in this scary place when everything seems out of control and even their own bodies are betraying them."

"Why not become a doctor?"

"No disrespect intended, but doctors don't really do the same thing. Sure, they perform the surgery, prescribe the treatments and all, but they're not on the front lines, twenty-four/seven the way we are. When some poor kid's just puked up his guts, it's not the doctor who cleans it up, eases the kid's embarrassment, makes him feel like he's still normal. We're the ones who assure him that he's not some freak, that it's the disease messing with his body and nothing he can control."

"We're there for all of them, all the patients, all the time."

I look at him and all I can think is, wow. He's too good to be true.

"So are you gay?" I ask.

He frowns. "Why? Because I chose to become a nurse?"

I shake my head. "No. I know I'm guilty of generalizing here, but all the single, smart and gorgeous guys I seem to meet are inevitably gay."

"You think I'm smart and gorgeous?"

"Well, yeah. They don't have mirrors in nurseland?"

He's blushing, but I know he likes it. He clears his throat.

"So what about that date?" he asks.

"Look at me," I say. "I'm not playing the pity card now—so don't lecture me about my attitude—but really, let's face it. I won't be going out on the town anytime soon."

"I meant when you're feeling up for it," he says. "We could watch a movie in the common room, or have dinner in the cafeteria . . . or something . . ."

His voice trails off—I guess it's because I'm just staring at him.

"What?" he asks.

"I didn't think they still made guys like you," I say.

I can see the hint of another blush crawling up under his collar again, but he ignores it and plays it cool.

"But that's a good thing," he says. "Right?"

"Sure," I tell him, though I'm not certain of anything these days.

His interest in me right at this time is an enormous complication. Never mind him dealing with the Broken Girl—though he seems to be okay with that. What happens when he meets the Onion Girl that lives inside her? When he finds out what's going on in my head? The memory losses, my relationship issues, and—here's a big one—my trips into the dreamlands. He seems like a nice, normal kind of funky guy. Smart and gorgeous, like I already told him. Good heart, cares about people. Everything a girl could want.

But how soon before he goes running for shelter after he takes his first stroll through my head? We've never talked about that kind of stuff at all.

Well, why put off the inevitable? Might as well get it over with now.

"Do you believe in magic?" I ask.

He gets this big smile. "Do you mean, do I already know that you really believe in faerie?"

I blink in surprise. "Okay. That, too."

"I have a confession to make," he says. "I already knew who you were before you were admitted to my ward."

"You did?"

He nods. "I even own one of your paintings—'The Yellow Boy,' the one with the little dandelion faerie man leaning against the hubcap of a junked car."

"*You* bought that one? Albina lost her copy of the receipt so we could never figure out where it had gone."

"Albina?

"Albina Sprech. She owns The Green Man Gallery where the show was."

"Okay. I remember her now. I just didn't know her name."

We look at each other for a moment, then he clears his throat.

"So," he says. "You were asking me if I believe in magic and faerie and all . . . Let me put it this way: I don't not believe in it."

"That's a double negative."

"You know what I mean."

I nod. I've been there, wanting to believe—in my case, desperately—but unable to completely let go and accept the peripheral world until the empirical evidence was laid out in front of me. I could imagine the denizens of it, but it was a long time before I was actually seeing them.

"It seems to me," he goes on, "that there's more to the world than what we can see. Or at least there should be. But the trouble is I've never experienced it. I guess I'm too wrapped up in the world that everybody agrees is here."

"I don't agree."

He nods. "I know. And that's what first attracted me to your work. I read this interview with you—years ago in *The Crowsea Arts Review*—and it just spoke to me. This idea that whole worlds exist on the periphery of the way we think, or expect, or are told the world should be."

"Ever go looking for magic?"

He smiles. "All the time. But I get the sense that it's the kind of thing that you either stumble across, or it's got to come looking for you first."

"That's a good way to put it," I say.

"Though it seems you have to stay open to it as well, and that's hard. Your paintings make it easier to stick with it."

"Really?"

"Oh, yes," he says with a kind of enthusiasm that warms my heart. "When I look at your paintings, it always seems so possible again."

I get this sharp stab of regret. It's the first time since I got the news about what happened in my studio that it really hits me. All those paintings, forever gone. I never stopped to think that they meant as much to anybody else. I mean, unless the black holes come up and swallow them, I'll always have the memory of them. But what he's telling me now—that's half the reason I did those paintings.

"Did I say something wrong?" Daniel asks.

I shake my head, but I can't stop the tears building up in my eyes.

"I did," he says. "I can tell. I just talk too much. You probably think I'm just some rabid fan now . . ."

I try to snag a tissue with my left hand, but I can't reach it. I can't make my arm move properly. Daniel goes into nurse mode and gets the tissue, wipes my eyes, doing it all in such a way that it seems like a casual thing, no big deal, I could do it for myself but he wants to do it for me. I don't know quite how he pulls off this sort of thing, but it just blows me away that anyone can.

"No," I finally say when I feel I can trust my voice. "It's not that at all. I just started thinking about all those paintings I lost, that's all."

"What paintings?"

I realize then that I never told him. My friends know, but we don't talk about it and I didn't tell anyone else. So I tell him now and he gets this stricken look on his face that makes me want to comfort him, but I'm still the Broken Girl and all I can do is lie here and talk.

"It's okay," I tell him. "Well, it's not okay, but I can deal with it. I have to deal with it."

"Who would do such a thing?" he says.

Well, when your sister hates you enough, I think, but I don't even want to get into that.

"Who knows?" I say.

"Do the police have any leads?"

I shake my head. "Nothing concrete."

It's funny. He's always been perfectly okay with my injuries. But this has really thrown him and I can tell he's feeling all awkward now. He never pitied the Broken Girl, but his sympathy for the loss of those paintings is close to pity—this knowing that I might never be able to paint their like again—and he doesn't know how to deal with it.

"Let's do that date," I tell him, as much to change the topic of conversation as that I'd like to get to know him better. I don't hold out any real hopes—you can't when you're a Broken Girl—but I can't seem to let it go, either. I want to explore the "what if" that lies between us, though I already know where it's going to take us in the end. Why couldn't I have met him a month or so ago?

"When's your next night off?" I add. "Because my calendar's pretty much clear these days. We could do the movie thing."

I say it like a joke and he accepts it that way. I see him put away the shock of all those paintings having been destroyed and give me a smile.

Another point for him. What I don't need from anyone right now is more pity.

"How about tomorrow night?" he asks.

"Tomorrow night's perfect."

"Anything you'd like to see?"

"Something light and silly," I tell him.

After he's gone, I lie there and stare up at the ceiling. But I'm not counting the holes in the ceiling tiles this time. Instead, I find myself looking forward to tomorrow evening and that's weird, because I can't remember the last time I looked forward to anything. I wish I could pick up the phone and talk to Sophie or Wendy, but even not being able to reach for the receiver and dial doesn't bring me down.

It takes Lou to do that.

"Raylene Carter," he says after he's asked how I'm feeling and takes a seat in the chair Daniel so recently vacated. "Turns out your sister's got a record."

"How high did it get on the charts?" I ask.

"Ha, ha. I ran her name and came up with a solicitation charge in L.A. for which she pleaded guilty and did six months in county. That was back in '81. Since then, she's kept her nose clean—at least on paper."

"What's that mean?"

"I've got a friend on the LAPD—you remember Bobby Kansas? We used to call him Oz."

I nod. He walked the Lower Crowsea beat for years. "A young, red-headed guy . . ."

"Not so young anymore," Lou says. "And he hasn't got that much hair left, either, but yeah, that's him."

"What's he doing in L.A.? I thought he got transferred uptown."

"He did. But then he moved out west. He was going to work in the movies." Lou shakes his head. "Instead, he's a cop again and the closest he gets to a film set is working for the studios on his off hours, providing security for film openings and stuff like that."

"I wonder if he and Geordie have run into each other?"

Lou looks at me for a moment, then files my comment as irrelevant and goes on.

"Anyway," he says, "I asked Oz to dig a little deeper for me. He came back with the same charge I got off the computer, but also a lot of associated material. Turns out she surfaced in a case he had dealing with a porn actress named Pinky Miller who went berserk on a set and knifed a few people in '95."

"Porn?" I repeat, my heart sinking.

Lou nods. "Your sister wasn't in the movies herself, but this Miller's her best friend and she was definitely a part of that scene. Miller did time—six years in the pen with the usual time off for good behavior—but your sister kept her nose clean. Or at least she didn't get caught. She turns up again a little earlier as a witness in a shooting at a copy shop—this is '94. She was still working there at the time Miller did the knifing, but she also had a side business by then, writing computer programs and selling them on the Internet. Nothing major, strictly small-time shareware stuff."

Lou's been reading from a spiral-bound notepad. Now he looks up and fixes me with that cop look of his.

"Here's her arrest photo from '81," he says, pulling it from the back of the notepad and handing it over. "Looks a lot like you at that age."

I nod. She could be my twin.

"Funny," Lou says. "The two of you having different surnames."

"I changed mine," I tell him. "Legally," I add when I see his eyes narrow.

"This back in the days when you were under Angel's care?"

"Can't we just leave it as old history?" I say. "Please? I mean, whatever happened back then, hasn't the statute of whatever run out by now?"

I can see he has to work at it, but he gives me a reluctant nod. I know what's going on inside his head: all that old history between the two of them, Angel playing loose with the same law he was determined to uphold. It's what broke them up and I don't think he's ever forgiven her for that. Or himself for letting her go. Considering the two are mutually incompatible, you can see how it'd leave him messed up, even after all these years.

"Does she have a car?" I ask.

Lou nods and looks down at his notepad. "A '68 Cadillac convertible with California license plates."

"Does it say what color it is?"

He gives me an odd look. "Pink."

It's the car Sophie saw near my place, I think. The one Wendy said showed up on Cassie's cards. So it really is my sister behind all of this. Lou catches whatever's going on in my eyes, though he mistakes where it's coming from.

"You remember something about the accident?" he asks. "According to the report we got back from forensics, the car that hit you was a dark blue Toyota Camry."

I shake my head. "I don't remember anything more than I told you."

He continues to study me, finger tapping against the open page of the notepad.

"There's something going on that you're holding back," he says.

"Woo-woo stuff," I tell him. "Dreams and premonitions."

All true enough, and he buys it. And because that kind of thing makes him uncomfortable, he doesn't push it.

"You know I'm only trying to help you, Jilly."

"Of course I know that," I tell him.

"If there's anything else you can tell me about this sister of yours . . ."

"Lou. I haven't seen her in over thirty years."

"But Sophie says she could have a mad on for you."

"I really don't know," I say. "I abandoned her in that hellhole I grew up in, so maybe. It could even be likely. But I think it's pulling at straws. I mean, if it is her, why would she wait so long to get back at me?"

"Time does funny things to people," Lou tells me. "For some, it lets them forget. For others, it just makes the old hurts bigger and more painful."

I don't have to ask how he knows. You just have to see him and Angel in the same room to understand.

"We're still trying to get an address on your sister," he says after a moment, "but we're running into a wall. She moved out of her L.A. apartment in February of this year—when Miller got out of prison—and so far as Oz can tell, neither of them have been heard from since." He pauses, then asks, "You think they came back here?"

"Here or Tyson," I say. Then, reluctantly, I share a last bit of information with him. "Sophie says she saw a pink Caddy convertible on my street not too long ago."

Lou doesn't say anything for a long moment. Then finally he nods.

"I'll put an APB out on the car," he says as he gets up.

"Lou?"

He pauses in the doorway and gives me a questioning look.

Don't be hard on her, I want to say. From the little he's told me, her life after she left that hell that was our home just went from bad to worse. I don't want to add to her pain.

But if it is her, if she is responsible . . . I can't take the chance of any-body else getting hurt.

I don't know how to tell him any of that.

"Thanks," is all I say.

He nods, and then he's gone.

After he leaves, I'm back to staring at the ceiling again. I'm like a Yo-yo Girl, today. Up one minute, down the next. Daniel coming by, all sweet and full of possibility, then Lou's bad news . . .

I think of what Joe told me, what feels like years ago now, how I have to deal with the old hurts before he can get someone to help me mend the new ones. So by setting the police on my little sister—is that adding to the burden, or lightening it?

I just want to get away from it all, but even the cathedral world has gotten complicated. Between that nasty Tattersnake and the threat of my sister, the Amazing Wolf Girl, not to mention Toby running off, all bummed out the way he was, the dreamlands don't hold much promise of relief.

Do I even deserve relief? I ask myself, free to do so now because Sophie and Wendy aren't here to try to convince me that what's happening with Raylene isn't my fault.

What I need is a miracle, I think. Or those wizard twigs that Toby was going on about . . .

His voice comes back to me, talking to me about the magic those twigs embody. *The more you want it or need it, the harder it is to get.*

But that doesn't mean it's impossible. Hard doesn't mean impossible. It just means difficult. And if there's one thing I've never done it's back down when times got hard.

So I close my eyes and I think about that cathedral tree, the place where I left off my climb, and as I drift away, I wonder if I'll make it there this time, and if I don't, where I'll end up instead.

It doesn't feel like it'll matter right now. Because wherever I end up in the dreamlands, I'll be mobile and able to take care of myself.

I can just leave the Broken Girl behind like she never was.

If only the rest of my life was as easy to fix.

6

Returning from a late lunch, Wendy sat down at her desk and found a message from Angel waiting on her voice mail.

"Hello, Wendy," it began. "Jilly asked me to give you a call. She wants to know if there's something bothering you and if she's somehow the cause of it. If you could come by and talk to her after work, she'd appreciate it." There was a pause, then Angel added, "*Is* there something bothering you? You know you've always got a willing ear with me—and I say that in friend mode, not as a social worker." Another pause. "But do talk to Jilly if you get a chance."

Like many people, Angel's voice when leaving a phone message was different from her normal speaking voice. You could still hear the warmth, but the sentences were clipped and there was just a hint of the discomfort that some people get speaking to a machine instead of a real person. But the meaning had come across, loud and clear. Jilly knew something was up between them.

Well, they were so close, the three of them, how couldn't she?

Sighing, Wendy erased the message. She thought about what Cassie had said to her last night, how she should talk to Sophie and Jilly about it, but what was the point?

"It's not something that can be fixed," she said as she cradled the phone.

Not unless she could join them on the other side of nevernever where the lost boys fly and her namesake kept house for them.

But I wouldn't keep house, she thought. No way. I'd be out having adventures. Let the boys clean house and do the cooking for a change. She'd hand Peter Pan the duster, drop her apron to the floor, and off she'd go.

Off she'd go and she wouldn't look back.

She blinked, and looked around the office.

Was that what Jilly felt? she wondered. Was that unfettered feeling of utter freedom that had gripped her, just now, for one daydreaming moment . . . was that what Jilly experienced in those faerie dreamlands?

She picked up a stack of galleys that needed proofing. Chewing on the end of her blue pencil, she tried to concentrate on her work, but her thoughts kept returning to that feeling. Just for a moment there her heart had seemed to swell far beyond the boundaries of her body, encompassing anything and everything. It was probably what an epiphany felt like, though if she'd learned anything from it, it was only empathy for Jilly and why, given half a chance, she would be happy to just vanish into the dreamlands.

If that's what you feel, she thought, then maybe I understand how you could want to go over there and not think about coming back.

She tried practicing what Cassie had told her, to look sideways at things and see if some hidden landscape might appear in the corner of her eyes, but all that happened was that she kept missing typos and had to go over the pages again.

Joe

Morning comes to these red rock canyons, same as it does every place. Today it shows up with a big yellow sun peeping over the edge of the horizon, the first rays shining right against my eyelids and that's it, I can't sleep anymore. For a while I turn my head from the light and think about the feeling that's followed me out of my dreams, trying to decide if Cassie really needs to see me, or if it's just wishful thinking on my part. Finally I get up.

I leave Whiskey Jack and Bo sleeping by the fire. Walking around the rocks that are sheltering our campsite, I stare at the light play across those tall red hoodoos while I take a leak. I'm just getting going when I hear somebody giggling.

Turning my head, I see a little manitou that looks like it stepped out of one of Jilly's paintings, an urban sprite, but completely at home for all that she's been transplanted to this place. She's sitting casually on a nearby rock, maybe a foot high, perfectly proportioned, with a heart-shaped face and spiky pink hair. Her violet eyes match the silky shirt she's wearing over a little black skirt. On her feet are black platform boots with impossible heels.

"What's so funny?" I ask as I finish my business and zip up.

"You're so big," she says.

Here's the thing you never read about in all those fairy-tale books: we're the horniest bunch you'd ever run across. From canids like Whiskey Jack and Reynard, always on the make, to little punk faerie like this, everything always seems to come around to the pillow dance. The urge can build up strong in the dreamlands. I figure it's something in the air. I'm a one-woman man myself, so I don't spread it around the way some of us do, but whenever I get back from *manidò-akì*, the first thing I want to do is take that big-hearted woman of mine in my arms and head for our bed.

"Considering your size," I tell this little sprite, "everything about me would seem big."

That just makes her giggle some more.

"So what's your name?" I ask.

"Nory."

"I take it you're not local."

"Why do you say that?"

"Your getup," I say. "You look like you're heading out for a night of clubbing."

She brightens right up. "Oh, I do love to dance," she says.

No surprise there. Dancing's right up there, almost as popular as sex.

"But sadly," she adds, "I'm here on business."

"And that'd be . . . ?"

She stands up from where she's been lounging on the rocks, back straight, hands primly clasped in front of her. When she starts to deliver her message I realize she's a derrynimble, a finding sprite. They can find pretty much anyone or anything. It's a handy talent as I know, since I've got a touch of it myself, though not to the same degree as they do. The way it works for them's got something to do with the middleworld, the space that lies between *manidò-akì* and the World As It Is, but I've never made a real study of it.

I remember hearing that someone in Mabon had started up using them as messengers and couriers, but I hadn't put any real stock on it. Derrynimbles are normally too flighty to be of any real practical use for much of anything. This is the first one I've seen on the job and with the way she started off giggling when we first met, I wouldn't have changed my mind except that she delivers Sophie's message like it's Sophie standing there in front of me, instead of some pink-haired sprite that's not much taller than the length of my forearm.

She sticks to her prim little pose when she's done, an expectant look on her face. I'm wondering if she's expecting a tip, and if so, what a derrynimble would consider an interesting tip. Come to think of it, what currency does the courier service use to pay her?

"Am I supposed to send an answer back?" I ask.

She shakes her head. "You just have to give me a kiss, to prove receipt of the message."

"A kiss."

"There has to be actual physical contact."

I lean forward and touch my index finger to her brow. She sticks out her tongue, then grins, does this sideways step, and disappears.

I come back to camp, shaking my head. Bo's still sleeping, sprawled out on a raggedy blanket he pulled out from behind the woodpile last night, but Jack's awake. He's stirring the coals of our fire into life, getting ready to boil up some water for coffee. I see he's already helped himself to my tobacco and got himself a smoke going. He looks up and gives me a smile.

"When did you start talking to yourself?" he asks.

"It's the damnedest thing," I tell him. "You hear how someone in Mabon's started up using derrynimbles as messengers?"

He nods. "I heard. But what're the chances it could ever work out? I mean, derrynimbles. Like they'd remember what they were doing long enough to actually deliver a message."

"Well, I just got one," I say. "Cute little thing brought it, standing there on a rock watching me have a leak."

"How cute?" Jack asks.

"Seriously cute—if you like your women a foot tall."

Jack laughs. "She have a big sister? And I mean that literally."

See what I mean? One thing on the mind.

"She didn't talk about a sister," I say. "But she did have a message for me from Sophie. Sophie probably doesn't realize it, but I think she's given us the lead we've been looking for."

Jack forgets his libido. He gives Bo a nudge with his foot and says, "Listen to this."

Bo's like most canids—slips from deep sleep to alertness with the snap of a finger. He sits up and looks from Jack to me.

"Joe got him a message," Jack says. "By way of a derrynimble."

"Bullshit," Bo says. He reaches for where Jack left my tobacco pouch lying beside his own blanket. "They haven't got the brains for it. The only thing they can deliver is what my mama liked to call social diseases."

"Well, this one brought me a message all the same," I say.

Bo grunts, but whether in acknowledgment or not, I can't tell.

"So give," Jack says.

I watch Bo roll himself a smoke as I repeat Sophie's message. With the pair of them cadging off me, I'm surprised I haven't already run out of tobacco. Bo gets his smoke going with that lighter Jack won off Cody.

"So the pack leader's her little sister," he says as he lays the lighter down.

"*Could* be her sister," I say.

Sophie—by way of Nory—was pretty emphatic on that point.

"But it looks good."

I nod.

"And they figure she's in Newford?" Jack asks.

"Or Tyson."

"You remember her scent?"

"As a wolf, sure," I say. "But out of the dreamlands, when she's human, I'm not so sure I'd recognize it. Depends on how good she is at hiding it."

Changing shape changes your scent, too, at least it does on an individual basis. But you have to consciously think about hiding your clan affiliation. Corbæ, canid, urse . . . we can usually recognize each other, doesn't matter what shape we're wearing.

Jack nods. "So I guess we split up and cast around for her in both places."

"Count me out," Bo says. At the question in my eyes, he adds, "I lose this human look whenever I cross over. Hard to stay unnoticed walking around a city on four legs."

"Yeah, especially when they're coyote legs," Jack says. "Somebody curse you?"

Bo blows out a stream of smoke on the back of a sigh. "Back in the 1880s. I ever find that sucker . . ."

"So you'll hold the fort on this side of the border," I say before Bo takes us off on a tangent.

I see Jack catch himself from asking Bo more about this curse and get back on track to the business at hand.

"How well do you know Tyson?" he asks me.

"Haven't done more than pass through it a few times," I tell him.

"I'm the same with Newford, so I'll take it, you take Tyson."

It's good planning. When you know a place too well, you tend to miss things a stranger doesn't, like, there's no sense in checking out this alley, those blocks, that part of town because you think she'd never go there. But all too often, that's exactly where she'd be.

"All we're doing is observing," I say, looking from one to the other. "No cowboying. One of us finds her, we get the others before we make a move."

"Unless she takes a swipe at us," Jack says.

I nod. "That goes without saying."

Whiskey Jack and I leave Bo at the fire and go our separate ways. I spend most of the day making a slow pass through the town, from downtown Tyson, over to the Ramble and Stokesville. I even take a turn through all those new suburbs that are spreading like weeds on the south side of town. I make good time, slipping in and out of the middleworld when I need to get from one part of town to the other quickly. The middleworld's a handy place for that sort of thing—not to mention, just plain everyday spying. You can see out fine, but most people can't see in. Don't even know you're there.

I catch hints of canid presence, but whenever I track one down it turns out to be somebody with the blood, yeah, but so thin they can't even see me peering out at them from the middleworld. Twice I come across a pureblood—or as pure as you're going to get outside of *manidò-aki*—but they're minding their own business and don't have any connection that I can see to Jilly's sister. They're not hiding their scent, and I don't recognize either of them.

I can't ask people, but I talk to a lot of dogs, especially in Stokesville and on the edges of the Ramble where there's more of them and they run free. They're not exactly articulate, but a couple of old yellow hounds point me in the direction of the Ramble so I go back there. I don't find

Jilly's sister or her friend, but I do run across a backyard with about a dozen pit bulls staked out on short chains. It doesn't take a lot to realize that someone's breeding them to fight.

Their heads lift when I come into the yard, but they're smart enough to see I'm out of range of their chains and they've probably been trained with beatings not to start in on barking every time something unusual happens to show its face. I look at the back door of the clapboard house, waiting for someone to come out. No one shows and I have to admit I'm disappointed. I'd like to discuss how I feel about this kind of thing with whoever's set it up. I force down the urge to hunt him down and do a little drumming on his face and turn back to the dogs.

"You want out of here?" I ask them.

They regard me with flat, hard gazes until one honey blonde gives a slow nod of her head.

Anyone watching would think I was crazy to just walk up to her the way I do. I'm not worried. I can tell the canid blood runs strong in her. She knows I'm here to help.

I can't break the chain that's keeping her staked in place, but I don't have to. I just kneel down and undo her collar. She bumps her head against my arm by way of thanks. I don't make the mistake of trying to give her a pat. These aren't pets. And besides, they're cousins. Do you go around patting your cousins on the head?

The next one starts to snarl at my approach. The honey blonde pushes by me and gives a quick short bark that shuts him right up. He trembles—with anger, not fear—as I reach for his collar, but doesn't snap at me, doesn't move except to back away once his collar's lying in the dirt.

I free the rest of them, the honey blonde following me from stake to stake until I'm done.

"You're going to have a hard time of it," I tell them.

They just look back at me with expressions that don't give away anything.

I think about leaving them here to fend for themselves. How long are they going to last with no one to look out for them? Even in this part of town no one's going to stand for a pack of dogs running wild. Not to mention mistreated the way they've been, they might take it into their heads to get a little bit of their own back, just on general principles.

So I show them a way into the dreamlands, take them to a stretch of alleyway I noticed a few streets back where the layers of the middleworld are thin enough to push through, if you know enough to recognize the way. The honey blonde ushers the pack through. When it's her turn, she hesitates for a moment, then comes over and bumps her head against my leg, the way you might punch a friend on the arm. I lift a finger to my brow and I swear she grins before she bounds off after the others.

Then they're gone and I go back to looking again.

Late in the afternoon, I catch up with Jack. I find him north of Newford, up by where old Highway 14 passes the Sleep Comfort Motel. He's sitting right on the border of the middleworld and what Jilly likes to call the World As It Is, looking out at the parking lot of the motel.

"Any luck?" Jack asks when I settle down beside him.

"Nothing useful."

I offer him my tobacco pouch, but he shakes his head. I wonder if he's feeling sick until he offers me a ready-made smoke from his own pack. I think I can count on the fingers of one hand the number of times he's had his own smokes and I take one for the sheer novelty of it coming from him.

"How about you?" I ask after he lights me up.

"I don't know what I've got," Jack says. "You smell it?"

I shift to my dog face and lift my head, take in the air. For a moment there's nothing. Then the wind turns and I smell what's got him holed up here, watching that motel.

"You had a closer look?" I ask.

"Did a walk around, but I couldn't pinpoint the den."

I let my dog face fade and we step out of the middleworld, taking an easy turn around the motel, walking slow and casual, like we have every right in the world to be here. No one pays us any attention.

The canid smell is strong, but I see what Jack means. I can't zero in on the source either. It's just this wolf smell, hanging in the air around the motel.

"You know how we say we can smell the rain?" Jack says.

I nod, seeing where he's going with that. It's not the rain you smell, but the reaction of vegetation, or the land itself, to the precipitation.

"That's what we've got here," Jack goes on. "We're not smelling those dream wolves. We're smelling the reaction of their presence on their surroundings."

"But they're denning here," I say.

"No question. Or they have been until very recently."

I have another look around the parking lot.

"I don't see the pink Caddy Sophie was talking about," I say.

Jack waves a hand at all the box stores and fast-food joints that line this part of the highway. Time was, I remember, when the Sleep Comfort Inn was outside of town. Now it's pretty much right in the thick of it.

"She could be playing it smart," he says, "and just parked it someplace nearby."

"You want to have a look?"

He shakes his head. "I think it's time we fetched Bo and have another meeting about where we go from here."

"We can't go rousting everybody in that motel," I say.

"Let's just get Bo. We can talk it out with him."

We cross the highway and come to the big sign advertising the muffler shop that's sitting across the road from the motel. At least that's what it looks like in this world. In the middleworld, it's still all bush around here. I give a look around, but no one's paying us any attention, so we cross back over.

"Think one of us should stay and keep watch?" I ask.

Jack shrugs. "Why bother? We've both marked that scent now and we can find it again. And if it moves, we can track it."

I give a last look at the motel, then we head back for Cody's mesa in those red rock canyons where the three of us got together last night. I think of Cassie as we go, but I figure we won't be gone long this time. I can see her tonight when we get back. If she was trying to get hold of me like I felt this morning, it was probably only to pass along the same message that Sophie did.

But I do miss her.

Raylene

I spend most of the day fine tuning this new synchronization program I've been putting together—just to keep my mind off of all of this crap with my sister. I always find the best way to come at a problem is to just settle in on some other damn thing that's got itself no connection to what's really on my mind. I guess it lets the back of my head come up with a fix-up that the front of my head can't see. Pretty much anything'll do the job, but programming's the best thing I ever found me to just take everything and slow it down till any problem I got's just one more thing in the world, not the whole damn world itself.

Lately I've been working with Linux. I like the fact that the operating codes are all open source. Linux programmers give you the sense that we're all one big happy community and I like that, 'cept I know everybody's still looking for a way to make a buck and I ain't no exception.

Pinky's idea of doing something constructive is to sit around in her bra and panties, watching TV and chain-smoking. Come eleven, she pops her first beer.

"What exactly are you doin' with that machine of yours?" she asks during a commercial.

"Thinking," I tell her.

She laughs. "It's gettin' pretty bad when you need somethin' like that to help you with your thinkin'."

I don't bother to explain. I just smile back at her and keep at it.

This program's starting to seriously annoy me. Them little handheld Palm computers are popular these days, but not everybody wants to synchronize their data through Windows programs on their desktop. So I'm trying to set up something that'll work with other programs, like Eudora for the people who don't use Outlook. I've been at it for a while and I can't even get me a decent beta version. I've checked the code a thousand times and everything reads just fine on the screen, but every time I try to run it through my Palm simulator program, I still get clean facts coming in one end and strings a gibberish spewing out the other once the sync is done.

I sigh.

I been at it all morning and I'm not getting any closer to either fixing it or figuring out what to do with that sister a mine. Finally I shut down the computer and close the lid.

"You done workin'?" Pinky asks.

"I'm going out," I tell her. "You want to come?"

"Where you goin'?"

"Don't know yet."

She glances at the TV screen, where some actor I don't know is shilling his new movie to an interested-looking woman I don't recognize neither. I think it's some local show. I remember when all I could do was stare at the TV, day in, day out, but I don't guess Pinky's depressed like I was. Or if she is, she's not showing it in any way I can see 'cept for suckling at the TV and drinking her beer, and she's done that pretty much forever.

"Naw," she says. "I'm just gonna watch this awhiles."

So I leave her at it.

I decide to go driving with no direction in mind, but I guess I shoulda knowed there's no such thing as an aimless action. Some part of us always knows what we're doing, even if it can't explain why. That being the case, I guess I shouldn'ta been surprised to find myself up past Tyson on the Indiana Road, sitting in the car on the side of the road and looking

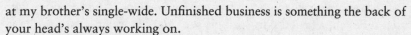

at my brother's single-wide. Unfinished business is something the back of your head's always working on.

I remember afore we went to sleep last night, Pinky turned to me where we're lying in our beds and asked, "How come you want to kill your sister but not your brother? He's the one was puttin' it to you when you was a little girl."

"She knew better," I said. "She had to understand what she was doing. Del—well, he's evil, all right, and dumb as a fencepost. But I reckon he just didn't know no better."

"And that makes it right, what he done?"

"Course it don't make it right. It's just . . ."

I don't know and I can't explain.

"Anyway, who says I want to kill my sister?" I asked.

"I thought you did."

I shook my head. "I just want to put her down. I want her to know what she done and to feel my hurting. And I don't want to be sharing no dreamlands with her."

I think about that as I sit here on the edge of the road looking at the trailer park. I guess I still feel that way about my sister. But I can't explain my feelings about Del. I know I don't even come close to liking him. I'm maybe even a-scared of him a little—somewhere in back of who I am now where the little girl I used to be is still living. I sure wouldn't mourn his dying none. But where I want to hurt Jillian May, I can't even muster up much of anything for Del 'cept maybe a kind of pity.

I guess it'd be different if I thought he was still playing his old games. If there was some little girl here in the park he was doing it to, like he done it to me. Maybe that's why I'm here. Just making sure of that. But it don't feel like it's why I come. And it's not likely I'm gonna catch him up to no good just by sitting here watching his trailer. For one thing, this pink Caddy ain't exactly inconspicuous, parked here the way it is.

I remember on one of them talk shows I used to watch how they was always going on about forgiveness, how you needed to forgive the one that hurt you so that you can get on with your own living, but that ain't in my repertoire neither.

So I don't know why I'm here, and after a whiles I figure I might as well go back to the motel. But then I look in the rearview mirror and see me a girl walking up the road. I put her at about fourteen, but I could be off a year or two either way. She looks like me and Pinky did when we was her age, wearing too much makeup and looking like a prostitute with that tube top, a denim skirt so short she might as well not be wearing it, and platform sneakers. She gives the Caddy an admiring look as she comes up aside of it.

"Hey, there," I say.

She stops, but she don't say much of nothing.

"You live here in the park?" I ask her.

"This month," she says. "Mama don't get the rent together soon we'll be out on our asses again."

"I been there."

She admires the Caddy again, gaze lingering on its lines.

"Don't look like that from here," she says.

"Yeah, well, looks can be deceiving."

"Not 'round here."

"I guess not," I tell her. "You want to go for a ride?"

She only hesitates for a moment before coming 'round to the passenger's side of the car. I guess she figures me being a woman, she's not taking her no chance at getting hurt. I don't bother to set her straight, but some of the purest evil I run into come in the shape of one of the female persuasion. Take my mama . . .

"What's your name?" I ask as she settles in her seat.

She runs her hand along the white leather of the seat, enjoying more than the texture. I know what's going through her head: daydreams of how someday she'll have her a ride like this and no way anyone'll catch her 'round these parts again.

"Lizzie," she says. "What's yours?"

I tell her as I start up the Caddy and we pull away.

"This your car?" she asks.

I nod. "Where you want to go?"

"Anywhere but here. Newford. Chicago. New York. L.A. You name the place and I'm game."

I want to laugh, but I know she's serious—just as serious as me and Pinky woulda been back in the old days, we get offered a ride in something like this.

"How about someplace a little less ambitious," I say.

She grins and leans back into the seat. "Just drive and I'll be content."

So we do that awhiles, not talking, just enjoying the wind in our hair, the wheels humming on the pavement under the Caddy's wheels.

"What were you doing there at the park?" she asks after a while.

"You know that blue and white single-wide with the busted awnings over the windows?"

She nods.

"I thought I might know the guy that lives in there."

"He a friend of yours?"

"Not likely."

"That's good. I was thinking maybe you was some old girlfriend of his. Show up with this ride and he'd be as like to sell it under your ass just to get him some liquor."

"So he's dangerous?"

She laughs. "Are maggots dangerous? He's just some no-account loser, always crying 'bout the good times he once had and how they all got took away. We call him Bottle on account of you pretty much never see him without one."

"He bother you at all?"

"You mean like wanting a party favor?"

"Something like that."

Lizzie shook her head. "He looks plenty, but we got his number. He try and grab me and I'd just cut off his dick."

"You're a feisty one, ain't you."

"He mighta married into the Morgan clan, but they're all dead and gone and no one's gonna put up with any crap from him now, least of all me. I heard he was a hardcase and raised some hell when he was younger, but you take a look at him now and he's just some fat old drunk who's got nothing left of them days but memories and some jailhouse tattoos."

She turns then to look at me.

"He hurt you once?" she asks.

"Why do you say that?"

She shrugs. "Dunno. You just look like you got some old painful history sitting there in your eyes."

I laugh. "And you got you an old woman sitting there in yours. How'd you get to be so smart?"

"You learn pretty quick to read a body in these parts," she says. "Read 'em wrong, and if you're lucky, you'll at least live to regret it."

"Somebody hurt you?" I ask.

"We all hurt each other," she says. "That's the way the world turns."

"I guess that's the truth."

I keep seeing myself in her. And here's the strangest thing: I want to help her out afore she gets to where me and Pinky got ourselves. Never much thought of myself as a social worker. Hell, I never much thought of much more'n me and Pinky. But I got no time for this now.

"I gotta get going," I tell her. "Want me to drive you back to the park or let you off somewhere else?"

"Take me with you," she says.

I look at her for a long moment afore I have to turn my attention back to the road.

"I can't do that," I tell her.

"Why not?"

"Well, for one thing, you're underage and I don't want to have the cops on my ass for abducting a minor."

"Nobody'd even miss me."

I shoot her another look.

"What is it you think I do?" I ask.

"I don't know. But it's gotta be better than my life."

The sad thing is, she's probably right.

"Tell you what," I tell her. "I got me some business to finish up, but when I get that done, I'll swing on by the park again and we can talk some more about all of this."

"Yeah, right."

I pull the Caddy over to the side of the road so I can give her my full attention.

"Listen," I say. "We don't know shit about each other, so I'm not going to ask you to trust me or nothing, and I don't think you should even if I did. But if I say I'm gonna come back to get you, then that's what I'm gonna do. Now you can believe it or not—it don't make no never mind to me—but one thing I know for sure: you're not coming with me now."

"Why would you come back?" she asks.

" 'Cause I been in your shoes and I woulda thought I'd died and gone to heaven, somebody ever offered to help me outta here. So maybe I'm doing it for the little girl I was that never had no one come along and offer her what I'm offering you."

I don't know why I'm saying this—no, that ain't the truth. I know why. It's like I told her. I can't explain why this little girl got me wanting to help her, but I know I do want to do what I can for her. Maybe it's to prove I ain't like my own sister. But I don't know what I'm gonna tell Pinky.

"Okay," Lizzie says. "I'll wait for you."

"I won't let you down."

"Yeah, well, the jury's still out on that one."

Neither of us have a whole lot to say on the ride back to the trailer park. I pull over and catch hold of her arm afore she gets out of the car.

"I don't come back for you," I tell her, "it's that I'm dead or in jail."

She nods, but she don't believe me for a moment. I don't know why it's so important to me that she do.

"And then what?" she asks.

"Then we'll talk. 'Bout what you want. 'Bout what I can do to help you get there."

She looks at me for a long moment.

"There's something I can't figure out here," she says. "I got me this feeling that me believing you're coming back means more to you than it does to me. Why you reckon that is?"

"I know what it's like, waiting on someone who's never gonna come for you. That ain't gonna happen here."

"You know what?" she says. "I think maybe I do believe you."

Them's only words. But I can see in her eyes she means it. Then she leans across the seat and gives me a quick kiss—like a girl would her mama in that make-believe world on TV where families actually care 'bout each other—and she steps outta the car. She gives me a wave, then goes sashaying down the dirt lane between the trailers. I watch her go and I think, she looks different. The set of her shoulders and the swing in her walk, it's like they're radiating hope.

For the first time in longer'n I can recall, I feel good. I don't know why this little Lizzie gal makes me feel that way, but she does. I let my gaze drift over to Del's single-wide.

"Fuck you, Del Carter," I say. "Whatever you got coming to you is gonna be delivered by somebody else's hand."

Because I ain't gonna risk no jail time over him. Not when I got me somebody I can maybe look out for now. Not like Pinky and I done for each other all these years, but somebody whose life ain't all screwed up yet.

"You 'member them dog boys we met over in the other place?" Pinky says when I get back to the motel. "One of them was wearing this T-shirt said somethin' about not buyin' no Thai products."

I'm just through the door when she starts in on this and I can't figure out what it's got to do with anything.

"He chased us off that kill of ours," she adds. "Back in them woods we go to when we're dreamin'."

I kick off my shoes and settle on the sofa.

"Sure," I say. "What about him?"

"He was out there in the parking lot today," Pinky says. "Him and his pal—least I think it was his pal. They didn't neither of 'em have dog heads today, but I 'member that shirt on accounta you makin' this point of talkin' 'bout it. They did them this slow ramble 'round the parkin' lot and then they crossed the highway and just up and disappeared."

"What're you talking about?"

So she goes through it again for me, with more detail this time, and I get a worry on. What're they doing, tracking us down like this?

"Where were they when they disappeared?" I ask.

Pinky gets up outta her chair and I join her over by the window.

"They was right there," she says, pointing. "Under the sign for that old muffler shop."

I can't see nothing special from here. There's some raggedy bushes under the sign, musta looked pretty once when someone was taking care of them. Now they're being choked out by weeds and litter. The asphalt in behind is all cracked and overgrown, the shop's boarded up, and there's a couple a junked cars along the side of the building.

"And they just disappeared?" I say. "They didn't just walk on outta sight or nothing?"

Pinky shakes her head. "One minute they was there, big as life, and the next they was gone." She snaps her fingers. "Just like that."

I need me a closer look at this. I put my shoes back on and go out into the parking lot, Pinky trailing along behind me.

"What're you expectin' to find?" she asks as we cross the highway and stand under the sign for the muffler shop.

"I wish I knew."

I walk all around that sign and in and outta the weeds, looking for I don't rightly know what, 'cept I'm pretty sure I'll recognize it when I see it. But everything looks pretty much like you'd expect. It's driving me crazy. I know there's something here—so damn close I can taste it like a bit of hot pepper on the tip of my tongue—but it ain't nowhere I can see. I kick a beer can and it goes skittering across the asphalt. Pinky lights a smoke.

I start to turn toward her, to ask if she can show me exactly where them dog boys vanished, and that's when I catch a glimpse of something out of the corner of my eye. It's nothing I can really describe, just a kinda thinning in the air, like a shimmering heat wave you see on the highway of a time. I turn to look at it straight on and it's gone, so I shift my head, moving slowly. And there it is again, sitting right back there in the corner of my eye again.

I feel a tugging from it, like something in me's drawn to it, something deep and hidden most of the time. It's like wherever it is inside me that the wolf lives recognizes that shimmer and wants to walk right into it. I give Pinky a look but she's not paying any attention. She's just smoking her cigarette, staring back at the motel, bored.

I put her outta my mind. I put everything outta my mind and come up on that shimmer easy and sly, not looking at it straight on, moving sideways toward it like a crawdad' might. I come right up to it and the air feels different. Thick and thin at the same time. I kinda give it a push. I feel it touch me all over like walking into a spiderweb. There's a moment of dizziness and then I just about fall on my ass.

I catch my balance and my eyes go wide and I just start in a-grinning 'cause the world of motels and highways is gone. No, not gone. It's like I'm looking out of a window at it. I'm standing in scrub bush, but looking out at the cars and semis going by on the highway. There's the motel across the highway. But I'm not in that world.

I turn and look over the tall grass and scraggly trees to where there's this kinda glow maybe a hundred yards away—where the muffler shop should be. That's the dreamlands, I tell myself and I know I'm right. I can feel them, taste their smell in the air from where I'm standing. This place I slipped into is some in between place, a kinda waystation separating the two, I guess.

And as I'm thinking all of this, I can feel something shift inside my head. It's a way of looking at things, I reckon, 'cause I know that when I step back into the world I left behind I'm never gonna have me no trouble getting back here again.

I notice Pinky then. She's looking stupidly around herself, can't figure out where I'm gone. She turns in a slow circle. I wait until her back's to me and there's no traffic, then I step out and tap her on the shoulder. I swear she jumps two feet in the air.

"Jesus fuck!" she yells. "I think I peed my panties." Then she gets this real puzzled look. "Where'd you come from anyway?"

"I found the way across," I say.

No, I think. Not the way. A way. There's these thin crossings everywhere, you know how to see 'em, and I know now. Don't ask me how. I guess doing it once unlocked something in my head, 'cause as I'm standing here I can see how there's these shimmers in the air all over the place. I catch 'em, from the corners of my eyes, every which way I turn.

I try to show Pinky, but she just can't see any of them. I can't figure that out at all. Finally I take her by the hand and pull her through. The dizziness hits her harder'n it hits me and I get the sense she's somewhat scared about all of this. Me, I feel like I been given the keys to the world and I guess in some ways I have.

When we cross back to the muffler shop's parking lot, Pinky still can't find them places even though I'm seeing them all over the place. I practice walking through them, popping in and outta Pinky's sight until I realize anybody happen to glance this way—and with Pinky in her half-unbuttoned blouse and skintight Capri pants, that'd be any guy that ain't gay—is gonna see what I'm doing and wonder.

So I head us on back to the motel room. There's even one of them shimmering places right inside of here, up by the wall we share with the unit next door. I have me another go through it, stepping back and forth and just a-laughing. I take Pinky the first time and we walk right on through into the dreamlands, you can tell right away. I'll admit to a touch of unease the first time, but when I look back and see that shimmer, all my fears just wash away. Pinky's not near so happy as me. When we're in that in-between place she can't shake this feeling like she's gonna hurl, but once we get through to the dreamlands she comes 'round.

After we get back, Pinky sits her down in her chair and lights up a smoke, but I keep on a-playing with the shimmer.

"You're givin' me the creeps," Pinky says.

"Why?"

"It's like you're walking right through that wall and disappearing."

"That's 'cause I am."

"It still gives me the creeps."

She can't see this shimmer neither, though I can bring her through with me. She has to be holding on my hand, is all.

I finally get over the novelty of it and set me back down on the sofa again.

"That damn old juju woman lied to us," Pinky says.

"I don't think so. She just didn't tell us everything. She told us two of the ways to cross over, and just didn't bother letting on there was any others."

"Why you figure she do that?"

I shrug. "Miss Lucinda strikes me as a woman who likes to cause trouble. We do it one of her ways and it's either trouble for us, or for them dog boys. Either way she gets her a laugh."

"I don't know," Pinky says. "I don't trust me none of this."

"You got a right to be suspicious," I tell her. "It don't pay to trust nothing. But that don't change what we know now."

"How come I can't do it? I mean, you can take me over, but I don't see a damn thing. When you're takin' me through, it's like we're gonna walk smack into that wall. And the whole time we's over there, I get the feelin' like I'm gonna puke."

"It went away once we got all the way over."

"I suppose. But I don't like bein' there like this. You know, just a couple of gals. Something comes at us, how're we gonna protect ourselves?"

"We got knives," I tell her. "And we got the shotgun and a box of shells."

We picked that up first thing when we got to Tyson.

"I'd be a lot happier with a little more firepower'n that," she says. "A couple of pistols and an Uzi, say."

I shake my head. We been through all of that. Even a handgun's too much trouble to get one legal-like, and I don't feel up to spending the cash to get us an unregistered one. 'Sides, we can't be going around with no arsenal, not with our records.

"Well, I been thinking," I say.

Pinky shakes her head. "You're always thinkin'."

"Now we got us a way to deal with my sister," I go on like she never said nothing.

"How you figure that?"

"What'd she do last time we come upon her?"

"She disappeared like them dog boys did."

I shake my head. "No, she woke up."

Had to be that way. If she could cross over like I just learned, she wouldn't be walking nowhere. She'd just be a-lying there, crippled and helpless.

"So?" Pinky says.

"Well, imagine what'd happen if she couldn't wake up? Say someone was to feed her a few sleeping pills—not enough to hurt her, just to keep her under. She wouldn't be able to get away from us then seeing's how she'd have no place to wake up to."

"Hell," Pinky says. "Comes to that you could just grab her sorry crippled ass and haul her into the dreamlands with you, that's sayin' you can find one of them shimmers in that room she's in."

"I got me a feeling you can find them pretty much anywhere, you know how to look."

"But then we're gonna get us some cash and retire from all this shit, right?"

I think about the promise I made to Lizzie, but now isn't the time to bring that up.

"We'll do anything we damn well want," I tell Pinky. "Anything at all."

She gives me that old grin of hers.

"Now you're talking," she says.

Seeing's how we don't know how this is gonna play out, we prepare for anything. I take my duffel bag. Rolling up the shotgun and the box of shells in some clothes, I stick them in. I change to jeans and running shoes.

"You got any decent walking shoes?" I ask Pinky.

"I got my pink sneakers."

"They'll do."

Our next stop is a drugstore where we buy the sleeping pills in case we want to feed them to my sister. I also pick up some bottled water, granola bars, and then add some candy bars for Pinky. She wants to stop at a liquor store and bring something a little stronger, too, and pouts when I tell her no, but she tosses a carton of smokes into the basket and lets it slide.

The whole time we're in the store and we're driving I'm checking for them shimmers. I see more of them than I don't and that makes me feel good about Pinky's idea. I kinda like the thought of my sister lying crippled in the dreamlands just a-waiting on me to decide on what I'm gonna do to her. And that way I can explain real clear how she brought all of this on her own self.

It's getting close to nine-thirty by the time we're finally pulling into the parking lot at the rehab building. Good timing, I think. We don't have to pay for parking and most of the spots are free. And once inside, well, visiting hours are over and all we got to do is get by the nurses.

We get outta the car and I reach into the back for my duffel bag.

"Ray, honey," Pinky says.

I look over at her.

"You're gonna be smart here, right? We're either gonna pull that sister of yours into the dreamin' world, or we're gonna feed her a few sleepin' pills. You ain't gonna go all postal on me in there, are you?"

"I got everything under control," I assure her.

But she won't let it go. "Yeah, I'm sure you do. But every time you so much as look at a picture of this woman, you stop firin' on all cylinders, honey. Now I ain't the one to say what you should or shouldn't be doin'," she adds when I start to shake my head. "It's just, if there's a chance this is gonna get messy, maybe we need to do us some real plannin' first. You know, like park the Caddy closer, or better yet, get us somethin' a little less conspicuous for while we're doin' the job."

"You don't have to worry none on my account," I say. "I'm thinking clear."

"Okay. You know I'm only sayin' this outta worry for you, right?"

"I know, Pinky. You're the only damn person in this whole wide world I'd ever stop and actually trust with anything important."

She gets that grin of hers then.

"Okay," she says. "Let's get this show on the road."

I been in the rehab building after visiting hours afore, but never this early. Usually I come creeping in late at night, having me a look at that sister of mine and I can't account for why I'm doing it. But tonight's different. I got Pinky at my side. I got the shotgun in my duffel in case things go wrong. Hell, I got me escape routes like no dumb cop's ever heard tell of afore.

I keep my eye on them shimmers. They're in the parking lot. They're by the side door we go in. There's a couple in the hall we're walking down and if there ain't any in my sister's room, at least there's one right outside the door on the other side of the wall.

"She's still lookin' kinda fucked up," Pinky whispers.

I nod. I'm waiting to see if the red rage is gonna come over me, like Pinky was worrying over in the parking lot, but I don't feel much of nothing, looking down at her here on her bed. I'm not saying I suddenly come over all sappy-eyed and feeling sorry for her. I just don't want to start punching in on her face the way it comes over me whenever I saw her picture afore this. But that don't mean I'm gonna walk away neither.

"I guess," I say, finally replying to Pinky. "But she's got to know herself some mental anguish if any of this is gonna mean anything."

"You figure we can touch her without her wakin' up on us?"

"I dunno. But it ain't gonna make much difference, is it? She can wake up and scream, but by the time a nurse gets here, we're gonna be through that shimmer and in someplace they can't begin to follow."

"So we're takin' her?" Pinky asks.

I been thinkin' 'bout this ever since Pinky brought it up, and it looks better every time I let it take a run through my head.

"Well, we ain't here to give her no good sister award."

"She don't look like much," Pinky says. "I can pick her up on my own. You go do whatever it is you need to do to get that shimmer ready to take us away."

I take a last look at Jillian May, lying there so peaceful on her bed. She's far gone—deep in the dreamlands, I reckon. I doubt she'll even stir when Pinky lifts her from the bed.

"Ray?"

I nod and walk back into the hall, have me a look both ways. I don't see nobody.

"Okay," I call softly back to Pinky.

I'll give her this. Right from when we was kids, Pinky mighta been built like some elegant showgirl, but she was always strong and she still is. She just picks that sister of mine up like she don't weigh nothing and steps back from the bed. Jillian May's head lolls on one side of Pinky, her feet on the other, the arms hanging like they don't know where they're supposed to go. And she don't wake up. Hell, I don't even hear her breathing change none.

Pinky carries her to where I'm standing. I got me the duffel in one hand and put the other on Pinky's shoulder, steering her into that shimmer she can't see.

"Hey!" I hear somebody yell from down the hall by the nurses' station.

I don't even bother to take me a look. I just walk us into the shimmer and we're gone.

Jilly

Once upon a time . . .

Either my navigation skills have improved, or whatever fateful whimsy that sent me to the Inn of the Star-Crossed the last time I was here is looking the other way, because this time I arrive right where I want to be, high up on the many roads-wide convergence of branches of that tallest of the cathedral trees. Or maybe I had one of my blackouts while crossing over the last time. I think of that because when I do arrive at this place, I can't remember why I'm here, what I came to do. But this time it comes back to me quickly enough.

I look up and I can't see the top. It's going to be a long way up to those wizard branches of Toby's.

This juncture of branches still makes me feel like I'm on a raft, all these branches coming out of the trunk at this one point to form what feels like a large natural platform, the slight sway of the tree itself mimicking the slow rise and fall of a river's current. I look away through the break in the branches, my gaze traveling over the tops of the other trees that make up the Greatwood, off to the west where foothills climb up to the distant mountains. I note the inn and marvel again at how clearly I can see it from here, because it's not as big as you'd think it would have to be from this vantage. Finally, I turn back to the rat's nest of branches and vines that cluster around the trunk.

Time to start climbing, I think.

I'm actually looking forward to the physical exertion. I think I'd actually enjoy digging ditches at this point in my life, since the Broken Girl I really am can't do a damn thing. She still can't even get up out of bed by herself. Or feed herself, for that matter. My brain coughs up a whole litany of the things that the Broken Girl can't do anymore until I begin to feel depressed and completely overwhelmed.

"Oh, just stop it," I tell myself.

"I can't, I can't," someone replies in a broken voice.

That's when I realize it's not just myself and the birds and little forest critters up here on this platform of branches.

I recognize Toby's voice, but it takes me a moment to find him where he's huddled mournfully in a nest of intertwined branches and vines near the trunk of the tree. He lifts his face to me as I approach, tears streaking his cheeks, his eyes all red-rimmed and swollen.

"I'm just so bad," he says.

I crouch down so that our faces are level, though I'm looking at him through a raggedy crisscross of twigs and strands of vine.

"Why are you so bad?" I ask.

"I . . . I'm everything you said I was. I *was* just your friend so you'd help me become more magic. So I wouldn't fade away and die."

"Well, that's understandable," I tell him. "You were scared. I know all about being scared."

"No, I'm just bad and bad. You . . . you should find yourself a real friend."

I reach through the tangle of vegetation and put my hand on his knee.

"Friends are supposed to be there for each other through thick and thin," I tell him. "If I'd been a good friend, I would have just helped you get those magic twigs without making you go through twenty questions."

He sniffles. "You didn't ask me that many."

"It's just an expression."

He wipes his nose on his sleeve.

"Come on," I say. "Why don't you get out of there?"

"I suppose . . ."

Even with my help, it takes him a moment or two to extricate himself from the thicket. When he's finally standing beside me, he's still acting all hangdog and sad, shoulders drooping, gaze on the ground, won't look me in the eye. So I give him a hug, which is fine at first. I can tell it perks him right up. Unfortunately, it perks him up a little too much. I let him go and step away.

"Whoops," he says.

He sticks his hands in his pockets and tents out his pants a little to hide his boner. But he's grinning while he does it.

"See, I told you I had a penis," he says.

I have to smile back. "I never doubted you for a moment."

"If you ever change your mind about wanting a boyfriend . . ."

"You'll be the first I tell," I assure him.

He's still got that mercurial temperament, I see. Going from whimsical to serious—or in this case, sad to cheerful—in the blink of an eye. But I don't mind. I hated seeing him so depressed.

"How long were you hiding in there?" I ask him.

He shrugs. "I don't remember. Days. Weeks. How long were you gone?"

"Hardly weeks."

"Did you miss me?"

"Actually," I say. "I did."

"Me, too. I promise to be a good friend from now on."

He takes his hands from his pocket and his pants fall back naturally, unimpeded by the evidence of his earlier excitement.

"So what do you want to do now?" he asks.

I point upward.

"No, no," he says. "We don't have to do that anymore. I told you. I'm going to be a good friend. Not someone who just wants you to do things for him."

"But that's what I want to do," I tell him. "It's why I'm here."

"You need magic now?"

"Everybody needs magic," I say.

"Everything already is magic," Toby says. "Just most people don't see it. Maybe what we need is miracles."

I look at him, trying to remember if I ever told him about the Broken Girl I am when I'm not here in the cathedral world. But all I say is, "Miracles are good."

"And rare," Toby agrees. "Can you earn them, do you think?"

"You mean by climbing up to these wizard twigs of yours?"

He nods.

"I guess there's only one way to find out."

So up we go again. It's like climbing a net woven of vines and branches and I revel in the sheer physicality of it. I never get the feeling we're in any real danger, but it seems whenever I start to feel too cocky, a vine gives way underfoot and I dangle for one heart-stopping moment until my foot can find purchase again. Then I'm careful again for a while.

"I met your friend the Tattersnake," I tell Toby when we stop for a rest.

The branches aren't as wide anymore, though still the width of a good-sized path. The foliage is dense once again and all we can see is the tree itself, its branches, the thick covering of leaves.

"You can't really be his friend," Toby says.

"I kind of found that out. Why do you think he's got such a chip on his shoulder?"

Toby shrugs. "That's just the way he was made up. All the Eadar come to life with the personality they were imagined to have, though you can change it if you want to put the effort into it. That is, if your maker doesn't continue your story and make changes himself."

"Does that happen a lot?"

"Enough to be worrisome. It's horrible to wake up one day feeling like a completely different person and you know you're that way just because your maker got bored with how you were."

I give him a questioning look. I don't want to pry, but an insatiable curiosity has always been one of my failings.

"Did that happen to you?"

He nods. "More than once," he says, not hiding his bitterness. "In one story I'm a puckish sprite. In another this wise wood spirit. In yet another, as randy as a satyr."

So that's why he can seem so mercurial, I think, but I don't comment on it. He seems upset enough about it without my adding to it. Instead I just make a sympathetic noise.

"They never think of us," Toby goes on. "Not all of them. They don't care if we have no real sense of who we are. To them, we're just something they make up to amuse themselves with, nothing more."

"Maybe they don't know."

"Probably they don't," he says. "But that doesn't change how it is for us."

We leave it at that as we start our climbing once more.

"The Tattersnake was a villain in his story," Toby says the next time we take a break.

I don't know how far we've come, but we've been climbing for at least a few hours. How tall can this tree be? I feel like we're a pair of Jacks, climbing a beanstalk. Maybe there won't be wizard twigs at the very top. Maybe we'll find another world there instead and if there are wizard twigs, they're secreted away in some giant's big wooden chest, wrapped around with chains and locked with magic spells.

I lean back into my perch. "William Kemper—he's the—"

"The innkeeper. I know."

"He says that the Tattersnake is the way he is so that people will remember him. So that he won't fade."

Toby smiles. "Well, he's certainly memorable. We're the only two left from our stories, you know."

"You shared the same story?"

He nods. "But he was always the villain."

"And you were the hero?"

That makes him laugh. "Not me. I was always the sidekick."

"So who was the hero?"

He gets a sad look. "I don't remember anymore."

It's like my black holes, I think. Maybe worse. Because he knows he knew it once, while for me it's just holes. I don't know what was in them.

"Well, obviously you're pretty memorable, too," I say.

"I suppose. But I'm not any one thing and that seems particularly sad to me."

I shake my head. "That just makes you normal. Most people aren't any one thing. They have all sorts of faces they present to the world. Two people can meet and talk about someone and not even realize they're talking about the same person."

"But inside they know who they are, don't they?"

"I suppose. Though I'm not so sure of that myself. I don't know that I've ever known who I really am."

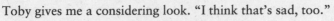

Toby gives me a considering look. "I think that's sad, too."

"I guess it is, when you think about it."

"Then let's not."

I look into his grinning face, all his seriousness fled, and give a slow nod. But now I'm thinking how it's so much worse for him and feel even more depressed. To stop thinking about it, I start climbing again, letting the physical exertion steal away all busy concerns that are rattling around in my head. But that only makes me think of how the Broken Girl I left behind doesn't even have that. The nurses in the rehab are always insisting I pace myself. They won't let me drive myself to the point where the exercises are all I can focus on.

I end up leading us at such a furious pace that finally Toby has to ask me to stop.

"Why are you in such a hurry?" he asks when he starts to catch his breath.

I'm out of breath, too, but all I want to do is keep going.

"I'm not, really," I tell him. "I'm just trying not to think. If I'm concentrating on hand- and footholds, I don't have room for anything else in my head."

He gives me a sympathetic look. "It doesn't go away just because you're not thinking about it."

That's what the healer who talked to Joe meant, I realize. When she said I had to heal the inside of me before the outside could be properly healed. It's all that baggage from when I was a kid. I can't heal the Broken Girl, because I haven't let the baggage go. But I can't let it go because there's no place for it to go.

"So what do you do with it?" I ask, curious as to what he'll say, who it'll be that says it. The puck? The wise wood mystic? The satyr?

But, "I don't know," is all he says. "I wish I did."

After a while we start climbing again and I let Toby set the pace this time. The branches are now the size of a normal tree's, but we still have the tangled net of vines growing close to the trunk for us to climb up. I wonder what we'll do when the vines run out, but when I look up, they continue as far as I can see.

And so does the tree.

I haven't seen any wildlife for ages and the birds are so exotic I can't recognize them at all. I don't think they exist anywhere else. Green birds, purple birds, red ones. Some with animal faces. Fox and lizard and mole. Some with human. Most with a curious combination of the two.

The next time we take a rest we have to wedge ourselves into the nooks made by branches, Toby above, me on the one below.

"How much farther do you think it is?" I ask.

He shakes his head. He doesn't know any more than I do and he's just as tired.

I try not to think of what we'll do when the branches become so frail they won't hold our weight anymore, but the tree goes on.

"It's not necessarily a possible task," he says, and I realize he's worried about the same thing.

"But we're not giving up."

I'm not sure if I mean it as a statement or a question, but he replies all the same.

"I can't," he says. "I've never made it this far before."

That strikes me as odd. Sure, this has been a strenuous exercise, and who knows if we'll even be able to climb to the very top, but it doesn't strike me as having been an impossible journey up to this point.

"Why not?" I ask.

He looks down at me from his perch. "Whenever I've tried before, the way became impassable. Sometimes the vines would give out. There'd be no handholds and the trunk would be too wide to shimmy up. Or I'd come upon such a nest of vines that it was impossible to get around. A couple of times the birds would come at me like diving swallows, except they'd cut at me with their talons and beaks."

"I wonder why it's different this time."

He laughs. "It's you—why else? The tree and its guardians recognize that light you carry and are allowing us through. At least so far."

Again with the light. I've never understood what Joe meant by it, though when he says that Sophie has it too, I can see something in her. There's always this nimbus of a glow about her, radiating an otherworldly glimmer the way really healthy people radiate their physical well-being. I put it down to her faerie blood. But me? I look in the mirror and all I see is me. No light, no glow, no shine.

"Well, at least it's good for something," I say.

Toby gives me an odd look. For a moment I think he's going to make a comment, but then he stretches his shoulder muscles and asks if I'm ready to continue.

"Lead on," I tell him, and up we go again.

I'm not sure how long we're climbing this time. I'm not judging our progress anymore either because I'm too busy concentrating on hand-and footholds, wearily pulling myself up, inch by inch it seems. So when Toby stops, I bump my head against his rear.

"What's the matter?" I ask.

"Look," he says, pointing up.

I change my grip and twist around so that I can see past him. I can't believe we've come this close and I wasn't aware of it. The top of the tree isn't more than ten feet above us. Past it is a sky so blue it makes my eyes tear to look at it. But the most amazing thing are the topmost branches— no more than twigs, of course. They're hard to look at, too, because they're glowing with an intense amber light that's shot with filigrees of bright golds, turquoise, a deep red, and flashes of emerald.

When my gaze settles on them, my head fills with the sound of singing and all my fatigue is washed away. The voices aren't human. The sounds don't come from the throats of anything I can recognize at all. But it's singing all the same. A swell of celestial sound that would be cheesy if this was a movie, but here, in this place, it fills me with this incredible sense of humility and awe.

I have to look away. The voices do a slow fade, echoing and resonating deep inside my ribs. When I lift my gaze again, it's to grin at Toby.

"We made it," I say.

He's grinning, too, but then he directs my attention to the branches above us. We're on the last part of the trunk and it's not much more than a half foot across at this height. Right above Toby there's a clump of growth, a tangle of vines and sprouting branches. Those are the ones that continue on and not one of them has a diameter of more than a few inches. There's no way they'll hold our weight. At the very top of a half dozen of them are those bright, singing twigs.

"This far," Toby agrees. "But to get any farther . . ."

"We can't give up now," I tell him. "Let's change places."

We have an awkward moment as he descends and I scramble up to where he was. I test the largest of the branches but it bends alarmingly with only the slightest weight put on it.

I look up again at those glittering twigs. My head fills with their chorus. This time I can almost understand the words. It's as though they're related to a language I knew once, but have long since forgotten. The voices pulse against my spirit like hands on a drum, my spirit the drum-skin, taut and resonating. An echoing tattoo wakes in me and what I feel I can't begin to describe. There aren't words for this. I just know it's magic. A deep and old magic that I'm being allowed to experience and remember forever. A miracle, even, that will never fall into the little black holes that rise up to swallow other parts of my life.

The sound of the voices continues to swell and grow until I have to turn my head away again. But I'm determined to reach those twigs now. How, I don't know. I'm still holding on to the branch. It's still slender and unable to bear my weight.

It'll have to be more magic, I guess. Which I don't have. That leaves only luck.

I remember something Joe once told me when I asked him how the People could eat meat when they're so closely related to animals—not just the way you or I might say, we're all mammals, but to know that many of them are actual family.

"We all need sustenance," he told me. "The wolf, the puma, the eagle as much as the rabbit, the deer, the salmon. Even the trees and grass require nourishment that's dependent on the lives of others. Nature was never benevolent or fair. But by the same token, we have to live together in this world and cruelty is neither gracious nor defensible. So when you take from the bounty that others provide for you, bless their gift, treat it with respect, give it dignity. And always ask before you take, give thanks for what you receive."

I wrap my arms around the trunk and close my eyes, press my cheek against the rough bark.

"Oh, tree," I say softly. "I don't know that I deserve it, but surely Toby does. I'm just going to take two of the smallest twigs and no more. I hope that's okay. We're not going to do anything bad with them. We're just going to use them to fix what's broken inside us."

I look up again and the chorus fills me once more, but I don't hear anything different in it. I don't hear yes, I don't hear no. The only mes-sage I seem to get from the voices is that there is wonder and beauty everywhere.

Biting at my lip, I slowly stand up, balancing precariously in that nest of vines and branch beginnings at the very top of the tree. I reach up and pull at one of the branches, bringing it down to me. As it comes down, I inch my hands up, putting a deeper bow in the branch and bringing the top closer to me. I'm doing fine until those glittering top-most twigs are almost at hand, but then I lose my grip and the branch goes snapping back.

I start to lose my balance. Without even thinking about what I'm doing, I do the right thing. I don't try to flap my arms to regain my balance. I just crouch down and bury my hands into the nest of vines, gripping them tightly.

When my pulse steadies, I stand up again, slower than before.

"Jilly, no," Toby says.

But I ignore him and go through the process once more, gradually bringing those topmost twigs back into reach again. When they're finally close enough, I take a deep breath and grip the main branch more tightly with one hand, reach for the twigs with the other.

It's hard to see what I'm doing. This close, their light is completely blinding. The singing chorus fills my world, becoming a sound that I can smell and taste and touch as well as hear. When I put my hand around a pair of the twigs, the very touch of their smooth bark makes me shiver and my heartbeat quickens.

"I . . . I hope this won't hurt," I say as I give the twigs a quick twist and break them free.

I realize I'm holding my breath, waiting for something horrible to happen. But nothing has changed. I stuff the twigs down the front of my shirt.

"Thank you, tree," I say. "I'll never forget your generosity."

Then I let the branch go and crouch down again.

It takes me a while to regain my equilibrium. For long moments the chorus of voices continues to ring in my head. Not until it fades to little more than an echo and then is finally gone do I look down at Toby. He's staring at me open-mouthed. I clear my throat, smile at him.

"Let's go down," I say.

The descent isn't any quicker than the ascent was, but it feels easier. We continue until we get to a branch that's wide enough for us both to sit comfortably on. Grinning, I pull the twigs out from under my shirt, but my good humor fades when I look at what I've got in my hand. The twigs are dull and brown and silent. I have the horrible feeling that whatever enchantment imbued them once, it disappeared as soon as I broke them off from the tree.

"I killed them," I say. "The magic's gone."

"We have to *believe* it's still there," Toby tells me.

I look into his earnest face and give a slow nod.

"Okay," I say. "I can do that."

I give him one of them and almost drop my own when his shoots out a light made up of all the colors we saw in the twigs above—a searing flash of amber, filigreed with spirals and twisting threads of turquoise and gold, red and green. The singing chorus awakes like a switch has been turned on and hits a sudden crescendo. I can almost see words form in the interplay of the colored threads. Not with letters I recognize, but made up of runes like you see in ancient stoneworks. The flare holds, bathing both our faces with its unearthly light, then dies down, winks out.

Toby's palm lies empty, but there's a mark on his palm. Not a white scar, but an amber stamp, like a birthmark. Or a tattoo, like the ones he has on the backs of his hands. He stares at me with wide eyes and looks more—I can't explain, really—more solid, I guess than he ever has before.

"Are . . . are you all right?" I ask.

He opens his mouth, but no sound comes out at first. He gives a slow nod, then runs the fingers of his other hand over the mark on his palm.

"I feel the same . . . but different," he finally manages to say. "Like I'm . . . more me. Or only me. Or . . . I can't explain. It's like I'm not fading anymore." He's beaming now. "You made me real," he says.

I'm happy for him. Truly I am. But then I look at the twig I'm holding and it's still just a dead twig. Toby's gaze drops to it as well and his smile falters, fades.

"I guess it couldn't fix what's wrong with me," I finally say.

"We could try again," he says. "Get another one."

But I shake my head. "No. Joe pretty much told me that only I can fix what's wrong inside me. I'm just going to have to figure out how to do it, I guess."

He starts to respond, but then I get a sudden stomach cramp and I jerk forward, almost falling from our perch. The twig drops from my hand. Toby catches it and even in my pain I watch to see it flare and get swallowed into his skin. It does neither.

A dud, I think. A broken twig for the Broken Girl.

Another sharp cramp grabs my abdomen and I stifle a cry. I'm feeling nauseous now, vertigo wheeling through me, making my head spin.

Toby stuffs the twig in his pocket and eases forward, putting his arm around my shoulders.

"What's wrong, what's wrong?" he cries.

I can't answer as another cramp hits me, but it turns out to be the last. The vertigo and nausea start to fade as well. But I'm feeling very strange now. Dislocated. Here and not here, all at the same time. And I have this sudden urge to go somewhere. I can't say where, but my head and my body and my spirit all know exactly where I'm supposed to go. I just have to get up and let them take me there. I can't *not* let them take me there.

"Jilly?" Toby asks.

"I feel sick," I finally manage to tell him. "No, that's not right. I don't feel completely *here* anymore. I guess I shouldn't have taken those twigs . . ."

Though I guess that's only partially true. The one I gave Toby certainly helped him. I'm the one that was rejected by the magic. Or maybe I'm paying for what we did. Maybe all the polite asking and thank yous weren't enough. Maybe some things aren't supposed to be taken like a common harvest, no matter how hard a climb it is to reach them.

"Story of my life," I say.

I lift my head to see a look of horror on his face.

"What is it?" I ask and try a joke. "Did I grow another nose?"

"You . . . you've become an Eadar . . ."

"What?"

"I know that look—I've lived with it all my life. You're not real anymore." He shakes his head. "But that's not possible. People don't become Eadar. You're either made or you're born. There's not supposed to be an in between."

But I'm hardly listening to him. That's not true. I hear everything he's saying, but none of it really computes. It can't compete with this tug and pull, the ever-growing *need* that's burning in me. It started out strong, but it's getting stronger by the moment. I have to go. Right now. I feel like I'm stretching apart and if I don't go to whatever it is that's calling to me, I'll simply get pulled so thin that I won't exist anymore.

"I can't stay here," I tell Toby.

He shakes his head. "How can this have happened?"

"It doesn't matter," I say. "I have to go."

He's so shaken that he can hardly concentrate on what I'm saying.

"Go where?" he manages to ask.

"I don't know. But something's pulling me . . ."

I think then about the Broken Girl. Something must have happened to me back in the rehab, some new crisis. Maybe the wolves found me there. Maybe my body just up and failed.

"Good-bye," I tell Toby and let myself wake up.

Nothing happens. No, that's not true. My whole body is shivering and shaking with this need to go. There's plenty happening, it's just all inside me and nothing I have any control over. Maybe this is what being an Eadar means—a constant, awful feeling that you're always at someone or something else's beck and call. I want to ask Toby if this was how he felt, but I can't even frame the sentence.

So I duck from underneath his arm and start to descend again. As soon as I'm moving, the terrible ache of this need to go lessens. I guess it's because I'm on the move.

"Jilly!" Toby cries from above.

"I just have to go," I tell him. "If I don't, I'm going to come apart."

I look up long enough to see that he's following me, then concentrate on my descent.

It's a long way down.

We still stop to rest, but I can't do it for very long, no matter how much my shoulders and arms are aching. As soon as we stop, I get all twitchy, and the longer we're stopped, the worse it gets. My limbs start to quiver and tremble and my head fills with this awful need to go go go. We don't talk much, either when we're resting or descending the tree. When we're moving, it takes all my attention just to keep my exhausted grip on the vines and make my way down. When we're resting, I'm too busy concentrating on shutting off this need to keep moving so that my body can get a little rest.

"It's like someone has snared you with a geas—a compulsion spell," Toby says at one of our stops.

I can tell the rapid pace I'm setting is wearing on him. We were both tired enough on the climb up. If we keep up this pace, one or the other of us is going to make a mistake and go plummeting down.

"I don't know what it is," I tell him. "I just can't get it to shut up. The longer we sit still, the worse it is."

"But who would do such a thing? You must have powerful enemies."

"I don't know about powerful," I say, "but the 'dislike Jilly' factor seems to have gone up quite a few notches ever since I've been able to cross over into the dreamlands."

"I know a field where vervain grows, but it's far from here."

I have no idea what he's talking about and tell him so.

"To break the geas," he says. "The vervain's blue flowers and scented leaves combat sorcery."

"Whatever," I say.

We've been sitting still too long and I feel like I'm going to explode. It's too hard to concentrate on this conversation, for all its relevance and possible importance. So these blue flowers can maybe break the spell. We don't have any of them. All we have is this compulsion geas thing sitting in my head and it won't let me go.

"I have to get moving again," I add.

I don't wait to see if he's ready. I just grab hold of the vines and swing my legs over the edge of the branch we're sitting on, feet looking for purchase.

Eventually we reach the forest floor, the cathedral trees towering all around us. Toby leans against the massive trunk of the one we've just come down from, catching his breath. I don't have the luxury. I turn in a slow circle. The pull is strongest from the south. As soon as I turn in that direction, it's like someone's snagged a giant fishhook right inside my chest and now they're reeling me in.

I start walking. I hear Toby sigh, then he comes straggling along after me, dragging his feet. I know what he's feeling. My arms and shoulders are burning with muscle ache, my legs are trembling from exhaustion. But I can't stop. The geas makes me want to run, but I force myself to keep my pace reasonable. I have no idea how far I still have to go. It could be miles and I don't want to collapse partway there.

I think of the fairy tale where the people dance until they die and now I know just how they felt. You can fight the compulsion for a while, but eventually you have to start moving again. There's no respite, no chance to rest. Ultimately, you keep going until your heart bursts, or your limbs give out, or you just generally cave in. And even then, you'll lie there on the ground, twitching and quivering.

How long do we walk? I don't know. But the cathedral trees finally give way to smaller growths, smaller being relative to the enormous size of the Greatwood's trees, of course. The ones around us now would still be considered huge by any normal standards. There's undergrowth here as well, and a dampness in the air, muffling our passage. Leaves and other debris from the trees form a moist carpet under our feet and the only sound we make is the brush of sapling branches against the fabric of our shirts and trousers, the odd twig that snaps underfoot, and our breathing which sounds ragged and harsh—in my ears at least.

Just when I think the fairy-tale dancers' fate is going to be my own, we finally top a rise looking down into a granite-strewn gulch and as quickly as it came, the immediacy of the geas is gone. I can still feel it, but now it's like the low hum of an appliance, something that can settle into the background if you stop paying attention to it. I drop quietly to the ground—as much from exhaustion as to avoid the attention of the figures below. A moment later, Toby collapses beside me.

I roll over onto my back and rest my head against the damp leaves, my limbs splayed out. I don't know when I've ever felt this beat before. I don't want to think about what I've seen below in the gulch.

"It's eased off," I tell Toby. "The need to keep moving."

"That's good."

We keep our voices pitched low so that they don't carry past our own ears.

"It depends on your definition of good," I say.

After a while, Toby lifts himself up on his elbows and peers down at the threesome. He studies them for a long moment before lying down beside me again, his face turned toward me.

"They were responsible for the geas?" he asks.

I nod. Though I can't say if it's something that they did on purpose.

Toby studies me now. "Do you know them?"

"A couple of them. The . . . dark-haired ones."

"They could be your sisters," he says. "The sleeping one's older and the other's more buxom, but the family resemblance is—"

"The sleeping one's not older than me," I say. "She just looks that way because this"—I touch a hand to my face—"is how I see myself, so it's how I appear here. Younger. Healthy."

He gives me a puzzled look.

"She's me—in the world I come from. I call her the Broken Girl." I tell him briefly about my accident. "The other one's my sister. I haven't seen her in years, but apparently she's learned how to turn into a wolf since then. Acquired the ability to use this compulsion spell you were talking about. Figured out how to cross back and forth between the worlds. Oh, and she hates me something fierce."

I say it lightly, but I can't hide the pain in my voice and eyes.

"And the third?" Toby asks.

I don't know her, but from what Lou told me, I can guess. She looks like a hooker with that body poured into tight pink Capri pants and her white sleeveless blouse unbuttoned past her bra, wearing her hair in a dated bouffant shag. The only incongruity is her running shoes, also pink.

"I think her name's Pinky Miller," I say.

"She looks—"

"Like white trash."

That gets me another puzzled look.

"Cheap," I say. "Like she's just waiting for you to ask 'How much?' before you get down to business."

I'm surprised at the bitterness in my voice. I don't even know the woman. I'm happy when Toby doesn't focus on her.

"This explains why you seem to be like an Eadar," he says instead.

Now it's my turn for the puzzled look.

He nods his head over the rise. "Your dreaming self and otherworld self shouldn't be sharing the same world. It makes for a conundrum that will only create deeper and more profound discordances if left unchecked. The geas . . . the compulsion you felt, and must be still feeling—"

"Though not as intensely."

"Is your other self calling your dreaming self back into it. You need to be one entity, not two."

"And how does that work?"

"Physical contact should be enough to allow the two of you to merge."

"And then I'll be what?"

"As you are in the other world, except here."

I crawl back up the slope and stare in sick fascination at the Broken Girl. My sister's yelling something at her limp form but I can't hear what she's saying. Pinky's sitting on a stone outcrop and seems to be cleaning her nails.

"Is there no other way?" I ask Toby.

"If there is, there's no time to lose," he says.

I turn to see him get up and do his fade into the underbrush. I watch him vanish through the trees, not quite believing he's deserted me once more. I can't even muster any anger toward him this time. It's hard to blame him. Now that he's real, the last thing he's going to want is to saddle himself with a cripple who can't even feed herself.

I start to feel nauseous. To be the Broken Girl here . . . I'd soon find myself yearning for that helplessness I know in the World As It Is. There, at least, I have support—the rehab staff, my friends. Here I've got nothing. If I end up back in that body, all I'd be able to do is maybe crawl around on the forest floor for a while until I die from exposure or an attack by some predator. And even if I could get to someplace like Mabon, I'd still only be the Broken Girl with no escape at all—no place to go in dreams and seek relief because I'd already be in the dreaming world.

But at least now I understand why my sister's brought the Broken Girl here. She's probably going to abandon me the way I abandoned her. I guess I shouldn't complain. It's a fitting revenge and it's not like I don't deserve it.

I just wish Toby hadn't left me. This is a hard thing to face alone.

Like Raylene had to, my guilt says.

There's nothing I can say in reply to that.

Joe

Bo's not at the camp when we get back, but the fire's still smoldering so we know he hasn't gone far. It's late afternoon here in Cody's heart home, going on evening, and we find Bo at the edge of the mesa, dangling his feet over a drop of a couple of thousand feet, staring out across the red rock canyons. As the sun continues to lower, the shadows get more and more dramatic. It's the kind of view that can swallow you whole, leaves you feeling bigger inside than when you first stopped to have yourself a look.

"We had company while you were gone," Bo says without turning around.

"Anybody we know?" I ask.

Bo finally looks away from the view and draws one knee up against his chest, holds it there with his arms, fingers linked.

"Remember in the long ago," he says, "when they used to tell a story about Nokomis having a sister?"

I shake my head. "Before my time."

"I remember," Whiskey Jack says. "Nobody ever saw her and she didn't have a name."

Bo nods. "But people had names for her. They'd call her Fate. Or Destiny."

"Or Grace," Jack adds.

"I thought Grace was a state of being," I say. "Or maybe even a place. Though I guess I've heard people talk about it as a light."

"In the shape of a woman," Bo says.

Jack sits down beside him, lets his own legs dangle. "Cody always said she was the one who gave birth to the humans."

"After he impregnated her," Bo says.

"But he didn't force himself on her."

Bo nods. "Yeah, when it comes to women, Cody never has to force anything. Funny, thinking of him settled down with a magpie."

"Funny thinking of him as settled down, period," Jack says.

I squat on my haunches between the two of them and let my gaze lose itself in the red rock canyons, tracing the lengths of the hoodoos, starting at the top of one, dropping way down to the canyon floor where the shadows lie thickest, then going up the one beside it, back to where the sun's still waking highlights in the red stone.

"Everything changes eventually," I say. "That's about the only constant we get. It just takes some of us longer."

Bo gives me a look and smiles. "Listen to the philosopher king," he says to Jack.

"So this Grace you're talking about," I say. "Is that who came visiting?"

"I don't know. She looked like Nokomis, but she didn't have her scent. Didn't sound like her, either. You know, the way the old woman thinks. I just saw her in the Greatwood not too long ago, so she's kind of fresh on my mind."

"I'm guessing there's a point to all of this," Jack says.

"What did our visitor have to say?" I ask.

Bo sighs, doesn't look at us.

"That we should let things be," he says.

Jack and I exchange glances.

"You mean she condones these killings?" Jack says.

"She didn't come right out and say that. What she said was that there's too much magic in this world, not enough in the other. These things have to balance out."

"But the killings . . ."

"I asked her about that," Bo says, "and she gives me this look—it's like, how dumb are you?—and then wants to know when it was I forgot that dying doesn't end anything; it just changes where you are."

We all fall silent for a long moment.

"I've got to think on this," Jack says.

I know just what he means. He offers us smokes and we all light up, studying the canyon once more. I don't know where they go in their heads, but I've got two memories floating in mine. One's from long ago, that night my uncle and I came upon the unicorn, singing to the moon. The other's a lot closer in time. It's of me and Jack disturbing that pack of dreaming wolves and chasing them off of their kill. I don't know as the World As It Is deserves magic if it's got to be paid for in the blood of innocents.

And if that same pack is hunting Jilly, this whole thing is too personal for me to ignore.

I take a last drag on my cigarette and put it out. Pocketing the butt, I stand up. Bo and Jack turn to look at me.

"I'm going home," I tell them.

"Are you letting it go?" Jack asks.

"Yes, no—hell, I don't know. I don't think I can, but I need to talk to Cassie about it." I hesitate a moment, then add, "I tell you this, though. It's getting under my skin. These wolves. The killings. Some old spirit coming along, telling us what we should and shouldn't do, what's wrong and what's right."

Jack nods. "Yeah, I'm not too comfortable myself with the idea of the greater good having more weight than an individual's right, especially when it comes to killing. You start thinking along those lines and where do you stop? Unicorns today. Maybe canids or corn girls tomorrow."

I nod. "You see something wrong, you fix it today."

"A lot of those old spirits don't see the human factor."

"We're not human," Bo reminds us.

Jack turns to him. "You know what I mean. They don't have anything invested in living in the here and now. They just kind of float on through life with their sights fixed on all the big issues. I'm not saying they're wrong, or even purposefully cruel. They're just not considering all the little pieces that make up the puzzle."

"Yeah," I say. "If there's a problem with the balance of magic between the worlds, there's got to be other ways of dealing with it. That spirit's thinking it's natural selection, I guess, but it's too much like the start of a forest fire for me. Sure, you know that in the long run the forest'll come back bigger and stronger than before, but what about all the lives that are lost while it burns? We're supposed to look the other way and let them die?"

"When you put it like that . . ." Bo says.

"I still need to talk to Cassie," I tell them. "She's plugged into some whole other kinds of mystery and she's got an eye for this kind of thing."

Jack nods. "The question isn't, are we going to do anything, but what's the best thing we can do?"

"That pretty much sums it up for me," I say.

"We'll be waiting for you here," Bo says.

Jack nods. "And you tell that good-looking woman of yours hello from me."

That earns a laugh.

"Like hell I will," I tell him. "Last thing I want is you sniffing around my back door."

Jack smiles and turns to Bo. "Kind of sad, isn't it? Man has such little faith in his woman. Course, he knows that when she sees a handsome man like me, all memory of him's just got to go sliding right out of her mind."

I leave to the sound of their laughter, chuckling myself. We all know Cassie's not one to be swayed by anything but her own mind. It's one of the reasons I love the woman as much as I do.

2

NEWFORD, MAY

Arriving after visiting hours was getting to be a habit, Wendy thought as she walked from the bus stop to the rehab building at about nine-thirty that evening. She'd planned to come much earlier, except they'd had a disaster at work. Marley Butler's computer, which held all the final files for the next issue of *In the City*, had crashed while she was working on some designs for that same issue. While their resident computer tech worked on getting the machine running properly again, everyone in the office had been going through their own computers and the various backup discs scattered through the office, trying to reconstruct the next issue as best they could in case Ralph couldn't get Marley's machine up and running again.

In the end Ralph had worked his usual miracle, but a number of files remained corrupted. By the time they'd gone through everything, replacing the corrupted files with clean ones, it was almost seven-thirty. Since none of them had taken a break since the disaster first occurred, they went out for dinner as a group and it was just a little past nine before Wendy was able to get away and catch a bus up to the rehab.

In a way, Wendy hadn't minded the delay the problems at work had created. The truth was, for all of Cassie's urging, she wasn't entirely sure it was really the best idea to talk to Jilly right now. How was she supposed to convey how she was feeling so left out without the very fact of her bringing it up creating even more problems between the three of them? It wasn't as though she could ask—or even wanted—them to stop their wonderful dreamland adventures. How could she make Jilly feel guilty for the freedom those visits provided for her?

Wendy just didn't want to be left behind.

Sighing, she made her way through the parking lot. She got to the front door, then paused. A little nagging thought made her turn around and look behind her. There was something in the parking lot—something important—that she just now realized she'd seen but it hadn't really registered . . .

She scanned the pavement, gaze roving from the pools of shadow to the light cast by the parking lot's lighting until her gaze fell on the long pink Cadillac parked a few spots down from one of those oversized all-terrain SUVs that the yuppies seem to need just to drive from one part of town to the other. She stared at the Caddy for a long moment. How could she have missed it?

That was the car she'd seen in Cassie's cards, the one Sophie had seen near Jilly's apartment. The one that belonged to Jilly's little sister, which meant Raylene and her friends were—

"Oh, my god!" she cried. "Jilly!"

She turned and wrenched open the door of the rehab building. Halfway down the long hall, right by Jilly's door, she saw figures. A tall, blonde woman carrying a limp, bandaged figure in pajamas. Another, smaller woman with curly dark hair ushered the pair of them through a doorway directly opposite Jilly's room.

"Hey!" she called after them.

They didn't even turn, just vanished into the doorway. Wendy started to run down the hall, but one of the nurses came from behind the counter at the nurses' station and caught her arm.

"Visiting hours are long over," she said firmly. "And we certainly don't appreciate your shouting—"

Wendy tugged free and ran down the hall. Behind her she heard the nurse ask someone to call for security, then set off in pursuit. Wendy skidded to a halt in the doorway to Jilly's room to find the bed empty. Heartbeat drumming, she turned to look back across the hall where she'd seen the figures disappear. There was no doorway there, only a blank wall. The doorways, when she looked, were staggered down the hall, none of them facing each other.

But she was sure she'd seen them go from this room into another through a doorway that was directly across from Jilly's door.

"I've called security," the nurse said as she caught up with Wendy and grabbed her arm again. "Now will you please—"

"You idiot woman," Wendy said.

"Perhaps you think—"

"You called security? Good. Maybe they can tell us who kidnapped my friend. Though if they're as good at figuring things out as they are at keeping watch, what's the hope in that?"

"What?"

Wendy pointed to Jilly's empty bed. "My friend's gone."

The nurse's hand fell from Wendy's arm. "But she can't even feed herself, little say walk."

"Well, duh. I saw two women carrying her. That's why I was yelling. I thought they went through a doorway across the hall, but there isn't one there."

"They must be in one of the other rooms," the nurse said.

She went to the nearest doorway to look in while Wendy went to the one on the other side. All she saw were two sleeping patients. She bent down to look under their beds. Nothing. Opened the bathroom door. Empty.

"You just saw this happening?" the nurse asked her when they met again in the hall.

Wendy nodded.

The other nurse and security guard came trotting down the hall. The guard started for Wendy but the nurse she was with waved him off.

"Someone's taken one of our patients," she said.

As they discussed what to do next, Wendy ran back to the nurses' station and picked up the phone. From the front pocket of her jeans she took out the business card that Lou had given each of them a few weeks ago. She had a bad moment trying to dial out—it took an eight rather than a nine to get an outside line—but soon she had the phone ringing on the other end of the line. She went out as far into the hall as the cord would allow and looked out through the glass doors. The pink Caddy was still in the parking lot.

"That's their car," she told the security guard when he and the nurses joined her at the station. "The pink Cadillac. Hello, Lou?" she said into the phone receiver as her connection was made. "You'd better get down here. Someone's kidnapped Jilly from the rehab center."

3

It's quiet when I step into the apartment. I can smell the leftover traces of a cedar smudgestick and the fresh sweetgrass that's lying in a basket on the coffee table, waiting to be braided. The only light is cast by candles. Cassie's funny. When we were living in squats, she was always wishing we had electric lighting. Now that we've got it, she just keeps on using the candles.

I see Cassie lying on the sofa and I think she's asleep, though that wouldn't be like her with all those candles burning. Then I realize her eyes are open and she's smiling up at me. She stretches like a cat and reaches up to me with both arms. I stand there for a moment, appreciating the sight, then I slide down on the sofa with her and for a time there I don't have any worries at all. All I've got is my woman on my mind.

. . .

"Bo said she was known as the Grace?" Cassie says later.

We're sitting in the kitchen, having a little whiskey that we wash down with sips of coffee.

"Actually it was Jack called her that," I say. "Bo came up with Fate and Destiny."

"Do you think such abstractions can actually have walking, talking personas?"

I shrug. "Anybody can call themselves or be called anything. Doesn't mean it's true."

"But it could be."

"With spirits, anything could be. You know that the same as me. Everything about *manidò-akì* kind of circles around a central core of 'why not?' "

Cassie nods. "I've just never met the personification of Love, say. Or Dreams. Like the Greek and Roman gods."

"I'm not saying they exist or they don't," I tell her, "because I don't know. But everybody's got something they're good at and some of them'll take a name from that."

She smiles. "Like you with your bones."

"At least you didn't say boner, shugah-baby."

That earns me another smile, but she also reaches across the table and cuffs me lightly on the top of the head with her open hand.

"Don't be rude," she says, like she wasn't saying anything stronger herself an hour or so ago, back there on the sofa.

"Getting back to the matter at hand," she adds, "what if this woman was right? What happens if you go ahead and deal with these dream wolves? Will she come after you?"

"Depends on how strongly she feels about it, I guess. And how strong she is." I pause for a heartbeat, then add, "You think I should let it go?"

"What? With Jilly caught up in the middle of it? Not a chance. I was just measuring the odds."

"I never bet when it comes to the old spirits," I tell her. "There's no percentage in it because you can't tell what they're going to do."

I'm about to go on about how I don't see Nokomis having a sister, anyway. You hear Raven or Cody tell it, from when everything came to be, she was always the world underfoot—the land, the water, and the moon reflected in it. If she had a sibling, it'd be Micomis, who was the sky and the sun and fathered the thunders, though most of the stories I've heard say they used to be related only through an old marriage and it's Micomis who's got the siblings—his brother thunders.

So I can't say who came by the camp to see Bo—not who she was, or how old and powerful.

But the phone rings, making Cassie jump and all that goes unsaid. Cassie gets up and lifts the receiver on the second ring. I watch her face, knowing it's bad news from her expression as she listens, just wondering how bad.

"We'll be right there," Cassie says.

She cradles the phone and looks at me.

"That was Wendy," she says. "Calling from the rehab. Jilly's been taken away by her sister and a blonde-haired woman."

I'm getting really tired of all these sisters popping up, I think.

"She call Lou?" I ask.

Cassie nods. "Before she called us. He's on his way."

"So are we," I tell her.

I stand up from the table and go back into the living room to put my shirt and boots on. Cassie goes into the bedroom and comes back to toss me a clean T-shirt, then heads back in to get dressed herself. There are times it can take her an hour to get ready, and all we're doing is going to the bookstore. Tonight I've barely finished lacing up my boots and she's dressed and waiting for me.

No bright colors for her tonight. Plain blue jeans, a dark green jersey, a buckskin jacket, brown walking boots.

"I didn't know you even owned stuff that drab," I tell her, trying to lighten the tension we're both feeling.

But she's not like the cousins in this and doesn't crack a smile.

"I'm worried about Jilly," she says.

That's not an explanation for what she's wearing; it's to tell me to stop screwing around and let's get rolling.

So I take her hand and we step into Meadhon, the middleworld, to find a quick path to take us over to the rehab center. Cassie closes her eyes to slits, tightens her grip on my hand. She doesn't like this place, the way you can see both *manidò-aki* and the World As It Is at the same time. "Give me one or the other," she always says. "Just not the between." But tonight we need the speed it can give us. We're halfway across town, but it takes us only a couple of minutes of quick walking to reach the rehab, step out of the middleworld and up to the front door.

There's already a cop on the door.

"Lieutenant Fucceri called us in," I tell him when he steps up to block our entry.

It's not true, but it doesn't matter. It gets us into the building and if this is going down the way I think it is, Lou's going to need our help.

I look back and see the cop scratching his head, still trying to figure out how we came out of nowhere and into his view so fast.

4

Some more guards from the security company's head office showed up while Wendy and the head nurse on duty stood by the nurses' station, waiting for the police to arrive. The security people left a man guarding the pink Cadillac and others at the exits, while the remaining men made a sweep of the building and the grounds outside. They came up with nothing.

That's because they went into the otherworld, Wendy thought, having already figured it out while she was waiting for help to arrive. There was no other explanation. But try telling that to Lou.

"You say this is where they went—right into the wall?" he asked when she showed him the stretch of hallway where she'd seen Raylene and Pinky disappear with Jilly.

"I know how it sounds," Wendy said. "And—okay, I was a-ways down the hall at the time. I admit that. But I saw them come out of Jilly's room and walk directly across the hall. And then they disappeared. I thought they'd gone through a doorway. Once we saw there wasn't one right there, we thought they had to have gone into one of the two rooms on either side of this stretch of hall, but we checked them both and—"

"We've checked all the rooms," the head nurse broke in, "as well as the basement, all storage areas, the kitchen and exercise area, the lounges, the grounds."

Lou nodded. "And since they were on foot, how far could they have gotten?" He laid a hand against the wall and pressed. "But there's no way they walked through this wall."

"That depends," a new voice said.

Wendy turned to see that Joe Crazy Dog and Cassie had joined them.

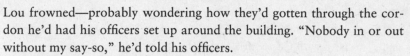

Lou frowned—probably wondering how they'd gotten through the cordon he'd had his officers set up around the building. "Nobody in or out without my say-so," he'd told his officers.

Cassie came over to where Wendy was standing and gave her a hug.

"You're okay?" she asked.

Wendy nodded.

"I guess this is your kind of thing," Lou said to Joe in a tone of voice that added an unspoken "And I don't like it one bit."

Joe nodded. "Seems like it."

Everyone knew how Lou felt about anything that didn't fit into the way the world was supposed to work. He'd been in Newford long enough to have run into any number of inexplicable phenomena, but he still managed to put each one in its own little box marked "anomaly" and then carry on with his unswerving belief in a rational world. People like Joe, or Christy and Professor Dapple, made him uncomfortable because they were willing to accept what he couldn't, and that played against his own hard-held view of the world.

He and Joe usually avoided each other when they were both at some gathering put together by Jilly. It was easier that way. But tonight they had no choice and Wendy saw that Joe, at least, was obviously doing his best impression of someone who had only helpful efficiency to offer. Considering how intense he could be, not to mention how wild, Wendy could never figure out how he managed to pull this sort of thing off. But once again, it seemed to work. Lou studied him for a long moment before giving him a grudging nod.

"What did you mean when you said it depends?" he asked Joe.

"I meant it depends on how you view the world and what you expect to see when you look at it."

Lou sighed. "Now's not the time for one of the prof's lectures, especially not a secondhand one."

"You see a wall," Joe said, going on as though Lou hadn't spoken. "But I see a door."

With that he stepped up to the wall, then started walking through it as though it wasn't there. Wendy heard the nurse gasp. Lou swore. Her own reaction was to grab Cassie's hand just before she disappeared behind Joe. She could feel Cassie try to jerk her hand free as Wendy's fingers closed around hers, but Wendy tightened her grip before the other woman could pull free. The wall came up to her face and she flinched, but then she went through it just as Joe and Cassie had and she was standing hand-in-hand with Cassie in a forest she didn't know where.

Cassie turned to her. "Oh, Wendy," she said.

For a moment Wendy found it hard to concentrate on much of anything. They'd gone through this weird fuzzy area where she'd felt as though she was going to lose her dinner, but that was already fading. Now she was just in awe. She was here. In the spiritworld. She was actually, really and truly, here.

She realized her mouth was hanging open and closed it. She tried grinning at Cassie and Joe, but her charm wasn't working, or at least not on Joe if his frown was anything to go by. He could give Lou serious lessons on how to look fierce.

"You can't stay here," he told her. "I need Cassie to go to Cody's heart home to fetch Jack and Bo, while I see if I can track where they've taken Jilly. We don't know how many we're up against, but the last time I ran into them, that sister of Jilly's had a good-sized pack of wolves at her beck and call. We just don't have the time to baby-sit you."

"I . . . I only wanted to help," Wendy said.

"And see the dreamlands," Joe added.

"Well, yeah. That, too. But I'm not, like, helpless."

Those stern eyes of Joe's softened for a moment.

"I know," he said. "Normally you're not. But in this place, you are. Trust me on that. We can't be looking out for you and helping Jilly."

"But—"

"She can come with me," Cassie said. "I'm just going to that mountaintop of Cody's, right? How dangerous can it be?"

Joe regarded them both for a moment, then gave a slow nod.

"Okay," he told Wendy. "Stick to the paths and do whatever Cassie tells you to do. Can you promise me that?"

"I do. I promise."

Joe turned to Cassie. "I need them here as fast as they can come."

"I'll do my best," Cassie said. "But you know how Jack can be. He's going to make me go through a whole song and dance before I even get to tell him why I've come."

Joe nodded, then faded into the woods, moving as silent as the memory of a ghost.

"He's not really mad at me, is he?" Wendy asked.

"No. He's just worried. Now come on."

Cassie took her hand and led her off along no discernible trail that Wendy could see.

After her initial excitement of actually being in the dreamlands, Wendy grew a little disappointed. The forest she and Cassie were tramping through wasn't much different from the wooded foothills of the Kickaha Mountains where she used to go hiking with an old boyfriend who'd been a real nature buff. There were more deciduous trees and less undergrowth, but it was neither the Greatwood with its cathedral trees that both Jilly and Sophie had described to her, nor the fairy-tale wood she'd imagined, in which one might catch glimpses of sprites and faeries and other sorts of magical woodland creatures. The air did feel remarkably clean and she understood what Jilly had meant about almost feeling as though it could sustain you all on its own, but it wasn't quite the magical experience she'd been hoping for.

Don't complain, she told herself. They weren't here for her own personal pleasure, but to help Jilly.

And yet, and yet . . .

She almost said something to Cassie, but she was still trying to decide the best way to frame what she wanted to say without sounding ungracious, when she realized how cold it had gotten. Blinking, she looked around herself. When had the trees lost their leaves and the air grown so chilly?

"We should have brought heavier jackets," Cassie said. "I didn't realize the way we'd have to take would get so cold." She glanced at Wendy. "Are you okay?"

"Um . . . I guess . . ."

"Don't worry. It'll change soon."

And it did. They came up a rise and somehow as they topped the ridge the forest was gone. The air grew warmer and they descended into a vast meadow of wildflowers.

"Okay," Wendy said. "This is weird."

Cassie laughed. "I forgot. This is all new to you."

"Pretty much. And it's nothing like Sophie and Jilly described it as."

"That's because we're going through the quicklands—places where time runs faster than it does in the World As It Is. It means you end up going through a lot of different kinds of landscapes and climates at what feels like an accelerated rate. Each one of them is what Joe calls an *abinàs-odey*—a heart home. The places that people go to in their dreams where they feel safest and most real. We all have one—you, me, the cousins, everybody—and large parts of the dreamlands are just one big quiltwork of these places."

"Well," Wendy said, "I was wondering where the magic was and now it's here. But it's . . . different from what I was expecting."

"Expect the unexpected—that's what Joe says."

"Is everybody's heart home like this?" Wendy asked. "I mean, forests and mountains and, you know, wild places?"

"There are as many different kinds as there are people to be home to them. It just depends where you go. That city of Sophie's—"

"You mean Mabon?"

Cassie nodded. "Whole sections of it are the heart homes of people that have become attached to her original imagining. There are homes all in darkness, underwater, in landscapes that appear to be one huge factory, or even places that seem to be no more than confusing tangles of pipes and inexplicable machines . . ." She shrugged. "They're whatever can be imagined—anyplace that someone might find true comfort. Most of us only visit them in our dreams and don't remember having been there when we wake up."

"I sure don't," Wendy said.

Though she could recall times when she'd woken up with this indescribable sense of well-being, slightly tinged with bittersweet, but that was only because she knew she was leaving the source of that feeling behind.

As they continued to walk through the shifting landscape, Wendy still found the sudden changes of locale and climate disconcerting for all that Cassie had now explained the twisty dream-logic behind them. She supposed what was oddest was how she couldn't see the seams. One moment they were climbing up a rocky slope in what felt like spring weather, the next they were making their way through the thick undergrowth of a new forest in a summer heat, but she could never seem to focus in on that exact moment when one changed to the other.

Finally they came out of an evergreen forest to the red rock slopes of a canyon.

"We're almost there now," Cassie told her. "And our surroundings should stay fixed."

"I kind of liked the way they kept switching around."

"Maybe you were born to walk the dreamlands after all."

Wendy gave her a smile. The slope they went up was steep and they'd been walking at a quick pace for over an hour, but she didn't feel the least bit winded.

"I feel like I've come home," she said.

Cassie nodded. "And somewhere in this quiltwork of the dreamlands, you'll *really* get that feeling —at least I hope you'll get the chance, because too many of us never get to visit our heart home when we're awake and in our physical bodies."

"Have you been to yours?"

Cassie nodded.

"What's it like?"

"Nothing like this. This is Cody's place, though from what Joe's told me, he's set it aside and a bunch of canids have taken it over."

"Canids are like corbæ, but they're wolves—right?"

"Wolves, foxes, coyotes, dogs . . ."

Just then they came up onto the mesa top and Wendy got her wish to see some of the magical inhabitants of the dreamlands. There were two men sitting by a fire, both dark-skinned and dark-haired, dressed in casual clothes. One of them looked pretty normal but, under the black brim of his hat, the other had a wolf's head in place of a human's.

"Oh, my," Wendy said and took Cassie's hand.

"It's okay," Cassie told her. "This is who we've come to find."

Don't stare, Wendy told herself. They might take offense.

But the two men were looking her over with their own unfeigned curiosity, especially the one with the wolf's head. He stood up and doffed his hat in an exaggerated courtly gesture.

"I swear," he said. "You pray often enough and sooner or later you get what you were asking for. Ladies, we are yours for the taking. You only have to say the word and we'll be your love slaves forever."

Cassie laughed. "Always the charmer, hey, Jack? But you've got to work on your script. I mean, it makes me feel like I'm in some bad seventies bar instead of this beautiful place."

"Beautiful? It doesn't hold a candle to you and your gorgeous friend."

"And it'd help if you lost the dog face," Cassie said.

Wendy blinked as the wolf's features morphed into that of a handsome, dark-skinned man. The transformation so riveted her that she almost missed their names when Cassie introduced the pair to her.

Bo gave her a wave from where he still sat by the fire.

"Nice to meet you," he said.

There was nothing so casual for the more flamboyant Whiskey Jack. He smiled warmly, hat in hand, his teeth flashing white. When he walked toward her, arms opened to give her an embrace, Wendy didn't know whether she should straight-arm him or more politely hide behind Cassie. She was never fond of people who were so touchy-feely right off the bat. It didn't matter how charming they might make themselves out to be, they just made her squirm.

"It's not simply nice to meet you," he was saying. "Trust me when I say that, in this lonely place, it's an honor and a privilege to—"

Cassie intercepted him, saving Wendy her decision. He wrapped his arms around Cassie, winking at Wendy over her shoulder.

"If only you weren't my best friend's gal," he told Cassie.

Cassie good-naturedly returned his hug, then disengaged herself from his embrace.

"See the problem," she said to Wendy, "is that canids like these—and especially our good friend Jack, here—live in their libido, twenty-four seven."

"And that's a problem because?" Jack asked.

Cassie ignored him. "That's the part the stories seem to miss or gloss over. Take 'Little Red Riding Hood.' When they say the wolf ate her grandmother—"

"Now you're just being rude," Jack said, but he was smiling.

"Anyway," Cassie went on. "The point is, they don't mean to be so lecherous, it's just hardwired into their genes—"

"I love it when you talk dirty," Jack told her.

"And they rarely force their advances on anyone."

Jack turned to Wendy. "It's that we don't have to," he said.

Bo finally stood up from the fire and came over to where they were talking.

"You know it's always a pleasure seeing you," he said to Cassie, "but I'm guessing you're here for something a little more serious than putting Jack in his place."

"My place, your place," Jack said with a laugh. "I'm easy."

"Joe sent us," Cassie said. "Those dream wolves you've been chasing

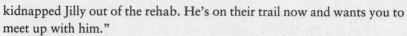

kidnapped Jilly out of the rehab. He's on their trail now and wants you to meet up with him."

Wendy was astonished in the change that came over Jack. He went from teasing joker to serious in the blink of an eye. Where before she wanted to back away because he was too forward, now it was because he was too scary. Joe could do that, too, though his teasing was usually silly rather than lewd. She wondered if this ability to switch moods so quickly was another canid trait.

"How long ago?" Jack asked.

"We just left him."

Jack nodded to Bo. "Come on, partner. Let's finish this business."

"We left him at—" Cassie began.

"We can find him," Jack said.

They took a few steps and then vanished, as though they'd slipped behind a curtain of air. Wendy stared at where they'd disappeared.

"How'd they do that?" she asked.

"Once the People have been to a place, then can usually just will themselves to and from it. It's something that comes naturally to them— like their shapeshifting. We can do it when we're dreaming, and we can learn how to do it outside of dreaming time, but it's harder for us."

Wendy looked past Cassie to where the red rock canyons seemed to go on forever. The view was so magnificent it seemed to stop her breathing. The red stone vibrating against the green of the junipers and ponderosa pines, the immense sky overhead, so blue it could make your eyes sting. She'd never seen anything remotely like it back home except in picture books and nature specials.

"We should get back to the rehab, I guess," she said, unable to keep the regret out of her voice. "Lou's going to be having a fit."

Cassie nodded. "We should, but I just want to try something."

Wendy followed her to the edge of the mesa. Cassie cupped her hands and gave a sharp, resonating cry that seemed to rise from the bottom of her chest and soar out into the canyon.

What . . . ? Wendy thought as Cassie repeated the sound a couple more times.

But then she was unable to do anything except take a startled step backward and stare.

A giant dragon lifted up from behind the line of hoodoos directly in front of them, golden and shining. Wendy stared at it in an astonished awe that grew only more profound when the dragon suddenly broke up and she realized it had been made up of hundreds of birds, flying in formation.

"They're golden eagles," Cassie said. "Joe's told me they like to put on this show if you ask them politely enough. I don't know what that sound he taught me means, but it sure seems to work."

"I . . . I never . . ."

Cassie grinned at her. "Me, neither. I thought he was putting me on when he told me about it." She took Wendy's hand. "That's something to remember."

Wendy could only nod.

"Unfortunately, now we have to go back to the real world," Cassie said.

"It won't seem as real as this," Wendy said. "This seems like the template on which our world was based."

Cassie gave her fingers a squeeze in agreement. Then she led her away.

5

MANIDÒ-AKÌ

I hope I wasn't too rough on Wendy, but there just isn't the time to be polite. Who knows what these wolves want with Jilly? I only know it can't be good. And to make things worse, they've hidden their trail. The damnedest thing is, I don't even think it was willful. It's not a canid trick—I'd see through that. It's something else, something that slides away from my mind every time I try to look at it straight on.

I remember what I said to Lou, back in the rehab.

It depends on how you view the world and what you expect to see when you look at it.

That works here the same as it does back in the World As It Is.

Thinking about Lou makes me realize how little he's changed over the years. He was always steadfast and true—a rarity in a man these days, little say a cop. I know Jilly's grateful for how he took her off the street back when, but it's him being who he is that keeps them friends.

Cops just see too much of the wrong end of the world. You can see how it wears them down. They can't match the stats up on the rez, but more of them eat their guns than you'll find in a cross section of regular citizens. The ones that don't are either in AA, or still drinking, or have closed down their ability to feel much of anything.

All these years gone by, and Lou still cares. Plays everything too tight by the book, so far as I'm concerned, but you've got to give him credit. The only thing he's lost is any kind of lightness in his heart. I guess in a job like his, that's the first thing to go. It's why cop humor's so grim.

I shake my head and bring my mind back to the problem at hand.

What did I expect to find here?

That's easy. Jilly and the wolves that grabbed her from the rehab.

Why can't I find them?

Because they've hidden their trail.

Hidden it how?

I roll a cigarette and light it, studying the woods around me.

Something hidden. Something secret.

And then I know. It's *the* secret, the one that binds them, Jilly and her sister. Jilly and Angel both refer to victims of abuse as Children of the Secret, how the secret gives these victims a connection the rest of us can't have—something deep in their bones that answers to each other when they meet, doesn't matter how long ago they had to live through their own private hell.

So I'm thinking, that's where they've gone. Into someplace only they can access, these Children of the Secret. To find them, I have to get myself into that head space if I can, but I don't know if it's possible, and I don't think I have the time. But then I realize I know someone who can help me and she won't be as hard to track down, because she's not hiding from me.

Like I've said, I'm no derrynimble, but I do have a gift of being able to find things in the dreamlands.

I close my eyes and concentrate on her. It's kind of like how Holly Rue—that friend of Jilly's with the used bookstore—describes how you can access other people's computers over the Internet. You send out a little search program and it goes pinging against firewalls until it finds a computer that isn't protected and sends the information back to you.

What I'm sending out instead of a program is a need to find something, but otherwise it's not much different. It's just as random and there's not really all that much mysterious or magical about it. When it bangs up against what I'm looking for, it sends an echo back and I know where to go.

I get a quick return on this search. Doesn't surprise me—she's only been in the dreamlands for a few hours and everything being new to her, she wouldn't have gotten far. I take a last drag of my smoke, put it out, and store the butt in my pocket. Then I find me a quicklands trail and head off to find her.

6

NEWFORD, MAY

Lou was pacing back and forth in the hall outside Jilly's room when Sophie arrived. She got the feeling he'd been doing it for a while. As they drew nearer, the policewoman who'd escorted Sophie from the front door of the rehab center cleared her throat.

"Sorry to bother you, Loot," she said, "but this lady was saying—"

She broke off when Lou turned and waved her off.

"It's okay, Barb," he said. "Thanks for bringing her."

"Where's Wendy?" Sophie asked as the policewoman returned to her post. "I came as soon as I heard, but the cab took forever to get to my place."

Lou pointed at the blank wall across from Jilly's doorway. Sophie's gaze followed his finger, then returned to his face.

"I don't get it," she said.

"You and me both, Sophie. All of a sudden everybody's walking through walls, except they don't end up on the other side. Nope. They're just gone."

"Gone?"

Lou made a helpless gesture with his hands. "There's a room on the other side of that wall, but there's nobody in it."

"*Wendy* walked through a wall?"

He nodded. "Along with Cassie and Bones. And before that—at least according to Wendy—it was Jilly's sister and her partner carrying off Jilly."

"But—"

"I know what you're thinking," Lou said. "It's nuts. But I saw them go. They stepped right into that wall like it wasn't even there, and then they were gone."

Sophie ran a hand across the plaster of the wall.

"If it's a trick," Lou said. "It's a damn good one."

"It's not a trick," Sophie said.

Lou nodded slowly. "So, are you going to follow them?"

"I wouldn't know how."

"I think I'm kind of relieved," Lou told her.

"Relieved?"

"Because if you went, I'd have to go with you and . . ." He shrugged. "This world's already weird enough for me. I don't need to add the problems of another to it."

"It's not all bad over there," Sophie said.

"So you have been over?"

Sophie gave him a small smile. "Only in my dreams." She looked away from him, back at the wall. "You say Cassie and Joe followed after Jilly?"

Lou nodded. "With Wendy in tow."

"Well, that's something. Joe'll know what to do. I think he was born there."

"So it's not just a shtick—his reading fortunes and making like he knows more about the world than you and me can see?"

"He's for real," Sophie told him. She sighed. "Though it's not something I've ever been comfortable admitting to—knowing about this sort of stuff, I mean. But I guess I've always thought of Joe as this trickster figure who's got one foot in our world, another in the dreamworld. Jilly says he's way older than he looks and—how did she put it?—potent."

"Tricksters," Lou said. "They're like con men, right?"

"I suppose they can be. But Joe's on our side. No matter what's going on over there, he won't let anything bad happen to Jilly."

"He'd better not," Lou said.

Sophie nodded. But she knew it wasn't going to be up to Joe. While she had no idea what was really going on anymore, she was sure of this much: things had spun way out of anybody's control.

Except for maybe Jilly's sister.

7

MANIDÒ AKÌ

The honey-blonde pit bull doesn't seem too surprised to see me come walking out of the woods into the meadow where she and her pack have set up camp. I made a point of calling out before I came into sight—to give them warning, but also to let them know I'm aware of their presence. As I step into the clearing, the dogs rise to their feet and watch me with those flat gazes of theirs. I know a couple have slipped off—I can hear them circling around behind me in the bush.

I go down on one knee once I'm in the clearing to bring my head closer to the level of theirs and wait, palms open at my side, nothing threatening. The pack doesn't move until the two circling behind me are in place. Then the honey blonde approaches me.

"My name's Joe," I tell her. "We didn't take the time to introduce ourselves properly the last time."

I wait a moment, but there's no response. I know she understands me, but I don't know if she can make herself understood. She's got some old blood in her, but it's thin and she's probably never tried to communicate with anybody except for the members of this pack—her fellow prisoners, back in the World As It Is.

I'm pretty sure she recognizes a kinship with me—the one that goes back to my mother's side. My mother was some old yellow camp dog up in Kickaha territory, the story goes. Had a lot of the old blood in her, but nothing to help connect her to that side of her heritage. She'd slip in and out of her shape—yellow-haired woman, yellow-haired dog. No control.

I was told she was in human form when she met her a handsome black-haired man with old corbæ blood in him. She couldn't talk—I don't know why; didn't have a voice in her dog shape either—but they got along the way folks have since the beginning of time when they're attracted to each other. She stayed with that crow man long enough to give birth to me, but then the canid in her got too strong and she went back to the camp and I got raised by my father and my uncles and aunts on the corbæ side.

One of my aunts told me later that my father used to go back to her on a regular basis, follow her around the camp in crow shape, but she never shifted back. It's not a happy story, but it could've been worse for me. I could've never been born. Or I could've had parents like Jilly's.

Does this honey-blonde pit bull see any of that story when she looks in my eyes? I can't tell.

I would've come to them in dog shape myself, but that would've put a whole different dynamic in place. I would've looked different, smelled different. Hard to say if they would've recognized me before taking me down. I'm not saying they're particularly vicious. It's just that, bred the way they were, treated the way they were, attacking first is pretty much hardwired into their thinking.

"Just in case you're wondering," I say, "we're square. You don't owe me anything. I didn't need anything more for setting you free than knowing you're out of that place I found you and living free."

She's watching, still listening, still silent.

"So what I'm asking now is a favor," I tell her. "Nothing more. You can say yes, you can say no, and I won't think the worse of you. But if you can help me out here, I'll be beholden to you, no question."

Then I tell her my problem.

The pack never loses its wariness while I'm talking. It's all stiff legs and flat stares. I decide maybe we need something here to put everybody at ease.

"I'm going to put on my own face," I say to the honey blonde. "See if you can keep your boys from jumping to the wrong conclusions."

With that I let one of my true faces show, that of a yellow hound— what I got from my mother's side. It's not one I wear often.

"There's not a lot of dignity in it," I tell Cassie the one time she asked. "A man with a dog's head—it reminds me too much of all those paintings you see at garage sales of dogs playing poker."

"And a coyote or a wolf's better?"

I remember grinning. "Maybe, maybe not. But it looks a bit more mythic, don't you think?"

"I think I like your real face better." She touched the palm of her hand to my cheek. "This is your real face . . . isn't it?"

"It's my real human face," I told her.

Dog, crow, man. Talk about your mixed breeds. I've got it all sewn up.

The pit bull pack bristles as I let the rest of me change. Now they've got a strange dog in their midst. I hear one of them growl, over on my right. There's movement behind me. But before anyone gets too antsy, the honey blonde gives a sharp bark and nobody moves. She and I do the dog thing and smell each other's asses—it's not my favorite part about this shape—but I seem to pass muster. I have to go through it with the rest of the pack. When the last one's done you can feel the tension ease.

The honey blonde bumps my shoulder with hers. When she sees she has my attention, she heads off toward the woods. She pauses at the edge of the clearing and barks. I nod and trot off after her. The rest of the pack stays behind.

I could maybe use their help, too, depending on how many wolves Jilly's sister has got running with her today, but I don't press my luck. I figure the honey blonde helping me is already more than I could hope for right now. Once I told her we were square—and I know she could see I meant it—she didn't owe me a damn thing. It's only her big heart that's got her doing this for me. Or maybe it's what I told her, about Jilly.

After all, the honey blonde's one of the Children of the Secret, too. She's strong. A survivor. But the real measure of her heart is that she's willing to put something back, to help someone who can't help herself. In that she's closer to Jilly than Jilly's sister will ever be.

then. Was it so bad? I even had a date, for god's sake, with the first normal, sweet guy I'd met in years.

Okay, so we wouldn't be able to do the kissy-cuddling thing. Truth is, we wouldn't be able to do much of anything except watch the movie together and talk. But in a way, with my history, that wouldn't necessarily be such a bad thing. There was the possibility that, given time, we could become pals. And then, if anything else came out of it, maybe the part of me that shuts down when relationships get too intimate wouldn't engage because it would already know Daniel. It would know he was sweet and no threat and nothing like every man in the early part of my life had been.

I sigh. I don't know why I'm even bothering to think of any of this.

No, that's not true. I do know. It's to stall, plain and simple. It's to not have to go down into that gulch and confront the worst parts of my life: the Broken Girl and the Deserted Sister. Because I know that, bad as things are at the moment, as soon as I go down there, everything will be so much worse.

But there's no point in stalling. It's not like the cavalry is about to come riding through the trees to rescue me. Nobody even knows that I'm here, or what the situation is, except for Toby, and he didn't exactly stick around to lend me a helping hand.

So I stand up. I take a steadying breath.

Face the music, I tell myself.

And I start down the side of the gulch, feet sliding on the damp leaves that carpet the steep slope, holding on to the trunks of saplings to keep my balance as I go down. I make it almost halfway down before either my sister or her friend Pinky Miller notice me.

Raylene's the first to look up. Her eyes widen a little, but she doesn't seem to be too surprised. Pinky's in the middle of lighting a cigarette.

"Damn," Pinky says and scrabbles in a duffel bag that's lying near her feet.

I don't know what she's looking for, but when she pulls a shotgun out and aims it in my direction, I stop dead in my tracks, ten, maybe twelve yards away.

"You might want to load that ol' scattergun," Raylene says in a mild drawl. "The shells are still in their box, wrapped up in a black T-shirt."

Jilly

I lie there in the damp leaves for a long moment after Toby's deserted me, then I finally get up and try walking away myself. I don't manage to take more than a half-dozen steps before that geas thing grabs ahold of me, almost physically yanking me back. When I turn around to face the gulch, the compulsion eases into a steady, summoning pulse once more. I still feel the need to go down to where my sister's haranguing the Broken Girl, to go down and let my dreaming self become swallowed by helpless flesh again.

The geas hasn't gone away; it just doesn't actually *hurt* anymore.

It's funny how your perspective changes as your circumstances do. Only a few hours ago my low point was being trapped in my bed as the Broken Girl. But I still had the support of my friends. I was still in a medical facility where all my needs were looked after. I was still able to fall asleep in my bed there and go wandering the cathedral world as my dreaming self.

As things stand, I'd be happy to wind the clock back a few hours to

She never takes her gaze away from mine. I can't read anything in her eyes—what she's thinking, what she's feeling. She doesn't give anything away.

I can't tell if Pinky's busy looking for the shells or not. Maybe she's found them already and is loading them into the shotgun. Maybe she's about to shoot me. I don't know.

I've lost my ability to focus on more than one thing at a time. Everything's telescoped down into this one moment of contact.

All I see is my little sister and just like her I don't look away either.

I can't.

2

Toby stopped at the top of the ridge to catch his breath, the forest lying dense and thick behind him. His every muscle ached—some in places he hadn't even known he had muscles—and he was tired, so tired, but that was hardly a surprise. Between climbing the tree in the Greatwood with Jilly and their subsequent descent, the long trek following the pull of her geas, and finally the pace-eating jog he'd kept up since he'd left Jilly on the ridge above the gulch, he hadn't had more than a few moments rest for longer than he cared to consider. It was most definitely beginning to tell on him. Unfortunately, the one thing his immediate future held wasn't the chance to relax.

Below him through the trees, he could see a clearing, a large field of goldenrod, yarrow, and Joe Pye weed growing up out of a sea of yellowing grasses and thistle. A beautiful place, to be sure. But it wasn't the field he'd been looking for.

Somewhere back along the way he'd come, he'd stepped onto the wrong quicklands path. Now he'd have to backtrack until he found the right one. He could feel the minutes slipping away, running short. An hourglass draining to its last few grains of sand. If he took too long, he'd never get back to her in time.

Unless he went by the factory world.

If he was one of the People or a dreamer, he could have just willed himself to his destination and none of this would even be an issue. But that wasn't an option. While he might now be real, due to Jilly's earlier courage and stamina, he was still a native of the middleworld with many of the limitations that came from having such an origin. But he couldn't give up now. Jilly had risked much to help him. How could he do less for her?

Still, the factory world.

He hated the place, but there was no quicker way through the dreamlands—the Eadar knew this, if no one else did. All the quicklands paths crisscrossed one another there.

Taking a last look at the welcoming view below him, he turned back into the forest and walked a half-dozen paces in among the trees until he found the path he needed underfoot.

It didn't take long for the trees to die around him. At first the lush boughs above simply changed to yellowing leaves, as though he was walking into autumn. But soon even the foliage was gone and he traveled under empty, dead boughs, the ground underfoot changing from leaves and grass to dry dirt that rose in plumes of dust behind him. The next clearing announced itself long before he could see it with a dissonant roar of hammering and clanking that grew louder with every step he took in its direction. Then the trees were gone and he walked under gray, oppressive skies, the air thick with a metallic taste and smelling of sulfur and iron.

Soon there were buildings all around him, some falling in upon themselves, others rearing skyward for story upon story of dull, graying brick and stone, glass and steel. The ever-present thunder of unrecognizable machinery going through inexplicable tasks came from them, their only tangible result appearing to be the chaotic noise that ensued.

Nothing grew or seemed to live in this place and visitors were few and far between, even with so many quicklands paths meeting one another here as they did. The toxic fumes and proximity of so much iron-bearing metalwork was anathema to many denizens of the dreamlands. The ground was rutted and pocked with hidden sinkholes where pools of cyanide and chemical waste lay in wait for the careless traveler.

Toby hurried along to the central square where the quicklands paths met, sleeve held up to his face so that he could breathe through its cloth. Twice the dry dirt gave out under him and he only just managed to scramble free of a sinkhole, dark liquids bubbling below. When he finally reached the square, the clamor of machinery had built to a deafening pitch. The noise and stink made it hard to concentrate.

Find the thread, he told himself. Blue and green. The echo of a sweet meadow.

Just as he found and stepped onto the quicklands path, he heard his name called. Turning, he saw the Tattersnake approaching him from a far corner of the square. Shivering, Toby returned his attention to the task at hand. Taking the path he'd found, he stepped into a blessed silence. It was long moments before the ringing in his ears died down enough so that he could hear the natural sounds around him—wind sighing though boughs laden with broad, flat leaves, and there before him, the sweet-smelling field of vervain, their blue blossoms dancing on the breeze. The stink of the factory world would take a little longer to fade from his clothes and hair.

Stepping off the path, Toby put his back to a tree and waited, hoping that the Tattersnake wouldn't follow. Luck wasn't with him.

The Tattersnake appeared on the path just as he had, bringing with him a momentary echo of the factory world's machinery and stench that hung in the air until both were swallowed by their present surroundings.

"Well, now," the Tattersnake said. "And where, I asked myself, is good Toby Childs, the Boyce, off to in such a hurry? Such a hurry he's in, he doesn't have the time to pass a few words with an old friend." The dark eyes mocked Toby. "But then we're not friends, are we? I'm the sort that one can't be friends with—isn't that what you've said?"

"I . . . I'm not afraid of you."

"You should be. Here we are, just the two of us. Bainbridge is long dead, so there won't be any more stories. No more rescues by plucky Maggie Redweir or any of Bainbridge's other pathetic little heroines. They've all faded away, unremembered, except for you and me."

An odd thing happened as the Tattersnake spoke: Toby found himself remembering. All those stories he'd tried to hold in his head but had lost over the years, they all came back to him. All those heroines he'd accompanied on their quests to put the Tattersnake in his place. He had often wondered why only he and the Tattersnake appeared in each of Margery Bainbridge's stories, though the heroine usually had a name similar to the author's, as well as the author's red hair.

Why was he able to remember all of this now?

The Tattersnake never seemed to forget any of it. And when he spoke of it, Toby would remember too, but only vaguely, and he could never hold on to the memories. But it had all come back now, from the spray of freckles across Maggie Redweir's nose, to the strange motley coloring of her little dog Nock. It had all come back and sat there in his head with the assurance of never going away again.

He would have loved to think about it all, but he still had a task undone and the Tattersnake to mollify so that he could get about his business. Then he realized that the Tattersnake was regarding him with an appraising look and his nervousness returned full force.

"There's something not quite right about you today, Toby me boy," he said. "What could it be, could it be?"

"I'm fine, really. Thanks for asking. But now I have to—"

"You . . . you're real," the Tattersnake broke in. "How . . . ?"

"The gift of a twig from the topmost branch of a Greatwood tree."

The Tattersnake frowned at him. "That's only a fairy tale."

"So were we," Toby told him. "So you remain."

"Give me the twig."

Toby had a sudden shiver of fear. He was still carrying in his pocket the twig Jilly had dropped, but the Tattersnake couldn't have it. That twig belonged to Jilly. It might not have worked once, but who was to say it wouldn't work the next time they tried?

"It . . . it's gone," Toby said.

He held out his hand and showed the Tattersnake the pattern that the twig had left on his palm. The expression on the Tattersnake's face was pure envy, Toby realized.

"Perhaps I'll just cut it out of you," the Tattersnake said.

"You can't," Toby told him, speaking quickly. "It wouldn't work. The twig is gone and gone. It's part of me now and won't do anyone else any good. You know how magic works. If it could be undone at all, it would have to be undone by the maker. Can you force a Greatwood tree to your bidding?"

The Tattersnake remained silent, staring at Toby's palm until Toby finally put his hand in his pocket.

"You could get one, too," he said. "If I could do it, then surely you would have no trouble at all."

But he would have already tried, Toby realized, for all that, moments ago, he'd said it was just a fairy tale. He would have tried, just as Toby had, and he would have had just as much success, which was none.

"So you're real," the Tattersnake said. "Doesn't matter if anyone believes in you or not, because there you'll still be, all the same."

"I . . . I suppose I am."

Toby was worried where all this was going. He didn't have this time to spare. He couldn't stay, but he couldn't simply walk away, either. No one walked away from the Tattersnake at the best of times. But now, with this look about him, this mood he was in. Contemplative as well as dangerous.

"So you can do what you want, when you want," the Tattersnake went on.

Toby nodded.

"Which makes me wonder, what are you doing here? Collecting vervain, I imagine, but what would an Eadar-become-real need with vervain? The only use I know of vervain is to break a spell."

Toby didn't know what to say without giving everything away, so he chose prudence and remained silent.

"Well, my little man?" the Tattersnake said. "Nothing at all to say for yourself? Maybe what you need is a few good sharp raps against your noggin to help you find your voice."

It was always this way with the Tattersnake. He would appear out of nowhere—as he had in the factory world—and bully Toby with cruel words and threats and impossible questions, until eventually he got bored. Sometimes he'd cuff Toby before he walked away. Sometimes he'd knock him down and give him a kick or two as well. There was no telling how it would go. It could be long and Toby was never brave enough to stand up to him. But today he had to. Today he had no time for the Tattersnake's petty cruelties.

The trouble was, being real didn't make him any stronger or bolder than the formidable Tattersnake. But Toby didn't feel particularly clever either, the way all those heroines in Bainbridge's stories had been. They were always able to outsmart the Tattersnake—outsmart him and get away and have him look foolish as well.

No, he thought, with his returned memories. They hadn't all done so. Maddy Reynolds in "The Blue Mask of Wintering" hadn't been clever.

That was the last of Bainbridge's stories and in it Maddy had simply stood up to the Tattersnake. And when she had, he'd blustered and threatened and ranted, but finally he'd backed off and slunk away.

"You have to stand up to bullies," she'd told Toby in that story. "Let them see that you're not afraid. That you'll take their blows, but you'll give back as good as you get. You might wind up with a black eye, but they'll think twice about bothering you again—trust me on that."

Toby smiled, remembering.

Trust me on that.

Maddy was always telling him to do that. And she was usually right.

"Something humorous come to you?" the Tattersnake asked.

That dark look was in his eyes, the one that said today it would be more than cruel words and laughter. Today it would be fisticuffs or worse.

Toby swallowed hard. He thought of feisty Maddy, with her swinging walk, her long red hair tied back in a braid, and that determined glint of stubbornness in her eyes. The memory of her helped give Toby the courage he needed now.

"What I'm doing here is none of your business," he said in a far braver tone of voice than he was feeling.

"Is that so?"

Toby stopped himself from biting at his lower lip and simply nodded.

"Maybe you're real now," the Tattersnake said, "but I can still hurt you, my wee brave little man."

Toby found himself shaking his head.

"You can't," he said. "Not anymore. Only with words."

The Tattersnake took an intimidating step toward him, but Toby held his ground.

"Think about it," he told the Tattersnake, making it up as he went along. "I'm real and you're not. What do you think will happen to you when you try to hit me?"

"Why don't we find out."

"Fine," Toby said.

He continued to hold his ground when the Tattersnake lifted a fist, though it was all he could do not to cringe. The Tattersnake held that pose for a long moment and Toby could see indecision warring with anger in the taller man's dark eyes. Finally caution won out and the Tattersnake smacked the fist into the palm of his other hand and glared at Toby.

"What do you know?" he demanded.

"Only that the quickest way for an Eadar to fade is for them to attack someone who is real."

"You've been chewing mushrooms, you have."

Toby shrugged. "Think what you want. A dire attacked me on my way here, but it faded away to nothing when it bit me. See." He held up his arm and pushed back the sleeve. "The teeth didn't even leave a mark."

Dires were the ghostly remnants of some other story, gray-furred wolfish men with stooped shoulders and embittered souls. They'd haunted the middleworld for years—or at least they had once upon a time. Like other Eadar that Toby and the Tattersnake had seen come and go, there were few dires left now and those few were fading fast.

"If I find you've been lying to me . . ."

Toby gave another shrug. His feigned nonchalance was coming easier now.

"I've my own business to attend to now," he said. "So if you'll excuse me . . ,"

"I think I'll come along."

Toby shook his head. "I can't allow that."

Before the Tattersnake could respond, he took a quick step toward the taller man, his own fist cocked now. It was all he could do not to show his own surprise when the Tattersnake hastily backed away. Perhaps Maddy had been right. Perhaps all you had to do was stand up to a bully.

"Go bother somebody else," Toby said, "before I decide to make you my business."

The Tattersnake lifted his hands, palms out. "Easy now, Toby my good man. No need for rash actions. I'm already on my way."

Toby watched him back away, schooling his own features to remain impassive until the Tattersnake stepped on a quicklands path and was gone. Then he allowed himself to breathe once more. His legs shook so much that he wanted to sit down, but he wouldn't allow himself the luxury. Instead he forced himself to hurry down to the vervain field and began plucking plants until he had an armful, whispering "Sorry" and "Thank you" to every one he pulled out of the ground.

But all the time he was thinking, I stood up to him. The Tattersnake! I made him back down. I actually made him run away!

It was as though the day had suddenly sprouted wings and flown off into the night, leaving the sun to look down from the sky and scratch its head in confusion. How could it even be possible? He was nothing. He was nobody . . .

He shook his head. No, that wasn't true anymore. He was real now.

The astonished sense of well-being filling him didn't—*wouldn't*—go away. Only his worry for Jilly stopped him from doing cartwheels across the field and made him concentrate on braiding the vervain plants into a wreath.

He would add yarrow to it, he thought. For the healing. And perhaps rowan as well. But then he remembered the twig in his pocket. Surely the magic that had made him real could heal Jilly's sleeping twin, the Broken Girl. The twig and the vervain, together they would cure her. The twig hadn't worked before because it had only been Jilly's dreaming self that had tried to use it. It seemed so obvious to him now. She needed to be whole and complete, both parts of her joined, for it to work.

3

"Well, I'll give you this," Raylene finally says. "You got balls, coming here with all the cards stacked against you."

Her voice breaks the spell that had our gazes locked and lets me blink. I sneak a glimpse at Pinky. She *is* loading the shotgun.

"I should never have left you there," I say. "In that house."

"You got that right."

"But I was just a kid myself, you know. I got so messed up when I finally got away that it was years before I was thinking straight again."

"And that's supposed to make everything okay?"

I shake my head. "No. But I want you to know that I came back for you."

"Bullshit."

"It's true. But you were gone and the house was empty."

I see something cold and dark rise in her eyes.

"You can ask Margaret Sweeney," I say.

"That old bag wouldn't give nobody the time a day."

I shrug. "Think about what it was like for her—all of us white trash moving into her neighborhood, treating the land she grew up on and loved like it was a junkyard. And she was supposed to like us?"

"Jesus, now I'm supposed to feel sorry for her? If she was such an angel, why didn't she do anything about what was happening to me?"

"She didn't help me either," I say. "Maybe she didn't know. Or maybe she was scared of Del, too."

"I ain't scared of Del."

"Neither am I—not anymore. But I was."

"You should've done what I did and cut the bastard. Maybe then he would've left all of us alone."

"You stood up to him?"

She pats the front pocket of her jeans. "Me and my good friend, Mr. Switchblade."

"I could never find the courage."

"I guess that's where you and me are different, big sister."

"I'm sure we're different in a lot of ways."

"Christ, I hope so."

We fall into the hole of a long moment of silence, just looking at each other again. She seems as curious as I am, though it's not enough to take the dark anger from her eyes. I try again.

"I really did come back for you," I say. "I know it was too late, but when I left that place I ended up becoming a junkie hooker. There are whole years that are just this awful blur in my head. But as soon as I cleaned up my act and was able to think clearly again, I came looking for you. Believe whatever else you want of me, but that's true."

"You're just saying that," Raylene tells me. "I got you running scared now. You'll say any damn thing to save your skin."

I shake my head. "I'd die for you."

I hear myself say it and I'm surprised. Here's me, so divorced from family that I changed my name, changed my whole life, to get away from them, and now I'm saying the thing that blood relatives say at times like this. But I guess the family tie is strong—except it's not the one of blood.

It's that we're both Children of the Secret and that's maybe the strongest bond of all. We could be complete strangers, but because of the horrors we've undergone, we know each other better than anybody else can. And since what happened to her was my fault—I'm the one who abandoned her—I'm the one who has to make good.

But I don't know how.

Raylene

It's funny, but when my sister comes sliding down the hillside toward us, that red rage I got every time I saw some damned picture of her just ain't in me. I don't know where it's up and gone. I find myself hungry to look at her—not like afore when I was sneaking me peeks of her lying in her hospital bed, but like this, face-to-face. Me looking at her looking at me. She knows who I am. I know who she is.

And then she starts in on her explanations and I answer her back, smart-lipping and no give, and that deep dark anger, it's just not there. Oh, I'm still pissed, but now I'm not so rightly sure just exactly what it is I got to be so pissed about. Because she's right about this much: she *was* just a kid. What could she do but run off and get herself all fucked up like she done? And maybe she come back looking for me, and maybe she didn't. It don't seem to matter so much no more.

Don't get me wrong. I ain't about to turn this into no Hallmark moment or nothing. But I see her standing up there on the side of that hill and I wonder how I could ever have expected more of her. Hell, the reason she probably took it as long as she did back in that hellhole we called home was on account of me. I suddenly find myself remembering all of them times she warned me to keep away from Del, and me, I just didn't listen till it was too late.

Where would I have been without Pinky giving me that knife? I was older'n my sister by then and I sure wasn't putting up any kinda fight my own self. I had Pinky, but Jillian May, she didn't have her nobody 'cept the raggedy-ass little kid I was who probably made things worse for her instead of better.

And then she delivers her killer line.

I'd die for you.

And damned if she don't mean it.

There's folks can lie to you with a straight face, but my sister don't appear to be one of them. There's so much emotion in her eyes when she says them few words and I guess the clincher is, I can tell she's about as surprised she said what she done as I am.

All I can do is stare at her.

Where we're going with this now, I don't know. And the sorry thing is, I don't get to find out.

"You 'bout done now?" Pinky asks.

I look over at her. She's standing there, got that shotgun cradled in her arms like it's a baby.

" 'Cause I don't like me the look of how all of this is goin'," she says.

"How all what's going?"

"Her," Pinky says, nodding at Jillian May with her chin. "You goin' all stupid on me now, Ray? Look at yourself—she's got you bewitched and you're too dumb to even notice. I got me the same feelin' right now that I did settin' on Miss Lucinda's porch."

"So what're you suggesting we do?" I ask. "Shoot her?"

"It's a notion."

I give Jillian May an apologetic look. We got us stuff to work out, no question, but what Pinky's proposing ain't no part of it.

"Wasn't it you telling me not to go all postal just a few hours ago?" I ask Pinky.

"Yeah," she says. "But that was in some damned old hospital in the middle of the city. We're nowhere now. No cops. No rules. Nothing."

"Pinky—"

"Christ in a cornfield, Ray. All of my life I've had to listen to you cryin' over how your sister done you so wrong. Every damn thing went bad in your life, you laid it at her door. So now what're you goin' to do? Let her walk? Where the hell's the closure?"

Thing I forget, with her just a-hanging around most of the time doing nothing more strenuous than smoking and drinking and watching the TV, is how cold she can be. She might not give the impression of being too dangerous on a regular day, but she's shot a cop and cut more'n one man with that knife of hers—cut her some women, too.

"You been watching too many of them daytime talk shows," I tell her.

She just shakes her head and puts the stock of that shotgun to her shoulder.

"I'll show you closure," she says.

"Pinky, no!"

I don't even think about what I'm doing as I run to her. This's got nothing to do with what my sister said 'bout her being willing to die for me. It's about stopping something wrong, that's all. Plain and simple.

But I ain't in time.

Pinky shoots.

I ain't in time.

To stop her from pulling the trigger, I mean.

But I'm plenty in time to get in the way of that shot.

I take it right in the chest and it blows me off a my feet like some giant hand come down outta nowhere and flicked me with a finger.

I don't see my life go by afore my eyes. I wouldn't've wanted that anyways.

But as I'm lying there with the life leaking outta me, I find myself thinking about that sorry-assed little girl I met by the trailer park. How I'm going to be breaking my promise to her.

She's gonna think of me same as I thought of my sister all those years and it ain't even my fault, me dying like this.

That's if she bothers to think of me at all.

"You're dead!" I hear Pinky scream and I don't know if she's yelling at me or my sister.

And then I don't know nothing more 'cept that I'm falling into this big black hole, only the damn hole seems like it's above me and I'm rushing toward this spark of light I can see that's 'biding there at the end of it 'bout as far away as a thing can be.

Joe

That honey-blonde pit bull takes me right to where they are, Jilly and her sister and the sister's friend. I've been hoping we can find a clean end to all of this, but we arrive way too late for any of that.

We come out into a gulch in time to see the tall blonde take a shot at Jilly and damned if Jilly's own sister doesn't step into the line of fire and take that load of buckshot herself. There's a moment of shock when we're all frozen in place. They don't even realize that the pit bull and I are here. The blonde lowers her shotgun and is just staring at her dead friend. I focus on Jilly, see the horror in her face. As Jilly starts down the slope toward her sister, the blonde lifts her head. She screams something and that shotgun of hers comes back up to her shoulder.

It's only Jilly's dreaming self that she's taking bead on, but Jilly's body is here, too. Who knows what'll happen to her if her dreaming self gets killed?

I start for the blonde, but the pit bull's quicker. She launches herself at the blonde and slams into her just as the shotgun fires. The buckshot goes wild, pinging against the rocks and trees. The blonde loses her balance and goes down—half twisting her body to see what hit her instead of doing the sensible thing of looking where she's going to fall. The crack of her head as it hits a granite outcrop makes my stomach do a flip and I know she's not getting back up again.

The pit bull landed easily. She's in ready mode before all her feet are back on the ground. She approaches the dead woman on stiff legs and gives her a sniff, then backs up and whines. Looks like she's no more fond of killing than I am. When she turns to me, I'm already in human form.

"You didn't know," I tell her. "And she had to be stopped. I would've done the same if I'd been closer."

Those dark eyes of hers fix their gaze on me and I can see it doesn't matter that it had to be done. She's going to be holding on to this for a long time. I know what she's thinking. With every life taken, we're all diminished. That's something too many people don't get. Yeah, we've got to stop violence and killing—but you're only adding to the problem when the way you solve it is by more of the same.

The honey blonde turns to look at Jilly, who's bent over the body of her sister. My gaze follows. Jilly looks up, her hands red with her sister's blood, her eyes filled with confusion and hurt.

Jilly

I'm no stranger to violence, though it's been long years since I was a teenager, living on the street where people getting hurt or dying was an everyday occurrence instead of something you just read about in the morning paper. Those days are gone and it's simply not part of my life experience anymore, my recent accident notwithstanding.

The accident.

When Pinky points that shotgun at me, I go right back to that night. I freeze, just as I did when the headlights caught me. Then the shotgun goes off and Raylene gets shot. Her stepping in front of the spray of buckshot meant for me hits me as hard as the impact of the car did.

I lose all awareness of Pinky and the shotgun, of the danger to myself. Only one thing matters. I scrabble and slide the rest of the way down the slope until I'm down on my knees on the damp grass and leaves, crouching beside my sister. I touch her with a trembling hand. Everything I know or can feel or can think about narrows into this singular focus on what's happened to her. I don't want to look, but I can't turn my gaze away.

I stare at the ruin of her chest. The way her head lolls at an unnatural angle. The splay of her limbs. The horrible fact that she's not breathing. That her eyes are rolled up, showing their whites.

That she's dead.

I want to call her back from wherever's she's gone, from wherever she's been taken. I try to put my arms around her and lift her up, but she's a dead weight. Her blood makes my hands go slick and I can't get a good grip.

I don't know how long I'm gone.

When I finally remember Pinky and look up, I blink in confusion. Joe's standing over her still body with a pit bull the color of pale yellow ocher at his side.

I open my mouth, but my voice doesn't seem to work.

When did they get here? What happened to Pinky?

I dimly remember a second shot. Did Pinky shoot herself?

I can see the shotgun in the leaves and brush not far from where she's lying. Joe's hands are empty. That leaves only the Broken Girl, but she's still the unconscious lump she was when I first got here. Knowing her as well as I do, she couldn't have lifted a gun, never mind pulling the trigger.

I get a sharp pull in my midsection—

come to me, come to me

—when I look at the Broken Girl and quickly turn away. My gaze returns to Joe to see he's approaching me. He crouches down on the other side of Raylene's body, those half-crazy, half-laughing eyes of his filled with sympathy.

"I'm sorry it ended this way," he says.

I open my mouth again but I still can't find my voice so I give him a slow nod. I watch his fingers as he rolls himself a cigarette. He lights it and inhales, blows out a stream of blue-gray smoke. When he offers it to me, I shake my head.

"We've got to get you back to the rehab," he says. "Everybody's pretty worried."

My gaze drops to Raylene's face. I reach out with bloodied fingers and close her eyes, one by one. The marks I leave behind on her eyelids look like red war paint. I clear my throat and finally get control of my voice.

"Fuck the rehab," I say.

He looks as though he's about to argue, then nods.

"Yeah," he says. "Healing's way overrated, isn't it?"

"That isn't fair," I tell him. "And you know it."

"I suppose. Though the longer your dreaming self is separated from the rest of yourself, the harder it's going to be on you. You pay for this kind of shit, Jilly."

I shake my head. "It's too much to pay."

"I don't mean what happened here."

"It doesn't matter," I say. "It's happened anyway, hasn't it? My sister's dead. I think I was actually getting through to her, but now she's dead. I haven't seen her in forever and now I'm never going to get the chance to know her any better."

"Not much to know," a second voice says.

I look up to see that the gulch has suddenly gotten way more crowded. I recognize Nanabozho from having met him before in the Greatwood. The other man, the one in the black hat who spoke, isn't familiar, but from stories Joe's told me in the past I make him out to be Whiskey Jack. Another canid.

They seem to have appeared out of thin air—which doesn't startle me, not at this point, knowing what I know about the People, but it's certainly taken the pit bull that came with Joe by surprise. There's a low growl coming from the bottom of its chest. I realize that I've been aware of it in my peripheral hearing for a while—from when the canids first showed up—I just wasn't listening to it, if that makes any sense.

Joe turns to the dog and murmurs, "It's okay."

But it's not okay. How can anything be okay?

Then I focus on what Whiskey Jack said.

"Maybe not for you," I tell him, "but it was the world to me."

"Oh, for Christ's sake. You're acting like she was a saint."

"Jack," Joe says, a warning in his voice.

But Whiskey Jack ignores him.

"She was killing our cousins," he says. "And you know why? So she could bathe in their blood. Make herself young. Make herself high, her and that pack of wolves she was running with."

I look at Joe and he gives me a reluctant nod.

"She was doing a lot of killing," he says. "We've been hunting her and her pack for a while now. We didn't know it was her when we first started looking. We just knew she had to be stopped. One way or another, the killings had to end."

His voice is mild, soft, like he's trying to gentle the hurt, keep me calm. Though I get the sense it's not just for me, but for Jack, too.

"She was my sister," I say.

"But she was doing wrong."

"I don't care." I look back at Jack. "You don't know what she had to go through as a kid."

"I don't need to know," Jack says. "You think that's some kind of excuse? People treat you bad and that gives you a license to do whatever you want to anybody else?"

"No, but—"

"Joe says you both went through some hard times," he says. "So tell me this: how come you turned out so stand-up and she didn't?"

"I could've gone down the same road she did," I tell him. "The difference is, I had people to help me, to pull me out of the gutter and show me there were other choices. All she had was that psycho with the shotgun."

"Bullshit. She was just born bad."

I stand up. I want to wrap my bloodstained hands around his throat and squeeze the life out of him.

"Nobody's born bad," I tell him, my voice tight with anger.

"She was going to kill you," he says.

"We . . . we don't know that."

But now I'm on unsure ground. I don't know why Raylene brought me here. I remember the hate I saw in her wolf eyes. I think of all the paintings she destroyed—she had to know they were the ones that would mean the most to me. I don't know if she was planning to actually kill me, but I know she wanted to hurt me.

"Well, I'm sure of it," Jack says.

"Get out of here," I tell him. "You got what you wanted. My sister's dead and everything's good now in dreamland, so why don't you just go away and leave us alone."

Jack doesn't say anything for a long moment. I get the sense he's about to turn and go away, but then everything changes again.

2

Hearing all the voices coming from the gulch as he approached, Toby crept the last few yards, crouching down behind a fallen tree when he reached the top of the ridge. He peered down, then hastily pulled his head back out of sight. Canids. Two—three. So many of them. His pulse, already pounding because of the long run back from the vervain field, quickened still more.

He swallowed thickly, afraid almost to move. But the more he heard, the more he knew he couldn't stay hiding up here.

As her dreaming self, Jilly wouldn't be strong enough to stand up to so many of the People, all at once. But she had that light in her, shining so strong. The spirit of the Greatwood was on her side—it had to be. Hadn't it allowed her to claim the twigs the way she had? If she could be reunited with her broken self, if what she called the Broken Girl was healed and the two were one, hale and strong, perhaps she would have a chance.

So reluctantly, he rose to his feet. With the vervain wreath in hand, the blue flowers and sweet-smelling leaves intertwined with cream-colored flower heads of yarrow and that one piece of Greatwood magic, he topped the ridge and started down into the gulch.

3

NEWFORD

Sophie sighed. Tonight was like the vigil when Jilly had been in her coma all over again except there weren't as many of them in attendance this time. And there wasn't a comatose body on the bed.

They waited in the hall of the rehab building where Jilly had disappeared. She, Wendy, and Cassie sat on the floor, all in a row, she and Wendy with their legs pulled up to their chests, arms around their knees, Cassie with her legs stretched out, crossed at the ankles. After registering shock at seeing Wendy and Cassie reenter the rehab through the same section of hall that they'd disappeared through earlier, Lou had spent most of his time pacing back and forth until Angel arrived. Now the two of them stood farther down the hall, conversing in quiet voices.

Sophie glanced in their direction. When it came to Jilly, they were like divorced parents. Lou had taken her off the street and brought her to his social worker girlfriend who had gotten her into a detox program and then helped her finish high school and get into university. Though Jilly treated them both as friends now, in those early years they had been like surrogate parents—the ones Jilly should have had, instead of the ones she'd gotten.

When Lou and Angel broke up, Jilly had confessed to Sophie that she felt like the kid caught up in her parents' divorce. She loved them both and knew they loved each other, so the acrimonious breakup had been all that much harder to take. Jilly carried the child's guilt for a parents' divorce as well. While she knew she wasn't personally responsible, it *was* because of Lou's and Angel's differing perspectives on how Angel's clients such as Jilly should be treated that had led to the breakup.

But tonight, as had happened when Jilly was in her coma, their differences were set aside and they were united in their worry and grief.

Sophie had considered calling some of Jilly's other friends, but hadn't known what she'd say to most of them. She was now willing to accept that this kind of thing could happen, that two women could waltz into the rehab and carry Jilly off into the dreamlands by stepping through a wall, but to try to explain it to anyone else besides Christy or the professor would take far more energy than she could summon.

Better to wait, she told herself. At least get through the night. Cassie had assured them that Joe and his friends would be able to rescue Jilly, so it was just a matter of holding tight. Any moment now, Joe would come back from the dreamlands with Jilly and any explanations that were needed could be given by Jilly herself in her usual exuberant style.

But the minutes dragged into hours and there was still no sign of either of them. Sophie wasn't giving up, but her anxiety grew in direct proportion to the passing of time. It was two-thirty now, almost five hours since Jilly had been spirited away. She didn't want to think about what could be taking so long. She knew all too well that danger lay as thick in the dreamlands as wonder.

She glanced at Wendy, sitting beside her. Although Wendy was carrying a soft radiance about her from her own brief visit into the dream-lands, she'd been oddly subdued ever since her return. Sophie reached over and gave her hand a squeeze.

"It'll be okay," she said, putting all of her own hope into the assurance.

"I guess. It's just . . ."

"Just what?"

Wendy sighed and shook her head.

"I feel like such a shit," she said. "Now that I've been over there, I know how it is for you. How could you *not* want to be there?"

"What are you talking about?" Sophie asked.

"I was just feeling . . . left out."

"Of what?"

"Of the three of us. There were you and Jilly, both going into the dreamlands now, and I was turning into the third wheel."

"It would never have been like that."

"I know," Wendy said. "But it felt like it. And the worst thing is, I could have prevented all of this."

Sophie gave her a blank look.

Wendy sighed. "Jilly knew something was up. Maybe she guessed how I was feeling, or at least knew I was feeling something weird. She sent me a message through Angel to come and talk to her about it, but I got caught up at work and then, instead of coming over right after, I went out to dinner with everybody."

"I still don't understand how that puts you at fault."

"Don't you see?" Wendy said. "If I'd come earlier, I would have been here when those horrible women took Jilly away. I could have stopped them."

"Or you could have been hurt."

"Maybe. But before I did I would have raised a stink and maybe the security guards would have got here in time."

"Oh, Wendy," Sophie said, putting her arm around her friend's shoulders. "I can see why you're feeling the way you do, but you really can't blame yourself for this."

Tears welled in Wendy's eyes.

"It's just . . ." she began, then had to start over. "I don't want maybe the last thing Jilly thought of me to be that I was angry with her or some-thing."

She got a pained look on her face, as though by simply expressing her fears, she might have made them real. Sophie hugged her.

"Jilly'd never think that," she said. "And we'd never have left you behind in anything."

"Joe will bring her back," Cassie assured them from the other side of Wendy. "Trust in him."

"We do," Sophie said.

But the waiting was still so hard.

4

MANIDÒ-AKÌ

Everybody turns when Toby comes down the slope, one hand holding on to saplings for balance and to slow his descent, the other carrying a wreath of blue flowers, leaves, and twigs that seems to glimmer and glow.

You didn't desert me, I think.

In the midst of everything else that's going on, that seems like a big deal. An anchor that I can hold on to with my sister dead on the ground in front of me and these two canids with their hard cruel words. At times, they make it so that I can hardly breathe. Then I want to lash out at them, at myself, at the dead bodies of Pinky and Raylene, the one for killing my sister, the other for dying.

I focus on the wreath that Toby's carrying. At first I think it's for Raylene and I wonder how he knew she'd died, but then I realize what it is, who it's for, where he went to in such a hurry when he ran off. He went to that field of magic flowers he'd told me about. He plucked the blossoms he found there and wove them into a wreath for me. To break the spell that the Broken Girl has over me.

But we're way past that now.

"I know that little man," Nanabozho says. "He's always sneaking around in the Greatwood, spying on people."

Jack nods. "An Eadar."

There's something in the way they're talking that makes me realize Toby wasn't so far off in his judgment of the People. They're discussing him the way people do the scrawny stray cats in my neighborhood, which isn't with affection. I'm happy to see that Joe doesn't seem to feel the same—I'm not sure what. Mild antagonism, maybe. Or a kind of annoyed indifference. And then I realize that the pit bull never even growled at Toby's approach.

"What are you doing here?" Jack asks Toby. "Who are you spying for today?"

"He's not a spy," I say. I get up from where I'm kneeling beside Raylene's body. "He's with me. He's my friend."

And then Toby's standing beside me. He straightens his back and gives back as good a hard stare as he's getting—which surprises me, considering how he usually runs away from any encounter with one of the People.

"I'm not an Eadar anymore," he tells them.

Joe gets to his feet as well and all three of the canids study Toby for a long moment.

"Well done," Joe says finally.

I don't know what the other two canids are thinking, but I get the distinct impression that "well done" isn't a part of it. I'm beginning to get a bead on them and I think I know their type now. They don't like change—at least not when they haven't instigated it themselves, and especially not when it doesn't leave them at the top of the food chain. I wonder what new snide remark they'll make.

"There's a scent in the air," Nanabozho says instead. "Something familiar, but I can't put a name to it."

He disappoints me the most. I'd liked him when he came by to talk to me in the Greatwood. Now he's as much a stranger as Whiskey Jack, his cousin in the flat-brimmed black hat.

Jack's nodding in agreement. "Old. Deep."

"And worrisome," Nanabozho adds. "But I don't know why."

I glance at Joe. I can see his own nostrils flaring, those eyes of his that never miss anything looking around. When he sees my gaze on him, he shrugs.

"There's something in the air," he agrees, turning back to his cousins. "But worrisome? It doesn't feel like that to me. It feels more like my *abinàs-odey*—my heart home—though it's far from this place."

"And that doesn't worry you?" Jack asks.

"No, it just makes me curious."

Jack shakes his head. "Something's here that knows us too well."

"I've nothing to hide from anyone," Joe says, "so I have nothing to fear."

"This is older than that," Nanabozho says. "This is older than secrets and fear. It reminds me of my visitor, back at Cody's mountain."

The three canids exchange glances and I want to ask them what they mean, who they're talking about. But Toby plucks at my sleeve, distracting me. When I turn to him, he hands me the wreath.

"Put it on the Broken Girl," he says. "It will break the spell, I know it will. But I also think it will heal her. And you. Both of you."

When the wreath is in my hands, I start to understand what the canids are feeling. It's like the air around us has gone completely still. As though the forest, the rocks, everything, is holding its breath. And then I see the twig from the Greatwood tree, woven into the flowers. It's not just a wreath of that healing vervain Toby told me about earlier, there's another, older magic involved in what he's thinking—something that's sure to work. The twig didn't do anything for me as my dreaming self, but on the flesh and blood of the Broken Girl it should be effective.

She could be healed, whole again.

I could be healed.

My gaze drops from the wreath in my hands to the body of my sister lying on the ground at my feet.

But by that same token, I find myself thinking, if there is such powerful magic in that twig that can work on dead nerves and broken flesh, might it not also work to raise the newly dead? These are the dreamlands, after all. The land of fairy tales. Toby said the magic of the Greatwood twigs could create a miracle. What better use for a miracle than to save my sister?

Now. Here. Where I can. To make up for where I didn't before.

As soon as it comes to me, I know it's what I have to do.

"Are you certain of your choice?"

I blink at yet another new voice, but this one seems to come out to me from a secret place, out of the inheld breath that everything around me is holding. I find that I'm sitting on the ground again, the wreath held against my chest. Slowly, I lower the rough circle of leaves and blue flowers to my lap and look up from my sister's body.

A moment ago the gulch was crowded. There was the Broken Girl and Toby. The corpses of Pinky Miller and my sister. The three canids and the dog that came with Joe. Now it's just my dreaming self, sitting back on my knees beside my dead sister. Everyone else is gone.

But I'm not alone.

The woman who spoke stands where Joe had been only a heartbeat before. She reminds me of Nokomis, the White Buffalo Woman I saw that one time in the Greatwood. I'm sure it's her, even though I never saw her with a human face such as the one this stranger has. There's just this familiarity about her and there's no one else remotely similar to her in my experience. The stranger's face is round as the full moon, surrounded by a cloud of dark, curling hair, thick as a forest. Her complexion is a coppery brown while her eyes are old beyond measure, distant and mysterious, deep and warm at the same time.

We're not in the gulch anymore, either. Around me are the cathedral trees of the Greatwood—or trees like them. These appear even older. Taller and broader of trunk, if that's possible. Cloaked with mystery, yet shining with an inner light that seems to emanate from the bark itself.

I return my attention to the woman. She has the same light in her eyes. She smiles and the shiver of fear that's been creeping up my spine falls away. I'm not so sure she's Nokomis now. I'm not really sure of anything anymore.

"Who . . . who are you?" I finally manage to ask.

That beatific smile of hers widens slightly. "I don't have a name, child, though I've been given many. If you need a reference for me, think of me as the spirit Raven called up to inhabit the first forest in the long ago—those echoes of the forever trees where life began."

"So . . . you *are* Nokomis."

She shakes her head. "We are more like sisters. She is the earth, I am the wood. There are others like us . . . in the first ocean, the first river, the first hill . . ."

"How come she has a name, but you don't?"

"She doesn't have a name any more than I do. Nokomis is simply a name she has been called."

"You don't like names?"

She shrugs. "We ignore names for how they can lock you into a set state of being. We are always shifting, you see—never one thing or the other, but many things all at once. I have been called Mystery and Fate. I have been called the White Deer Woman." She looks down at the body of my sister that lies between us. "I have been called Choice."

It comes back to me, that first thing she asked. The words that drew me out of the gulch, where I'd been standing with the others, to this place that seems so much older and deeper than anywhere I've been in the dreamlands so far.

Are you certain of your choice?

Kneeling down beside my sister's body, I lift the wreath Toby brought me and hug it against my chest. The woman looms over me until she lowers herself to the ground on the other side of Raylene, moving with such grace that she appears as cloudlike as her hair, gently floating, a stranger to gravity.

"Are you asking if I think it's the right thing to do?" I say.

"If you wish."

That seems like an odd answer, but I find myself shaking my head and responding to her instead of asking what she means. I feel oddly disassociated and realize I've been like that since the canids first arrived back in the gulch. The grief for my sister waits like a tsunami, an enormous wave, poised above me, ready to fall. But for now I can both feel it, and be in this other moment at the same time. Talking with a stranger rather than folding in on my grief and letting it bear me away.

"I don't know if it's right or wrong," I say. "Back . . . where we were before . . . they told me she's been doing terrible things. But I feel this needs to be done anyway. It's what I have to do since I already abandoned her once. If this can work, how could I turn my back on her again? Everybody deserves a second chance, don't they?"

I try to read an answer in her eyes, but the mystery in them only seems to deepen.

"Perhaps," she says. "If they would actually make use of it. Do you think your sister would?"

I look at Raylene's still features, the blood smeared across her eyelids.

"I . . . I don't know," I say.

"And then," she goes on, "you must also consider, would your brother deserve the same chance?"

I'm shaking my head before the words can come out of my mouth.

"No," I tell her, emphatic. "What he did to us was purely evil."

"But surely he wasn't born bad either? You said yourself that no one is."

I close my eyes. She's making this too hard.

"I feel like you're trying to talk me out of this," I say.

She shakes her head. "I only want you to be aware of why you are making this choice." She pauses, then adds, "Do you forgive your sister for the things she's done?"

I shake my head. "It's not for me to forgive—that's something she'd have to take up with the ones she hurt. I can only forgive her for what she's done to me and hope she'll do the same."

"And if she doesn't?"

"It doesn't matter. I'll still forgive her."

"What if I told you that she would mock you for making this choice?"

"It's not about what she or anybody else thinks," I say. "It's about what I have to do."

I look down at Raylene again and run the back of my fingers along her cheek. Her skin already feels cold.

"Why are we here?" I ask. "Why did you bring us to this place?"

I look back at the woman sitting on the other side of my sister's corpse as I speak. That glowing shine in her eyes . . .

"You're the light I saw at the top of the Greatwood tree," I say before she can answer my other questions.

"I am of that light," she says. "Only the Grace herself can claim to be it."

"You let me collect the twigs. But why? Why me? Why couldn't Toby reach them without my help?"

"You are of the light, too," she tells me. "You have my light in you."

This is the thing Joe's always talking about. I wonder if he knows this moon-faced woman with the light of cathedral trees glowing so bright inside her.

"Like Sophie," I say.

She shakes her head. "Sophie is a daughter of another of my sisters—you know that. I've seen the painting you did."

She's talking about *Lost Mother Found*, the canvas I painted after Sophie's first adventure in the fairy-tale world. It shows a woman with the face of a full moon, her entire body suffused with a warm golden light, holding Sophie. It was my way of reminding Sophie of what she'd found in that other world, but while she'd hung the painting in her bedroom, she'd scoffed at the idea of there being any magic in her blood.

This woman before me and the one in my painting certainly have a strong enough resemblance to be sisters, though how I managed to do that, I have no idea.

"Sophie's faerie spirit was born into a human skin," the woman says. "Moonlight held by flesh. But you and I, we have a different light. You could say we are kin."

Everything goes still inside me at those words. Then this feeling rises up in me—old and familiar. How I used to pretend that my parents weren't—couldn't—be my real parents, because real parents would love their kids, wouldn't they?

I clear my throat. "Are you saying I was adopted . . ."

I trail off as she shakes her head.

"No, I mean I chose to gift you. You and your sister."

"But why?"

I sound like a broken record. Why, why, why. But I can't stop asking

"I was in that tree that you lay under so often as a child," she says. "I would listen to the stories you told. I saw the belief you awoke in your sister's eyes. The truth you recognized in your own. So I knew you were kin and gave you the light."

"Both of us?"

She nods. "You met all my expectations, but your sister . . ." Her voice trails off into a sigh. "I knew there would be trouble when she burned down the tree. But a gift such as this, once given cannot be taken back."

I remember that road trip back to Tyson that I took with Geordie, all those years ago; how devastated I had been when I saw that only a blackened stump remained of my beloved childhood friend.

Raylene had done that?

"The light I gave you can be a great joy," my companion goes on, "but it can be a burden as well, for it carries with it a responsibility to reach beyond yourself. When I gift such as you, it's in the hope that you will do the same. That you will shine your own glow into the darkness and pass its magic on." She favors me with a beatific smile. "You, once you found your way out of the darkness, have proved true. Many don't. It is so easy for your people to forget that everything has a spirit, that all are equal. That magic and mystery are a part of your lives, not something to store away in a child's bedroom, or to use as an escape from your lives."

"So you're a Muse as well?"

"There are those who have named me as such."

"But you don't because you don't like to be locked into a particular persona."

"Exactly. Still, I have gifted many over the years—with the light of the forever trees, however, not with talent. Your talent you are born with, or earn on your own, of course."

I'm happy to hear that. I know that inspiration can come from anywhere, from inside and all around us. But the idea that the artistic gifts we use to express ourselves might come from outside of us rather than within would be too depressing.

"Like you, many have proved true," she goes on. "Storytellers and artists and musicians." She smiles. "I suppose the other thing too many forget is that we were all stories once, each and every one of us. And we remain stories. But too often we allow those stories to grow banal, or cruel, or unconnected to each other. We allow the stories to continue, but they no longer have a heart. They no longer sustain us."

I think back to what the professor told me about how people need to be storied. How if they miss out on stories when they're younger, it creates a hunger in them that they can't sate. They don't know what it is, what they need. They only know they need something. They have to be re-storied before they can find any kind of peace.

And then I remember something Christy, forever collecting quotes the way he does, told me. He knows about this stories-as-sustenance business, too. He once read me a few lines from one of Barry Lopez's books, something about how there were times when people needed stories more than they needed nourishment, because the stories fed something deeper than the needs of the body.

"I wasn't telling stories," I say. "I was just painting."

"And each one was a story. Each one a reminder that there is more to the world than what one expects to see."

I give a slow nod. I suppose she's right. That's what Daniel said, too, and it's probably the reason I kept fleeing into the dreamworlds after the accident . . . not knowing if I'd ever paint again, at least I could be in a story, even if I couldn't make them anymore.

And I realize that's the choice she's talking about, this mysterious woman who claims to have known me since I was a child when I was hiding from my hurts under the boughs of my own forever tree. I can call it that because if all forests reflect the first forest, then all trees must reflect the first tree, and that tree of mine connected me all the way back to the beginning of things, to what Joe and the People call the long ago.

But knowing that doesn't help me now.

I have to choose between continuing the stories that first came to me from that sheltering tree, healing the Broken Girl so that she—so that *I*—can paint again. Or saving my sister's life.

But I've already made that choice.

The moon-faced woman with her clouds of hair and the forever tree light in her eyes can talk to me forever, but I won't change my mind.

"Will it work?" I ask her. "This wreath that Toby made for me?"

She nods.

"For Raylene as well as me?"

"Only for one of you."

"I know that. I just wanted to know if it would work for either one of us."

"It will," she says. "You have only to choose."

I meet her gaze. "I already have. Before you ever brought me here."

"I know. I think, perhaps, that is why I brought you here. To have the chance to speak with you before you leave."

I can see where this is going. I think I've known this all along.

"I won't be able to visit the dreamlands anymore, will I?"

She hesitates, then gives a slow shake of her head. "Probably not. Or at least not for a long time. Miracles always have a price, though not one measured in coin. I . . ." She hesitates a moment. "The light of the forest is only in me, I can't command it. If it were up to me I would give you as many twigs as you needed, but the light is more sparing with its gifts."

I give her a small smile. "Otherwise they wouldn't be miracles anymore."

She nods. "The hardships we endure are what temper us, what make us who we are."

I'm wondering if she means I should be grateful to my brother and all the others that hurt me when I was growing up, since the horrors they inflicted on me are what eventually made me who I am. But she's already shaking her head. Maybe she can read my mind, maybe she only sees it in my eyes. I don't suppose it really matters.

"Oh, no," she says. "There is no plan, no future laid out for any of us beyond what we make for ourselves. If you embrace the darkness, it only lessens you as well."

"It was the accident that let me cross over into the dreamlands, wasn't it? Not the light. Something got shifted around inside my head when the car hit me."

"The light connects you to this place," she says, "but you needed to find the doors yourself. In that my gift was the bane of your desire to step into the dreamlands. It shines so bright that when you cross over in your waking body, it makes you a target to those who might take advantage of your inexperience." She sighs. "Your sister is not the only predator to hunt in the dreamlands."

"That's what Joe's always telling me."

"But the light helped your dreaming self cross over," she says. "And in that form you are not so vulnerable to the dangers that might find you here."

"And when I heal Raylene . . . ?"

"The process will take of your light as well. There's no telling how long it will be before it shines as bright as it needs to be once more."

I nod.

"Thanks," I tell her. "For taking the time to talk to me before I have to go back into the Broken Girl—I do have to go back into her, don't I?"

"If you leave her unattended much longer, especially in this place, you won't have a future."

Maybe that would be best, I think. Because a future as a cripple . . . unable to paint, unable to even visit the dreamlands . . . what kind of a future is that? But I'm already pushing that thought away as soon as it comes whispering up out of the shadows in my head.

"You could still recover," the woman tells me. "Let us assume the best, not the worst."

"I know," I tell her. "Don't worry. I don't give up. I haven't before, and I'm not going to start now. It's . . ." I give her a bright smile that I don't feel. "It's just this gift I have."

"One of many, child."

Whatever.

"So, anyway . . . thanks," I tell her.

I take the wreath and lay it on my sister. I think for a moment nothing is going to happen, but then, just as it did with Toby, the light comes flaring out of the leaves and blue flowers, out of the cathedral tree twig that I broke off from the highest branch of the Greatwood's tallest tree. That flash of amber with spiraling and twisting filigrees of red and green, turquoise and gold. I hear the chorus again, can almost see the untranslatable words. The warm otherworldly light bathes my face, for one moment, another, until finally it dies down, goes out.

And when it goes, I feel something leave in me as well. Some of my light, I guess.

My hands are empty. Like the twig did with Toby, the wreath has been consumed by the light and dissolved into my sister.

Raylene still lies motionless, but I can see a pulse in her throat, the rise and fall of her chest. I touch her face and the skin is warm. Alive.

Her clothes are still bloodied, but when I lift the raggedy T-shirt, blown apart by the shotgun blast, her skin is smooth and untouched underneath except for one splash of color—a mark just below her breasts like the one on Toby's palm. An amber stamp like a birthmark or a tattoo in the shape of the twig, only hers is surrounded by a miniature wreath.

I look up to the woman, but she's gone.

I'm back in the gulch with everybody staring at me.

"What the hell have you done?" Whiskey Jack says.

He takes a step toward me, but Joe blocks him with an arm, then points behind me, up the slope. Jack goes still.

"It's her," Nanabozho says. "The woman from Cody's mountain."

I turn to see the moon-faced woman standing among the saplings on the slope, halfway between the ridge and where we are. Her expression is sterner now, but Jack's not intimidated by her.

"So that's it?" he says. "She comes back to life and the killings go on?"

The woman doesn't say anything for a long moment. When she does speak, her voice, like her gaze, is so much sterner than it was when we were talking in that place she took me to.

"There will be a balance," she says finally. "There always is."

"And what good does that do those that are already dead?"

"Have you learned nothing from Cody's misadventures?" she asks. "To stand up against injustice is what the brave do. But revenge never aided anyone."

"Except it feels good," Jack tells her.

She shakes her head. "Ask Cody how good revenge feels."

Before anyone can reply, she turns and continues up the slope. Silence falls over the gulch until she's out of sight. Then Nanabozho sighs.

"Well, we've been wrong before," he says.

"Not this time."

As Jack speaks, I get up to stand between him and my sister.

"Maybe retribution's not the answer," he goes on, "but the killings have to stop and there's only one way we can do that."

"Nobody's going to hurt her," I tell him.

That dog of Joe's comes sidling up to stand by me. Joe steps closer, too. Toby's on my other side.

"You don't understand," Jack says. "She's been killing for too long now. We don't have a choice anymore. She's got the taste and she won't stop until she's put down."

"This is my kid sister you're talking about—not some animal."

"I've got more respect for most animals than I do her kind."

"She died trying to save me."

Jack looks down at Raylene.

"She doesn't look too dead to me," he says.

"Give her another chance," Joe says.

"You want more killings on your head?" Jack asks. "I don't. We've got a simple situation here. The woman did wrong. Not once, but over and over again. But we can stop this here. And if by doing it she pays for the past killings, too, then that's justice being served so far as I'm concerned."

"I'm the reason she went bad," I tell him. "Any punishment meant for her should be mine."

"Okay," Joe says. "Let's all just calm down here. We don't need to hear any more talk about punishments or retribution or anything else along those lines."

Jack looks at him. "Who died and put you in charge?"

"Weren't you listening to what that spirit said?"

"I was listening. Just like I was listening to what Bo told us she said back at Cody's place. I didn't like what I was hearing then, and I don't like what I'm hearing now. Hell, you were right in there with us, asking why we should follow some kind of edict laid down by one of the old spirits."

"I'm not asking you to listen because of who she is," Joe says, "but for what she was saying. We all know how well it's worked out for Cody anytime he went looking for retribution."

Jack shakes his head. "You've gone soft, Joe."

"And you've gone too hard."

"Joe's right," Nanabozho says. "Back off on this one, Jack. Next thing you know we're going to be fighting between ourselves and who wants that?"

"So what do we do?" Jack asks. "Leave her to kill some more?"

"We don't know that's going to happen," Nanabozho says. "My advice is we let it go for now. We keep an eye on her. She looks like she's going back to her old ways, we find a way to stop it. But I'm guessing she won't. While you two've been arguing, I've had a good look at that girl. You see the light in her?"

Jack and Joe both turn their attention to Raylene.

"It's different," Jack admits. "It's not dark like it was before."

I'm looking, too, but I can't see whatever it is that they see.

Nanabozho nods. "She got the dark cleaned up in her by whatever they did to bring her back. I'm guessing she's going to be doing some serious hard time when she wakes up—just dealing with all she's done."

"And the unicorns?" Jack asks. "The kin that've survived?"

"She's going to have to make peace with all of them, the living and the dead."

Jack looks like he's going to say more, but then he lets his shoulders lift and fall, all nonchalant. He looks from me to Joe and Nanabozho, then turns off the anger like it never was.

"Okay," he says. "I can wait. I got me a date with a puma girl anyway."

He takes out a pack of smokes and offers them around. Everybody takes one, even me. I cough when he lights me up with this fancy lighter of his and I suck in a lungful of the noxious stuff, but I've got a reason to be doing this. I think it's like a way to seal some bargain between us—a tobacco offering, or a Kickaha peace pipe. When I catch Joe's eye, he nods his approval, so I know I'm right.

"We're gone," Jack says.

He tips his finger against the brim of his hat. He and Nanabozho take a few steps away and then it's like they've turned a corner that isn't there and they simply vanish from our sight.

Once they've left, I bend down to put my cigarette out against a rock and offer the long butt to Joe. He sticks it in his pocket. Toby touches my arm.

"Why did you do it?" he asks. "The miracle was supposed to be for you—to heal the Broken Girl."

"I know. But I couldn't let my sister die. I owed her some kind of salvation."

"But now you . . ."

I give him a hug.

"It doesn't matter," I say, talking into his hair. "I'll be fine. Thank you, Toby. You've proved to be the truest friend."

I let him go when I feel him start to get hard against my leg. Even now, after all of this. He's incorrigible. He gives me a smile as I step back and sticks his hands in his pockets to tent his pants, but I know what's happening in there and Joe just smiles. The pit bull isn't paying any attention. It's looking back down the gulch to where Pinky's body lies, a very contemplative, undoglike look in its features.

"So what do we do now?" Toby asks.

"Jilly has to go back," Joe says.

I shake my head. "Not until Raylene wakes up."

"Every moment your dreaming self and the real you are both here in the dreamlands, the tie that binds you to life grows thinner."

"I know," I tell Joe. "That's what the spirit told me, too. But I have to talk to my sister before I go back. If she stays in the dreamlands, I might never get the chance to talk to her again."

"We'll get you back over here," Joe says. "Once you're healed. It'll just take some time."

But I'm not so sure. Once I'm healed . . . I don't know if that's ever going to happen. And as for ever getting back here, when I was with the spirit, confirming my choice to help Raylene instead of myself, she made it sound like coming back was a possibility, but I still got the distinct impression I wouldn't necessarily ever be able to return. Or if I did, it wasn't going to be anytime soon.

I know it's dangerous to stay on right now. I can feel the Broken Girl. There's a constant pressure, an ache to get back into her, to be complete again. But I have to do this. Then a thought comes to me.

"Couldn't you just take the Broken Girl back?" I ask Joe.

I see him think about that. Finally he nods.

"It would help," he says. "But you can't stay out of her for too much longer. You've both been here too long."

I nod. "I won't. Thanks for coming after me, Joe. And for standing up for my sister."

"I hope I did the right thing."

"Me, too."

Because I don't know. I'm not so sure as I let on that Raylene's going to come out of this changed. All I know is that just before Pinky shot her, Raylene was actually listening to me. We were connecting. And then she tried to save me, stepped in front of the shot that was meant for me.

"Let's hope for her sake she *has* changed," Joe says. "Because if she hasn't, Jack's going to come down hard on her." He pauses, reluctant, then adds, "And I'd have to be with him on that."

"I understand," I tell him.

He steps up to me and lays his forehead against mine, hands on my shoulders. I remember he told me once, that's the kiss of life.

"Please," he says, "Don't stay here too long."

Then he turns and walks farther down the gulch to where the Broken Girl lies. The pit bull waits a moment, its attention on me now instead of Pinky's body. When I reach down to pat the dog, it avoids my hand, then steps in, bumps its head against my leg.

"Where'd you get the dog?" I call after Joe as the pit bull trots after him.

He stops to look back. "I didn't get her anywhere," he says. "She's a friend who stepped in to help."

"What's her name?"

"She hasn't told me."

"Well, thank her for me," I say.

Joe smiles. "She's got ears," he says. "Thank her yourself."

I do and the dog barks once at me.

I watch as Joe goes down on one knee beside the Broken Girl, face turned to the dog. He says something I can't hear and she does what she did to me, bumps her head against his knee. Then she steps away like the canids did, one moment there, the next gone. I'm getting so used to this, I don't even blink.

Joe lifts the Broken Girl in his arms.

"Remember," he calls to me.

"I know. Get back as quick as I can."

And then he's gone, too, carrying his burden back into the World As

It Is. The pull I felt toward the Broken Girl changes when she's gone. It turns into a hollow feeling, deep inside my chest.

I look at Raylene for a long moment, but she hasn't changed. Sleeping, I guess. I hope. Her color's still good and her breathing is normal.

I turn to Toby.

"Want to help me bury my sister's friend?" I ask him.

"No," he says. "But I will."

The ground's too hard, and we don't have tools anyway, so we start to pile stones on her, raising a cairn like Toby says they did in the old days. It's hot, sweaty work, but it helps to keep me from thinking what's going to happen when Raylene wakes up. What will I say to her? How will she feel toward me?

I don't know what to expect. But I don't know what exactly it is that I want either.

5

NEWFORD

"Thank god," Sophie said when Joe came walking out of the wall, carrying Jilly in his arms.

She scrambled to her feet. The odd manner of their appearance, the impossibility of their walking through solid matter as they had, barely registered. All she could focus on was Jilly.

Behind her, Wendy started to cry and Sophie understood. She had tears of relief in her own eyes. Turning, she helped Wendy to her feet and the two of them stood with their arms around each other.

"You're okay?" Cassie asked Joe. "Both of you?"

He nodded. "For now."

Angel and Lou hurried up from where they'd been standing down the hall. Lou helped Joe take Jilly's weight and carry her back to her bed. The rest of them crowded into the room after them.

"Can one of you get a nurse in here?" Joe asked.

Cassie nodded. "I'll go."

Wendy touched Joe's arm, looking as grateful as Sophie felt.

"Oh, god, we were so worried," Wendy said. "It's been hours. We thought you'd never find her and bring her back."

"It's not over yet," Joe said. "Her dreaming self is still on the other side."

Sophie understood the ramifications of that immediately, but a confused stillness fell across the room, sending ripples of uncertainty through the rest of them.

"What the hell's that supposed to mean?" Lou asked.

Sophie could see the relief he'd been feeling drain out of him.

"He means her spirit is still in the dreamlands," she told Lou.

"Why . . . why didn't she come back with you?" Wendy asked.

"Unfinished business," Joe told them. "But this time it's Jilly's choice—something she says she needs to do. Nobody forced her."

"So it's not over?" Angel asked.

Joe shook his head. "Not yet."

He sat on the edge of the bed, stroking Jilly's brow with his fingers. Angel went to where Lou was standing at the foot of the bed and wrapped her arms around him, burrowing her face against his shoulder. He held her, patting her shoulder, but his gaze remained on Jilly. Wendy took Sophie's hand. Glancing at her, Sophie gave Wendy's fingers a squeeze, then they put their arms around each other's waists, standing close for the comfort. They, too, studied Jilly where she lay so broken and still, searching for, praying for some sign of resuscitation.

Joe looked past them to the door. "Where's that nurse?"

Raylene

It's funny. Here I am dying, but for the first time in my life I feel like I'm really at peace. I never felt like this before, not even when I was a little kid, back afore my sister went and took off, or when Hector and me was together. Don't matter where I went, if'n I was alone or in a crowd, I always knew I was carrying around some kinda black mark on my soul. I done so many shitty things in my life it couldn't be no other way.

I was never no sociopath freak, don't know better, thinks the whole damn world's just a-circling 'round her. I only acted like I didn't know. Like I didn't care. But I knew I was doing wrong. And maybe I never let on or nothing, but that knowing left a shadow on me—Catholic guilt, I'm guessing. You can't never get away from what the damn priests and nuns try to drill into your head.

Only I guess I found me a way now: die, and it's all gone.

I don't feel forgiven—that'd be asking too much of anybody. But I do feel forgotten. Like the world's going on and nobody's thinking 'bout me, for good or bad. I'm just off of their radar and I like it.

Or maybe it's just the world spitting me out like a melon seed it don't want to swallow. I don't care. All I know is I'm falling up through this smear of black nothing, heading straight for this one pinprick of light that never seems to get no closer, but I'm coming up on it all the same. For once in my life, I feel completely at peace.

Until something starts to pull me back down again.

I fight it, but it ain't no use. Whatever's got ahold of me is just a-pulling me back. It's got itself dug in like some old mule that won't be budged, not no how. And I know what it is. It's my own damn dying self, got itself resuscitated. All of a sudden, I can feel my body again. All the holes are closing up like I never had no load a buckshot tore through me. The blood's starting to move in my veins, my lungs are drawing in air. I can feel the black mark of guilt set up shop inside me and just like that, my moment of peace is gone.

I was dying, and now I'm not, simple as that.

There's a flicker flash in front of my eyes—strobing lights like at them clubs Pinky likes to take us to, and then I'm back inside my body. The ground's hard under me, the tatters of my T-shirt are wet and sticking to my skin. I sit up and stare down at all the blood I got on me. Then I lift my head and have me a look around.

I'm in a forest, but the big woman sitting on the ground nearby grabs my attention right off and I don't look no further.

She's like one of them New Age earth mamas, you know, a big—I mean, big—woman, wearing the sack dress, got her a face as round as the full moon with a mess of curly dark hair just clouding up around it. I know her type. She's got that air 'bout her of somebody who's been meditating too long, or just smoked her a nice fat spliff—way mellow. The eyes are kinda spooky, though. Deep and dark and they have them a glow back in behind of them that almost seems familiar, though I know I never seen her before.

"You got anything to do with bringing me back?" I ask her.

The woman shakes her head. "Your sister did. She gave up her own chance at good health so that you might live."

I have to think on that a minute, work it through.

"You mean she could've helped herself," I finally say, "but she's gone and left herself stuck as a cripple just to help me?"

The woman nods.

I shake my head. "What a chump."

I look around some more. We're not in that holler in the dreamlands where Pinky and me took my sister. The trees here are godawful big and the air feels kinda thick and heady. We run through places like this with the pack, but none of 'em felt this old or ... I don't know. Just away from everything. And I mean away. I don't hear nothing—not a rustle, not a bug, not a bird—coming outta the woods around us. It's just me and this creepy New Age woman with the moon face.

"Where is everybody?" I ask. "Come to think of it, where the hell are we anyway?"

She doesn't answer me. Instead she says, "I would have thought you'd be grateful for her sacrifice."

I'd laugh, only it ain't close to funny.

"What for?" I tell her. "I was happy being dead. I was at peace, for Christ's sake."

"One doesn't need to die to find peace."

"Yeah, well 'one' don't need to talk like no swami guru neither, but it happens, you being a case in point."

She gives me this calm, sorrowful look. I guess it's supposed to make me feel like we're friends, like she cares about me, but it don't do nothing for me. I can count my friends on one finger and she ain't it.

"Why are you so angry?" she asks.

"I got lots to be pissed about, starting with finding myself back in my skin instead of finally being free of the mess of my life."

"Yes, of course," she says. "What your brother did to you was—"

"Fuck you, lady. You don't know jack about me or anything I could be feeling, 'cept for being pissed at being alive and having to listen to you and that's only 'cause I'm spelling it out for you."

She's like one of them social workers used to come see me when I was doing my six months in the L.A. county jail. They were all these soft-spoken little bitches wouldn't know a trauma if it come up and bit 'em in the arse. Course moon mama here's got enough bulk to make up two or three of them, but otherwise she's cut from the same bolt of cloth. But then she goes and surprises me.

"You're right," she says. "Never having been human, never having experienced what you did, I can only imagine how it might have felt for you, what it would drive you to."

Wait a minute, I'm thinking. Let's back up here.

"What do you mean 'bout 'never having been human'?" I say.

She gives me this look. "What did you think I was, child?"

I don't like the child business, but I answer her anyway.

"Some do-gooder trying to fix what's too broke to be fixed," I tell her.

"Are you so sure of that?" she asks. "That you can't be fixed?"

I shrug. "I'm confused 'bout a whole lotta shit, lady, but that part ain't too hard to work out. I'm the one's been living this life you only get to see from the outside."

She gives me a slow nod and rises to her feet. The movement takes me by surprise. 'Stead of lumbering up from where she's been sitting, grunting and groaning with the effort like some old hog got its legs knocked from under it, she just kinda floats up into a standing position.

"Well," she says, "There's nothing to stop you from finishing the job your sister's sacrifice interrupted."

"Guilt don't work on me," I tell her.

Those dark eyes fix their gaze on me, cold and hard like a thundercloud.

"What makes you think I'd be interested in making you feel guilty?" she asks.

She's looming over me, so I get to my feet, but it don't make me feel any bigger. She got a way of making me feel small that's got nothing to do with her size. I ain't playing to it, but I got to admit I'm curious.

"Then what do you want from me?" I ask.

"Nothing," she says. "I was only interested in speaking with you before you woke up."

"Wait a minute—you mean I'm dreaming right now? This ain't a done deal?"

She gives me a weary look.

"You did die," she says. "Your sister did sacrifice a normal life to bring you back. You *are* alive once more. None of that has or can be changed now. This is only a way station between when you lost consciousness and are returning to it. Never fear. As soon as you wake up, you'll be free to seek oblivion once more."

I just shake my head. "See, you really don't get it, do you? I ain't no suicide bomb. I figure everybody's got a time they're going to die and it's nothing I'd go looking for. I just ain't made that way. But this was my time. I was gone and I never felt so light and free, letting go all the garbage of my life and floating free. *That's* what got took from me."

"Then by such consideration," the woman says, "obviously, it wasn't your time."

There's still dark thunder in her eyes, but her voice is calm. Damned if I can find a hole in her argument either. Finally I give her a slow nod.

"Well, I guess it'll make Pinky happy," I say. "She's never been all that big on making decisions by herself."

Though she was good enough at pulling that trigger, I find myself thinking. But that weren't the natural order of things. Independent thinking never stood Pinky to no good. All it ever did was get her in more trouble.

Then I realize the woman's just looking at me. Her eyes have finally softened, but there's a whole world a something going on between us that I can't begin to get me a handle on.

"What?" I ask.

"Your friend Pinky is dead," she says.

It takes a couple of moments for that to register.

I can't look at her. It was bad enough all them years I did without her when she was doing her time—but at least we had us our visiting days and we could run with the pack. I can't imagine a world without her in it at all. She's been with me from the beginning. Hell, wasn't for Pinky, I could still be my sick freak brother's girlfriend, trapped back there in Hillbilly Holler. Without her . . . well, I guess now I know how come I was dragged back into life. The world had it one more joke to play on me.

Goddamn. I can't believe she's gone.

I feel the pressure building in behind my eyes. My chest's so tight I got trouble breathing.

Goddamn.

I swallow hard. No way I'm breaking down in front of nobody, 'specially not this moon-faced woman with her eyes gone too kind now.

"How . . . how long I been gone anyways?" I manage to ask.

"Not long," the woman says softly. "An hour or two."

I nod. Like it means anything. No matter what we got to say here, Pinky's still going to be dead. But I need to keep this conversation going. It's all that's keeping me from falling to pieces. I'm like a china mug, tottering on the edge of the table. A touch of wind, somebody makes the wrong move, and down I'll go a-tumbling to shatter on the floor.

"Did she die hard?" I ask.

"She went quickly," the woman said. "After you were shot, she made a second attempt to kill your sister, but this time a dog knocked her down. She fell badly, struck her head on a rock, and died instantly." She hesitates a moment, then adds, "I'm sorry."

"Yeah, right. You don't know me and you never knew her. What do you got to be sorry about?"

"Any death diminishes all of us. You can't pluck a blade of grass without changing the landscape. It might not be immediately noticeable, but the change is there, nevertheless."

"You're not just talking 'bout Pinky, are you?"

I'm thinking 'bout all them proud horned horses we took down, me and Pinky and the rest of the pack. The unicorns with their blood like a drug. They were a hell of a lot more'n any blades of grass.

"I see what it is about you now," the woman says. "You jump to conclusions and once you have, it becomes carved in stone. Immutable truth. Or at least in your worldview."

"I don't know what you're talking about."

She just ignores me. "Whatever ills you might have done are between you and whomever you might have wronged. I came here not to judge you, but for conversation."

"Yeah, well, I ain't much for small talk."

"Neither am I. I gave you a gift, one that you have mostly ignored. When you didn't, you used it unwisely."

"You mean the dreams?"

"I mean the light in you," she says. "The dreams came from that light, though not what they were or what you would do in them."

"Well, maybe you should've took the time to include an instruction manual."

"That isn't how it works."

"Course it ain't." I shake my head. "You're all the same. Don't matter if you're some big-shot spirit—that'd be you, right?—or some big-shot moneyman from my world. Everything's got to go your way. And everything *can* go your way 'cause you're holding all the damn aces. The little guy ain't got a ghost of a chance where you're concerned. We can't play by your rules, 'cause we ain't got your grease, but if we try to change the rules so that we can at least get in the game, you just shut us down."

"You are hardly one of the downtrodden," she says. "You made the choices to be who you are."

"You think I *wanted* to be my sick freak brother's sex toy?"

"No. But what of the choices you made after that?"

"Fuck you. Ain't my fault I got dealt a lousy hand. But at least I played it out."

"Since you wish to use card games as an analogy, did you ever consider folding and playing a new hand?"

"It don't work that way," I tell her. "Not when you're at the bottom a the food chain like me and Pinky was."

"Your sister's origins were no different."

"Yeah, well, whoopie-do. Look where it got her."

"Yes, do," the woman says. "She has friends. She's lived a good life. She's helped people. She took the gift of my light and created art that served as doorways to open the imaginations of others."

"But she still ended up a cripple in a bed who can't even feed her own damn self. So now what the hell good are her arty little friends or how she's lived? You don't think them friends of hers are going to get tired of looking after her and do the slow fade out of her life?"

"Do you think her present condition was premeditated?" the woman asks. "Do you truly believe that by living as she did, she earned the fate she has now?"

"You tell me."

"It was bad luck. No more, no less. It can happen to any of us."

" 'Cept it don't happen much to your kind, does it? You get to breeze through life and let the rest of us make do wallowing in your crap."

Those thundercloud eyes've been back for a while now, but I don't muchly care. What's she going to do to me? Kill me? I been there. Hell, I been through the worst this world's got for me. Ain't no threat she can make'll scare me.

So we stand there and glare at each other. And maybe I see something like sadness for me, sitting in there behind the mad, but it don't stop her from doing what the people up top always do to nobodies like me that're scratching out a life down below.

"I cannot take back the gift of my light," she says, "but Animandeg is not the only one who can close doors," she tells me.

"Who?"

She steps up and before I can back off, she's making like she's at some heavy metal concert, holding her middle and ring fingers with her thumb, the other two fingers sticking straight out. Sign of the devil or whatever. But when she touches my brow with the two fingers that stick out, I feel a little jolt in my head, like a static charge. I push her hand away with one of my own, fill the other with my switchblade. I thumb the button and the blade snaps out.

"Touch me again," I say, "and you're going to lose that hand."

She doesn't move, just fixes me with those dark eyes.

"When next you leave the dreamlands," she says, "there will be no return for you."

"Maybe I just won't leave."

"Perhaps," she agrees. "But if you remain, it would do well for you to make peace with those you have wronged."

"Anybody has a beef with me, they're already dead."

Though I guess death's not the same here as it is back in the world where I come from. Hell, I'm standing here, ain't I? Except:

"Yes," she says. "They are. But they have kin. And they have friends—you know, the sort of people you mock your sister for having."

"Hey, I understand friends, lady."

But she only shakes her head and then she's gone. She does this side-step and she disappears I can't tell where. I walk all around where she was standing, looking for the edges, but there's nothing there. No way to track her. No way to get outa here my own self.

"Fuck you!" I yell, don't matter she probably can't hear me.

I stand alone under those damn monster trees and I just keep yelling until I realize I'm lying on my back again, my eyes closed. I'm still saying "Fuck you," but the words are no more than a whisper.

I open my eyes and I know where I am now. Back in that little holler where I left my sister. Where Pinky got herself killed.

I sit up slowly and see my sister with some little dorky-looking guy, like a cross between a computer geek and one a them faggy boys hangs out at the Renaissance Faires. The pair of them were building them-selves a pile of stones, I guess, but they're stopped now, both of them looking in my direction. The dork seems curious. My sister's some-

where between happy and scared and I reckon both feelings got to do
with me.

"Raylene," she says softly.

I get up. I figure I should be feeling shaky or something, 'cept that
ain't the case. I'm feeling no different than I ever done, 'cept for having
died and come back and for Pinky still being dead her own self.

There's just the two of them and me here.

"Where is she?" I ask them. "What've you done with Pinky?"

"We . . . we're raising a cairn for her," my sister says.

"A cairn . . . ?"

But then I get it. Them rocks they been piling up—Pinky's under 'em.
I fight the wave of pure misery that comes flooding over me, push it back,
hold steady. Like I done when Hector died, or when I was doing my time
in county. You never let 'em see a weakness in you.

But goddamn.

"We . . . were doing it to honor her," my sister says, looking not too
sure of herself anymore. "So that nothing would disturb her body."

That flood of red rage I usually feel for her goes through me like a
lightning bolt, but it don't hold. It just drains away, leaving me feeling a
little dizzy. Whatever else is fucked up in my life, I know I can't lay the
blame on her. Guess I always knew it. I just didn't want to deal with it.

" 'Ppreciate your doing that," I tell them.

I wish I had something to do with my hands. I end up shoving 'em in
my pockets.

Jillian May turns to the little dork standing beside her and says something I don't quite catch. But I figure it out when he gives her a nod, me
another look of pure curiosity, then takes off into the woods. I guess she
wants to finish the conversation the shotgun blast ended, just the two of
us, nobody else sitting in.

I look at that old pile a stones that are covering Pinky.

The two of us and Pinky's ghost.

Okay. I can do that. Anything to stop thinking about how maybe I
got to admit it's my own damn fault how things turned out for me. I got
me a head full of hurts right now, but for the first time I can remember,
there ain't some finger in my brain, pointing at someone else.

I walk over to where she's waiting and look her over. Like me, she's
carrying the years well. Hell, she don't look much more'n twenty, tops.

I take me a seat on a big old stone that gives me a view of the holler, the way it goes winding down between the hills in a mess of rock and cedar and pines, but keep my back to that pile of stones that are covering my poor dead Pinky. Jillian May hesitates a moment, then comes over and sits near me.

"You're looking pretty damn plucky for someone who's supposed to be crippled," I tell her.

"This is just my dreaming self," she says. "Joe took my body back to the rehab."

"Joe'd be one of them dog-faced boys?"

She nods.

A big piece of quiet falls down between us. I guess we don't the neither of us know where to begin. I start in easy, coming up on what I want to talk about from the side.

"So how come you never painted any of them boys?"

She gives me a surprised look, then shrugs. "I don't know. I just never thought to do it, I guess."

"They're a big piece of something strange, though."

"They're old spirits," she says, "except for Joe. He's younger than the others I've met, but still a lot older than you or me. Most of them have been around since the very beginning, when Raven made the world in the long ago."

"You buy that?"

"What?"

"That someone just made the world. God. Raven. Whatever you want to call him." I think about that New Age earth mama with the moon face and the dark eyes who just walked out on me. "Or her."

Jillian May gives me another shrug. "The world's a long complicated story," she says, "but it had to start somewhere."

"I suppose." I take me a breath. "I guess I'm sorry 'bout them paintings of yours."

She doesn't say nothing for a long pair of heartbeats, then finally asks, "Why did you do it?"

Then it's my turn to have to look for the right words.

"I guess I hated you something bad," I tell her, "and them paintings was just standing in for everything I didn't want to remember 'bout you. You know, back when we was kids and getting along and all. Before you went and took off. I saw them paintings and it went and brought the whole damn mess of it all back."

I see her swallow hard.

"Do you still hate me?" she asks.

"I can't rightly say," I tell her, being honest for a change. "I don't know much of anything these days."

"I know that feeling," she says.

Which surprises me. I know she's had it hard, what with being crippled by that car accident and all, but I always reckoned she was just one of them people always knows who she is, how she fits into the world, what she's going to be doing with her life.

"Tell me how it was for you," I find myself saying. "After you took off that last time and I didn't see you no more."

So she does, though she looks at the ground or up into the trees while she's talking 'stead of looking at me.

I hear about this little girl, running away from home, getting shunted between foster homes and juvie, always trying to get away, just taking off whenever she can, until this one time she run off, she don't get caught and brought back. But that don't turn out a whole lot better. Now instead of getting molested in the foster homes or beat up by the other kids in juvie, she's living on the street and eating out of garbage cans. Then when she finally hooks up with some guy, he starts in a-pimping her soon as the money and dope runs out.

Her voice, the way she talks, none of it's looking for me to feel sorry for her. She's just doing like I asked, giving me the story and it ain't pretty. Between being a junkie and a hooker, she was so messed up in them days that I come to understand how she didn't have her the wherewithal to be worrying, or even thinking, 'bout this little kid sister she left behind.

I say something about how this guy Rob would've been looking at a knife in the gut, he tried any of that shit on me. My sister just shakes her head.

"That's because you're brave," she says. "You were probably born that way. I had to learn to be brave."

"Naw, that's something Pinky taught me."

We both fall quiet at the mention of her name but neither of us turn to look at that heap a stones behind us.

"I've never had any luck with men," my sister says after a moment. "I guess it's not so surprising, after Rob and Del and all those state-sanctioned pedophiles in the foster homes. I know there must be good foster parents, but I never got to meet them. And then there were all those johns . . ."

Her voice trails off and she gets this lost look in her eyes like she's back there again, living in that time. She catches me looking at her and shrugs.

"After all of that," she says, "I started making my own bad luck, I suppose. Or at least it seems that way. Guys I'd go out with would always turn out to be married or creeps or something. And I could never be intimate with them—not without first shutting myself off inside."

"You were making the mistake of thinking sex's got to be meaningful," I tell her. "It's just supposed to be fun."

"Do you really believe that?"

"Worked for me," I say. I hesitate, then have to add, "Or it did until I met Hector."

I tell her 'bout him. It's funny. That's something I never done before, not with no one, not even Pinky. I mean, tell how it really was between Hector and me. Sweet and deep and like nothing I ever knew before and sure as hell ain't never going to be feeling again.

"That's so horrible," she says when I tell her how he got himself shot, how I just shut me down afterward.

She reaches out and lays her hand on my arm. I know she's been wanting to do something like that right from the start, or better yet do the sister hug thing, but it ain't in me. I can maybe understand how she come to leave me behind for all of them years, but there ain't going to be any kind of bonding happening here.

I look her in the eye, then down at her hand. She takes it away, holds her hands on her lap, fingers twisting around each other.

"So how'd you get off of the street?" I ask.

She tells me 'bout this cop and his social worker girlfriend. About going into detox. Finishing high school. Going to university. Making friends. Finding a real life. Making a difference.

She's matter-of-fact 'bout all of this, too. There's no bragging 'bout how she done so good. She's just sharing her story. When she gets to how she and this guy Geordie come back to Tyson to look for me, but all they find is the empty house and the burned-out tree in the field out back, I find myself wondering, what would my life have been like if we'd managed to hook up then?

"Why did you burn down the tree?" she asks. "Was it like with the paintings?"

"I reckon."

She nods and looks away, past me.

"I ain't particularly proud of setting out to hurt you," I tell her.

"I know," she says. "But there was magic in that tree."

"Yeah, you had a hundred stories 'bout it."

She shakes her head. "No, there was real magic. I didn't know myself until today."

She tells me about how the little dorky guy brought this wreath of magic flowers and twigs to heal her, how she used it on me instead. But before it worked, she got took to this other place, this deep mysterious forest, where she met her this old spirit. Funny thing is, she's well into this part of her story afore I pick up on how this must've been the same woman I met on my way back to being alive again.

Hell, no wonder that earth mama was so pissed off at me. I went and burned down her special tree.

"I met her," I tell Jillian May when she's done. "Just afore I woke up here, I was in that same place with her. But we didn't get along near so well as the two of you did. She was some disappointed in me, but like I told her. She wanted things to work out different, she could've been a little more forthcoming 'bout it all. I mean, how the hell were we supposed to know what she give us?"

"I suppose."

"It's too late anyways," I say.

Jillian May shakes her head. "I don't think it's ever too late."

Yeah, like I can just turn my life around now after all I done.

"How come you never hooked up with this Geordie guy?" I ask instead, pushing the conversation onto steadier ground. "Sounds like the two of you were particularly tight."

"We were just friends for the longest time," she says. "And now . . . now he's with someone else."

"Don't mean you can't make a play for him."

"I couldn't do that."

I think about that a moment.

"Yeah, I guess it wouldn't be right," I say.

Considering how she turned her own self around, I'm kinda surprised she ain't more judgmental 'bout my life and the things I done. But all she seems to want to do is understand me. She's not even trying to correct the way I talk.

"Did you really . . . you know, kill all those unicorns?" she asks.

"I guess. But we was wolves. That's what wolves do. You hunt. You bring down game."

She nods, but I can tell she don't like it. I can't say's I blame her. I look at what we done, me and the pack, and it don't seem right to me neither, not no more. Sure wolves hunt. Out there in the wild country, it's always gonna be survival of the fittest. But we wasn't hungry. We was hunting them critters for the plain fun of it and then getting us high on their blood. Ain't a whole lotta dignity in that for 'em and it don't say much good 'bout me and Pinky and the others, that's for damn sure.

But it's nothing I can take back now. I can feel bad about it, and I do, but it don't change nothing for them that's dead and gone.

And we got the same problem with my sister here. I feel bad for her, too, but I can't change what's been done. I can't take back all them years of hating her. I can't fix all them paintings I cut up. I can't do nothing 'bout that burned down tree. I can't trade my life for her health.

"You know we ain't never going to be friends," I tell her. "We don't got much in the way of common ground 'cept that one thing and I'm not real eager to sit around and talk about that sorry-ass freak brother of ours for the rest of my life."

She nods, but not like in agreement.

"We're just too different."

"Different never stopped me before," she says.

"Well, I guess time will tell. You going back?"

"I have to," she says. "If I don't, I'll die back in the World As It Is and then I'll have to move on anyway. I might as well see this through."

"I ain't going back. That spirit, she told me once I'm gone outta here, that's it, I can't come back."

"She told me pretty much the same thing."

" 'Cept I know there's other ways to cross over," I say, thinking 'bout what Miss Lucinda told me and Pinky.

I tell my sister about that, run through the whole damn list of materials you need and how you get 'em and all.

"Sounds complicated," she says.

"I reckon it's supposed to. Course there's another way. Miss Lucinda also told me you can just have yourself a sip of the blood of one a them animal people and it'll do pretty much the same thing."

She gets this horrified look on her face.

"Is . . . is that how you learned how to cross over?" she asks.

Funny, I never thought about how the blood of them unicorns could do the trick. But then I realize it can't be. I might've been able to take that feeling of well-being back with me, and I guess it did something to make me and Pinky lose our sags and wrinkles, but the thing about dreaming is, you can't take nothing back 'cept what's in your head.

Course that don't explain how come me and Pinky had us the glow of youth like we did. Like I still got, I guess.

"I remember that time when I saw you as a wolf," Jillian May says. "You were chasing this fox with the face of a little man . . ."

"We never caught him," I tell her. "We never took down one of them hybrids. It was just deer and little critters like hares and mice and such. And them unicorns, of course."

I stand up. I can see we're about to start going in a circle with our talking and I don't have me the stamina for that kinda thing. Not right now, not today. Maybe not never. Pinky's too soon dead and I ain't never been one for opening up anyways.

"You take care," I tell her as she gets to her feet.

I know that urge's coming over her again to do the hug thing, but I can't. I stick out my hand instead and we shake.

"Where will you go?" she asks.

"I can't rightly tell. Wherever my feet take me, I suppose."

"There are other places besides these forests," she says.

I guess she's worried I spend too much time in the wilds, I'm gonna go feral again.

"There's a city called Mabon," she goes on. "It's big and all kinds of people live there—people native to the dreamlands as well as dreamers."

"Maybe I'll pay it a visit."

She points west. "And over there, in the foothills of the mountains, there's this inn. The innkeeper's really nice."

"I don't know that I'll be looking for any kind of company," I tell her, "but I'll keep it in mind, too."

She don't want me to go, but we both know I can't stay. I'm feeling anxious, some kind of pressure building up inside my chest, though I can't tell why.

"What about you?" I find myself asking. I'm about to say what *can* you do, but I catch myself. "What are you going to do?"

"Try to get better," she says. "That's all I've got right now."

A little smile touches her lips, goes right up into her eyes, and it changes her face. I can see why people are attracted to her. There's something about her just makes you want to know her, to be her friend.

"And I've actually got this guy interested in me," she goes on. "One of my nurses from the hospital, though I don't know what he sees in me. I just hope he doesn't turn out to be some kind of serial killer."

"You like him?"

She nods. "Except he's too good to be true."

I think about Hector and feel that old ache start up inside a me.

"Well, give him a chance," I say. "What've you got to lose?"

She laughs, but there's not as much humor in it as there was in that little smile of hers a moment ago.

"I guess you're right," she says. "When you're where I am, there's not a whole lot further you can go down."

"I didn't mean it that way."

"I know you didn't."

"You think there's any chance you're going to . . . you know, walk again?" I ask.

"I don't give up," she says. "Not on anything."

I know she's not just talking about her crippled body. She's talking 'bout us as well.

"Yeah, well, I hope it works out."

"I'll think of you," she says.

Lying in bed, not much else she's going to be able to do but think. But I don't tell her that.

"Me, too," I say.

I start to go, but she calls after me.

"Raylene."

I turn to look at her. There's something in her eyes I can't read. But discomfort's a part of it.

"You weren't driving that car that night . . . were you?" she asks.

"I wanted to kill you, you'd already be dead."

She nods. "I . . . I just had to ask."

"And ain't that a sorry thing between sisters," I say.

"Raylene, I . . ."

But I turn away again and head off, quicklike, afore she finds some more words to cast out and reel me back to where she's standing. I got no more words. I got nothing but this ache inside me, getting bigger by the minute. So I just scramble on up the slope of that little holler and do the best I can to lose myself in the forest.

And I don't never look back.

Jilly

I wish I hadn't asked Raylene about the car. Long after she's gone up the slope and been swallowed by the forest, I keep wanting to follow her into those woods, find her and try to explain. But each time I stop myself. What would I say? The fact that I had to ask the question says it all.

I didn't trust her.

And that's not the only thing that's leaving me so confused.

All those things Raylene did were awful and wrong—I understand that, even if the canids think I don't. And while I'm not sure that everybody deserves a second chance, did Raylene ever have a first one? From the day I left her in the hell that was our childhood, there was no one to stand by her, to show her a way out. All she had was that psycho Pinky Miller, and we saw where her friendship took them.

But now that she's got the second chance, there's still no one to stand by her. When she left, I could see that so much anger and hurt remain in her and I know she's capable of great violence. So did I do the right thing in bringing her back to life?

I don't know.

I know I had to do it. I know it wasn't just because she's family, because she's my little sister and I owe her big time for deserting her the way I did. I did it for the same reason I'll help anybody—but especially other Children of the Secret.

But I wanted to be there for her, to give her the moral support she's going to need in the days to come, just as I got that kind of love and support from Lou and Angel, and later from my other friends. Instead, I basically kicked her out of my life and now she's got no one again.

How's she going to get through this on her own?

It makes me so frustrated I could cry, but I can't cry. Because if I cry about this, then I'll cry about everything, and there's far too much to cry about. I might never stop.

I don't know how long I stand there staring up into the trees before I finally sit down once more. I really should return to the rehab. They're all going to be worried about me. But surely Joe and Sophie, at least, will understand. They know what it's like to be here. They can guess how much I dread being back inside the Broken Girl again. Inside her and trapped, and this time with no more interludes in the dreamlands like I had before.

The sound of a twig breaking underfoot snaps my gaze back up the slope, but it isn't Raylene picking her way down to where I'm sitting. It's Toby. He slides down the last couple of feet and sits on the rock where Raylene had been sitting.

"Hey," he says.

"Hey, yourself."

"She made you unhappy, didn't she . . . with all those things she was saying."

"You were listening?" I ask.

Though I don't know why I should be surprised. Faerie have a whole different idea about propriety. At least he's got the good manners to look embarrassed about his eavesdropping.

"Don't be mad," he says. "I just wanted to see what people who are real talk about with each other."

I sigh. "And now you know. We mess up each other's lives. Being real isn't all it's cracked up to be."

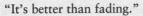

"It's better than fading."

"I suppose. But we make each other so unhappy."

"You don't have to be real to be unhappy," Toby says.

"This is true."

We sit in silence for a while, listening to a light wind whispering through the trees around us.

"Do you really have to go back?" Toby asks after a while.

I nod.

"And you won't be able to return?"

"Apparently not. It's something to do with giving up too much of my light to bring Raylene back to life."

"Why did you do it?" he asks. "She was so ungrateful."

I start to tell him what I've been thinking, about how I always try to be the kind of person who'll be there for anybody in need, but I realize that's not entirely true in this case.

"I didn't really do it for her," I say, not sure if I can explain. "I did it for me. It didn't matter whether she'd be grateful or not; it was something I had to do for my own peace of mind. And not because of what Joe said about how if I can heal the old hurts in me, there are people he knows who will be able to heal the new ones."

"Did it work?"

I shake my head. "Not really. I've made a kind of peace inside myself—you know, with my guilt over how I treated her. But it doesn't change the fact that I *did* abandon her—not once, but twice now. And it doesn't change what our brother did to both of us. I don't have it in me to forgive or forget that."

"I don't know why you feel you need to."

"Because all it really is is this useless baggage I carry around that affects not only my physical health, but my emotional well-being. I just can't with a man the way I should be able to. For the first fifteen years or so of my life, every man I ever met just used me. I should be able to put that aside. It's the past, done and finished with. And to some degree, I can. But not once I get close to a man. As soon as we start to get intimate, I just shut down inside."

I don't know why I'm telling him all of this. I don't know what an Eadar might or might not feel. Toby's acting as though everything about being real is this wonderful novelty, so maybe being an Eadar really is different. My own brief experience was so locked into the geas pulling me back to the Broken Girl that I can't tell much from it.

"Maddy once told me that trust and faith are the hardest to hold true," Toby says. "Love itself is easy."

"Who?"

"Maddy Reynolds—she was a character in one of Margery Bainbridge's books."

"Those were the books in which you were born?"

He nods. "When I became real, I started to remember them all again."

"I don't know if love is so easy," I say. "Maybe infatuation is—but even that gets complicated when it gets too strong."

"It seems everything is complicated when you're real."

"I guess so. Unless you remember and hold on to the connections."

"What connections?"

"The fact that we're all connected. Everything has a spirit and it's all connected. If you think about that, if you live your life by it, then you're less likely to cause any hurt. It's like how our bodies go back into the ground when we die, so that connects us to the earth. If you dump trash, you're dumping it on your and my ancestors. Or to bring it down to its simplest level: treat everything and everybody the way you want to be treated, because when you hurt someone, you're only hurting yourself."

"Because we're all connected."

"Exactly."

"But why don't the people doing the hurting feel it?" Toby asks. "How come they keep doing what they do?"

"I don't know. Because they're not aware, I guess. But I still believe it'll all come back on them. That's why I've never been interested in having any kind of revenge on anybody that hurt me when I was a kid. I can't forget, and I don't forgive, but I do believe there's going to be a reckoning down the line . . ."

My voice trails off and I suddenly realize just how tired I am. Physically from our adventure in the Greatwood tree, and then the long run to reach this gulch. Emotionally from finally being reunited with my sister, only to watch her die, have her brought back to life, and then estranged from me once more. I can barely keep my eyes open and my head feels like it's full of dust and cobwebs. Only the pain in my heart is sharp and bright.

I turn to Toby and take his hand.

"I have to go now," I tell him. "But I want you to know that you've been a good friend. You're a good person. Don't ever let anyone tell you differently—especially not yourself."

He squeezes my fingers. "You, too."

I have to smile. "Yeah, I guess I could follow my advice, couldn't I?"

"I'll never forget you," Toby says. "You gave me my life."

"Personally, I think you were always real."

"You won't come back?" he asks. "Not ever?"

"I don't know that I can."

"Then I'll come find you."

"I'd like that," I tell him.

I take a last look around. These are only the smallest echoes of those trees in the Greatwood, but there's still a magic in them. I take a last breath of that wonderfully thick and sustaining air. I lean forward and kiss Toby on the cheek.

And then I let myself wake up.

Joe

So Jilly makes it back okay. The nurses check her over and pronounce her none the worse for her misadventure, but both Cassie and I can see how that bright medicine light she's always carried inside her is greatly diminished. She looks the same as ever to everybody else, I'm sure, but for us it's a little like looking through a mist. Healing her sister might have required the medicine of the Greatwood and the vervain her friend Toby gathered for her, but it also used up a lot of her own spirit light.

She won't be dreamwalking in *manidò-akì* for a long time. And from what the nurses told me on our way out, she won't be walking in this world either, or doing much of anything, until that paralysis clears up. I ask how long it might take and the nurse won't look me in the eye. That tells me all I need to know: maybe never.

But nobody's thinking about that when she first wakes up. Everybody's just happy to have her back.

"I'm really beat," she says after the first flurry of excitement wears down and the nurses have left her to us. "I need to sleep—not to dream," she adds, looking at Sophie, then me. "I just desperately need some rest."

Lou and Angel are the first to go. I can hear Lou complaining about "How the hell am I supposed to write any of this up?" as they head off down the hall.

Sophie and Wendy each give Jilly a hug before they go, and then it's just Cassie and me.

"You know, don't you?" Jilly says.

Cassie nods. "You gave up a lot for her."

"But that old tangle of hurts and pains is still inside me," she tells us. "All I managed to do is add to it." She gives us a tired smile that hasn't got a whole lot of humor in it. "So I guess there isn't going to be any magical healing happening anytime soon."

"You're just going to have to do it on your own," I say. "But I know you can do it."

"Can I?" she asks. "I mean, really?"

"You don't give up," I remind her.

"Yeah, I know. But it's hard."

"We'll be here for you. All your friends. We're going to get through this."

She manages a little nod.

"It's going to be weird," she says. "Sleeping, but not dreaming. I mean crossing-over kind of dreaming."

"We'll work on that," I tell her. "Soon as you've got all of this behind you, you and I are going over there in our own skins, walking large. Your medicine light's going to come back, bright as it ever was, but we'll find a way to mask it so you don't call the wrong kind of spirits to you when we're over there."

"I'd like to believe that."

"It's my promise to you."

"Except I don't know that I'm ever going to put all of this behind me," she says. "I'm scared that I'm always going to be the Broken Girl."

"There's more to you than that," Cassie says. "There always was and there always will be."

"I guess . . ."

I can tell she's already drifting off, so we make our farewells. When I lean over to give her a kiss on the brow, she asks, "Do you think she's going to be okay?"

I know who she's talking about.

"That's going to be up to her," I say.

I get a small sad nod as she drifts off. I straighten up, then Cassie and I head down the hall to talk to the nurses before we leave.

MANIDÒ-AKÌ

The sun's still below the horizon in the World As It Is when Cassie and I finally get away from the rehab, but it's already past dawn on Cody's mountaintop mesa where we join Whiskey Jack and Bo. Jack might've talked about heading off to see that puma girl of his, but I knew I'd find them here. They've got a fire going and coffee on. Bo's dug up a pot and enough tin mugs to go around, don't ask me where. We sit quietly around the fire, drinking coffee strong enough to strip paint and smoking cigarettes, though Cassie's only had the one puff for politeness sake. Tobacco means a whole different thing, here in *manidò-aki*. And it doesn't affect us the way it does humans, not even with all the chemical crap and additives the tobacco companies slip in.

Jack's making out like he's in cheerful mode, but it doesn't wash for me. Hell, he hasn't even made a single pass at Cassie, and lord knows she's looking good this morning.

"Didn't work out the way we were expecting, did it?" I say after a while.

Bo shrugs. "I didn't know what to expect."

Jack takes a final drag from his cigarette and flicks the butt into the fire.

"It's kind of funny," he says. "The one time I try to do good and . . ." He shrugs. "Well, we didn't manage to do much of anything except tick off some old spirit."

"Just making a stand makes a difference," I say.

"You think?"

"I know."

He nods. "I suppose you would. But I guess now I know how Cody felt all those times he tried to make things right."

That makes Bo laugh. "You kidding us? Maybe we didn't change anything, but we didn't screw up the world either."

Everybody's got a story about Cody's attempts to make the world a better place, from how he's the reason the humans are here, to his inadvertently welcoming sickness and death into the world. Most of the time his motivation is good; he just goes about it in about as wrong a way as you can. He's the main reason canids don't get themselves involved in issues much.

Jack's pack of ready-made smokes are gone by now, so he bums my tobacco pouch and rolls himself one, passes the pouch to Bo.

"So did we learn something from this?" he asks as he lights up.

Nobody says anything for a moment.

"Maybe that nobody's necessarily what we expect them to be," Cassie says. "Everybody's got the potential for great good and great wrong in them, but it's the choices we make that define who we really are."

That gets her a blank look from Jack.

"I mean the way Raylene hated Jilly," she explains, "but she still took the shotgun blast for her."

Jack gives a slow nod. "I was thinking more along the lines of how it's better to mind your own business, but I suppose that'll work, too."

"You think the one good thing this Raylene did balances out everything else she destroyed?" Bo asks.

"No," Cassie tells him. "But it's a good start."

I finish off my coffee. "Time we were going," I tell Cassie. I look at the boys. "You keep out of trouble now," I tell them.

"We don't even know the meaning of the word," Jack says, grinning.

Bo laughs. He gets to his feet.

"Yeah, time I was going, too," he says. "I've been borrowing this place of Cody's for long enough. Maybe I'll have me a look into getting rid of this curse of mine. It's been too long since I've been able to walk on two legs outside of *manidò-akì*."

"You want some company?" Jack asks.

"I would have thought you'd have some girl waiting for you somewhere," Cassie teases him.

"Naw," he says, shaking his head. "I'm into causes these days."

"Lord, help us," Cassie says.

Instead of heading directly for home, Cassie and I take a longer route, walking for a while in those red rock canyons, appreciating the sun in our faces, the warmth that sinks right down into our bones. Sometimes I think that everybody photosynthesizes light, not just plants.

"You're awfully quiet," Cassie says after a time.

I put my arm around her shoulders.

"I'm just thinking about Jilly," I say. "I was hoping it'd turn out better for her."

"It's hard on her," she agrees.

"And I guess I'm feeling a little like Jack," I add. "Let down, I mean. I pride myself on being able to take on a problem and fix it, and that hasn't been the case from the get-go here."

Cassie slips her arm around my waist.

"Welcome to the real world," she says.

Jilly

I fall asleep in the middle of talking to Cassie and Joe. When I wake up later, I'm sure I'm dreaming. I haven't crossed back over into the dreamlands, because I'm still in my room in the rehab, and anyway, I can't cross over anymore. But nevertheless, this doesn't seem real.

I hear a tap-tap on the window and see two faces pressed against the glass, looking at me.

Crow girls.

The windows are plate glass and they don't open, but they do now. They swing wide and the two small dark-haired girls hoist themselves up from the lawn outside to climb into my room. They stand at the end of the bed, holding hands, their hair all spikes, their raggedy black sweaters hanging loose, almost to their knees.

"Oh, Jillybilly," one of them says.

"That's like a rockabilly," the other explains, "only not so goatish."

"Or as musical."

"You don't have a beard, you see."

"It would be all too silly if you did."

"And you don't have a guitar either."

"Unless you have one hidden under your pillow."

"I don't," I tell them.

They get up onto the end of the bed and sit cross-legged beside each other, looking at me.

"Why are you here?" I ask.

"To say we're sorry," the one on the left says.

I know their names: Maida and Zia. But I can never tell them apart the way that Geordie or Joe can.

"Veryvery sorry," the other agrees.

"What do you have to be sorry about?"

"That we can't help you."

The one on the right nods. "We've tried and we've tried, but it's just no use."

"We're useless girls," the other says.

"When they were handing out usefulness, we thought they said moosefulness."

"So we hid."

"We didn't want to be moose."

"Or even mice."

"Though sometimes we like to eat mice."

"When they're all sugary," the one on the left explains.

"Made of candy, you see."

"And we do like a chocolate mousse."

"Oh, yes, chocolate's always good." The one on the right digs in her pocket and comes up with a brown lump of something that has bits of lint and less identifiable matter stuck to it. "Would you like a piece?"

"No, thanks."

She breaks it in two, handing half to her companion before popping the other half in her mouth.

"I don't think you're useless," I tell them as they contentedly chew on their chocolate.

"You're too kind," the one on the left says.

The other nods. "Veryvery kind. Everywhere we go, people say, that Jillybilly, she's too very kind."

"They really do."

"But we can heal things, you know."

"All sorts of things. Big and small."

"Wide and thin."

"Sweet and sour."

"But not when the hurt's like the one in you."

"It's okay," I say. "I know this is something that there's no magical answer for. Sometimes that's just the way it works out."

The one on the left turns to her companion. "Kind *and* brave."

The one on the right sighs. "Now we feel even worse."

"Lying here all on your own, being ever so veryvery brave."

"I'm not on my own," I say. "I've got lots of friends to help me through this."

They lean over their respective sides of the bed, and peer underneath.

"*Where are you hiding them?*" the one on the left asks when she's sitting up again.

"They go home at night," I explain.

"Of course."

"We knew that."

"We should go home, too."

"Thanks for visiting me," I say.

They nod. Then they each reach into their hair and pull out a short dark lock that turns into a black crow feather in their fingers. They lay the feathers down on the bedclothes that cover my legs.

"If you ever think we can help," the one on the right says, serious now, "hold these in your hand and call our names."

"You know our names, don't you?"

I nod. "Maida and Zia. Only I can never tell which is which."

That makes them giggle. They each point at the other and say, "She's Maida."

"I'm glad you cleared that up for me," I say.

That makes them giggle more.

"Don't forget," the one on the left says.

"I couldn't ever forget you," I assure them.

"And don't you pay attention to what that old tree sister said."

The other nods. "Anybody can fly."

"Anybody can dream."

They're talking about the spirit I met in the forest, the one who gifted my sister and me with the light when we were children. I feel hope rise in my chest.

"You mean I'll be able to go back to the dreamlands someday?" I ask.

"Anything can happen someday," the one on the right says.

"Call us when you're ready."

"We're like doors."

"You can step through us to wherever you want to go."

They hop off the bed and approach me from either side. First one, then the other kisses my brow. With a wave and a grin, they run to the window and jump out. Somewhere between when their feet leave the windowsill and they should be landing on the ground, they turn into crows and fly away, trailing caws that sound like laughter.

I stare at the window, watching the large pane of plate glass slowly close once more. Then I fall asleep—or slip out of dream sleep into a dreamless one. I'm not sure which. But in the morning there are still two black crow feathers lying on the bedclothes.

Raylene

MANIDÒ-AKÌ

I never really been over here in my own body afore and it's disconcerting. Everything feels different. It's mostly the smells and sounds, but my eyes don't work near so well neither, not like they done when I was a wolf. When I'm a wolf it seems my whole body's inputting information. It's coming through the hair covering my skin. It's coming from some extra senses I can't even explain.

The wolf feels free. Runs free. Every movement's like the flow of water. Right now, I feel like I'm wrapped in burlap and I don't much like it. But there ain't a whole hell of a lot I can do about it neither, so I do what I always do, and that's carry on.

Once I left my sister, I didn't go far. I was going to run as far as I could and never look back, but it ended up I only went me a short ways into the woods, then circled back to where I could keep me an eye on doings down below in that little holler. Having done the clean exit like I done, it'd be somewhat of a letdown if I come walking back, but there's no way I'm leaving my stuff behind.

For one thing I got me this bloody T-shirt that I don't want to be wearing Christ knows how long, so I want a change of clothing from my duffel. And then there's the ol' shotgun. Without a wolf's teeth and fangs, I'm going to need me protection against the critters and whatnot they got inhabiting this place. For starters, there's them dog-faced boys who already told me they was a-gunning for me.

I got me some food in there, too. Granola bars. Bottled water. And then there's Pinky's smokes. I ain't one for sucking on cancer-sticks, but maybe I can use 'em for trade or something.

So I sit me down and wait and afore too long, my sister does the fade-away and it's just her little friend down below. He sits there for a bit—lost in his head, maybe, I don't know—then gets up and walks over to the duffel. Show time, I think. I get up my own self and yell down at him.

"Don't you even be thinking 'bout poking through my stuff!"

He gives me this one shocked look and then he's outta there like a scared jackrabbit, he's moving so damn fast. I don't much care where he goes, just so's he's gone.

I slip and slide my way down the slope to where my duffel is and grab me a clean T-shirt, strip off the old one. I don't know if that little fella's hanging around getting him an eyeful or what, but it don't matter none to me. He can look all he wants. But he tries to grab him a handful and he'll be losing that hand, guaranteed.

I look down at my chest, still marveling that I ain't even got me scars from being shot like I was. That's the first time I notice I got me a kinda tattoo—what looks like a twig, circled by a wreath of little leaves. I touch it with my finger and it feels warmer'n the rest of my skin.

Weird.

I put a new shirt on and it feels good against my skin.

I lay the bloody shirt on top of them stones covering Pinky, then I start to have me a look around some, afraid them dog-faced boys might've took the shotgun. I spy it lying where Pinky must've dropped it. It don't seem no worse for the wear, but I crack her open and sight down the barrels all the same, making sure they ain't got all clogged with dirt or nothing. Then I eject the spent shells and feed in a couple of fresh ones. I store the casings in my duffel—this far from nowhere, you never know what could be useful.

I take me a last look at that pile of stones covering Pinky.

"I'm going to miss you," I tell her, but I don't reckon she's around to hear.

Dead's gone, the way I see it. Hell, I was halfway there my own self, so I know what I'm talking about. There's no hanging 'round, waiting to say how-do to them that's left behind. You die, you got other business. Like falling up into that sweet light that got took away from me.

I get me another pang of hurt to add to all them sorry feelings rattling around inside me when I think of that light.

"Hope it took you, Pinky," I say.

Maybe we'll see each other again on the other side of the light but I ain't holding my breath, waiting on it.

I heft my duffel in one hand, the shotgun in the other, and I set off into the woods again. I remember what my sister told me 'bout some inn, so I head off in that direction. I ain't much in the mood for socializing, but I wouldn't mind me a bed to sleep in, and maybe something hot to drink.

I wonder what passes for money in this place?

It's a long trek and, time to time, I get the idea someone's following me, but I never do catch me a glimpse of no one. Could be my sister's little friend, I guess. Or maybe one of them dog-faced boys. Makes no never mind to me, just so long as they keep their distance and leave me alone. I don't want to use this shotgun, but I ain't a-feared to neither.

I figure I walked me a couple of days, easy, getting to that inn. It's hard to tell 'cause the light don't change. I never really sleep, but I have me a rest from time to time. Finish off my granola bars. Drink all my water. I pass a stream or two and I reckon the water's clean, but I ain't too sure I trust it so I hold off until I've gone a few hours without a drink and I don't care anymore. The next stream I come to, I fill them water bottles and have me a good long drink. Don't feel much of nothing 'cept my thirst's gone and I ain't so hungry anymore.

Back around the first couple of hours, I tore my other spare shirt to make me a sling for the shotgun and I took to carrying the duffel on my back, using the handles like they was back straps. I would've just kept the shotgun in the duffel, but not knowing the first damn thing 'bout what I might run into in these woods, it seemed a safer idea to keep it handy.

The last stretch is a killer. The slope leading outta the woods don't seem like much of nothing, but once you're walking it, it feels like it's just gonna head on up forever. But I finally get me to the big gray-stone building I seen from below. I consider stowing away the shotgun afore I step inside, but end up going in, carrying it in my hand.

The inn's nothing like I expected. I guess I was thinking along the lines of the Sleep Comfort Motel, up on Highway 14, north of the city, but this is fairyland and what I get is a thatched roof on top of fieldstone. It's sure enough big, though. I'll give it that.

I walk through an archway into a cobblestoned courtyard that's like some picture book—it's even got itself one of them old-fashioned wells, smack there in the middle. I can smell fresh bread and some kinda spicy stew and it sets my stomach rumbling. There's a sign 'bove a door on the left says:

Inn of the Star-Crossed

From the noise drifting outta the door, I figure this'll be the café or restaurant or whatever they're going to call it, so I head in that direction. When I step inside it's like I'm in one of them fairy-tale books my sister used to read to me. I mean, there's some humans sitting at that big mess of tables and benches and all I find inside, but mostly what we got here is every which kind of elf, dwarf, and animal-faced creature you can pretty much imagine. I don't figure I'm going out on much of a limb here to say that any normal body like my own self is going to feel herself to be a little outta place.

And soon's I come in, it's like I stepped into some ol' western movie— you know, where the stranger comes walking into the saloon and the whole damn place goes quiet, everybody just a-looking at you, taking your measure. Well, I can give me as good as I get and I just go from face to face, staring 'em down until everybody's minding their own business again and I can make my way to the bar. They start in talking soon enough, and I know they're talking about me, but so long as all they're giving me is sidelong glances, I don't much care. Unlike my poor dead Pinky, I purely hate being the center of attention at the best of times, but at least this way I can pretend I'm not.

I drop my duffel on the floor when I get to the bar and lean the shotgun up against the wood afore I take me a seat on a stool. The guy behind the bar's like one of the bikers hangs out on Division Street, back home in

Tyson—what I liked to call loser strip—'cept he's not practicing being tough the way they all do. He just gives me a smile and comes down to where I'm sitting.

"So you're back," he says.

"I don't think so. You must be thinking on my sister."

He studies me a moment, then nods. "Sorry about that, but there's a close resemblance."

"Yeah, people tell me that all the time."

"William Kemper," he says, offering me his hand.

I give him a shake. "Raylene," I tell him.

"So what can I do for you?"

"Well, I'm hungry, and I'm thirsty, and I wouldn't mind me a room for the night."

"I can provide you with all of that."

"Being an inn and all," I say.

"That's our business."

"Trouble is, I'm not exactly carrying what you might think of as money."

He smiles. "So what do you have?"

I've been worrying on that the whole last hour or so I been coming up the slope to get to this place, and finally decided that first off, I'd try offering up some of Pinky's smokes. That don't work, I'll offer to wash dishes or something. Only other thing I got of value is the shotgun and I figure I'll be needing me that.

So I get off the stool and dig a pack of smokes outta the duffel and set 'em down on the bar between us. That earns me a look I can't put no name to.

"We don't consider tobacco currency here," he says.

"Yeah, I kinda figured they wouldn't be worth much, but a gal's got to try."

He shakes his head and pushes the pack toward me. "It's not that. Tobacco is sacred. It's one of the ways we talk with the older spirits."

I give him a considering look and then slide that pack on back again to his side of the bar.

"Well, you take this here as a gift," I say. "Like I'm giving you an AT&T card, gets you a few minutes of spirit talk, no charge."

"A gift," he says. His voice is kind a quiet, like we got some big deal going on here.

"Well, sure," I tell him. "Why not? It ain't like I'm going to smoke 'em." I dig in my pocket and drop some bills and coins on the bar. "You consider any of this currency?"

He ignores the money, but he picks up the cigarette pack and puts it in his pocket.

"Tell me what you want," he says. "Food, beer, a room—it's on the house."

"You're shitting me."

He shakes his head. "The gift of your tobacco lays a heavy debt on me."

"No way," I tell him. "I just gave it to you, no strings attached. I'm willing to pay my way, just so long's I got something here's got any worth to you. Otherwise, I'd be willing to work it off."

But he's still shaking his head.

"It's because the gift was freely given that I'm indebted," he says.

I give him a long look, waiting for some punch line, but I see he's serious.

"Okay," I say. "Much obliged. I'll have me a drink and something to eat, and a bed for later."

"Beer?" he asks.

"You got anything nonalcoholic?"

"Tea, coffee, soda, water."

"Coffee'd be real fine."

"Coming right up," he says.

I end up staying me a time at the inn. That first night I drink my coffee, eat the stew and bread William brings me, and then go up to the room he says I can use and I'm out like a light. I no sooner lay down then I'm gone. No dreams, nothing. Just a long stretch of I ain't there no more till I wake up in the morning.

When I come downstairs there's only a handful of—hell, I don't know what you call it when you got this mix of people and things that sure ain't people. Beings, I guess. There's a pair sitting by the window, kinda slippery-looking, dark-skinned and wet, dripping with weeds, water pooling under their feet. At another table in the center is some guy could've been a stockbroker or banker, 'cept he's wearing sandals and a dress made of leather, belted at the waist with some kinda little bag hanging from it. Then there's the woman with the head of a goat and a couple of giggling little something or others, four feet short of a yard, sitting right on the table they're so damn small. Like little girls with wings, only they got them eyes so old.

I don't even get me much more'n a passing glance from any of them.

Anywise, when I walk over to the bar, William brings me a coffee and a serious breakfast—sausages and eggs, potatoes, corn, some kinda mash, and pretty much a loaf of bread, toasted up just right and slathered with butter. After I eat I try to see how I can make myself useful, you know, washing up or sweeping or something, but William he won't have none of that. I try to explain how I don't like to be beholden to nobody, but he just tells me how it's kinda late for that now, ain't it.

So I spend my day walking around the slopes above and below the inn, my head trying to get me to think about a mess of things, but I won't let nothing settle. It's like doing time in the hole, back in county. I just got to shut me down for a whiles till I'm ready to deal.

Come the evening I have me some supper, then I sit in a corner, drinking tea and watching the freak show. Thing I notice straight off is, 'cept for a few of these little fairy gals, everybody's pretty much got them a long face and there ain't a whole lotta fun being had. I ask William 'bout it and that's when he explains what the name of the inn means. People come here down on their luck. I reckon that's why I fit in so well.

I stay in the common room until closing time, until everybody else is gone and it's just me and William, and then I don't ask him nothing, I just start in on cleaning up the tables, mopping down the floor. He tries to get me to lay off, but I look at him like I'm some kinda immigrant, don't speak the language.

"I can't hear you," I tell him.

He tries a couple more times, but finally he lets me be.

So that's how the time passes for me, I can't tell you how long. More'n a few days, for sure, but less'n a couple of weeks. Everybody pretty much leaves me alone and I don't talk to no one 'cept William and we don't talk about nothing important. A couple of times I see one of them dog-faced boys, watching me from a corner, but I ain't killing nothing, and they don't push on me, so we don't got us a problem.

Then one night this handsome guy comes in, the kind of guy thinks he owns any place he's in. He's got him the dark hair pushed back from his forehead, the deep blue eyes with the longest lashes I seen on a man. Clean-shaven and dressed all in black. He orders himself a drink from the bar, then turns around and gives the room a good look-see, kinda smiling to himself until his gaze hits me where I'm sitting in my corner, minding my own business.

I look away, but it's too late. He's already coming in my direction.

"Ruefayel," I hear William call after him, like he's warning him 'bout something, but I guess this Ruefayel just ignores it 'cause next thing you know I got him in my face, just a-standing over me.

"So you're back," he says.

I look up. "Whatever I am, it ain't none of your business," I tell him.

He's got him a chip on his shoulder, and I guess I'm spoiling for a fight, though I couldn't tell you why 'cept he rubs me wrong. Right from when he come in, I wanted to wipe that smirk off of his face. We're a bad combination—you don't need to be no genius to see that.

"I told you before," he says. "We have unfinished business."

I already knowed how he's got me mixed up with my sister, but I don't bother to set him straight. I can feel this need in me to let off some steam—I guess it's been building up a time now. I got way too much pressure pushing inside me, everything from dying and coming back when I didn't want to leave that welcoming light, to Pinky dying and staying dead and the whole confusing mess with my sister. And I ain't begun to touch on none of it yet.

"So why don't you finish it," I tell him.

He slams his drink down on the table and starts to reach for me, but he's way too slow. So's William, who's coming out from behind the bar. Afore either of them can blink, I'm outta my seat, switchblade open in my hand. I slip around his side, grab his head with one hand, and lay the cutting edge of my knife against his throat.

"Go on," I say and put a little pressure on the blade.

That knife of mine's honed like a straight razor. You drop a hair across the blade and it'll cut it right in two.

"Why don't you teach me a lesson," I tell him.

It's funny. The whole time this is happening, it's like I'm two people. One's got this bundle of anger and unfinished business suddenly bursting outta her. She's ready to cut this moron's throat open and she ain't even going to blink when he's lying dead on the floor at her feet.

The other one's watching it all like it's happening to somebody else. She's thinking, this is exactly the kinda crap that made me the no-account piece of white trash I am today. The kinda gal who's happy when she's dying 'cause it means she don't have to deal with no more shit in her life. She don't have to make no payback for all the hurts and wrongs she's done 'cause she's going away into that warm and welcoming light, halle-fucking-luyah.

I give that Ruefayel a shove away and he goes stumbling, hits a table and falls to the floor. I stand there looking at him. I ain't got no more killing left in me, but I guess he don't know that. He just scurries back a few feet, then gets up and takes off.

I shake my head as I watch him go. He ain't no different'n Del. Once you stand up to the likes of them, they just fold. The hard thing is stand-ing up to yourself—to what you end up becoming when you pay 'em back in the same coin they used on you.

I've put away my switchblade by the time William comes up.

"I'm sorry," I tell him. "I shouldn't've done that."

"Probably not," he says. "But he's had something like that coming to him for a while now."

"Still don't make it right."

He nods. What's he going to say?

I got nothing more to say myself. I mumble something about needing some air and head out the door myself. I hear conversation start up again in the room when I leave it behind me and realize I never even heard it all go still.

Ruefayel's not out here waiting for me. There's nothing but the night. I walk outta the courtyard onto the side of the hill and sit me down on a stone to look out at them twilight woods going on into forever in the dis-tance. And I start to get me thinking on my sister and me, and how we turned out so different. But that don't mean I can't change. I guess I got to do me a Forrest Gump. Make me some lemonade outta the lemons the world keeps handing me. It's such a load of crap, but I suppose there's something to be said for being able to wake up in the morning and not feeling ashamed of who you are, or what you done.

And I can start with keeping my word to Lizzie, that little gal I promised to come back for at the trailer park where Del's living. I don't know what she's going to think 'bout what I got to offer her. She's expecting me to drive up in that big pink Caddy and take her away to a life that's full of easy living. But it ain't going to be like that.

I know how to make an honest living—hell, I been doing it on the side for years with what I learned from Hector.

That's what I got to do now, full-time. That's what I got to teach Lizzie.

I don't know how she's going to take having to work for a living, but I guess there's only one way to find out. At least, we'll be starting out on the right foot, what with me not breaking my word and leaving her there to wait for me like I done for so long, waiting on my sister who never come—not so's I knew, anyways.

All I had me was Pinky, god bless her, and she weren't much when it come to making an honest living.

Oh, Pinky.

I have me a hard cry then, the one I been holding back forever, it seems. Crying for her and me and how we went so wrong.

I'm out there a long time, long after the tears are gone.

I come back in after closing to help William clean up. We don't talk at all till we're finally done and we're sitting at a table, having us some tea. I find myself telling him the whole sorry story of my life—that's twice I done it now in as many weeks, once with my sister and now with him.

"Everybody makes mistakes," he says when I get to the end.

"Yeah, but do they keep on making 'em the way I done?"

He nods. "Until they figure it out they do. Don't be so hard on yourself. You haven't had a whole lot of breaks."

"I got no right to expect any kind of sympathy from nobody," I tell him.

"You could start with giving yourself a little."

"It don't work that way," I say.

'Cept how the hell would I know? I always been too busy trying to work me an angle—that is when I ain't just wallowing in depression like I done for way too many years back in L.A. afore I got me that job at the copy shop.

"You won't know until you try," William says.

"I suppose. But if I can't forgive myself—how can I expect anybody else to?"

"Don't concentrate on that," he says. "Instead, be the person you want to be. Take it a day at a time. Allow yourself some history of doing the right thing."

"Start small."

He nods.

We sit awhile longer, then I finish my tea. Time I was going.

"I was wondering if you could tell me how I can get home," I say. "Back to the world that's on the other side of this one, I mean."

He explains how the archways work—you just have to focus on where you want to be on the other side and when you step through, that's where you'll be.

"Works the same way for coming back," he tells me.

"I won't be coming back."

"You don't know that."

"Yeah, I do," I say. "I met me some old spirit in the woods told me when I leave the dreamlands this time, I ain't never getting back in again."

He doesn't say anything for a long moment.

"I liked having you here," he tells me then. "You made a good start on being that person you want to be."

" 'Cept for when I tried to cut the throat of one of your customers."

"Except for that," he agrees.

I stand up and go to shake his hand, but he gives me a hug instead. Funny thing. I got this whole issue with personal space, but I don't feel none of my usual anger and anxiety right now. I just hug him back. It's like grabbing a big piece of something comforting and real.

"Let's get your stuff," he says.

I shake my head. "I don't need none of that—'specially not that shotgun." I take the switchblade outta my pocket and try to give it to him. "I won't be needing this neither."

But he won't take it.

"Just because you're turning over a new leaf," he says, "doesn't mean there won't be those who'll try to take advantage of you. You could still need that. Remember, there's no shame in fighting back when the cause is right."

"What cause would that be?" I ask.

"The one that allows people the freedom of being who they want to be. There are those who'll do anything to rob us of that freedom—that's something that doesn't change no matter what world you're in. We can't ever let them win."

"So you're condoning violence?"

He shakes his head. "No. But we have the right to defend ourselves when violence is done to us."

This just confuses me.

"Don't that make us no better'n them?" I ask.

"Turning the other cheek only lets them win."

"Yeah, but I thought a good person was supposed to learn to forgive."

"You have to be alive to be able to forgive," he tells me.

I take that thought with me, back to the world on the other side of this one.

Jilly

I guess I thought that when the paralysis finally eased up, my life would go back to normal again, but it doesn't work that way. Though I get the feeling back in my arm and leg, it's still all pins and needles a lot of the time and I don't have any real strength or coordination in them at all.

The best thing was when the cast came off my arm. I went from completely helpless to suddenly being able to do all those things we take for granted: feed myself, comb my hair, just being able to pick something up. Sometimes I hold a pencil and roll it back and forth between my thumb and fingers—just for the pleasure of being able to do it. But I haven't tried to draw yet.

I do get to sit in a wheelchair, though. I got them to remove the footrest on the left so that I can move myself by using the wheel with my good arm and kind of steer with my foot on the floor for extra leverage. I move at a snail's pace, and I get tired really easily, but I can't begin to explain what it means to be mobile again, even in this limited capacity.

My right leg doesn't seem to be regaining its strength the way my therapist was hoping, but we're working on it, every day.

I still get the headaches, but they're not nearly as frequent, and I've stopped losing little pieces of time, though I doubt that I'll ever recover anything out of those black holes in my memory from before. That weird imbalance between logic and intuition has continued as well. I just can't seem to deal with numbers at all, no matter how simple.

Of course my bruising's all gone and I've got about an inch of hair on the right side of my head where all I had was stubble. I've stubbornly refused to cut the rest of my hair to match the new growth. I don't care what it looks like. I have this illogical idea that if I cut the rest of my hair, I'll be giving something up. Not the hair itself, but something inside me.

I can't explain what, or why I feel that way. I just do.

Wendy says it looks funky, god bless her.

We're living in the professor's house now—Sophie and me. I tried to talk her out of it, but she just looked at me and said, "And you're going to stop me, how?"

At least she's still getting some work done. She's using the old studio that Isabelle and I once shared in the refurbished greenhouse out back. We called it the Grumbling Greenhouse Studio in honor of the professor's grumpy housekeeper, Olaf Goonasekara. Sophie and I are still calling it that now, but not when Goon's around. He's cranky enough as it is without our giving him something to really complain about.

It's because of Goon that I'm grateful Sophie's staying here with me. It's not like he's mean to me or anything, and we have lots of visitors coming by, but if it was just me and Goon and his unrelenting gloominess, I think I'd go mad. The professor is usually so wrapped up in one project or another that sometimes we don't see him for the whole day, so without Sophie, it would have been just Goon and me most of the time.

When I asked the professor once how he's put up with Goon's bad temper for all these years, he just gave me a blank look. Either he really doesn't see it, or they've been together for so long it simply doesn't register anymore.

It's not that far from the professor's rambling Tudor-styled house in the old quarter of Lower Crowsea to the rehab center, so most mornings during the week Sophie just pushes me there in my wheelchair. Evenings

I spend with friends and often Sophie will go out—especially if Daniel comes by. In the afternoons, I watch Sophie paint.

When I first asked Sophie to bring me back to the studio with her while she was working she was reluctant, thinking it would hurt too much for me to see her painting and not be able to do anything myself. But I love simply being in that environment, listening to her charcoal scratch on the canvas, the smell of the paints and turps when she's got the oils out. And though it's hard to explain, I get a real creative rush just being there.

See, sometimes when we're in there, I paint in my head. I don't mean that I imagine a painting. Rather I go through the whole process, sketches and value paintings, setting up my palette and brushes, the work on the piece itself. Or I might just work with ink washes and linework. I've nothing to show for the time I spend doing this, but that isn't the point. It's the doing of it. It feels so real and I can call these paintings and drawings back up in my head anytime I want to.

Sophie thinks I'm slightly mad, but then Sophie's always thought me slightly mad. She doesn't say anything, though. I guess she figures that she's not going to stomp on any bright spots I might be able to find in my life, no matter how preposterous they might seem.

Another bright spot in my life is Daniel, though because of his schedule, I don't get to see him nearly as much as either of us would like. That first date of ours was such a total disaster I'm surprised he ever wanted to see me again. I was already so depressed because of what happened with Raylene and losing the dreamlands and all that I was going to cancel, but Sophie and Wendy wouldn't let me. So I went ahead, but then the movie he brought over for us to watch in the rehab's common room—*The Spitfire Grill*, which normally I would have loved—just had me sobbing at the end.

"Bad choice, I guess," Daniel said when I was finally able to stop crying. "Now that I think of it, you asked for something light and silly."

I gave a little shake of my head. "No, it was a perfect movie. It was beautiful."

"Beautiful, break your heart?"

"That, too."

"I understand."

I remember thinking, no, you don't, how can you? Except maybe he does. Maybe everybody recovering from a serious illness or accident goes away to places in their head that seem as real to them as the dreamlands did to me. Maybe they have experiences there that are just as traumatic as mine were. And maybe they still, nevertheless, miss being able to go back there.

But if I was less than enchanting company that first night, I guess he saw something he liked in me because he gave me this long soulful kiss after he'd wheeled me back to my room and got me into my bed, and we're still seeing each other, aren't we?

But I still don't know what it is that he does see in me and I don't want to ask.

I don't think I'm nearly as brave and cheerful as the crow girls made me out to be that night in May when I dreamed/saw them in my room back at the rehab. The one thing that's really come home to me with my recovering from this accident is just how angry and self-pitying and depressed I can get.

My emotional nerve ends seem to be a lot closer to the surface of my skin than they ever were before. Too often everything and anything is a big deal. It can be from the way my coffee tastes in the morning to the way Goon might look at me; everything's a major emotional experience.

It drives me crazy.

And talking about crazy, for a while I found myself wondering if all those experiences I had in the dreamlands were even real. If Sophie had been like she used to be, denying anything remotely magic, I'd probably have stopped believing that I ever went over into that otherworld. But she's changed. I get her to tell me about the doings in Mabon every morning when we're having our coffee and if I start to sound even a little bit doubtful about my own experiences over there, she's quick to set me straight. Now when I tease her about her faerie blood she just smiles.

And then there's Joe, who just *is* the dreamlands so far as I'm concerned. It doesn't matter on what side of the borders you see him. Those crazy-wise eyes of his don't let you forget. And with even Wendy having been to that otherworld now, the dreamlands remain a big part of my life, even if I can't visit them anymore. Or at least I won't be able to for a long, long time.

I hold on to the promise that the crow girls made me. Sometimes I take out the feathers they gave me and think about calling their names, but I know I'm not ready. I wouldn't be able to get very far in the dreamlands in my wheelchair.

But I think about those cathedral woods and Mabon all the time. I guess the best proof of how I couldn't escape them even if I wanted to was the night Toby came to visit me.

Sophie and I were in the greenhouse studio, talking while she cleaned her brushes, when we heard a tap-tap on the glass door and there he was. He doesn't like it in the World As It Is—"Everything's too scary," he tells me—but he still visits from time to time. That first evening he brought me my sketchbook which he'd found in the Greatwood. When I flip through its pages, I *know* I was really there. I *know* I drew all those sketches from life, not from my imagination.

And it's not just me that knows it.

"That's Bo," Wendy says the first time she looks through the sketchbook. She's pointing at a drawing I did of Nanabozho in the Greatwood.

"He was the other canid I met with Whiskey Jack on that mesa I told you about."

I think it's so cool that she finally got a taste of the magic that Sophie's had for so long, and I had for a short time. And she didn't even have to dream herself over. She got to go there in her own body.

Sophie told me about what had been bothering Wendy, just before my sister and Pinky kidnapped me, and we've settled all that business now. The promise is, whichever one of us finally learns how to cross over on their own, she'll teach the others. We'll always be this little tribe of three small, fierce women.

Wendy might even be the one to go over first. She's been working on Joe, but he wants to wait until I'm better so that he can teach the three of us together. I've tried to convince him to go ahead and show the others—why should they have to wait for me?—but he stays firm.

I think he's nervous about the kind of trouble the three of us could get into over there so he's holding off as long as he can. He *knows* that if I become completely mobile again, there'll be no keeping us back.

．　　　．　　　．

I try talking to Daniel about all of this one night, late in the summer.

Sophie, Wendy, and Mona are in the house, playing some mad card game with the professor—one of those games he makes up and changes the rules of every few hands. Daniel and I opt for some time alone outside.

He wheels me out along the cobblestoned path behind the professor's house, which makes for a bumpy ride, but it's worth it for the little arbor it leads us to. The air is thick with the smell of flowers and cut grass— Goon was out with the lawn mower all afternoon, grumbling as he walked back and forth with it across the backyard. The sky is clear, full of stars that seem far brighter than they should in the middle of the city like this. But even the sounds of the city are muted tonight.

Daniel adjusts the wheelchair so that he can sit on the little iron bench but we can still hold hands.

"What if I told you that there really is a fairyland?" I say.

"I know you believe there is."

"No, I'm not talking about my believing it or not. What if I told you I've been there? That one day, when I get well enough, I could maybe even take you there to see for yourself?"

He surprises me by not even batting an eye.

"If the chance comes up for me to see that Greatwood of yours," he says, "I'm there."

"You believe me—just like that?"

"Why would you lie to me?" he asks.

I don't know where he was hiding all of my life, but I'm glad to have him in it now.

I pull him forward with my good arm until he's close enough to kiss. He's the first guy in forever that I can be close to and not feel myself shrinking away inside.

SEPTEMBER

By the official end of the summer, I can shuffle across a room with the aid of a walker. If my right arm wasn't so weak, I'd be using a pair of canes by now, but it can't support my weight on its own any more than my leg can.

On a Friday, the last one of the month, I'm doing my usual physical therapy at the rehab and Sophie's off running some errands and collecting my mail. I still find it odd to be keeping the loft on Yoors Street. It makes no sense to me, but the professor insists on covering the rent, and arguing with him is like arguing with a wall. Once he makes up his mind about something like this, he simply doesn't listen to you.

But it'll be ages before I can manage those stairs again—if ever. The best-case scenario seems to be that I'll regain a lot of use from both my arm and leg, but they'll never be strong again. I'll walk with a limp and probably won't be able to dance, or run, or go for my long rambling walks ever again.

I refuse to accept that, of course, but on my bad days, it weighs heavily on me. This turns into a bad day—though not because of my physical limitations.

"You got a letter from Geordie," Sophie says when she picks me up at the rehab.

Geordie's good about writing, but it's been about three weeks since I last heard from him and that letter was uncharacteristically downbeat, though he never really came out and talked about anything specific that was bothering him.

I tried calling him that night, but there was no answer and he had his machine turned off, so I dictated a cheerful response to Sophie, hoping to jolly him out of the mood he seemed to be in. I'm usually pretty good at that.

I'd be writing my own letters, but while I've been practicing printing and drawing with my left hand, my script is still pretty much illegible and my drawing skills seem to lie in the other hand, because nothing I draw looks remotely like what it's supposed to.

"Want me to open it for you?" Sophie asks.

"Sure."

She runs a finger under the flap and tears it open across the top, then hands it to me so that I can read it while she pushes me down the sidewalk. I know she's not reading over my shoulder—Sophie would never do that—but I guess something in my body language tells her. She stops pushing and comes around to the front of the wheelchair, hunches down on her ankles with her hands resting on the chair's arms.

"What's wrong?" she asks.

"Geordie broke up with Tanya," I say.

"Oh, no."

I nod. "He says while he's tried and tried, he just can't fit into the life they have there. But every day Tanya fits in better. He's coming back to Newford at the end of the month."

"What are you going to do?"

What she means is, what are you going to do about Daniel? But I don't believe that's even a question.

"Nothing," I say. "Be supportive. Be his friend."

"But you and Geordie . . . I know how you feel about him. And no matter what you think, he loves you as more than a friend."

I shake my head. "He loves glamour girls. I mean look at Tanya. She's a movie star, for god's sake. And remember how gorgeous Sam was?"

She comes back with her old argument.

"That's only because he didn't think he could have you," she says.

I shake my head again. "I don't think so. And anyway, it doesn't matter. My relationship with Daniel's the best I've ever had, bar none. I'm not going to throw it away because I still have feelings for Geordie."

"But—"

"And besides," I say. "I'm in love with Daniel."

At least I think I am.

"Does he love you?" Sophie asks.

"I think so."

Though he's never said so.

Sophie gets up and gives me a hug.

"Then I'm happy for you," she says. "For both of you."

I nod, schooling my face to stay calm because all I want to do is cry. I'm not even sure why. Everything I told Sophie is true. I really do care about Daniel and I don't see any future beyond friendship with Geordie. If it was going to happen, it would've happened a long time ago. And I'm happy with Daniel.

But there's this great well of sorrow inside me all the same, just pressing against my chest and making it hard to breathe.

"But poor Geordie," Sophie says as she starts to push the wheelchair back down the sidewalk again.

I nod. He's as much the Onion Boy as I'm an Onion Girl and now he's got another layer of pain and disappointment to add to the ones that are already there, messing up his life as surely as they've always messed up mine.

"Poor Geordie," I agree.

And maybe I mean poor me as well. Because nothing's guaranteed.

Daniel and I are doing great right now, but I'm still the Onion Girl. Maybe he's willing to believe in faerie and the dreamlands. Maybe he likes who he sees me to be. But there are still all those other layers lying in wait to trip him up that he doesn't know anything about. The hurt kid. The junkie. The hooker. What was done to me and what I did to others, especially my sister.

But then I guess we all have a mess of one kind or another lying somewhere deep inside us. There's no such thing as a perfect life. The trick is to accept each other's weaknesses and lend our strengths when we can.

Walk large, as Joe would say.

I smile. Right now, I'd settle for just being able to walk.

But I'll aim for large. One step at a time.

2

It wasn't Indian summer, because it wasn't officially autumn yet and surely you couldn't have the one without the other, but it was one of the balmiest evenings the city had experienced in weeks. Like large numbers of other office workers, when Wendy left her desk at the end of the day and stepped outside the paper's offices, she simply wasn't ready to go home yet. Instead she mingled with the crowds on Lee Street and finally snagged herself a small table on the patio of The Rusty Lion from which she could sip a glass of wine and people-watch to her heart's content.

There'd been a time in her life when she would have felt awkward, sitting at a table by herself like this, but years spent in the company of avowed individualists such as Jilly had managed to cure her of the misconception that a woman out alone for a drink or dinner was somehow to be pitied. She certainly enjoyed going out with friends, but there could also be something inexplicably exhilarating about such a moment on one's own. Freed of any conversational or other companionable responsibilities, you were able to watch the parade of the world go by without worrying that you might, however inadvertently, slight someone.

It was at times such as this that Wendy loved living in the city. Like Sophie, she'd grown up in Newford, and while she enjoyed visiting the countryside, she only really felt comfortable downtown, surrounded by people and buildings and traffic. The energy of the city seemed to twin the way the blood moved in her veins, the way air was drawn in and out of her lungs, although that brief visit she'd had to the red rock canyons of the dreamlands had left an enormous impression on her as well.

It was the first time she could remember that she yearned to go away to some primal place, unrelated to the city, and she wasn't sure if it had been those canyons themselves or the dreamlands as a whole that had woken such a longing in her. Probably both.

She was thinking of that when she spotted the striking couple coming down the sidewalk toward where she was sitting with her glass of wine. There were both dark-complexioned and exotic in a city that already had a wonderful ethnic mix, particularly in this area of town. The man was tall and handsome, like a riverboat gambler or a Mexican senor, in black cowboy boots, jeans and jacket, with a white shirt and bolo tie, wearing a black flat-brimmed hat decorated with a hatband of turquoise and silver. His companion was almost as tall and even more attractive. Her cowboy boots were red with faded blue jeans tucked into them. She had a white shirt as well, with a short deerskin jacket overtop. She wore no hat, maybe to show off her gorgeous blue-black hair with the two white streaks running back from her temples.

Looking at the pair, Wendy could feel a poem waking up inside her, the same way Sophie or Jilly would have been reaching for a sketch-book, or simply fixing the image in their minds to come back to later in the studio.

Just as they were nearing her, the man did something odd. He lifted his head and sniffed at the air, then his dark gaze met her own and he steered his companion to the iron-worked fence beside Wendy's table. He smiled at her, teeth white against his skin, and paused, leaning an arm casually on the railing.

"I know you," he said.

"I . . . uh . . ."

"No," he corrected himself, his voice a drawl. "I don't know you—I just know where you've been."

Okay, this was too weird, Wendy thought. If he hadn't had the woman with him, she'd have got up from her table and gone into the restaurant, or called the waiter over. Or maybe she wouldn't have. He was so mesmerizing that she couldn't seem to move.

"Where . . . where I've been . . . ?" she found herself saying.

He nodded. "The scent's still on you."

His companion laid a hand on his arm.

"Cody, don't," she said. "You're scaring her."

"Am I?" he asked Wendy.

"No," she said, too quickly. "Well, maybe a little."

"What's your name?" the woman asked.

Wendy turned gratefully in her direction. There was something way too unsettling in the man's eyes. But the woman's were just as dark—just as ageless and dreaming.

"Um, Wendy."

"It's nice to meet you, Wendy," the woman said. "I'm Margaret, and this is Cody."

Wendy's gaze returned to the man.

"Cody?" she said. "As in Cody who owns those red rock canyons in the dreamlands?"

Cody laughed. "Nobody owns those canyons, darling. But I've got a place there and that's what I smell on you."

Margaret was regarding her curiously while he spoke.

"But you don't have the blood," she said. "How did you cross over on your own?"

"I went with a friend," Wendy explained. "We had to bring a message to these guys who were camping there—Bo and Jack."

She went on to explain a little about how she'd snuck along with Cassie to cross over into the dreamlands and then how Joe had sent her and Cassie to the mesa.

"And now that place is in you, isn't it?" Cody said. "It's got its hooks into your heart and you can't stop dreaming about it."

Wendy nodded. "Something like that."

"Those boys are gone now," Cody said, "and I'm not using the place anymore. Margaret and I have found us another spot where our hearts beat a little quicker."

"I can't imagine any place that would be better," Wendy told him.

"I can see that," he said. "It's like you found your heart home there and you never even knew you were looking for it."

Wendy nodded again.

Cody glanced at his companion who gave him a small nod in response.

"Tell you what, darling," he said. "Why don't you look after that camp for me? Think of it as a permanent loan. I know I said nobody can own a place like that, but we all put claims on a landscape anyway, now don't we? You can hold that one for me and call it your own, too. I'm good at sharing." He grinned and gave Margaret a wink. "Hell, I'm good at a lot of things, aren't I, darling?"

Margaret elbowed him in the ribs—hard, it seemed to Wendy, but he didn't react in the least.

"What do you say?" he asked Wendy.

"Me? But . . . I . . ."

She had to take a deep breath to steady herself. This was all so amazing that she couldn't believe it was happening to her. But reluctantly, she had to shake her head.

"I couldn't," she said. "I mean, I'd love to, but I wouldn't know how to begin to get back there."

"I'll give you a key," he said, but he looked at his companion.

Margaret dug into the pocket of her jeans and brought out a small red stone, worn smooth and round from either erosion or simply from having been carried around in a pocket for years.

"Use this," she said, passing the red stone over to Wendy.

Wendy accepted it gingerly, expecting she didn't know what. But something. A flash of light. An immediate crossing over into the dreamlands. But the stone simply lay on her palm, catching the light.

"When you come up on a doorway," Cody said, "hold that key in your hand and put your mind into those deep red canyons. When you step through, it'll take you there."

"Any doorway?"

Cody shrugged. "Any one you can step through, darling. Between's a kind of magic that doesn't take a lot of preparation or skill."

"I . . . thank you," Wendy said. "Really. I mean that."

"I know you do, darling," Cody told her. "That's why I'm sharing it with you, though if you ask me, I think you already had your own hold on it, just no way to get back."

That was exactly how it had been feeling, Wendy thought.

"Now you take care of that place," Cody said.

Wendy nodded. "I will."

"And maybe we'll see you there sometime," Margaret added.

Then smiling, the pair moved on down the sidewalk. Wendy watched their backs until they were lost in the crowd, then looked down at the red stone she still held in her hand.

She had this sudden sense that the world had tilted underfoot while her attention had been distracted by the conversation she'd just had. She lifted her head, turning her gaze to the door that led from the patio back into the restaurant.

No, she thought. That was too obvious. People'd freak if they saw her step through and simply disappear.

That was saying it would even work.

No, she told that little rational voice inside her head. It *will* work.

She got up and went inside to the women's washroom. After making sure that she was alone in there, she took a breath, then moved toward the door of one of the cubicles, stone in hand, those red rock canyons firm in her mind. She pushed the door open and stepped through, then stopped dead in her tracks.

"Hol-ee . . ." she murmured.

On both sides and behind her was the women's washroom of The Rusty Lion. But before her, where the toilet cubicle should have been, she was looking through a door that led out into a stunning vista of red cliffs and canyons, pines and hoodoos, with a sky so big above it defied any measurement.

Grinning foolishly, Wendy stepped back and the vista disappeared. But she knew she could have stepped through. She'd felt the breeze on her face, smelled the red dirt and the pines.

Oh, wait until I tell Jilly and Sophie, she thought as she went back toward her table on the patio, red stone stowed carefully away in her pocket.

3

OCTOBER

Geordie came by to see me as soon as he got into town. I think he only stopped long enough to drop his luggage off at Christy's apartment before coming over to the professor's house. Since he'd given up his own apartment when he'd moved to L.A. to be with Tanya, I told him he could stay at my studio until I could use it again. Neither of us brought up the fact that as things stood, he might well have the place permanently.

Actually Geordie's been pretty good about my convalescence. Those Riddell brothers have never handled anything to do with illness very well—the whole thing just freaks them out. I mean, Christy's only been by twice since I got out of the rehab, though his girlfriend Saskia comes by at least once a week.

I know Geordie felt really uncomfortable at first, finding me in this wheelchair of mine that first afternoon. Or maybe I'm being unfair. Maybe it had nothing to do with me being the Broken Girl and everything to do with me being with Daniel now. I can see he's trying to be happy for me, but I look at him with Sophie's and Wendy's eyes and see what they've been trying to tell me all along: he's unhappy for himself; not just because of breaking up with Tanya, but because he does carry a torch for me.

When I think of all the years we could have been more than pals, it makes me want to cry. But I try not to let any of that show: that I know how he feels, that we screwed up and now our chance is gone. Because this is still Geordie, my best friend. I can't let anything change that.

"So, Geordie, me lad," I say to him. "What're you going to do now?"

He shrugs. "I don't know. A little of this, a little of that—just like always. I'll get some busking in before the weather gets too desperate, then see if I can get some gigs, maybe put together another band."

"We missed your music," I tell him. "We missed you."

"I missed you, too."

"You had to try. You had to see if it could work."

He nods. "But it's weird having your failure spelled out in the tabloids for everybody to see. Before I left, one of the papers was already running a story on Tanya and her new boyfriend—you know, with the photo spread and all."

"You know how the tabloids are," I say. "They just like to blow everything out of proportion."

"They had pictures of them necking in some restaurant."

"That sucks."

"Tell me about it."

We used to be able to sit together for hours, not having to say anything; other times we'd talk until our voices actually got hoarse. That's not happening right now. We don't have words, but the silence between us seems to require them anyway. I hate this.

"It's funny," Geordie says suddenly. He turns to look at me. "Ever since you had your accident I've had this weird feeling that it was all my fault. That if I hadn't gone away, none of it would have happened. I know," he adds before I can protest. "You don't have to tell me. I know how stupid that sounds. But I still catch myself feeling guilty all the same."

I look at him for a long moment. The thing is, I understand just what he's getting at. I'm not saying it's true, or real. But I've felt it before myself.

Then something horrible occurs to me.

"That's not the reason you and Tanya—"

"No, no," Geordie says, breaking in. "Tanya and I just live in different worlds. I don't know why we pretended we didn't. If she hadn't been slumming in mine, I don't think things would ever have gotten to where they did."

"But you loved each other."

"I think we still do. But we don't suit each other—and that's the bottom line. Believe me, we've had a lot of long nights talking it out."

"I'm sorry," I tell him. And it's true. I am. I mean it.

"Yeah, me, too," he says, then he leans back on the sofa and sighs. "I was just so . . . displaced out there. I thought I'd feel different when I got back home, but I don't. Everything's changed. You, me . . ."

"Except we're still best friends."

He doesn't say anything for a long moment. Then he sits up and looks at me, a small smile on his lips, a sadness in his eyes.

"We are, aren't we?" he says.

"Even when you're an idiot," I tell him. "Maybe especially when you're an idiot, because it makes me seem so smart."

"I'd give you a whack if you weren't already in a wheelchair."

"Now you can see one of the side benefits of recuperation."

This time the smile almost reaches his eyes.

"I really did miss you," he says.

It takes me a moment to school my features, to not let my own sadness show.

"I know," I tell him.

4

So Wendy's gone picture crazy. Every time she and Sophie cross over into the dreamlands, Wendy comes back with her pockets full of rolls of film that need developing. Most of them are of those canyons near

Cody's camp on the mesa. Breathtaking vistas with cliffs that drop forever or rise to heights that rival the trees in the Greatwood. With towering firs and pine trees, their dark greens vibrating brilliantly against the red rock. With those curious hoodoos, the rock formations that seem to have a hundred faces hiding in them when they don't look like castle spires and towers.

But occasionally she comes back with portraits or candid shots of some of the people they meet over there. Puma girls and strutting eagle boys. Spirits of the juniper and pinyon pines. And of course canids.

I particularly like this shot she's got of Whiskey Jack, lighting a cigarette, his head cocked to one side as he looks into the camera. She's captured that elusive blend of wisdom, tomfoolery, and sex drive perfectly.

"What is it with that guy?" she said the first time she came back from having met him over here. "He's got a libido as big as those canyons."

But she's not the only one to be taken by those magical views. Sophie's gotten back into landscape painting in a big way, working *en plein air* with my *pochade* box and small canvases, then using those paintings to develop larger, more finished pieces back in the Grumbling Greenhouse Studio.

"I think I've got a show here," she said one morning while she was taking a break and we sat in the studio looking at the half-dozen new canvases that were propped up along one of the worktables.

"And when people ask you where those canyons are?" I asked.

She shrugged. "I'll just say southern Utah."

At first they were both worried at how I'd take their being able to cross over. It took me a long time to get them to stop waiting for me to get better before they went themselves and even longer to convince them that I really was okay with it.

And I am.

They just don't understand how much this means to me, how it gives me something so tangible to shoot for—I mean, beyond being completely mobile again, which is the first priority, of course. I thought I might never get back there. I certainly can't cross over in my dreams. But now I know that all I have to do is keep working at getting better and I will be able to be there again.

I won't deny that I get jealous twitches. But I get jealous twitches just seeing people walk around, taking their mobility so for granted.

Tonight I have the professor's house to myself. Daniel's got a late shift, the professor is at a lecture, Wendy and Sophie have gone out to a club, Goon has the night off, and Geordie's got a gig. I've managed to convince them all that I'll be fine on my own for the few hours I'll be alone. And I am, though I'm a little at loose ends.

I try watching some TV, but it's just boring. I flip through some magazines, ditto. I'm reading *Owls Aren't Wise & Bats Aren't Blind*, a book debunking fallacies about animals that I got out of the professor's library. I've been really enjoying it, but it's a hardcover and I have trouble holding a book its size for a long time. And anyway, tonight it doesn't hold my interest either.

I perk up when the doorbell sounds. It's too late for a delivery, so it must be a visitor. I wheel down the hallway, wondering who it is. Angel, maybe. Or Mona. It doesn't matter—I'm just happy to know that I won't be alone. So much for resiliently hanging out on my own.

But when I get the door open, I find the last person in the world I expect to see standing there on the stoop. I have a momentary flare of nervousness that I quickly and firmly put aside.

"Hey, Raylene," I say.

She nods, looks down at my wheelchair. "Hey, yourself. I see you're still in the wheeling around stage."

"I'm improving."

"That's good to hear."

"What are you doing here?" I ask. "Not that I'm unhappy to see you, but the last time we . . ."

She waves a hand. "Yeah, I know. But things change. I'm turning over a new leaf and all that."

"Really?"

She shrugs. "I'm giving it a shot, anyways. Just thought I'd drop by and say how-do before I hit the road."

"Where are you going?"

I can't believe this. She leaves the dreamlands and comes to visit, and now she's already going again?

"Back out west," she says. "I got me a little business out there that I been neglecting. I ever tell you 'bout that software I been designing?"

"A little."

"Well, I figure I'd give it a shot—get serious 'bout something for a change. See if I can walk the straight and narrow, you know? And maybe even be happy 'bout it."

"Can you come in?"

She looks over her shoulder to where a pink Cadillac convertible is idling by the curb with its roof up.

"I got somebody waiting," she says.

"They're welcome to come in, too."

She gives me a long look.

"You really are some piece of work, aren't you?" she says. "You got all this crap in your life, but you're still cheerful, still being the good hostess and all."

"You'll have to get your own drinks," I tell her.

"I can do that. You sure it's no trouble?"

"Not even close."

She gives a slow nod. "I'll go get my friend Lizzie. We won't stay long."

"You can stay as long as you like."

"Damn," she says. "You really mean that, don't you?"

"Of course I do."

She steps closer to me and I think she's going to give me a hug, but she just rests her hand on my shoulder for a moment, then turns to get her friend.

We talk for so long that she and Lizzie have to stay in one of the guest rooms overnight and put off their trip until the morning.

Interview

Extract from an interview with Jilly Coppercorn, conducted by
Torrane Dunbar-Burns for The *Crowsea Arts Review*, at her
Yoors Street studio, on Wednesday, April 17, 1991.

*What do you think it is that makes you different from other artists? That
makes you so welcome among so many disparate disciplines, untouched
by maliciousness or gossip?*
[Laughs.] Well, I think there's plenty of gossip.

*But it's not mean-spirited. Whenever I hear you talked about, it's as
though you're a mischievous little sister—even to artists many years
your junior.*
I don't know. Maybe it's because I don't want to rule or serve, only
to be allowed to go my own way.

Isn't that the ambition of all artists? To make their own mark?
Is it? It seems to me that people make art for all sorts of different
reasons. I'm not interested in leaving a body of work behind. But I
am interested in promoting communication between everybody—
and not only through the arts. And I'm determined to show through
my art that there are alternatives to the way the world is these days.

You mean by showing us that there are faerie and magic?
The magical beings in my paintings aren't the point. The point is
that we're not alone. That we're surrounded by spirit and spirits. I
truly believe that if we do our best to live a good life, to treat each

other with kindness and respect, we can make the world a better place. The faerie are a representation of that betterness—is that even a word?

It is now, if you want it to be.
The faerie represent the beauty we don't see, or even choose to ignore. That's why I'll paint them in junkyards, or fluttering around a sleeping wino. No place or person is immune to spirit. Look hard enough, and everything has a story. Everybody is important.

"Death makes equal the high and low."
What's that from?

John Heywood, I believe.
Too bad we have to wait for death to make a balance.

Isn't that the truth. But to get back to the faerie and the other magical beings in your paintings . . .
They're just how I tell the story.

So the faerie aren't real?
[Smiles.] I never said that.